# EXIT FROM AMERICA

## D. F. BAILEY

*For Gary and Bev*
*~ From your story to mine ~*

Vinci Books

vinci-books.com

Published by Vinci Books Ltd in 2026

1

Copyright © D.F. Bailey 2013

The author has asserted their moral right to be identified as the author of this work in accordance with the Copyright, Designs and Patents Act 1988. This work is a work of fiction. Names, characters, places and incidents are the product of the author's imagination or are used fictitiously. Any resemblance to actual persons, living or dead, places and incidents is entirely coincidental.

All rights reserved. No part of this publication may be copied, reproduced, distributed, stored in any retrieval system, or transmitted in any form or by any means, including photocopying, recording, or other electronic or mechanical methods, nor used as a source for any form of machine learning including AI datasets, without the prior written permission of the publisher.

The publisher and the author have made every effort to obtain permissions for any third party material used in this book and to comply with copyright law. Any queries in this respect should be brought to the attention of the publisher and any omissions will be corrected in future editions.

A CIP catalogue record for this book is available from the British Library.

Paperback ISBN: 9781036703516

The EU GPSR authorised representative is Logos Europe, 9 rue Nicolas Poussion, 17000 La Rochelle, France
contact@logoseurope.eu

## By D.F. Bailey

Standalone Thrillers

*Healing the Dead*
*Exit From America*
*Fire Eyes*
*The Good Lie*

Will Finch Mystery Thriller Series

*Five Knives (Prequel)*
*Bone Maker*
*Stone Eater*
*Lone Hunter*
*Second Life*
*Open Chains*
*Run Time*
*White Sphere*
*Burnt Embers*

## Chapter One

A crash landing.

He would have preferred a more elegant arrival, something resembling the controlled descent of a sky diver or a paraglider. But after Iris's funeral, after renting out his house and obtaining a passport, after ensuring his monthly checks would be deposited into his new bank account, and then clutching the twin boys in a final embrace — following all that he'd endured and concocted — Doyle Mere was robbed twice in one day.

He felt as though he'd fallen from an errant satellite and smashed into the heart of San Francisco. Yet despite the bruising he'd taken, the realization that he'd landed hard and then shattered would only come several weeks later.

For the moment Doyle is preoccupied with directional issues. Where next, and how do you get there? Or more precisely, how do you begin the next phase of your life? These persistent questions have led him to the spot where he now stands: on a lip of dry grass next to the asphalt pathway curling along the edge of an elaborately clipped-

and-pruned space within the broad expanse of Golden Gate Park. He takes a moment to re-examine the San Francisco Recreation & Parks map, double-checking that this green stretch of land within the park is actually named Hippie Hill.

"Yeah, that's what they call it," he says aloud and laughs with a sense of disbelief. He refolds the map and tucks it behind his wallet in his back pocket and examines the open space before him. Perhaps twenty people are in transit, most of them entering the area from the east side of the park known as the Panhandle. A gray-haired couple decked out in matching T-shirts jogs along the sidewalk that scrolls into the distance. Behind them a lone woman pushes a baby pram down the walkway toward the Pacific Ocean, her legs canted at an angle to propel the weight of her rig forward.

From the opposite direction a teenager with waist-length dreadlocks drags a skateboard on its hind wheels as he approaches the patch of grass where Doyle stands. After a moment Doyle can make out the letters written on the skater's shirt — ¡Ouch! — a hand-painted script rendered with considerable care. In his free hand he twirls a foot-long lanyard around his fist. When he reaches the stretch of pavement next to Doyle the boy sets his board on the asphalt and then slides the cord into a patch pocket on his jeans. He tugs a yard of his hair over one shoulder and with a push from his right leg he sets off toward town.

"It's a breeze, dude!" He smiles as he zooms along the path and for a moment Doyle feels a bond with this kid.

The wave of affection surprises him. Apart from Louis Laporte, the apartment building manager he met yesterday after his arrival, Doyle doesn't know a soul here. Piqued with a sense of longing, he imagines that anyone reaching out to him could be a potential comrade. He failed to anticipate this yearning for companionship, the isolation in the midst of humanity that is now the pulse of his daily life. Selling most of his life-long possessions is one thing, but settling into Haight-Ashbury with nothing more than a duffle bag of clothes, a few books and his second-hand laptop, has inserted a melancholy note into his melody of renewal.

But if loneliness is to be his new companion, he's committed to exploring its dimensions in new and open places. That's why he chose San Francisco for his destination after he settled his affairs back home. And because it was Iris's playground, the magical backdrop of her youth and the inspiration of her personal generosity and her unlimited faith in humanity. Indeed, San Francisco was once a place of joy, of unfettered public elation. At least it used to be in the 1960s. Or more precisely, in the summer of 1967, most likely on a Saturday afternoon early that summer — but definitely in this very place, in Golden Gate Park where the celebration of existence itself blossomed into a global carnival of indulgent pleasure and innocence — a carnival that he missed by more than four decades. By his reckoning, following the Gay Nineties and the Roaring Twenties, the Summer of Love marked the last flowering of spontaneous public joy in the world. And while he failed to attend that unique intersection of time and place, Doyle is now determined to seize any remnants of bliss even though the best-before-date is long past due and the good vibrations have faded into the black hole of a declining republic and cascading economic collapse.

"Hey, mister, you want a bracelet?"

Doyle turns in surprise. In his reverie he failed to notice

the girl approaching him from the crest of the hill. He adjusts the strap of his shoulder pack and examines her. A pall of onyx-black hair hangs limply over her shoulders and accentuates the bleached wash of her face. Her lips are thin, unsmiling.

"Here, let me get you started," she continues before he can decline her offer.

"What's this?" Doyle flinches as she winds a leather band around his right wrist and spins a few loops about his fingers. She cinches them lightly and before he can say more she tightens the long strand and pulls his arm next to her own.

"My craft," she explains and holds her left hand aloft to display two intricately woven leather bracelets, one on her wrist, the other above her elbow. Doyle studies the Celtic patterns as she continues to tie a series of knots into the bracelet she's making for him. He convinces himself that the girl is innocent enough, that this is her trade and if she wants a few dollars for her labors he'll gladly pay her and in the meantime they'll share this brief moment of friendship, the warm, but usually forgettable bond that links buyers and sellers of home-made trinkets and charms.

"I like Celtic designs," he offers as she pulls the length of leather cord from a shoulder bag and weaves it into his bracelet.

"Are you Irish?" She briefly pauses her handiwork to offer a smile and he notices that one of her eyeteeth is missing. In the gap-toothed cavern of her mouth he detects impending exhaustion, perhaps an early death. She appears to be about twenty-five, but Doyle figures she's probably closer to eighteen and has recently succumbed to the habit of smoking heroin or crack or some eerie cocktail of drugs she purchased on Market Street. Be kind to this one, he tells himself.

"Well, my name *is* Doyle. From a clan that goes back twelve centuries," he adds in his best brogue accent so that she imagines he's a refugee from the latest version of potato famine, the death of the Celtic Tiger, otherwise known as the Irish economy. The truth is his father was half French and legally he's no more Irish than Ronald Reagan. But if it's blarney she wants, he'll be happy to dish up a few dollops to get her started.

"I'm Kandy." She glances over her shoulder as if she's expecting someone. "With a 'K,' like in Kansas. There. We're almost done." Although he's still firmly attached to the web she's cast over his wrist, she tightens a few more knots into place. "If you want, we can stop here and it's seven dollars. Or if you want a matching bracelet, it'll be ten for both."

"Ten for both?" Doyle narrows his eyes. He decides not to haggle. If seven bucks is the price of this late-edition piece of the 1960s, so be it; he knows it's as close to hippie authenticity as he'll likely find. "I'll take just the one," he says.

"You sure? I can do the second one pretty fast. Make it just *nine* bucks for both."

"Dead certain." He presses his lips together and gazes across the lawn. "One's plenty," he says evenly, as he examines the compounding mess of knotted leather bound around his wrist. With every embellishment the seven-dollar deal is looking more and more like a rip-off. Doyle's left hand dips awkwardly into his right rear pocket as he tries to fish his wallet from his jeans. The sooner he can free himself from this budding entrepreneur, the better. "Cut me loose from this thing now and I'll give you seven bucks, but that's it."

Kandy shrugs and glances over her shoulder again. She quickly weaves another strand of leather across Doyle's hand.

As a burst of adrenaline courses through his arms Doyle breaks into a light sweat. "All right! Look, Kandy, we're done with this. Now cut this thing off and I'll give you your seven bucks." Twisting his hips to the left he finally extracts his wallet from his pocket and holds it aloft along with the tourist map. But in the light breeze and the slick of perspiration on his hand the map slips from his fingers and flutters to the ground. He scrambles to snag it in mid-air and in this instant — in the juncture that his wallet and the map and his sense of balance collide — everything changes.

Before he can hear the tight spin of polyurethane wheels racing along the path, before he can see the flash of golden dreadlocks, Doyle's wallet is snatched from his hand. Breezing into the near distance ¡Ouch! passes Doyle's wallet from one hand to the other then tucks it into his pocket and jets down the asphalt path without looking back, his blond dreadlocks flagging in the wind.

"Hey!" Doyle jogs a few steps after him and then stumbles as he tries to untangle the cord from his hand. In the same moment Kandy drops the long strand of leather at her feet and runs in the opposite direction. Doyle watches her dart across the lawn toward the Panhandle. Part of him is inwardly shrieking Irish profanities. Another part is admiring Kandy's athletic form: long-legged, arms pumping, head level, shoulders squared. There was a time, he figures, before she decided to redeploy from Kansas to San Francisco to begin a career as a drug addict and grifter, that Kandy probably qualified for the final heat of the hundred-yard dash in the Kansas State senior high school track meet. And judging by the way she races over the hill and disappears on the far side, she may well have won it, too.

Louis Laporte immigrated to the USA from Rouen, France in 2002.

When Doyle told him that he was writing a memoir and looking for a quiet room where he could work in peace, Louis embraced him as a fellow artist. As a teenager Louis lived near Gustave Flaubert's home, a spacious urban chateau that now serves as a museum that celebrates the great author's childhood and his father's prominence as a physician. Louis was delighted to know that Doyle had read not only *Madame Bovary*, but also two lesser-known works, *Salammbô*, and *Novembre*. The men's instant affinity prompted Louis to reveal his own story beginning with his arrival in the Bay Area where he'd hoped to find work as an illustrator. He wanted to specialize in album covers and he designed a few CDs on spec for two Bay Area bands whose recordings were never released.

After he'd run through his savings he found employment as an architectural artist, rendering condo plans into tasteful marketing brochures for developers. During the real estate boom he joined the marketing team at Samuels, Connors & Brace. The company focused their business on vacation properties and leveraged the profits from their single, oversubscribed development outside Palm Springs to launch four new boutique hotels in Las Vegas. When the real estate bust hit, the company collapsed within three months.

"Those were the good years," he explained to Doyle. He spoke slowly in short sentences which occasionally revealed his accent. "And we all ate well," he said as he wove his fingers over his belly. "Some of it, some was *juste* too good, if you understand me." After the market collapse Louis picked up a few shifts serving tables in a French restaurant until he found his current job as a rental property manager which paid him two hundred dollars a month plus a rent-free room in Doyle's apartment building.

When Doyle retrieves Louis from his tiny apartment to report another robbery, and rage about the thieves who'd broken through the window off the back lane, Louis's dwindling sense of self-esteem is further reduced. He's had to disclose so many break-and-enter burglaries to the landlord and the police that he's come to see himself as a sort of local score-keeper of petty crimes. Now, with one more episode to proclaim, he can feel himself sliding into a gloomy depression.

"Come and see what happened." Doyle can barely believe it himself. Less than an hour after his fleecing in Golden Gate Park, he's now the victim of a *second* robbery.

As he stares at the mess in Doyle's room Louis presses a hand to his mouth. "I have less now than when I arrived from Rouen," he confesses. "But today, Doyhul, it looks like they took almost everything from you, too, my friend."

"Yeah. Almost everything." Doyle is shaken by the rubble scattered before them. When he exited the park without his wallet, he wasn't overly concerned. He'd lost maybe thirty dollars, he figured, plus his credit cards and his driver's license. He knew he could cancel all the cards, and even if it took a month for the banks to issue replacements, he'd get by because he'd stashed his new bank card and some cash in his money belt. The only nagging problem he could foresee was the loss of his driver's license. Yes, that could lead to all kinds of nastiness: identity theft, fraud, perhaps something unimaginably worse. As he walked back to his room on Oak Street, he ran through a mental checklist of possessions that he'd flown down to San Francisco in his duffle bag. But when he entered his room he realized the duffle bag itself was missing. Then he saw that someone had punched a hole through the glass next to the window lock, then slid open the casement, slipped through the window and stolen every moveable object that fit through the breach. Only the bed, the tube TV, the desk and the overstuffed love seat remained. Most of the amenities that came with the room were gone: the microwave oven, the coffee maker, the twin desk lamps.

Doyle shakes his head as he considers his missing property. All of his clothes, his books and notepads. He opens his shoulder bag to assure himself that by some slight-of-hand Kandy and ¡Ouch! hadn't rifled through it, too. He's relieved to see that he still has his laptop. And his reading glasses, a bottle of hand sanitizer, a transit pass, some loose change, Kleenex tissues, and (thankfully) the keys to his house back in Victoria. The discovery of his keys trips a memory of another missing item: his passport. He feels his stomach churn. He'd stored his passport in the zipped pocket inside the duffle bag. Without his passport and driver's license, he has no proof of identity. That could cause a problem. He presses two fingers to his lower lip and considers the possibilities. An image of being tossed into the back of a police van forms in his mind: naked, shivering, hungry. As of this moment, he murmurs to himself, you can be arrested as an illegal alien. Better report the stolen passport to the consulate and get them to issue a new one. But the instant that thought occurs to him, it fades when Louis mentions the police.

"I'll call the police, Doyhul," Louis offers. "Not that they do anything. These kinds of things pass through this neighborhood four or five times every day," he adds with a shrug and lifts both hands in exasperation and then folds them over this stomach. "This city has become a metropolis of shit."

"Maybe you're right," Doyle agrees. "I mean about the police not helping so much. Maybe it's better not to get them involved." But he's not convinced that San Francisco is a metropolis of shit. Apart from the twin robberies, he's found it an appealing place; near-perfect if you base your assessment on the once-grand Victorian houses and heritage buildings, all of them sporting bay windows and most of them freshly painted with color-pallet coordination. Shaking his head in disbelief he gazes at Louis and hopes he might feel their common bond. They're both foreigners. They'd both come here with similar aspirations. But look at them now: both dispossessed, sorting through the aftermath of crime. "All I need right now is to find a new place to live. Somewhere safer, I guess."

Louis studies Doyle a moment. His attitude brightens. "Maybe I *can* help," he says. "There's an opening over in Berkeley. The tenant phoned just this morning. The place rarely comes vacant — very desirable!" he adds, and as he waddles down the hallway to his office to retrieve the address in Berkeley, he calls over his shoulder, "And it's on the *top* floor, Doyhul. No more street-level, back-alley, *boites du mard* like this place!"

Doyle stands alone in the room. A thin ray of sunlight reaches through the broken window and illuminates the spray of broken glass on the worn carpet. Where to now? he asks himself. Where next? And furthermore, why is it that you can't seem to put these questions to rest?

Doyle trudges along Dwight Way, both arms weighed down with bags of groceries. When he nears People's Park, he crosses the road and approaches the two-story house that Louis recommended the previous day. He likes the Berkeley area and despite the dozens of homeless people who sleep on the lawns around the park and on the sidewalk in front of his house, so far he's managed to escape any new muggings or robberies.

As he climbs the steps to the front door he fumbles with his house keys, juggles his packages and eventually has to set them on the porch before he can unlock the door and step inside. After he gathers his groceries and starts up the inside staircase that leads to his attic rooms, a man with a tangle of black, curly hair appears at the end of the hallway.

"Hello." The stranger's voice reverberates down the lobby corridor. He glances at Doyle and smiles awkwardly. "I thought you might be someone coming for a session. The front door can be sticky," he explains and swivels his wrist as though he's struggling to turn a doorknob.

"Sorry. Just me," Doyle offers and continues up the staircase to his rooms. He sets his groceries and newspaper on the kitchen counter and after loading the perishables into the refrigerator he stands at the living room window overlooking the street. He's surprised by how much he likes his little loft, a cliché garret that has everything a memoirist could want: a bedroom with a firm mattress and a good reading lamp; a kitchen with its original porcelain sink; an adequate supply of clean plates, glasses, cutlery; a gas oven and stove with two burners; a set of copper-bottom pots and pans in good condition; a twenty-square-foot bathroom with a shower stall with a vented skylight; and a decent-sized living room with a functional sofa, four chairs and a dining table set next to a broad dormer window that provides an unobstructed view of the street.

As he considers the furniture, he decides to shift the blue arborite dining table away from the living room window so that his laptop is sheltered from the direct sunlight. From this vantage-point he can observe the stream of pedestrians strolling up and down the sidewalks and the circus of activity across the road in People's Park. Apart from the local residents, most of them appear to be students or homeless drifters: a salt-and-pepper mix of optimists and the destitute.

Early the same evening James Wayman and Mavis Helm tap at Doyle's door and present him with a loaf of banana bread. "I made extra," Mavis explains and passes the loaf, still warm in the baking pan, into his empty hands. "Would you like to join us for some coffee?"

"We're on the main floor," James adds, his index finger pointing downward. "Where you saw me this afternoon."

The aroma from the home-made bread fills him with a nostalgia of domesticity and comfort that lasts through the evening. He learns that James and Mavis were married during the summer and moved into the main floor apartment in August. Mavis is working on an MA in counseling psychology at Berkeley. James had been a yoga teacher in Los Angeles and then started the White Light Meditation Foundation sponsored by a Hollywood talent manager who'd been one of his yoga students. Last January, "on New Year's Day to be precise," he experienced a personal satori that is propelling him in a "new, undefined direction. The unknown about to be made known," James concludes, and he nods his head with certainty.

His new housemates are very left coast, Doyle decides, self-directed beings working on personal redeployments of their own. Just what he's looking for: the free spirits of 1967 with a modicum of contemporary common sense and social purpose. To advance his writing project it may be helpful to get to know them. But before his hopes become too elevated, Mavis reveals that there are certain local hazards to avoid.

"B-and-E's are endemic," she explains. She's adamant that everyone in the building must lock the doors to the house as they come and go. "Prevention is the only cure," she adds with a clinical emphasis that suggests no single person is responsible for the problem. Local crime is more like a medical condition than social breakdown, a bout of flu best treated with sympathy and common sense.

"But don't worry about the people in the basement," James continues, a counterpoint to Mavis's view of the neighborhood. He explains that three tenants occupy two separate basement apartments. Rosa Zanes, a nurse who works in a local HIV-AIDS clinic, occupies one suite and two engineering students from Taiwan share the other. The engineers are away more often than not, "and it might be a long time before you lay your eyes on either of them."

Mavis nods and smiles at him. "Overall, everyone in the building is fantastic." She waves a hand as if she's welcoming him into the clan. "I'm sure we're going to get along perfectly."

"I think so, too," Doyle says in response to her smile, an expression nearly identical to the look Iris wore whenever she opened her heart to strangers.

The next morning Doyle picks up the thread of his memoir and continues writing on his laptop. The narrative employs a bizarre guiding metaphor, but he doesn't care. He's simply writing about his obsession from a new perspective that he's certain no one has imagined before. It's based on the idea that human freedom, while it certainly exists, is much more limited than many people might suppose. Genetic factors (such as gender, skin color, height) when combined with environmental factors (like nationality, social mobility, poverty or wealth) will impinge upon you in ways that you cannot control. What you *can* control, to some extent, is your response to these circumstances. Even then, maintaining self-control can be extremely difficult.

Say, for example, your wife is dying of pancreatic cancer (here he pauses for a while, as he does four or five times each day, to think of Iris and the last time he touched her, the moment when he pressed his forehead to her forehead to bid her goodbye) and your emotions and behaviors fly out of control no matter how strenuously you fight to reel them in. The one thing you *can* do is to remove yourself from the orbit of distress that impacts you. In short, you can *redeploy:* insert yourself into a new place with a new set of circumstances and adjust your disposition accordingly.

This approach to life, he discovered, is perfectly symbolized by a condition known as the Kessler Syndrome. The Kessler Syndrome was first described in 1978 by Donald J. Kessler, who calculated that an accelerating number of collisions amongst the thousand-plus satellites circling Earth in geo-synchronous orbits is inevitable and that the first crash would likely occur early in the twenty-first century. The first accident, he predicted, would spray a mass of metal debris through the upper atmosphere. This shrapnel would then impact other satellites generating a geometric progression of wrecks that, in shorter and shorter intervals, would turn the entire array of satellite technology into space junk. On February 10, 2009 the first publicly reported collision occurred, at a breath-taking speed of 26,170 miles per hour, when Kosmos 2251, a defunct Russian bird, crashed into Iridium 33, a privately-owned communications blimp. At that moment the first prediction of Kessler's prophecy had been fulfilled.

Was there a remedy for this escalating disaster? Kessler suggested that the growing chaos of space debris should be tracked, their courses plotted, and impact projections defined. All satellites capable of redirecting their orbits should be redeployed in a sort of game that Doyle called *Dodging the Dropping Dominoes*. But it was a mug's game. Ultimately, Earth-based satellite communications would collapse in smash-ups that would illuminate the night sky with tracer-bullet flares and then one by one, blink into silence. In all likelihood, future satellite re-deployments would fail to dodge the ever-enlarging layer of shrapnel spinning through the stratosphere.

"Think about what that means," Doyle told his sons. "No more cell phones. No cash machine transactions. No video transmissions. No military surveillance. People will simply have to talk to one another in person, face-to-face!"

Rendered an historic artifact, the satellite array will become an enduring metaphor of human technological genius reduced to chaos. Doyle is certain of all this. Centuries from now the Kessler Syndrome will become the scientific equivalent of the story of the Tower of Babel. Except it will be better known. And a proven fact.

Mavis Helm stirs under the covers and presses her body against her husband. She can't remember him coming to bed, but she can recall his feet twitching in an irregular pattern that roused her from sleep. She rolls her right foot over his leg to calm him.

"James," she whispers as the quaking in his legs continues, "stop it. You're dreaming."

She opens her eyes. The dawn light is cast against the pull-down shade, a tattered blind that must be as old as the house. It makes her think of Egyptian papyrus, a yellow sheet that filters the light of day and warms the night chill with its pale illumination.

She drapes her arm over his chest, thinking how lovely and warm she would feel if he settled his arm around her, around her breasts or over her hip, stoking the heat deep within her body. But as soon as this thought arrives, she tries to dismiss it. Lately her life has been easier when she embraces the reality of the workweek stretching before her and she releases her untimely desire for James's affection. It's her version of the principle of non-attachment.

He moans slightly and she kisses his shoulder. He pulls away, wheezing as he tugs the covers up to his neck.

"All right," she says as he slips back to sleep. She's fully awake now and turns onto her back and reflects on her marriage to a man born fifteen years before she was even conceived. "Fifteen years *your senior*," her sister, Joleen, had said over the phone from Florida after Mavis announced her engagement. She then added, "Think about it: he probably had two or three *real* girlfriends before you started kindergarten." And maybe another dozen platonic attachments. Although Joleen never suggested this last possibility, the thought drifts through Mavis's imagination as she lies beside him.

Brushing a hand over his eyes, James rouses himself. "Mmmm?" He waits a moment and turns so that he, too, faces the ceiling. Then he inhales deeply. He likes to begin each day with a series of prana exercises. He pulls the air deeply into his lungs, suspends it for a count of ten and then exhales. Inhale ten, suspend ten, exhale ten. Always through the nose, never the mouth.

Mavis watches him briefly and then pulls herself from the bed. The air is cool, but she doesn't bother to wrap her housecoat over her shoulders. She's in a mood to tease him. She pulls on her slippers and pads across the room. When she gets to the door, she returns to James's side of the bed and bends at the waist to kiss his forehead, her breasts floating above his shoulders. His eyes open and he smiles as he absorbs the vision before him and he reaches for her.

"I'm going to shower," she says and slips from his grasp and dances toward the bathroom.

James closes his eyes and continues the cycle of deep breathing. A minute later he hears the spray of water hit the glass panel in the shower as Mavis pulls the door behind her in the stall. It pops with a tight, moist resonance as the rubber edges of the door and door-frame seal together. *Schluck.* They've been here just over a month now and the sounds of the house are becoming familiar to him. After a few seconds he steers the noise away from his awareness and he settles his attention on the flow of effortless breathing.

Soon he is one with the air.


James sits at the kitchen table eating toast and drinking the Americano that he prepared on the gas stove after Mavis finished her shower. When she joins him he tells her, "I had a dream last night. One I've never had before."

"I knew you were dreaming. Your feet were twitching so much they woke me up." After taking a sip of coffee Mavis adjusts her sweater. In her rush to prepare for work at the clinic she misaligned the buttons and buttonholes and arrived in the kitchen with her sweater lopsided. It has five, mother-of-pearl buttons up the front. They're gorgeous, she thinks as she pushes the three lower buttons into their proper place. The two below her throat she leaves open. "What was it about?"

"About levitating." He draws his attention away from her sweater and points his thumb to the back door. "In the backyard." As he eats the toast, he reveals as much detail as he can remember of the dream. What struck him was the *feeling* of the experience, he says. "There was this flow of energy streaming from my hands. It was incredible."

"The sign of a healer." She pulls her damp hair into one hand and with the other she ties it behind her neck. She fumbles briefly and then cinches the knot tight and eats a corner of her toast.

"You think so?"

"When it emanates through your hands? Yes." She blows a stream of air over the lip of her mug and sips at the coffee. "But it was a dream. Not reality."

James dips his head to the left and glances through the window. A few drops of rain spatter against the glass. "You're right. A dream, but still within the single continuity of awareness." He raises a finger for emphasis. "It's like the weather. One day it rains, the next it's sunny. They're opposite conditions, but part of a single system. Dreams and waking consciousness are part of one continuity."

Mavis continues to eat her toast and nods. He would say these things, little analogies, parables, insights — all of them pointing to the grand continuity. To oneness. Although doubts continue to plague him, she knows that he maintains a kind of faith, despite the absence of any deity in his system. It's all Nature for him. With a capital N. Or fundamental Darwinism as worshipped in the Church of Evolution. Try as she might, she can't quite accept all of it. There's a vacuum at the center of his cosmology; ultimately there is nothing to believe *in*. "But what is *oneness*?" she asked him shortly after they started to sleep together. "I mean, what is it really? There's no *it* in your spir*it*," she added and then she laughed to reveal that this was a half-joke, one that elicited a half-smile from him. "It's the paradox you have to embrace," he countered. "*That's* the part you have to believe in."

James finishes his coffee and glances away. "I think I'm going for a walk today. Maybe head down to the ocean to watch the surf. Want to come?"

She rolls her shoulders and frowns. A day strolling along the beach with James. How she would love that. But she has to meet Dr. Box in his clinic at nine, and then continue the work on her thesis proposal with her graduate supervisor back on campus. Besides, James knows her schedule, the new routine she's established to carry her through her MA degree. "Can't," she announces without explanation.

He understands. In fact, he admires her focus and determination. Before they'd moved from LA to Berkeley she was equally dedicated to her job at the high school. While the details of her work life may have changed, her work ethic has grown stronger than ever. "Of course," he says and shrugs and for a moment their eyes lock together and hold.

This is as close as they might get today, she realizes, but it's very close and it offers more intimacy than she's enjoyed with any other man. When they connect like this he never turns his eyes away and the two of them can go very deep, to a point where they're joined, a point of contact that reveals they are a single being. The experience takes her close to a oneness of their own making. It's comforting — *joyous* — and when she feels the comfort of it again, she smiles.

"All right. I have to think something through, anyway," he says and returns her smile and begins to clear the dishes from the table.

She studies him while he moves through the kitchen. He has a magnificent head, a head perhaps too large in proportion to the rest of his body. His forehead is broad and reaches high up to his hairline but it remains completely free of wrinkles, remarkable for a man of forty-seven. His jaw hangs solidly under his mouth and when he laughs his face is radiant, but now, in this contemplative mood, his lips are pressed into a tight line beneath his long, curved nose. Aquiline. She thinks of his nose as Roman, a philosopher's nose, whatever that means. His eyebrows are woolly and untamed, floating above his heavy-lidded eyes. And oh, what eyes! His eyes are a dwelling place, a place where, whenever she wants, she can measure the true depth of her marriage.


As Mavis packs her lunch, books and laptop into her bag, James stands on the front steps of their house on the corner of Dwight Way and Regent Street, opposite People's Park. The home is a solid, Victorian mansion built in 1907, with a west-facing orientation that catches the afternoon heat of the summer sun, or on a late September morning like this, reveals the prospect of a heavy storm that is about to wash through the city.

As he waits for Mavis he feels his feet fastened to the

porch, immobile and languorous, exactly opposite to the zest of electricity pulsing through his legs in his dream. He can sense the old doubts returning, long lines of hesitation cast into the ocean, their anchors dragging on the seabed and snagging him with each passing thought. It's happened before, when he feels he's approaching a new threshold that offers a way to move forward, then the suspicions begin to emerge and challenge everything that he considers secure and undeniable.

What *is* undeniable, is his certainty that this chronic skepticism is rooted in his childhood and the betrayal by his mother and aunt and uncle. He shakes his head and expels a deep breath. No, do not dwell on that nonsense, he whispers to himself. It leads only to remorse. But what if they'd been honest with him as a child? What if he'd been able to decipher the clues? If they hadn't waited until his eighteenth birthday to disclose that they'd adopted him as a new-born baby. And in the next moment, revealed that the nun whom they visited each Christmas was not his devout aunt, Sister Catherine — but in fact, his own mother. What if, *what if?* In the middle distance he can see the madness tied to this line of questions and he knows enough to back off before it sucks him under again.

Besides, there's too much to live for. So much that he'd built through discipline and focus. And good luck. And therein lay the magic of it all. The monthly endowment he received from the White Light Foundation revealed that his purpose was supported by a spontaneous, natural energy. He had not sought money or fame, but here it is, delivered to him by serendipity. At least he was aware that all of it could be snatched away at some point, as good fortune often is. In the meantime, he would exploit it to benefit others. Yes, above the dread and worry he can sense a series of waves flowing, a sense of growth, enlargement, opportunity. Things are about to change. Soon there will be more people wanting to hear the teaching. The weekly sessions of fifteen or twenty people that he leads in the living room would expand to hundreds of seekers just as it had in Los Angeles. He considers all this in a daze, his feet thick, immovable.

"Okay, I guess I'm off." Mavis swings the bag over her shoulder, not too eager to be on her way. "So where are you going to walk?"

"Maybe along the shore at Golden Gate Park. Unless it rains."

"You feeling all right?" She kisses his cheek and tries to read the look in his face. "The blues got you again?"

"Just for a few minutes. But I fought back, turned them into yellows and greens." He forces a smile and brushes away his uncertainty. "Really, it's not a problem."

"Okay." She kisses the other cheek.

"I'm leading a class at five. Will you be home in time to join us?"

"I'll try," she says and makes her way down the stairs to the curb, past the row of bodies sleeping next to the road. She crosses the street and climbs into her Prius. Without looking back, she starts the engine, guides the car out of the parking slot, and turns into the traffic.

James stands at the top of the steps and stares at the empty space she'd inhabited moments ago. A feeling of loss wells through his stomach. Mavis is perfect for him. But in the past few weeks he's inserted a barrier between them. He'll have to explain this to her, to ensure she understands that this new phase isn't a rejection of her, but rather his uncertainty about the visions he experiences almost every day.

*Depression. Bipolar disorder. Anorexia nervosa. Bulimia. Schizophrenia.*

Dr. Philip Box scans the diagnostic summaries of the patient files stacked on his desk. *Anxiety disorder.* He turns to another file describing a homeless sixteen-year-old boy: *pyromania.* And another: *depression*, again.

He knows this is a bad way to begin the week, scanning the caseload on a Monday morning, anticipating how to manage the line of patients before they walk through his door. He tosses the folders aside and glances through the office window onto Telegraph Avenue, watches a city bus pull to the curb and discharge its passengers onto the rain-drenched sidewalk. Compared to last year, the buses carry more passengers these days, a direct consequence of the on-going recession and an exhausted economy, he figures. Things are so dire that the State of California now pays him in IOUs. He absorbs the cost to his staff as a pro bono expense and deducts it against income he makes treating drug-addled sports, film and music stars. But even with the help of his accountant's legerdemain, he knows his routine Monday-morning act of charity is costing him money. Of course, he reminds himself, it has to. After all, what does charity mean unless you give something up?

No, Dr. Philip Seaton Gerard Box does not like what the world does to his patients. Not at all. But he understands that he can't change the world; all he can do is help them to adapt. It's a practical view of psychiatry, not terribly optimistic, but certainly a realistic approach. That is his job at its basic, social-utilitarian level, and in a good year he believes he restores twenty or thirty patients to their fundamental integrity. As for the hundreds of others who shuffle through his office, well, much like his own situation — with a long-standing ailment that time might, or might not, heal — each is a work-in-progress.

He braces both hands on the top of his skull and tilts his chin toward his chest in an effort to stretch the interspinous ligament that runs down the back of his neck. After the car accident last summer the acute pain that locked his head in place above his shoulders became chronic. His physiotherapist offered scant relief. Tylenol Three helped, but after one week, the twice-daily dose of codeine dragged him into a bleak fog. Yesterday he toyed with the notion of dosing himself with some serious medication, a shot of morphine, but then talked himself out of it. "You're not that stupid," he announces to the empty room, and continues to stretch the ligaments until his skin burns under the increasing tension.

He checks his watch and realizes that Mavis Helm will be arriving in about twenty minutes to sit in on another round of patient screening. Eleven years ago he agreed to serve as a clinical supervisor for the university's graduate school psychology interns and each term a student is attached to his practice one morning a week for ten weeks. To begin the internship they simply observe the flow of fractured souls streaming through his office as he determines their diagnosis and assigns them to various local therapists for on-going treatment. Once the interns demonstrate an understanding of the screening process, he allows them to assess one of his own patients. If they conduct themselves competently, he encourages them to propose a therapeutic program and assist in the treatment.

Like a few other interns, Mavis generates a sense of hope that their profession might heal some of the walking wounded. But beyond that, there's something special about her. Her obsession with Fritz Perls, for example, and his once-fashionable Gestalt Therapy. Some colleagues considered Perls laughable, but he knew that the World War One veteran (the old goose actually fought in the trenches *for the Germans!*) offered Mavis a path into the inner life, just as valid as his own entry into psychiatry thirty years ago via Sigmund Freud. Both Freud and Perls are now pretty well discarded by most contemporary clinicians, but they're not quite forgotten. Furthermore, Mavis brings insight and intelligence to psychology. She rightly believes that the therapist's psyche is itself a transformative agent and that to heal someone you have to enter the leper colony, put your own health at risk and communicate the strength of your commitment by absorbing your patient's pain. A rather feeble analogy, and a very mixed metaphor, he mutters to himself. In psychiatry and counseling psychology the tactics are different, but *that power*, the strength of belief, has to infuse the patient so that he believes there's a way forward. If you have that, and Mavis does, then the profession becomes a calling. A gift to the world.


Mavis sits next to the window at the left side of Box's desk, almost out of the patients' line of sight. He'd explained to her that he wanted her presence felt by the patients (never *clients*, she noted) but that she shouldn't become a distraction. "Don't intrude," he told her shortly after they'd met. "Just watch, make some observations, then I'll go over your questions at the end of each session, when we debrief." She rotated her wedding band around her finger and wondered what, exactly, he had in mind by the word *debrief*.

Their first three or four appointments together went reasonably well, and she began to grasp the screening method he used to move people through the system so they would be assigned to the appropriate specialists. He likened his role to a gatekeeper at the entry point to a vast therapeutic department store: Depression, third floor. Anxiety disorder, take the rear elevator on the right. He kept a few for his own practice and he usually booked a set of three appointments to see them personally. He tended to focus on behavioral problems like obsessive-compulsive and addiction disorders. These weren't really her area of interest, but the more Mavis observed Box, the more she appreciated what he was doing. The downside of working with a behaviorist was the growing doubt she harbored about the possibilities offered by her own prospective specialty, Gestalt Therapy. Her increasing uncertainty persisted over the first few weeks of her internship until the day when Fay Flood walked into Box's office and flopped into the chair opposite him.

"What brings you into the office today, Fay?" Box glances at her briefly as he scans her file. His locked head and shoulders turn in unison as he shifts his attention from her to her file and back again.

"Art." She nods her head with certainty, and smiles at Mavis with self-satisfaction. "Yeah-yeah. I'd say it was art that brought me here. The fact that I'm painting again."

Mavis studies Fay's face. Flush with energy, her eyes are intense and probing. A mass of dense brown hair falls past her shoulders and when she tries to pin a strand of it behind one ear, the mane springs back willfully to assert its independence. As Fay brushes her hair away once more, Mavis notices that a ring encircles each finger and that every fingernail is bitten to the quick. She guesses that Fay is perhaps thirty-five, but it's obvious that she's lived rough, lived the equivalent of two or three lives already.

"I see Dr. Benson treated you in the past." Box doesn't look up as he studies the file more thoroughly.

"Yeah. For a while, yeah." Fay pushes her lips together and narrows her eyes. "But that wasn't as productive as it could've been."

"No?" He places the file on his desk and leans backward as though he's trying to ease a weight from his shoulders. "Not productive?"

Fay looks at Mavis again, an invitation for her to add something to the conversation. But when Mavis offers nothing, Fay decides to change tactics. She opens her bag, an artist's portfolio, and unrolls a scroll of paper and lays it on Box's desk. "This is what I'm talking about. I'm back to painting again."

She stands and places a book on one corner of the painting and grasps the opposite edge with her hand. Box sets his fingers on a third corner of the paper and gazes into the image before them. A large figure, humanoid, sits in an awkward squat, its monkey-face pulled wide in a severe smile. The creature is neither male nor female; unsexed as opposed to unisex. The style is neo-primitive, similar to the many images Picasso created during his fascination with African art. The face, arms and torso are composed with solid, flat lines. Minor color shifts — brown, taupe, beige — create the impression of limited depth. A wooden quality fixes the creature's expression, as though it might be part of a totem. The painting has an undeniable technical excellence that draws the eye into the heart of its construction. Yet the most striking aspect of the painting is the growth that springs in two stages from the creature's lap. And it's this perverse growth, Mavis decides, that reveals Fay's inner torment. From the lap of the creature a small clone is emerging: simian, skeletal, malevolent. And from the head of this second creature a third, smaller being appears. The two secondary figures face the first, their mouths open, yammering for attention.

"It's called *Inner Trialogue*," Fay whispers to break the silence. "Because of the Trinity engaged in conversation. Most people never think of God, Jesus and the Holy Ghost talking to one another. Trying to sort things out." She looks at Mavis and Box. "Like you would in a real trial," she adds to emphasize the title's double-entendre.

Box lifts his hand from the painting and slides the book from the far corner. Fay rolls the paper back into a tight scroll and returns to her chair.

"Fay, tell me something." He pauses for emphasis. "Why are you here?" Box tries to hold her with his eyes, but as soon as he asks this, she glances away.

"I told you," she says when she recovers her composure. "I'm painting again. After two months, it's come back." She presses her chin toward him with certainty.

"What's come back?"

"The art. Aren't you listening? I spent the last month like a zombie. Everything" — she waves a hand next to her head — "everything that matters was buried under cotton. Worse than cotton. Under thick, steel wool. I couldn't *see anything anymore!*"

"Because of your meds?"

"Yes," she snaps.

Box waits a moment; he wants to defuse the tension before proceeding. He crosses a finger over his lips. A blade of pain flashes the length of his neck as he notches his head and shoulders to one side and then returns his attention to Fay. "And now that you're painting again, everything's fine."

"Yeah." Fay draws a long breath and settles both hands in her lap. "I probably have another twenty of these back at my place. I do at least one a day, sometimes three on a good day. Not all the same theme," she adds as if she needs to emphasize the importance of diversity. "And not in the same style."

Box nods his assent. "Good. So everything is good."

"Yeah. *I'm alive again.*" She licks her lips, tries to determine how much she should reveal and what to hold back. "But the drugs Dr. Benson gave me were killing the best part of me." She dips her head toward Mavis, a plea for sympathy. "I wasn't sure at first, but now that I'm painting again, I know it's true. Because of those drugs ... I was dying."

"Fay, believe me, no one wants to harm you." This time Box manages to hold her attention with his eyes. "What I'm worried about is what will happen to you without your Tegretol."

"What will happen is that I will paint more. And more. And more again."

Box shifts his shoulders and his voice falls to a whisper. "So then why are you here, Fay?"

She looks away, again weighing what to tell, what to hide.

"It's because you're frightened, isn't it." He delivers this insight calmly, as a statement, not a question.

Her jaw shifts under her mouth, left then right.

"You're frightened of what happens next. After you do three and four paintings a day." Instead of coaxing her forward with silence, he now comes at her in a rush. "Once you start doing twenty and then thirty paintings a day. When you get to the top of the hill and you see the crash coming. Am I right?... Fay?"

Her face flushes with a series of expressions: weariness, exasperation, entrapment. "Yeah," she whimpers with a slight nod. "Yeah.... *I'm fucking terrified.*"

"All right. Then let's help you with that. We can help you with that."

Fay lifts her bag into her lap and draws her arms around it, hugging it to her chest. "What can you do to help?"

"I'm going to ask you to see someone else. Not Dr. Benson."

"Good," she says with a sigh. "I can't see him again."

"Don't worry. Remember, we're trying to help you." His voice is full of genuine sympathy and he glances at Mavis with a look of assurance.


Moments later, to Mavis's surprise, Box writes a new prescription and then refers Fay to another clinic. After Fay exits the office with the slips of paper in her hand Mavis feels as though an opportunity is falling through her fingers. "I'd really like to take her case," she says, leaning forward in her chair as if she's ready to dart through the office door to retrieve Fay.

"I don't deal with bipolar disorders." He narrows his eyes. The decision is final. "I'm a behaviorist. You know that."

Mavis studies the severity in his face, the tightly clipped salt-and-pepper beard that defines the perimeter of his jaw. He has no mustache, just an inch-wide band of facial hair running ear-to-ear along the circumference of his narrow face. It reminds her of long-faced Amish men, of the solemnity of Abraham Lincoln. She considers another approach. "What if I work with the doctor you referred her to?"

"Simpson?" He considers this a moment. "I don't think

so. Besides, he's never taken an intern. He doesn't tolerate them well." His tone is dismissive. The unspoken corollary: you're lucky to be invited into my practice one morning each week to observe me as I sift through the unending line of lost souls.

Mavis glares at him, tries to understand his instant dismissal of her idea, of her need to work with someone she knows she can help. Fay possesses a talent that needs nurturing. That much is evident from her painting, disturbing as the image might be. But it's just as evident that Fay won't get any help from Philip Box. "All right." Mavis zips up her jacket as she prepares to leave Box's office and make her way through the rain to her car. "I'll see you next week."

As she opens the door the ceiling lights flicker and die. Box utters a gasp of resignation. "Not again," he sighs. "You'll have to use the staircase. They'll be pitch-black, but the elevators won't have any power either."

Once outside, she jogs through the downpour to her Prius, starts the engine and pulls into the traffic heading back toward the clinic and along Telegraph Avenue in the direction of the university. As she drives, her frustration from working with Box begins to simmer. Perhaps he's found a way to cope with the overwhelming load he carries by distributing the caseload to his colleagues across the city. Or maybe he generates these multiple hand-offs as a kind of personal bail-out, as part of his own therapeutic regime.

The moment she realizes that Box's capitulation is the source of her frustration she recognizes a familiar face standing at a bus stop. Waiting out the rain in a bus shelter a few blocks down the street from Box's clinic stands Fay Flood pulling her hair to one side, just as she'd done in his office. Mavis smiles. It's as though she's conjured her up.

She rolls down the window and leans across the passenger seat toward the curb. "Want a ride?"

Fay glances away, unsure who is calling her. Then she recognizes Mavis and steps next to the car.

"Get in." Mavis is surprised by her own voice, barking out an order rather than tendering an offer. "It's pouring out!" she cries and points to the rain dashing against the windshield. "And with the power down, you could be waiting here for hours."

"Okay. Sure." Fay opens the door and slides her portfolio onto the back seat as the car pulls into the traffic. They limp through the first three intersections — stop-go-stop-go — until the electric power grid bursts to life, the street lights establish control of the city interchanges again, and the traffic resumes its automated snarl.

She and Fay drive toward the university for five minutes before Fay announces that she has to return to her apartment. Rather than drop her off at another bus stop so that Fay can find her own way home, Mavis decides to skip her meeting with her thesis advisor, Lorraine Dansky, and accept Fay's invitation for a cup of coffee at her apartment.

She knows that this is a bad decision as soon as she makes it. But rather than appear fickle to Fay and change her mind and revert to her appointment with Dansky, she thinks that whatever time she spends with Fay will be more valuable than trying to weave together the dislocated strands of her thesis proposal.

She calls Lorraine Dansky on her cell phone (busy, fortunately) and recites an excuse into her voice mailbox. "I've got an upset stomach," she mumbles into the phone. "I don't think I can meet until later this week." Mavis has always suspected that nausea is one part intestinal, two parts neurosis, and therefore the perfect excuse for Dr. Dansky, who specializes in treating hypochondria. To conclude her message, she dredges a heavy cough from the bottom of her lungs to provide evidence of complicating factors.

Mavis follows Fay Flood up the narrow staircase to her apartment above one of the many abandoned retail shops in Emeryville. As she climbs the stairs she wonders what she might be getting herself into. Fay unlocks the door to her apartment and guides Mavis ahead of her. She drops her bag on the arm of an overstuffed sofa and wheels about.

"Welcome," she says and sweeps her arms wide, an invitation to enter her domain.

The room is not large but it contains the basic necessities for urban living: a kitchen area with a twin-burner stove, a deep stainless-steel sink, two chairs and a small dining table pushed next to the only window in the room, and a sofa facing a TV that is broadcasting *Degrassi: The Next Generation*. On the left, a door opens into a windowless bathroom. Two more doors, both closed, lead to what Mavis assumes must be two bedrooms. At the far end of the apartment stands an artist's easel. The walls are covered with dozens of Fay's paintings, drawings, sketches, all of them in various stages of completion. Not one looks like a finished piece.

"Sorry about the mess." Fay clicks off the TV and then quickly adds, "But I guarantee you, the coffee's good."

The coffee *is* good and Mavis sips it slowly as she relaxes at the table and gazes through the window into the back alley behind the building. The rain has let up and the rutted asphalt pools the gutter water into swirling rainbows of waste-oil slicks. Above the buildings on the far side of the alley, massive bands of slate-colored clouds roll in from the

Pacific. Views of the San Francisco skyline fill the distant horizon, and to the right, the twin arches of the Golden Gate Bridge stand above the entrance to the bay.

"The north light is best for painting," Fay says, confident that Mavis will admire this view of the bay. It surprised her the first time she saw it. Who imagined you could have a million-dollar view from a dime-a-day dorm in Emeryville? That's what the rent had been a hundred years ago when the Buxtons let out the two apartments above their meat shop. Since then, the entire block had been demolished and rebuilt, every building except this one. The well-worn "Buxton's Meats" sign is still visible on the brick exterior above the sidewalk. And the apartment still commands the magnificent view. "I've got lots of paintings of the bridge," she adds. "The light and mood change every day. It's as though I get a new chance at the truth every time I do them again."

"A chance at the truth?"

"Yeah, yeah." Fay sorts through a sheaf of art paper stacked next to the sofa and sets three sheets on the table. "Think about Claude Monet. He did dozens of versions of the same church doors in France. Set up his easel in the same place across the street from the church at different times of the year. Each one is perfect. But even though the image is identical, they reveal completely different truths." She pauses and then adds, "*Not* that I'm a Claude Monet. Or that the bridge is a cathedral ... though there are certain spiritual similarities." She smiles and Mavis realizes this is the first time that she's seen Fay's face light up with anything approaching spontaneity.

Mavis considers Fay's three paintings. She follows the lines of the Golden Gate Bridge, the steel cables rising to the familiar peaks, all set out with firm, hard strokes delivered in haste. In one image the colors are earthy, full of foreboding. In another they're bright, almost frivolous. The third conveys a sense of majesty, of a divine hand shaping the tight peaks, towers arching towards the clouds that brush against their tips. "They're very good," Mavis says with conviction. She's startled by the confidence they portray. She tries to align these images with the confused, half-broken woman she'd seen in Dr. Box's office two hours earlier. "When did you do these?"

"Maybe a year ago." Fay toys with the rings on her fingers, twisting each in turn as she stands admiring her own work. "Yeah-yeah," she whispers under her breath. Part of her has trouble believing she actually created these.

"Before the — "

"Yeah." She cuts Mavis off. "Before all that." Fay tries to pin a band of hair behind her ear, gives up, and then carefully stacks the paintings together and walks them across the room. She stands in silence a moment and then stores them in a new spot, in a wall-mounted cabinet above the TV.

It's as though she's discovering something new in these images, Mavis thinks, a precious quality that deserves better care. A new truth, perhaps. She decides to ask her about what made her paint, or how Fay decided *what* to paint when a shuffling noise, the sound of slippers scuffing across a floor, catches her attention.

An instant later a bedroom door teeters open and behind the half-ajar doorway appears a small, tentative face.

"Teejay, I told you: *not when I have company*." Fay strides to the door and peers into the dusty light of the bedroom. "You know the rules."

The door closes slightly, to a narrow opening, enough room for a set of dark lips to press against the doorjamb. "I have to go to the bathroom," a voice whispers.

Fay walks in a tight circle. She glances at Mavis and back at the door. "All right. Quick march. Then back to bed."

Mavis is startled to see a child, perhaps thirteen or fourteen, emerge from the half-lit darkness, turn quickly to assess Mavis, nod once, then dart into the bathroom and close the door.

"My daughter." Fay offers this as form of apology. "I had to put her on a time-out today."

Mavis considers this as Teejay loiters in the bathroom. She can hear the toilet flush and the sink taps turn on and off three times. If she's been restricted to the bedroom since Fay left the apartment to attend her session with Dr. Box, Mavis calculates the time-out amounts to at least four hours.

"That's enough, Teejay. You know where to go." Her voice is rigid, barely able to contain the surge of tension bottled inside her. To distract herself, Fay walks to the stove to retrieve the coffee pot and refill Mavis's cup.

The door cracks open and from the safety of the bathroom Teejay scans the living room, and then pushes the door wide enough to reveal her head. She looks directly at Mavis, who discerns the shape of Teejay's lips silently mouthing two words: *"Help me."*

When she sees this, Mavis stands up, approaches the bathroom and turns back to Fay. "You must introduce me. I insist."

Fay releases a deep sigh and looks from the child to Mavis. "All right. But we're going to be very polite. Right, Teejay?"

When it's clear that she can emerge safely, the girl tiptoes into the living room and stands before the two women. "I'm Teresa-Jacinta," she announces, "but everyone calls me Teejay." She casts her eyes away a moment and then looks directly at Mavis. "You're very pretty," she says with an innocence that is completely disarming.

"Teejay, no cheek." Fay's voice is guttural. A warning.

"Please," Mavis whispers and waves her fingers to temper Fay's mood. Then she laughs at Teejay's bit of flattery and takes the girl's hand in her own. "I'm Mavis Helm. And how old are you?"

"Twelve and a half," she says with certainty. "Exactly a half, this coming Friday."

Mavis smiles at her precision and stands next to the table and invites her to sit in the chair she'd occupied. Her neck is long and elegant, her breasts barely formed. She has a ballerina's posture, but as she settles in the chair Mavis realizes Teejay's lean body is beginning to fill out in the belly and lower back. Yet any hint of disproportion is dissolved by the perfect balance in her face. The cheekbones are set very high and her nose is slender and petite. Her eyes are especially beautiful: deep-set and unusually large, with steel gray irises. One word sums up the impression she imparts: *wise*. She's one of the reborn, Mavis thinks, without knowing what this might mean.

"And how old do you think I am?" Mavis wants to press forward with some kind of conversation. Anything to ensure Teejay doesn't return to time-out.

Teejay lifts her eyes to Mavis's face and then scans her sweater and the mother-of-pearl buttons. She looks at the coffee mugs on the table. She thinks she knows the correct answer, but weighs what might happen if she blurts it out. Her mother would march her back to bed and she'd have no supper. "A little younger than my mother," she says with confidence, knowing this is both true and flattering, and that it would mask what she's already guessed about Mavis.

The women chuckle at this and Mavis embraces Fay's

forearm with her hand and says, "You're very lucky to have her. She's perfect."

"Sometimes," Fay says, somewhat relieved. "I've been home-schooling her since school went back in session last month." She glances at Teejay and continues, "When I look at my life, I know Teejay is a blessing. My one and only."

"Apart from your art," Mavis adds.

Fay nods as her cheeks begin to flush. The mood has changed now and Mavis senses some warmth between Fay and her daughter.

"Can I see you again?" Mavis lifts her coat from the back of the chair and slings it over an arm. "The two of you, I mean?"

Fay glances about, embarrassed and somewhat confused now that her daughter has been brought into the relationship. "Yeah-yeah. Of course," she stammers when the silence lasts a little too long.

"Sometimes we go for walks," Teejay suggests.

"Then a walk it will be. Maybe this weekend." Mavis smiles, unsure how to end her stay. She steps toward the front door but before she can touch the door handle, Teejay darts beside her and beckons her with a finger. She wants to whisper something into Mavis's ear.

"Teejay." Her mother's voice drops a tone.

But the girl ignores the warning and holds her lips next to Mavis's cheek. "You're thirty-two," she whispers. "Just nod if I'm right." She backs away and looks into Mavis's eyes.

Mavis nods once, her jaw slack with surprise.

Teejay smiles as though she's just solved a difficult math problem on the first try. Then she turns on her heels, slips into the bedroom and closes the door behind her.

After leaving Fay and Teejay, Mavis sits in her car and eats her sandwich. Once she's digested the events of the morning, she drives to the university library to continue the work on her thesis proposal, a tedious process that she sustains without a break through the evening. The long hours serve as a kind of penance for skipping her meeting with Lorraine Dansky, she muses, and once she confesses this to herself she slams her books onto the table in disgust. *Can you not take one, single, solitary day off without feeling guilty?*

After she returns home she eats one of the hard-boiled eggs that she prepared on Sunday night and stored in the refrigerator next to the cheese and veggies. She likes to sprinkle the exposed part of the egg with a dash of pepper (a habit acquired from her grandfather) and with a teaspoon scoop the yolk and the white in tiny proportions from the shell, adding a little more pepper as she proceeds. While she eats she gazes at the blur of news on the TV: swine flu, corporate bankruptcy, ice sheets the size of cities collapsing into the ocean around the Antarctic, and most strange: a phenomenon the newscaster dubs *the Aflockalypse:* over ninety separate episodes of birds, hundreds at a time, dropping lifeless from the sky in different countries around the world. My god, she thinks, what a mess. When she's seen enough, she clicks off the remote and wanders to the bedroom at the back of the house.


An hour earlier James had gone to their room to write in his journal. Two or three times a week he sits propped against the headboard on their bed and writes with a pencil in a moleskin notebook. Writing is a decades-long habit, he told Mavis soon after they met. He's given the diary a working title, *Journal from the Center of Time*, and he has an idea that one day he'll shape the manuscript into something whole and find a publisher, one of the imprints specializing in meditation and life-energy, someone willing to gamble on publishing a new perspective on the human situation.

It's past ten o'clock when Mavis slips on her bathrobe, sits at the foot of the bed and begins to brush out her hair. "I told a lie today," she says when she has his attention.

"A lie?" He sets the journal in his lap and looks at her. "What kind of lie?"

She glances away and wonders where to begin. With the session in Box's office? Picking up Fay at the bus stop? "I told Dansky I was nauseous and that I couldn't talk about my thesis. But I just left a voice message. Nothing face-to-face," she adds with a weak smile as if to suggest that a voicemail lie is merely a prank, the equivalent of frivolous gossip or flattery.

"Careful, kiddo. Even white lies can lead to dangerous destinations."

"Meaning?"

"Meaning they're boomerangs. They can come right back at you. And they can hit you pretty hard, too." James studies her as she drags the brush through the cloud of blond hair. Three, four, five caresses. He loves this nightly ritual, the ministrations of feminine beauty. She glances at him between brush strokes and smiles at something, an inner thought, he doesn't know what. "So tell me what happened. Why no meeting with Dansky?"

Mavis rolls the brush in her hand, pulls the clot of hair into her fist and walks to her side of the bed. "It started at the clinic. We had this new client, Fay Flood, come in." She drops the wad of hair into the wastebasket, lays the brush on the night table and hangs her bathrobe on the hook behind the door. When she slips under the covers James wraps his arm around her shoulders and she nuzzles her head against his chest. She tucks a pillow between them and decides not to press beyond this boundary tonight, not until she reveals everything about Fay and her reams of art and her remarkable daughter.

She dismisses the anecdote about lying to Dansky and tells the story chronologically, inwardly attempting to analyze her attraction to Fay as she speaks. She really doesn't fully understand it, she confesses. Her fascination began with the painting, the piece she called *Inner Trialogue*. Fay is the first client she's seen in Box's office whose problems seem bound up in visual imagery. It's a perfect case for Gestalt Therapy because a comprehensive session could integrate all the inner threads of her mystery. She wants Fay to inhabit every image, to reveal her subconscious through the work, and then to confront the demons that have driven her into a manic depression and brought her to Box's clinic for help. In part she knows that Fay might serve as a case study for her thesis, that with Fay she can provide a new justification for interpretative psychology. She could make a new case for self-knowledge, a case against the twin monoliths of behaviorism and psycho-pharmacology that eclipsed insight therapy thirty years ago.

"Part of this — okay, maybe most of it," she admits, is about her own need to advance her MA degree. But when she met the child, her attention shifted abruptly. "There's something ethereal ... yet corrupted, about Teejay," she concludes, reflecting that both words seem to fit her perfectly. "That's her nickname. Short for Teresa-Jacinta."

"Jacinta...." James lingers on girl's name. "There was a Portuguese girl named Jacinta Marto. One of three kids who reported visitations of angels and the Virgin Mary during the First World War. She made three prophesies, and at the age of ten predicted her own death just hours before she died. From the 1919 pandemic, I think."

"Really?" Mavis lifts her head and studies him briefly. "How do you know all this?"

"My mother."

"Right. Of course." She makes a minor adjustment, pulls her body up along his torso, and then lays her head against his shoulder and sets the palm of one hand between her thighs. James's mother, Sister Catherine, is a devout Catholic. Pious, obedient, God-fearing. In fact, soon after James's birth, exactly five days following her own twenty-first birthday, she turned the care of her son over to her sister and brother-in-law and commenced her vows of perpetual faith to become a Dominican nun. It was the only response she could summon following her rape behind the church vestry late one Saturday night. But James insists that they ignore his family. As a result, Mavis has never met his mother, aunt or uncle.

"It's sad," she continues. "Fay and Teejay living on welfare and food stamps. Scrambling to find a therapist. A social worker checking on them every few weeks. No money. You'd think if there's a god, *She* wouldn't permit this kind of suffering."

"Hmm. A Christian fantasy with a feminist twist. Dansky might enjoy that."

Mavis lifts her head from his shoulder again and smiles when she sees that he's taken the bait. "I don't think Dansky believes in God. Feminism, yes."

"And suddenly *you* believe in God? Now that you need Her to intervene in human affairs?"

"Isn't that why anyone believes in God, so they can have an ear for their prayers? So they can believe in miracles?"

To believe in miracles. James smirks and turns his head

away. The ultimate wish-fulfillment mechanism. What a mass delusion: a thousand generations bowed in prayer, desperately yearning to be saved, to be healed, to be spared.

"There is only one miracle we can be sure of," he replies and he takes her hand in his own and lifts them together into the air above their heads. "It's the miracle of the here-and-now. The unbroken continuity of four billion years of evolution pulsing through our veins. That, and our awareness of it all. *Most important: our awareness of it all."* He draws her hand to his lips and kisses her fingers and then sets the palm of his hand on her face and turns her head toward him.

She sets her eyes on his and the moment she enjoyed in the morning returns. The comfort she experiences there, could it be an illusion, too? "Tell me what you think about us," she whispers.

He leans against the headboard to consider this and then bends toward her when he's composed an answer. "I think we're perfect together."

Mmm, yes. She presses her stomach against the pillow and then draws it away so that her belly slides against his. "And?"

"And ... that *knowing* how blessed we are is the center of our shared perfection. We have to keep that at the front of our minds." The tip of his index finger touches the middle of her forehead, the third eye he taught her to focus on when she began to meditate and then discovered her own white light.

The day's events settle on her now and she can feel herself slipping under their weight. She fights the drowsiness so that she can prolong this fading moment of intimacy. "Don't you think *blessed* is just a tad religious-sounding?" She tosses this out as another tease, anything to keep him talking and unraveling their story and his version of them together.

"I think you're tired, is what I think."

"Mmm." She yawns and with her eyes still closed she asks, "Just hold me, okay?"

James clicks off the lamp and pulls the covers over their shoulders. They turn in unison to face the window and he presses his face against the hair at the back of her neck and as he inhales the fragrance of her sex, he slips his arms around her so that he can cup her breasts. His fingers briefly tease her flaccid nipples and their bodies, spooning, lock together.

When she's certain he will not release her, she opens her eyes again and realizes neither of them has lowered the blind. She stares through the window. The night air is gray, opaque, a mask. The clouds press down onto the city, the streetlights flutter their pale orbs in the damp air. So many people are now making their beds on the streets: tired, broken, half-crazy with anxiety and fear. She feels lucky and she lays her palms over her husband's hands and presses them into her flesh and gives thanks that she's alive and well. *So* alive. How fortunate to have this life in this dry, warm bed with this man, this pantheist saint who is her husband.

Each morning Doyle buys a cup of fruit, a toasted poppy-seed bagel, and an Earl Grey Tea latté in the Caffe Mediterraneum down the block and around the corner from his apartment. None of the staff are able to explain the misspelling of Mediterranean. They shrug and smile as if it's an inside joke with a forgotten punchline. When Doyle learns that Allan Ginsberg wrote *Howl* on these premises, he assumes that Ginsberg is somehow behind the prank and soon Doyle is smiling, too, now that he's part of the café's insiders.

Whenever it's available, he grabs the table next to the window near the front door where he can enjoy a view of the crowds passing along the street as he scans the *San Francisco Chronicle*. This is his one indulgence, he tells himself, the pleasure of frittering away an hour each morning and the first step in building the daily momentum that leads him back to his rooms where he continues the work on his memoir. He's established a routine over the past week and now that he's settled in his loft he feels that his new life in Berkeley is underway. It took a day or two after the back-to-back robberies for him to purchase a few changes of clothes, a jacket, a new duffle bag, and the other odds and ends, like the French beret that he wears pulled to one side of his head, required to live the life of a Berkeley boulevardier. *A flanneur*, as Louis would say.

While he isn't yet free of Iris's passing, the future stretching before him seems unburdened, and for the first time in a month he feels open to new possibilities. The thought surprises him. He's sixty years old, a widower who's lost his wife of thirty-five years, the mother of his twin sons. He's at a stage when many men would retreat to familiar routines and shut the door on exotic possibilities, yet here he is, living alone in a new city like a twenty-something: free and ripe for new adventures. Yes, he nods, I'll take a new adventure. In fact, I'll try *anything* new, any time. Any day.

He glances around the café worried that he might have uttered this last insight aloud. He caught himself grumbling out loud as he walked along the street after the robberies in Haight-Ashbury. A sure sign of bad mental hygiene, despite the extenuating circumstances.

"Doyle?" James Wayman stands before him, one hand balancing a mug of coffee on a coil-bound notebook while the other grips his rain jacket.

Doyle folds his paper and leans forward. "James, wonderful to see you. Please, *sit*. I've been holding this table until you arrived." He smiles at this generous lie, a fiction intended to flatter his housemate. "What are you drinking?"

James drapes his jacket over the chair back, sits so that he faces the crowd and takes a sip of coffee. "Espresso. What about you?"

"London fog. It's Earl Grey tea with steamed milk and a shot of vanilla. Kind of a health drink for the caffeine crowd."

"Sounds like a necessary dose of comic relief."

"Comic relief? From what?" Doyle slips his newspaper into his pack to provide more room for James's mug and notebook.

"Lethargy. Terminal boredom." He smiles with a gesture that suggests the current latté culture, the narcissism of it all, is something he'd rather escape than inhabit. "We're in a state of decay, of social entropy."

Doyle shrugs and shakes his head. "Social entropy?"

"Our whole culture is atrophying. Withering away while everyone is poking their friends on the internet or making bets on the stock market. We've surrendered our lives to the grand illusion. To the last, desperate hope that technology will save us." He waves a hand in the air as if a mass hallucination floats a few feet above them and then pauses to study Doyle's face.

"Meanwhile," he continues, his voice self-assured, almost mesmerizing, "we face ecological, economic, and social collapse." He lets this thought sit, and then turns his palm and sweeps it about the room. "But as long as the espresso machines keep whistling, hey buddy, no need to panic!"

Doyle laughs at this and sits back in his chair, nods to suggest it's obvious. Undeniable. As an outsider he can see all this, it's apparent to anyone visiting from outside the USA. But when you're living *inside* the States, when you're actually swimming in the fish bowl, all that's important is snatching the next flake of fish bait floating toward you.

There's a momentary pause and Doyle leans forward. "The other night you said you had a revelation of some kind. So ... you have a solution to this social entropy?" He asks this evenly, careful to eliminate any note of skepticism from his voice.

"Maybe," James pushes his lips together and holds Doyle with his eyes. "Maybe a solution to the *personal* side of it." He blinks and finishes the muddy dregs from his espresso. "And if we all lived genuine, authentic lives then it might be a social solution, too."

Doyle swings an arm over the back of his chair. Who would he ever describe as genuine? As authentic? These are words used to sell collectible stamps and coins. James's grandiose vision seems almost laughable. Doyle shakes his head and smiles.

When James detects his doubts, he holds a hand in the air, as if to stop Doyle's train of thought from proceeding any further. "Look, this is all about *being*. Think of it as an active verb. Talking won't get you any closer to understanding what I mean. Come down to my apartment at five o'clock. I'm leading a session then. See for yourself."


The living room in James's apartment appears spacious even in the shadows cast by the waning afternoon light. The oak floors and fir wainscoting, the ten-foot-high ceilings, the front window edged with a plum, stain-glass trim that overlooks the street — all of it testifies to a long-departed, upper-middle-class splendor. By the time Doyle enters the room, about twenty people have taken their places on the floor. Most of them sit cross-legged, balanced between pillows or with their backs braced against a wall. Two or three sit in the overstuffed chairs near the window.

"This is Doyle Mere, everyone," James announces with his broad smile.

"Hello Doyle." The chorus of voices greeting him is followed by a round of laughter when everyone realizes they sound like a class of children welcoming a special guest.

Doyle presses his hands together and bows politely to everyone. *Namaste.* It's a gesture he's observed in movies from south Asia: a broad, open acknowledgement of welcome. He scans the room but does not see Mavis. Then he realizes that he's the oldest person in the group by at least a decade. After a moment of hesitation, he takes a place next to a black woman who pats the empty space on the carpet next to her. "I'm Rosa Zanes," she whispers to him and shakes his hand after he crosses his legs and leans his back against the wall.

"You live in the basement apartment, right?" When she nods, he points to the ceiling and adds, "I'm upstairs."

"All right, cell phones off, everyone." James holds a phone aloft and places it on the table beside him. More amused tittering is followed by the cacophony of digital blips and bleeps as a dozen people click off their phones and set them aside.

James stands in front of the fireplace, an old coal-burner that now serves as the setting for a large, healthy fern plant. He looks at his feet for a moment and everyone waits in silence for him to begin speaking. He raises his head and glances around the room, setting his eyes on each person in turn.

"Did everyone find some time to make contact?"

A sigh of assent ripples through the group and James nods and sweeps his hand before him, palm up, suggesting an easy confidence.

"All right." He draws a deep breath and then shifts his voice to a higher pitch. "I thought that today I'd tell you how I came to this time and place. How I came to be here, talking to you right now. It started at a turning point. Last year, on New Year's Day when I was walking alone down Ocean Front Walk in Venice Beach. It was about eight in the morning. The sky was overcast, the air was chilly, breezy. I suddenly realized there was no one else around me. Not a soul. I had the street to myself. Here I was in this very public place with only myself for company. That's when I had this strange insight: this split I'd created between me and *my self*. It made me laugh to *my self*, and then again I saw this division within me. Like I was two people: one making these comments and complaints and observations and jokes, and the other — inside me — who simply observed the running commentary."

James pauses and several people acknowledge similar experiences. "I've had that," Rosa says, "many, *many* times."

Doyle nods his head, too. The summer he almost drove himself crazy. He was twenty-two, had just finished his degree in geology at McGill University and was living on his own in the Yukon, panning gold twenty miles outside of Dawson City when he realized he couldn't stop thinking out loud. And then he couldn't stop *talking* about thinking out loud, and found himself trapped in a non-logical, recurring loop of mindless, solitary banter. Before this hebephrenic madness consumed him he decided to pack up his gear and walk along the Yukon River into town, where, as blind luck would have it, he met Iris at the youth hostel and began a life of near-perfect sanity that lasted the next thirty-eight years.

"Now the most important insight for me," James continues, "was not this split in my consciousness, but the words I used to explain it: that *I'd created* it." Several heads nod in agreement. "And this is where it gets tricky. The part of me that created this split, was a character I'd formed over the past four decades. That character was part of my identity. In fact, *he was* my identity. Don't be surprised. I've spent years working with Hollywood stars. When I lived in LA I taught yoga to dozens of athletes, musicians and actors. And believe me, they can completely take over your life with their drama!" He holds his hands aloft, then pushes them down as though he's restraining a dog jumping at his waist. "Okay, okay: that's just my persona speaking again. You can ignore him. I'll tell him to go away."

Doyle laughs with the others and adjusts his legs. He's truly enjoying this: the mood in the room, the story-telling, the casual atmosphere that allows everyone to confirm the insights of James's story with brief narratives from their own lives. James's oratorical talent is evident. For the first time, Doyle feels quite comfortable with these strangers who seem to hold nothing in common except a kind of shared anticipation. But anticipation of what?

"Once I had this insight," James continues, "*once I got it*, I realized all I had to do was release my *character* and the genuine, authentic human being that I am would emerge to fill the space of what turned out to be my false identity, or what I call my *persona*." He stops and turns from person to person, nodding when he reads the affirmations in each face. "Then, and I know this sounds crazy, like some kind of psycho-drug flash-back, but when I let the *illusion* of my identity go, I just stood there and the clouds that had been rolling overhead began to dissolve. A large open gap emerged above me and in the early morning I could see into space, way beyond Earth and the moon. I could see the blackness illuminated by the stars. And as I continued walking down toward the beach the sky remained completely open and clear. But as soon as I saw someone approaching me, when I realized the traffic was passing around me, the sky closed again. The wind came up, and finally after someone spoke to me, when I had to engage with the world again, I realized that I had to concentrate on suppressing my persona so I could respond with my *being*."

James then explains that this satori opened a new world to him. He now understood that the art of maintaining this state of being is to continuously inhabit the here-and-now, "to live in the moment without the interference of your own persona." The more he tried this, however, the more he realized how this false character would do anything to destroy his present-consciousness and force him to re-live the past or concoct new schemes and future plans. "Our personas are vampires. They love to live in the past and can relive past glories or re-script alternate scenes that might not have gone so well: that time when your lover broke your heart can be edited so that *you* finally have the last word. Or you plan elaborate scenarios reaching into the future to make money, sex, war — the endless matrix of human drama."

These last sentences prompt an intense response from a boy sitting against the far wall. "*Yeah. I get it,*" he snaps. "They're vampires because they suck us out of the present moment."

James turns to him and nods. "Exactly. And that's when I realized there was one component of my experience with yoga that could really help me. The meditation. To breathe in the here-and-now, to stop the monkey-mind in its tracks.

"Now let's be sure of something: there are no miracle solutions at hand. Even when you are in touch with the white light, you will re-emerge *into this world*." He points through the window, waves a hand at the expanse of humanity milling through the streets of Berkeley all the way to the suits in New York, the dream merchants in LA and the politicos in Washington, all of them buzzing away in the military-industrial-economic-media hive. "Because it's in *this world* that you must buy your daily bread and pay your rent. At least until we can make a change. Which is why the White Light Community was established: to change the world one-by-one. One person at a time.

"Now the most important thing," James continues, "is the fact that the Community isn't about me. *It's about everybody.* It's about learning a mental discipline so that every day there is a time and place for you to go inside and experience the natural wholeness that is connected to you. You don't need me, you don't need a guru. You simply need the will to nourish your own being. *Think of being as an active verb.*"

"Mmm, yeah," Rosa says and two or three people add their assent. "Let's do it now."

Doyle senses that the group anticipation he detected earlier is now ripe. Despite James's denial that he, personally, is in any way required to help them make contact, they all want him to lead them through the next steps. Without another word James sits in the place where he's been standing and crosses his legs. He closes his eyes and draws a deep breath and after a moment he exhales slowly. Doyle watches as the circle of people repeat the same procedure.

Soon he's the only person in the room with his eyes still open.

"Go inside," James says in a low monotone. "Close your eyes. Take a deep breath and then exhale naturally. There's nothing to fight. Leave the rest of your world outside the room. This time, *this place*, is for you. Breathe deeply. Slowly. Naturally. Straighten your spine and keep your eyes gently closed," he says and Doyle's eyelids finally slide together as he draws a deep breath and lets the air wash through his body.

Doyle begins to ease into the process as James leads them step-by-step in his steady, hypnotic voice: "Relax your neck. Let your head fall to one shoulder, then down to the chest, slide up to the other shoulder and then back as far as it can reach without causing any discomfort. Let it roll through another orbit and another and another. Change direction. Let the neck rotate until all the kinks and stress of the day are gone. Then set your hands on your knees, palms up. Touch the tips of the forefingers to the tips of your thumbs in *Gyan Mudra*. Once again, straighten your spine. Now, with the eyes still closed, focus on the mid-point of the brow. Keep the eyes focused there through the next half-hour until the session is complete."

James takes a moment to explain that because most thinking is based on words, the mantra can be any non-meaning sound that you chant whenever you realize your persona has lapsed into another round of internal debate. Just let the thoughts go. They are simply monkey-maya. Return to the mantra and into the embrace of non-thought. Eventually the mantra itself will slip away as your awareness harmonizes with pure being into the moment of *streaming entry*. You cannot force it, but soon your sense of time will dissolve and become irrelevant. "Now," he whispers, "settle your attention on your breathing. As you breathe, silently intone a mantra: om-ma-ra-ma." He repeats it several times until the sound is internalized in everyone.

But Doyle hears almost none of this. Nothing about the mantra, nothing about monkey-maya, nothing about streaming entry. He followed along to the point where his attention was focused on his mid-brow, the point of his forehead where he'd last touched Iris when she was still alive. He was transported to another time and place, another life, it seemed. He was in their bedroom with Iris as she lay propped against the pillows. She'd wanted to come home from the hospital to die. He'd called the twins, Wyatt and Jesse, and that same day they returned to the old house they'd inhabited together for so many years. Wyatt drove in from the marina where he lived on his sail boat and Jesse took the ferry from Salt Spring Island with his wife, Bess, and she carried their three-month-old daughter into the room, Doyle's and Iris's only grandchild. Baby Gale sat perched in the crook of Iris's bent elbow, babbling, reaching her fingers to Iris's lips and pulling on them as if they were a toy Iris had presented as a special reward for coming into her life at the last possible moment.

That evening Doyle sat alone with Iris on the bed and he could talk of nothing but the new baby. Through the fog of morphine Iris could utter no more than three or four words at a time. "She's ours, too," she said and moved her lips to say something more, something Doyle couldn't quite hear, and as he bent his head to her, instead of turning his ear to her lips he pressed his forehead to her brow and felt a small opening there. *A link*. In retrospect he wasn't sure what had passed between them, but he was certain that at this last moment a new connection established a bond that tied him to the instant of her death. Then she exhaled deeply, releasing all the air from her body in one long sigh, and later when he tried to explain this strangeness to the boys, he said that he could see the vapor of her being rise from her open mouth into the still night.

Fay Flood stares at Janice Slitz and wonders how to get rid of her. Fay has seen enough social workers over the past five years, but since August when she decided to home-school Teejay and began to draw upon the pittance of state welfare benefits, that's when the paper-pushers became persistent. Pressing into her world like they owned part of it. Just because she had to draw down a fraction of the tax pool, only her own fair share, she figures, the government now claims a piece of her private life. But no one is more invasive than Janice Slitz. No one gets under her skin so much or makes her more itchy.

"So Fay, have you put a budget together for this month?"

Fay can't stand to look at her. At her costume: the knee-high leather boots, a navy dress coat that covers her white blouse and the flounced scarf she wraps twice around her throat. Her pashmina. And then there's her coral fingernail polish and matching lipstick. Put it all together and she has the look of a dominatrix librarian. Or rather the *disguise* of a librarian, Fay decides. So she can cover up who she really is: a wannabe cop. Yeah, yeah. Who she really is, is someone pretending to masquerade some other life. A vacuum in a vacuum. Maybe Fay could paint that; the result would be a blank canvas with a double-loop title: *Void in Void.*

"Fay? Are you listening?" Janice walks across the small apartment to the window, wheels about and glares at Fay. She hasn't actually been invited to enter the room, but by the authority of her position she has a duty to ensure there's some accountability from the state's clients. Especially now that she's moved up to junior management and has to take on the Tuesday-through-Saturday shift. But more important, she wants to keep an eye out for the girl, Teejay. That's what everyone in the department is alert for these days: feral children. Tens of thousands of them out in the streets, hiding in abandoned factories and tenements, living rough and wild.

"Yeah, yeah. I'm listening. And I'm using the budget system you suggested." Fay decides that the best way to move Janice out the door will be to play her game for a while. "Everything's in separate money jars. Food, rent, clothing, bus money." She opens a cupboard door above the sink. There, sure enough, stands a line of recycled pasta sauce jars, re-labeled, and filled with loose dollar bills and change.

Surprised by this display of organization, Janice lifts the jar marked "bus" and glances inside. Two dollars and a clutch of quarters. Enough for a one-way passage into town. Probably not enough for the girl and Fay to make it through the next week, unless the girl sneaks her way past the driver. "And where's Teejay today?"

Fay presses her lips together and nods. She knew this question was coming and she's beginning to hate it, hate the insinuations that it implies. That she doesn't know her own daughter's whereabouts. That she's careless. Negligent. "That's a mother's business," she declares and tips her head to indicate that this is about all she's going to reveal on the subject of Teejay. "Do you have any children, Janice?"

Janice knows she doesn't have to answer this question but she can feel the wall going up around Fay and knows if she wants to get anywhere on this case, she'll have to remove a few bricks. She hikes her shoulder bag up next to her jacket collar. "No," she says and sighs without regret.

"Then it's going to be hard to have any conversation about that, isn't it? Mother-to-mother, I mean."

Janice is about to explain that you don't have to be a mother to care about children when she decides to shift gears. "What about the girl's father?" She realizes it would be more personable to identify him by name, but that would require her to reach into her bag and check this detail in Fay's file — and she doesn't want any distractions.

"Guzman?" She can barely spit out his name. "I kicked him out of here over a two months ago. He turned bad," she hisses. "Last I heard he got thrown in the drunk tank. Again. Maybe the city jail can provide you with his address."

"So he's not providing any support?" It's not really a question, she tells herself. More an acknowledgement of the world most of her clients inhabit.

Fay shrugs; there's no point in talking further about Guzman. He's the worst of her problems and she certainly isn't about to disclose any of that to Janice. If she did, Teejay would likely be apprehended and moved into a foster home.

"What about Dr. Benson?" Janice presses on. It was an email from Benson that prompted this visit. He contacted her to say that he hadn't seen Fay after her last session, nor had she renewed her Tegritol prescription. "He said he didn't see you this month."

Fay turns her jaw to one side. Obviously the mind-police were in complete control now. No matter that the world is barreling toward collapse. She has visions that reveal what's coming: wild fires, mass starvation, murder, rebellion. She's done her best to portray the disasters hurtling toward mankind in her paintings. The karmic retribution is long past due. The entire USA is going down, but despite that the mind-police are in full mobilization. "I changed my meds," she says after she finds a measure of composure. "A new prescription from my new shrink," she adds for emphasis. "Your files must be out of date."

"Oh?" This time Janice draws the file folder out of her bag. "So, who's your new therapist?" She scratches a line through Benson's name and while she's at it, adds a note beside the brief summary regarding Raymond Guzman: "check: drunk & disorderly?"

"Dr. Box. Philip Box. But I'm working with his partner, Mavis Helm," she adds and looks away.

"I haven't heard of her. Are you sure that's her name?" Fay nods, yes, and Janice enters Mavis's name into the file and sighs heavily. "All right, I'll get in touch with her and see where we go from here."

When Fay doesn't respond, Janice glances around the room. She feels breathless, an urge to retreat. Then she hears a series of footsteps climbing the staircase to the apartment. She expects to see Teejay appear at the door and decides to wait, to gain a small tactical advantage and enough time to assure herself that the girl is alive and well.

A moment later a hand taps at the still-open door and Mavis Helm dips her head into the room. "Am I early?" she asks. She glances at Fay and her guest, tries to decipher the odd tension between them. "I can come back," she offers when no one responds.

"No, no. You're right on time," Fay says with a satisfied grin. When she realizes what a mistake it would be to introduce Janice to Mavis, she stands and points to the door with her open hand and a look of contempt for her social worker. "And Janice is just leaving."

Ten minutes later Teejay returns to the apartment with the groceries that Fay asked her to pick up from Safeway. Mavis is pleased to see her, delighted to observe the same brilliance in her eyes and face, the same natural grace that she revealed during their first meeting, despite the tension between Fay and Teejay at the time. "You look a little better today," she says as a way to acknowledge her previous situation. "The day we met you were in bed."

"Thanks," Teejay says and she sets the bag on the table and places the milk and cheese in the refrigerator, and then draws the Calfresh food stamp card from her pocket and places it in the glass jar labeled "food." She decides not to respond with anything truthful, like *I wasn't really in bed*, or *Fay sometimes keeps me locked up for hours*. Instead, she smiles and says that she's really looking forward to the visit at Mavis's house for the day.

Over the past few days Mavis considered how to work with Fay using her artwork as a passageway to her inner world. Despite the warning from Philip Box, she decided the therapeutic possibilities are too important to pass up simply for the sake of operational protocols in the local therapist community. Without advising Box or her advisor, Lorraine Dansky, she arranged to pick up Fay and Teejay and drive them to her house on Saturday. James agreed to look after the girl for an hour or two while Mavis guided Fay through a session that focused on her art, particularly the piece she calls *Inner Trialogue*. She secured Fay's agreement to record their session together, and she'd set up a video recorder in the small room that she'd converted into a study. But first, in order to establish a relationship and reveal her genuine feeling that this wasn't strictly about therapy, Mavis offered to take both Fay and Teejay to lunch at Greco's. They would make an afternoon of it.

"Girls' day out!" Mavis cheers in a voice that she and Joleen often used whenever they had a day of freedom from their grandfather back in Florida. "A day away!" she cries as they step into the Prius.

"A day to play!" Teejay joins in, taking up the rhyme.

Fay smiles to herself. She can't believe how her mood has changed in the few minutes since Janice Slitz departed. She feels happy. Content to be heading off for an adventure with her daughter and her new friend. After she buckles her seatbelt into place she lifts her hands above her head, waves her ringed fingers in the air and calls out, "And a day for Fay!"


"Honestly? No ... I never really got that far with it." Doyle slants his head to one side and smiles weakly as he gazes at James. He could fake it, of course; invent a story about the transcendent experience he had during the group meditation last week but James is so genuine, so honest and endearing with everyone he encounters that to deceive him would be a form of self-betrayal. Besides, what did it matter if the meditation session didn't fulfill its promise? He's still alive and well, though perhaps not *exactly* transformed like Rosa Zanes and the other meditators.

James fills their cups with green tea. "So at what point did you drift off?" *Drift off* were the words Doyle used to explain how he'd lost the thread of the session and slipped into his inner world. When the group meditation came to a close, everyone was smiling with the benign expression that James had witnessed so often in the faces of those who'd made contact with the white light. Everyone except Doyle. *His* face was drawn in despair.

Doyle considers this question a moment. He knows the

answer, in fact, he knows the precise moment of departure when he drifted back to re-live those last few seconds with Iris. The more important question is, does he want to share this with anyone? After all, he came to San Francisco in order to disengage from all that. To redeploy. On the other hand, since he keeps returning to Iris night after night in his fitful sleep, it's obvious that his redeployment is not as successful as he'd hoped. He worries that he might be sinking into a depression and in this foreign place, in this foreign country, he could use someone to talk to.

"I'm not sure you want to know about it," he says at last. "It's a proverbial can of worms." He shrugs and glances around the room. The wood-paneled space seems larger now that only the two of them are sitting here, next to the fern in front of the fireplace. Five candles are alight, glowing in a brass candelabra on the mantle. Odd for the middle of the day, he thinks and he realizes that every time he visits, candles light up some corner of the apartment. Perhaps they provide comfort during the electrical blackouts that seem to strike about once a week.

James holds a hand to his mouth and studies Doyle while he mulls over this response. Here is a man in his late fifties or early sixties, he guesses, someone troubled by a preoccupation so overwhelming that he cannot escape its grip for a thirty-minute meditation. If he continues in this state he knows that Doyle has no hope of becoming a venerated old man. Perhaps no hope of growing old. "If you're worried that I'll reveal what you say, you can relax." He narrows his eyes and continues, "I can keep a secret. Even from Mavis."

Doyle leans forward in the chair, compresses his lips to a tiny opening and blows a long stream of air from his lungs and ponders how to respond. He slumps against the cushions and a deep foreboding begins to well through him, a sense that he might not be able to get out of the chair on his own. He worries that his mind might separate from his body, and his physical being will start to ignore direct commands. Someone — James — would have to grab him by the hand and yard him up out of the chair and lead him through the door to some unknown psychiatric ward. *And then where?* Where to redeploy once his body and soul have individually and separately capitulated to this growing ennui? It would be better to tell James all this than to recruit him for a rescue operation. Tell all and be done with it.

"All right," he announces when he reaches this conclusion. "And, yeah ... I'd appreciate it if you kept it to yourself."

James nods and he tips his head to the teacup. "Drink up," he advises. "I'm listening."

Doyle sips his tea and thinks another moment as the mellow jasmine warms his gullet. But his mind does not return to the last time that he touched Iris. Instead he begins to talk about the boys, the birth of his twin sons, Wyatt and Jesse. "The greatest surprise of all," he explains, "was that a new part of my life, the best part, began the day the boys were born on the kitchen floor in the two-bedroom cottage Iris and I rented the year we were married." He describes how he'd squatted behind her with his legs extended along her waist to her knees and how her shoulders were braced against his chest. He held both her hands as she pumped them in rhythm to the force that tore through her until she released the babies from her womb into the waiting hands of the midwife. She then snipped and tied off the umbilical cords, cleaned the babies' waxy flesh, bundled them in flannel receiving blankets, released a drop of tetracycline ointment into each eye and passed the children into Doyle's trembling hands. If he'd ever felt transcendent, this was the moment, the one time when he became effervescent, when he realized he was a mere speck of humanity, of time, of the world. And this precise awareness offered a perspective he'd never enjoyed before. At last he'd found his place in the great cycle of life. It was not only a place, but one of two pivot-points between which everything shifted and moved forward, the birth of the twins and then Iris's too-early death.

Doyle quickly covers the highlights that occurred between these two decisive moments: their move to Victoria on Vancouver Island, his job teaching high school geography, the purchase of their hundred-year-old house, the ongoing renovations that Iris hoped would never end because it provided a forum for their collaboration, a togetherness that never descended into scenes of personal rancor or argument. He describes the hobby he and the boys took up with the telescope on the deck at the back of the house. They became amateur astronomers, certified members of the American Association of Variable Star Observers Society, and Doyle developed a private obsession tracking the orbits of satellites after he attended a remarkable lecture by Donald J. Kessler. And there were the months he spent learning to sail with the twins and their summer voyage around Vancouver Island. He hints at the pride he and Iris shared when the boys finished university and finally went their own ways, when Jesse married Bess and finally when Bess delivered their grandchild, Gale — all of this, the decades-long span in the center of his life is simply the in-between part, he now realizes. The part between the first pivot-point and the second: the moment he last touched Iris before she departed to become a vapor risen into the heavens above him and into the care of God.

Not that he maintains any religious convictions, he quickly adds. Doyle considers himself spiritual but not religious. The description of his experience in the instant following Iris's death should be understood as an analogy. He suggests that her last breath could just as easily have risen to commingle with the remains of Kosmos 2251 and Iridium 33, but that is nonsense — *and* demeaning — and he immediately apologizes for saying this, not so much to James as to the memory of his wife. "I shouldn't have said that last part," he confesses. "I've been talking for so long that everything's tumbling out uncensored. I'm sorry." His voice falls under the weight of remorse and he averts his eyes from James.

James turns his face to the ceiling and considers their situation. Rather than say anything right away, he suspects it might be better to wait a moment, wait for Doyle to add a word or two, so that whatever James might say won't seem like a slight to Doyle's grieving.

"I'm not *really* sorry. It's good," Doyle adds with a sigh, "Good to get that all out."

James lingers another beat and then asks, "How long ago did she pass on?"

"Almost nine months now. On the twenty-third."

He nods and sips some tea. "And are your sons all right?"

"Yes." He's surprised to feel his lips forming a smile. "They're young. Busy. In the middle of things."

"Have you ever read Seneca?" James offers this question as though it were an afterthought. He wants to change the mood and he knows that Doyle is fully immersed in his grief and there is no merit in exploring its dimensions.

"Seneca?" Doyle shakes his head, no. "Maybe in my first year at college. I don't remember." He glances away.

The question annoys him; all of a sudden James has led him into foreign territory. Once again, he feels like an outsider.

"There's an episode in his correspondence with a woman, Marcia, who has lost her son before his twenty-fifth birthday. She's so deeply consumed by grief that she cannot go on. Seneca writes to her that we're all subject to the indiscriminate whims of the goddess, Fortune. No one can escape Fortune's impulses, he tells her, and that everything given to us can be swept away in an instant. Our only consolation is to accept our condition and make it the basis of wisdom. Seneca told Marcia that it's wise to grieve deeply, *but not forever*. We must live in the moment because life is fleeting and Fortune gives no warning before she strikes again."

Doyle wipes a hand over his face, drags his fingernails over the stubble of his four-day-old beard. During the past few days he's become too lazy to shave, another sign of impending depression, he decides. But could it be true? Could his grief last forever? Doyle considers this possibility as he examines James's large face: the mole on his cheek, the bushy eyebrows joined above his nose, the wave of thick hair cascading to his ears. "Do you think I'm stuck?" he asks.

James shrugs, hesitates a moment. "No. That's why you came here, isn't it? The first night you sat here with me and Mavis, you said you wanted to find something new. You're not stuck, but I think you're grieving so deeply that you haven't completely *arrived*."

Doyle presses a hand to his chin and his index finger climbs above his lips to touch the bottom of his nose. Yes, it's true. He isn't *integrated*. He knows he used to feel so *complete* before Iris died. But now, here in this house in Berkeley he can see the obvious: his life has been utterly shattered. "All right," he concedes. "But let me ask the ultimate cliché question: how do you, how does anyone, become whole?"

James smiles. He waits a moment, satisfied with the feeling rising through him. "By contacting the force of Nature within you," he replies and his smile widens brightly.

The solution seems laughable. Doyle smirks at first, then James starts to chuckle and they collapse into laughter. Soon the room fills with their howling.

When the apartment door swings open Mavis, Fay and Teejay — already in a buoyant mood from their lunch at Greco's — enter the room in a chorus of their own giggling. "Okay, *what* are you two *smoking?*" Mavis asks.

"No idea!" James holds his hands aloft. Then he adds, "Bliss!"

Doyle shakes his head in agreement. "Ecstasy!" he manages to blurt out between gasps. He's been seized by uncontrollable laughter and he abandons himself to it utterly. He's stumbled onto a vast beach of sheer joy, the lost ingredient in his life, and he wants to sift through every single grain of it.

Weeks later, James would realize that this was the first moment that the five of them were joined together as a group. Unlike Seneca, he didn't assign godlike powers to chance. On the other hand, he knows there are discrete intersections of time and space, and it pleased him to realize that their initial collective *pivot-point* (as Doyle would say) began with sheer nonsense. Despite everything that followed with Mavis, Fay, Teejay and Doyle, this moment gave him hope.

An hour later James and Teejay make their way to Rainbow's End Gallery which is featuring a retrospective of seven local feminist painters. After a walk-through of the gallery, he plans to take her for an ice cream cone, chat with her and then return her to Fay after she'd spent a few hours alone with Mavis.

However, the plan is far from perfect. The gallery is busy, but the art on display doesn't inspire Teejay. After twenty minutes spent sauntering past the collection she seems distracted, almost bored. "I like my mom's paintings better," she says as they exit the gallery and step onto the street.

"Why's that?" James asks as they stroll up the block towards Paradise Ice Creamery. "Didn't you like the cat portraits by Jill Zoloski? How she transformed all those animals into people? I *loved* the cats!" As soon as he says this he regrets it. The exaggeration is false, and worse, it's transparent. Certainly he enjoyed the images of the cat-people, surreal and fanciful as they were, but not as enthusiastically as his voice suggests. He can already sense the depth of Teejay's social intelligence, an aptitude so refined that she can detect hyperbole in a raised eyebrow.

"I liked them okay, but they didn't seem alive to me. Mom doesn't paint cats, but most of her work draws you in."

*Her work.* So serious. James smiles as they continue along the sidewalk. "So what do you do when Fay's painting? Mavis told me she paints a lot."

"School work." Her hand slaps along the spindles of a wrought iron fence as they approach the ice cream shop.

James foresees that this line of questioning will eventually lead to a void. He decides to say nothing, to eliminate any hint of interrogation, and let Teejay express her own interests. He glances at her and tries to absorb the inner dynamics of her life, the ways she's devised to navigate her world, to judge what might work and what would fail. She possesses a childhood grace but she has a determination in her face, in those slate gray eyes, that is decades old. She studies everything around her with a probing consideration and permits nothing to stand at face value. Her mind is full, but troubled, and despite her strength and acuity, she seems to be treading on problems that sink well beyond her depth. It's not easy to be Teejay, he decides.

Not another word is spoken until they reach the glass freezer displaying Paradise Ice Creamery's vast array of ice cream. Above it a hand-written sign states: "We have 48 47 flavors today."

"What are you going to have?" She looks into James's face, a little unsure that he's actually about to buy her an ice cream cone.

"Can't have the chocolate banana." The forty-eighth flavor of the day has been scratched from the menu by a thick line: Chocolate Banana. "I think a double cone. You want two scoops, too?"

She blinks and looks back into the display case. "I meant what *flavor*?"

"Hmmm." James studies the tubs of ice cream in the case. He tries to see everything before them through her eyes. He guesses that she would choose the strawberry. It shimmers with glossy ripe strawberries poking through the sheen of glazed ice cream. "You don't *have* to have two scoops. Unless you want to." He purposely avoids her question.

"But I can if I want to?" Her voice rises a note and she studies James's eyes.

"Yes. But only if that's what you want."

"I'll have two scoops," she declares when the attendant takes her order. "One strawberry and the other bubble gum. In a waffle cone," she adds and smiles at James.

Bubble gum. James can feel it. Feel the triumph of being twelve years old and receiving a treasure from someone who wants nothing more than the pleasure of providing a gift. He never understood the reciprocal dynamics of this transaction when he was twelve, of course, but now standing here, peeling off the few dollars required to make this bit of magic become a reality, he absorbs the joy of everything before him: of being forty-seven and twelve, of being provider and seeker, man and girl, father and daughter. This last thought jars him out of his reverie. He rarely imagines having a child of his own, but no matter, if Teejay wished it, if only for this afternoon, she would be his child and he would be her father.

"Do you ever pretend?" she asks after they're seated in the hot-pink plastic chairs that are bolted to an even deeper-pink table. Her tongue laps two or three circles around the balls of ice cream before she pauses for a breath and decides to qualify her question. "I mean *imaginatively*."

He's chosen two scoops of mint chocolate chip and in one lick he sweeps four chips onto his molars and crunches them with satisfaction. "Not as much as I used to," he confesses. "But I like to read books. You have to imagine the words as pictures in order to make any sense of them. So I guess I do pretend whenever I read."

Teejay considers this as she presses the ice cream into the cone with her tongue in order to keep it stable. "I write stories," she says and extends her free hand, palm up toward James. "Well, not stories exactly, but I write in my diary almost every day."

"Really? Me too. I've been writing mine for years. Do

you write on a computer or the old fashioned way, with a pen?"

She shakes her head. "We don't have a computer." She can feel a minor ice cream headache forming in the middle of her forehead and she momentarily suspends the splendor of licking the cone. Her fingers are getting sticky. She drags her tongue across her thumb and forefinger and wipes them with one of the napkins that James placed on the table when they sat down.

"Mmm. I don't either. Do you know who else keeps a diary?"

Teejay shrugs and returns her attention to the ice cream.

"Doyle. The man you just met in our apartment. But he's writing a memoir. And he uses a laptop."

"What's a memoir?"

"A story about your life, after you've lived a lot of it."

"He looks old."

"Maybe, but he's still growing. Inside, I mean." He thinks he should explain this, assumes it would be interesting to most twelve-year-olds. So she'll understand that the Mystery never stops teasing the mind. "People can still learn a lot when they get old. About themselves. And the world," he adds as his hand sweeps above the pink table. "And how they all fit together. Life's a puzzle and each of us has to fit together the pieces we've been given."

"Does your diary have a title?"

"Of course. But just a working title."

"Well?" She pauses to rub the back of her wrist against the expanding, radiant headache. "What is it?"

"It's private." James eases up on his cone. He wants to set it down somewhere and wonders if he'd been a little over-ambitious in ordering two scoops. "Okay, okay. I know that's not very nice. Tell me your title and I'll tell you mine."

Teejay tilts her head. "*That* is so *old*."

James laughs. "All right. My title is *Journal from the Center of Time.*" He raises his eyebrows, wonders what she'll make of this.

She muses on this a moment, nodding her head up and down in short increments and then resumes her attack on the ice cream. When she's pressed the strawberry scoop below the top ridge of the cone she says, "You could maybe make it shorter. You could call it something like, *Journal from Now.*"

James smiles, pleased that she'd unraveled the pun in the title. "And yours is?"

"Just *Dear Diary*. So far. I haven't actually given it a *working* title although I'm thinking of something like … *Where I've Been and Where I'm Going.*" She studies him briefly. "Aren't you going to finish that?"

"Can't." A grimace of defeat crosses his face. "You want it?"

She smirks, a look that reveals he must be crazy for not finishing such an excellent cone. Or crazy for offering it to her, which is simply disgusting. Or crazy because she'd already told him that she'd had two pieces of baklava for dessert after her lunch with Fay and Mavis and anybody with a brain knows that two ice cream cones on top of all that would also be disgusting.

James wonders if her look of disdain is intended to tell him that she's bored again. He dumps what's left of his cone into the wastebasket beside their table and returns to the subject of titles. "So where *have* you been?"

She tips her head and shrugs, this time suggesting that her travels have taken her nowhere special. "It's more about where I'm going, I guess. Or maybe where I hope to go. One day." In a final, concentrated burst she finishes the cone in three crisp bites, wipes her lips with the napkin and sets her hands on the table with satisfaction.

"And where's that?" James asks, realizing the conversation has reverted to a new interrogation. Damn it.

Another shrug. "Are you ready to go see Mom and Mavis?"

Mom-and-Mavis. She's joined them into a single unit: M-A-M. Before they leave the restaurant, James wants to learn one more thing about Teejay. "Hey, speaking about Mavis, she told me you guessed her age."

"Did I?"

"Yeah. Thirty-two. How did you do that?"

The customer line-up now extends to the front door. Teejay scans the people around her, recalling that rainy afternoon when Mavis arrived with Fay and saved her from an afternoon of time-out purgatory. "I just guessed," she confesses and shrugs again, a habit that James assumes she employs whenever people got a little too close to her inner life.

"You just guessed?" He stands, ready to go, and she rises beside him, the top of her head level with his shoulders. She looks awkward to him now, heavy in her waist — so out of balance with the agile grace of her shoulders and neck, the delicate lines of her face.

"Yes." She shrugs once more, a hint of impatience in her voice. "She was wearing this really nice sweater with five big, pearly buttons. Three buttoned up and two open at her throat. I just put the two numbers together."

Thirty-two. Mystery solved, and so simple, too. James laughs to himself and wonders if she can repeat this bit of clairvoyance. "Do you know how old I am?

Teejay studies him a moment and feels a twinge of pity. He's been very kind but he, too, is old. Much older than her mom or Mavis. He could even be Mavis's father. But she knows the two of them are married and she realizes she could never say *that* to him. Not out loud. She also knows she should say something polite because he has been genuinely nice to her. Kinder than anyone in months. She glances past his shoulder at the sign above the ice cream menu that identifies how many flavors are available today: forty-seven, not forty-eight. "Thank you for the ice cream cone," she says and looks steadily into his face.

"My pleasure." His face brightens. "I mean it."

She continues to concentrate on his eyes, on the way he has of letting you look at him without turning it into a staring contest. "I think you're forty-seven," she announces with complete certainty and before he can respond she adds, "and don't ask me how I know."

"What?"

Teejay points to the sign and when she sees him laugh she leads the way onto the sidewalk pleased to have made a friend of James. And pleased to have kept her secret to herself for one more day.

---

"Take me there." Mavis pauses a moment and leans into the space that Fay occupies. They sit in chairs facing one another in the office that Mavis set up the week after she and James moved into the apartment. Her grandfather's wing-backed chair is separated from James's Ergo-flex Gravity Chair by a small, round coffee table. On top of the table lays Fay's painting, *Inner Trialogue*. "Take me there," she says again, turning her head to the painting. "Tell me what it feels like to be the mother in your painting."

"The mother?" Fay combs her fingers through the bush of hair beside her ear. "She's in a whole lot of pain." Her voice is calm, contemplative. She studies the built-in bookcase filled with hundreds of books that Mavis has collected over the past decade and she silently reads a few titles: *Totem and Taboo, Irrational Man, Love's Body*. Sitting in the study with Mavis makes her feel as if she's been admitted to a place of privilege, a compact library where time has been stopped at the door. You can sit here and think and talk, and not be rushed or bothered with what lies ahead. She draws a deep breath and adds, "She might be worried because of what will happen to the child."

Mavis stares at the painting and considers the worry, the fear, in Fay's voice. Although she unrolled the painting and set it on the coffee table ten minutes ago, the images still claw at Mavis and she's surprised to discover that familiarity offers no relief from the painting's malevolence. She'd assumed the three creatures were sexless totems, but Fay revealed that they were a mother, daughter and infant. Mavis also assumed (wrong again, she murmurs to herself) that once the picture had saturated her attention, she could then look away and when she studied it again the image of the daughter sitting in the mother's lap, and the horrible growth, "the infant," extending from the girl's head — that all of it would lose some potency. But it doesn't. The effect is still raw and visceral. Remarkable. "So Fay, take a moment and try to *be* the mother. Tell me what she's thinking. What she's *feeling*."

Fay's eyes sweep the room, settle on a few more book jackets. *Escape from Freedom, Current Psychotherapies.* It's better to be sitting in this marvelous chair than to be in that painting. Better than being the mother, the centerpiece, in the nightmare of *Inner Trialogue*. "I like it here," she says. "It's cozy."

Mavis nods and holds Fay's eyes. She waits. Philip Box would wait, too. Waiting is a way of being. A way to nudge hesitancy into thought and thought into expression.

Fay straightens her spine and glances away. The stained glass trim on the window casts ripples of green and yellow light across the floor. Monet would like to see this, she thinks. Maybe he would like to live here, too. She turns each ring on her fingers in sequence. Three rotations each. The magic combination to protect her soul is one complete turn and two turns for Teejay — three altogether, each accompanied by a silent incantation: *Hail Mary, full of grace.* Despite the assurance offered by her faith she knows she has to go forward with this. Mavis is her guide and guardian; if her soul comes into jeopardy, Mavis will be there to pull her onto the far shore. She also knows that if she hesitates, or refuses to go forward, the thin crust of reality she's been treading along for the past two months will dissolve under her feet and both she and Teejay will plummet into the abyss, well past the point where any incantations or manipulations can save them. She draws another deep breath.

"The mother is surprised," she announces. She hears a tiny machine-like voice speaking from her throat and she coughs to clear it away. "She's surprised because she didn't see what was going to happen." That's better. Her voice is full this time and she glances at Mavis to determine if this makes sense. "She did manage to see a lot of other things that came to pass. Long ago, I mean. A few years ago she was a pretty good fortuneteller. But she didn't see this coming. So I don't think it's her *fault*, really. I don't think you can blame her." She turns her head to one side in despair as another part of her asks, *Oh? And how could a good mother not have foreseen this?*

"Fay, I want you to get closer now. I want you to *be* the mother. Tell me what she feels as if *you* are the mother. Say, *I feel....*"

Fay nods and examines the image of the mother in the painting. "She feels like — "

"*I feel like* — "

"Okay, *I feel* like ... dying." Fay's hand jolts to her mouth. Shocked to hear these words, she appeals to Mavis for help.

Mavis leans forward with a gesture that reveals they are about to go through a door together, but that Fay must lead the way. She repeats the last phrase to guide her: "I feel like dying because...."

"I feel like dying because of what I let happen to my daughter. I shouldn't have let that happen." She twirls the ring on her left index finger. One, two, three.

Mavis nods. They've crossed a threshold, but now where are they? "And what did happen, Fay?"

Fay dips her hand to the painting. "The daughter had the infant. But it's not the baby Jesus." Her voice drops a tone. "Nobody knows it yet, but the baby's going ... to be a *devil*." Her eyes open wide and she looks at Mavis with certainty. Now that she's finally said this aloud, she's convinced it's true. Suddenly she feels relieved. She divulged this horrible truth and she didn't fall through the floor into the abyss. But now she can feel the blood pulsing in her arms and chest, pulsing hard and fast.

The change in Fay is so visceral that Mavis can sense Fay's energy radiating into her own body. She understands the dynamics at play and she knows she has to press on while the door remains open. "Okay, now I want you to be the daughter, all right? Just like you did with the mother. Let her voice come through you. Tell me what she's experiencing." She waits a moment to let Fay adjust to the change and then prompts her: "So now the girl is talking. And she says, *I feel....*"

Fay turns her head slightly. A barrier stands in front of her and she tries to calculate its dimensions, determine if there is a way around it. She presses her jaw tightly, and through her teeth she whispers, "I feel ... cheated." She tests this to see if the words are accurate, then she understands that she has to make a slight change. "No: *he* cheated me." This emerges with more force. Fay draws another breath and continues. "He cheated me and *you didn't stop him.*"

Mavis weighs this carefully, balances the heat in her words with their meaning. "Who's the *you*, Fay? Who is the child talking about?"

"The mother." Again, Fay's hand dips to the painting. The zest of power streaming from her body shuts down. Once she hears this accusation from the girl, she realizes that she might not be able to continue. A tear wells in her right eye and she brushes it away with a thumb.

The sudden collapse in Fay's energy infects Mavis so that she realizes she must identify the source of her fear. The answer to that might come from the third figure in the painting. From the grandchild, the devil. "All right, Fay, I know you're tired, but I want you try just one last thing. This will be the last thing we do today and then we'll stop, okay?" She waits for some acknowledgement from Fay, and when she nods, Mavis continues. "I want you to tell me what the baby says. What the *devil* says," she corrects herself.

Fay sits back in the chair. She nods her head to show that she understands, that they must hear from the devil now, that learning what he has to say will complete what they're here to do. She adjusts her jaw again, rolls it back and forth a few times as she tries to hear what the devil has to say. "You made me." His voice is hard, bitter, accusative. "You made me ... and now you have to *love* me!" She pinches her lips together. *Enough*. Better never to repeat another word from him! She nods her head to confirm that he will soon be shut out forever and then she spins two rings to lock the vault.

Mavis studies Fay's behavior and when she turns another ring, Mavis asks, "Tell me something, Fay. What do your rings do?"

She looks at Mavis as if this couldn't be more obvious. "They open and lock the doors. For protection. Don't you lock the door when you come in at night? Especially when you have a child to protect," she adds when she considers that Mavis has no children. Just like Janice Slitz. So many young women are barren now. How could it be? Another sign that the end of days is drawing near.

"Of course." Mavis turns her eyes away and for the first time she realizes that Fay is dealing with an inner world far beyond anything she imagined. Philip Box had been too quick to diagnose her as bipolar. There are many other layers here. First, an obsessive-compulsive behavior (twirling the rings in specific combinations and orders) established to codify a form of magical thinking. But the magic that Fay incorporated into her life is so deeply felt that it could easily give way to a psychotic break. Perhaps *that* is the basis of her dread. It isn't fear of the devil, it's the fear of entering Hell. Unless she's able to bolt the door and keep it shut, she's terrified she'll collapse into the abyss of eternal Hell.

"Mavis?"

Mavis blinks and returns her attention to Fay. She smiles

slightly, puts on a look to assure Fay that Hell is simply an idea, a bad idea, a fiction invented long ago in order to rule by fear, not love. She tilts her chin to one side. "Yes?"

"I'm worried that I can't stay here," she confesses. "Me and Teejay. I don't mean in this room," she adds. "I mean in here." She touches the side of her head with her fingers and a look of dislocation crosses her face, an expression that reveals that she's forgotten a vital piece of information: *where do I live?*

Mavis weaves her fingers together and grips them so tightly the tendons in her arms begin to lock. She'd opened an inner door in Fay, a gate at the top of a high tower that opens onto thin air. One step forward and she could plummet into the underworld. Mavis reaches across the table and holds Fay's wrist with one hand and squeezes just enough to let her know that she's anchored. Bolted into the hear-and-now. "Don't worry," she says. "I've got you."

Fay's face dissolves. The dozens of muscles that keep her features in place loosen and collapse. Finally someone else is here to hold everything together and she knows she can rest for a while. She doesn't want Mavis to let her go. Not ever. She draws her free hand over her face to compose herself, to hide the tears that slip down her cheeks to her chin. She begins to cry. Like the child in the painting wants to cry, like Teejay wants to cry. She cries for both of them. One cry for her, two cries for Teejay, three cries altogether. She cries until she can barely breathe. As she begins to gasp for air, she feels Mavis's hand still clasping her wrist, a thumb massaging her skin so, so gently. When she realizes that she's still connected to something, that she isn't falling through the thin crust into the depths of the underworld, she manages to stop her tears. Then the part of her that controls her tears begins to stabilize her breathing, and after another moment she eases her shoulder into the corner of the wing-backed chair and takes shelter there. At last she feels secure and she pats Mavis's hand and gently removes it from her wrist. All this seems to take forever. She has no idea what day it is. She draws her knees into her arms and when she's comfortable she nuzzles her head against the leather upholstery.

"Mmmm," she purrs. Her voice alerts her to the dimension of her on-going existence. *You are here*, she whispers to herself. Time finds its rhythm and finally begins to beat again. She blinks two, three times to keep pace.

"Are you back with us now?" Mavis glances at the clock on her desk. Fay's crying jag has lasted almost twenty minutes. Throughout her collapse and revival Mavis said nothing. All she could do was tether herself to Fay and hold on.

"Nice chair," Fay replies. She chuckles a single, girlish giggle; happy with its own birdie sound.

"My grandfather gave it to me."

"Nice grandfather."

"Yeah. He was."

Fay expels a long sigh and buries one side of her head against one of the chair wings. She can see Mavis through her right eye. "So Mavis," she asks, her voice a mere whisper now, "where do we go from here?"


Ever since Mavis left home at the age of twenty to take an undergraduate degree at University of California in Los Angeles, Mavis's grandfather liked to communicate with her via postcards. She knew this eccentricity was old-fashioned but since Papa Helm was ninety-one and bull-headed in his ways, Mavis was happy to maintain their correspondence whenever he sent her a new card. He kept a condo in Boston, a summer cottage in Lake Tahoe and a townhouse in Sarasota where he passed the late fall and winter, about a ninety-minute drive from Joleen's four-bedroom bungalow in Tampa. Each time he moved from one place to the next, he sent Mavis a postcard to advise her of his whereabouts and to comment on whatever scene was depicted on the face of the card. Images of marlin fishing and skiing were his favorites. Not that he ever indulged in these sports personally, but he loved to suggest he was part of the action.

*Look at the size of this fish! Put up quite a fight, I'm sure. Joleen and her kids are fine. I'll be down here enjoying the sun until March. After that, back to Boston and then the summer in Tahoe.*
*Love, Papa. PS: Gerri sends her love.*

Gerri was Papa's long-standing companion and aide and Joleen suspected that through cleverness and stealth she'd managed to wiggle her way into the heart of Papa's last will and testament. Given Gerri's unstinting dedication to him, Mavis thought that was fair game, but she knew Joleen would be haggling with Gerri long after Papa's demise. The realization reinforced her commitment to remain in California, beyond reach (physically, at least) of her older sister.

Ten years had passed since she'd established a life on her own on the west coast. After completing her BA at UCLA she worked as a teacher's aide for five years at Venice High School, and although her career was beginning to feel "mature," (a word she preferred to "boring") she still enjoyed the students and knew that most of them liked her.

Late in June, soon after summer recess began, Mavis sat

in a Starbucks café writing a postcard in response to her grandfather's latest dispatch.

*Dear Papa, I finally have an afternoon to myself. Give thanks for small miracles. Think I'll wander around the neighborhood and have a picnic on the beach watching the surfers. Have a look at these two surfing the "pipeline"! Hope to do something special this summer, but can't imagine what it will be.*
*As always, Love, Mavis. XX*

After drinking her latté she strolled along the sidewalk toward the post office, mailed her card, turned toward her apartment, and then noticed a line of people entering the library lecture theater. Later she would wonder what had inspired her curiosity. Perhaps it was the unusual title imprinted on a placard taped above the auditorium door: *Making Contact: the New Humanity.* Maybe it was the expectant buzz of the people waiting for admission to the hall. In any case, she soon found herself inside the packed hall, looking for a place to sit when a man at the front of the room waved a hand and called out, "There're a few seats here in the front row."

James Wayman focused his attention on the clot of people at the door and then his eyes settled directly on Mavis. "Don't be shy," he called to her, "there's an excellent seat right here." Mavis made her way to the front row. James smiled at her and after a few minutes began his lecture.

First he focused on the difference between characters and humans, that we all invent characters which we inhabit as personal avatars and how important it is to realize that these roles are simply stuffed costumes, mere inventions, and that the key to achieving personal freedom, to discover your *new humanity*, is to inhabit the pure being of your self, not the persona invented by your ego.

Everyone was enamored by James's apparently persona-free presence. He had an ability to stand in front of hundreds of strangers and deliver this unique view of "being" in a completely convincing manner. Mavis had never experienced charisma like this before, a magnetism that drew everyone to him at once. His confidence, his voice tone, his animation, his genuine attention to the people in the room — all of it captivated her. Like almost everyone else, at the conclusion of the session Mavis was smitten.

She decided to enroll in his free, follow-up workshops. After the sign-up register circulated through the room she made a point of delivering it to him personally.

"You seem to be popular," she told him. "Looks like over a hundred people want to take your workshop."

"Well...." He glanced away and then forced himself to look at her. "I guess that'll keep me busy."

She was surprised to see his ears flush, the only hint of shyness she'd detected after listening to him speak for over an hour.

"And are you one of them?" he asked.

"Wouldn't miss it. By the way, I'm Mavis Helm. And thanks for saving a seat for me." She shook his hand and pointed to the chair where she'd been sitting. "I had an excellent view."

She turned away without saying another word and cursed herself. Why did she have to say *that?* She might just as well have confessed: forget all this crazy business about the new humanity and living in the here-and-now, *I love your body.*

A few days after her thirty-first birthday Mavis's attraction to James culminated at her grandfather's cottage on Crystal Bay above the north shore of Lake Tahoe. After she completed his three-week course in White Light Meditation — where she discovered a part of herself that she never imagined existed, but which was certainly, she had to admit, the most important and central source of her identity — after diligently focusing on and absorbing everything James had to impart, she felt very clever to convince him to join her at the lake cottage, alone, for a three-day weekend. When he accepted, she knew he must feel *something* for her, but she didn't know what. Was his *non-persona* persona (a delicate irony she suspected he didn't quite recognize in himself) falling for her save-the-world persona? Or did he see something else in her, *in them*, that she didn't know about? During the long drive into Nevada these questions played out in future scenarios in which she imagined herself as James's girlfriend ... partner ... wife ... mother to their children ... grandmother to the eternity of their recombinant DNA. The possibilities escalated into looping fantasies, the sort of crazy nonsense, if she revealed it to him, that James would have dismissed as multiple-monkey-minded maya.

Yes, she conceded, the trap of illusion had snared her well and true. And it got worse. Over the following months she entered a dream state furnished with warmth and safety and the anticipation of hours of tireless intimacy with her man. But she didn't care; the fantasy was just too sweet to ignore, one she cultivated with patience and tenderness, humor and complete trust. And complete lust.

Two months after Papa Helm died James asked her to marry him. Coming in the midst of her grief, his proposal took her by surprise and she burst into tears of joy and despair. Although marriage with James would be the perfect antidote to her mourning, she wished Papa could be there to witness her happiness and to see how much she'd become like him. But their resemblance wasn't physical, it was entirely psychological, comprised of personal attributes like focus, determination, attitude, perseverance. "Never give up," he'd told her. "Never give up on anything you want in this life." That was Papa. And Mavis.

Everyone recognized that Papa had lived a full life. Mavis, more than Joleen, knew it was a blessing that Papa had brought the girls into his home and raised them on his own following the accident that killed their parents while they were in Belize. Perhaps because Joleen was the older child, because she possessed warm, resonant memories of their mother and father, she developed a mild resentment of Papa. But Mavis could only recall her parents through the few photographs enshrined in the long hallway leading to the girls' bedrooms. While her parents were no more than phantoms, she loved Papa, and everything that he'd given her.

Ultimately, Joleen's suspicions proved to be correct. Gerri had quietly but quite successfully infiltrated Papa's last will and testament. "It's even worse," she said, "she's entitled to one-third of the assets! My lawyer said it's completely, totally, bullet-proof!" Despite the real estate market collapse, the three of them agreed to sell the condo in Boston, the Sarasota townhouse and, after a week of hesitation and debate, they decided to sell the cottage in Lake Tahoe, too. Jolene's agent advised them that the only way to liquidate the properties was to list them at fire-sale prices. Once that decision was taken, they accepted the first offer on each property and felt lucky to sell all three homes within two months. Before the crash Papa's net worth neared three million dollars, but after deducting the estate taxes and the legal, accounting and real estate fees, each of the beneficiaries received two hundred and eighty-three thousand dollars. In addition, Mavis kept some of the furniture from the cottage, including her cherished wing-backed chair. She put one hundred thousand into a bond, bought a new Toyota Prius, and set aside the rest of the money to pay her tuition and cover living expenses for the two years she needed to complete a masters degree in counseling psychology. It seemed like a lot of money, but after all the accounts were balanced, only a few thousand dollars remained. Her buffer.

Three months after his proposal, Mavis married James in a civic ceremony at the LA county court house. James's foundation chairman, Zack Philbin stood in as his best man and Hildy Franks, the librarian at Venice High School, served as her maid of honor.

She couldn't imagine marrying anyone other than James. Their marriage offered a turning point away from the past, away from Joleen and Florida toward this new life, wherever it might lead. Since James could oversee the operations of the White Light Foundation from anywhere, she enrolled in the graduate psychology program at Berkeley. They moved from Los Angeles to the Bay Area and installed themselves in the corner apartment building next to People's Park.

From here Mavis began her new life. A new life of someone living with intention, of choosing her own way forward. Bless you Papa, she whispered to herself as she went to bed on that first night in Berkeley and she closed her eyes and wished that nothing would ever change.

During some of their meditations together (perhaps one in five, he figures) James is unable divert his mind from sex. Instead of an orb of white light glowing at the center of his brow, the tyranny of his penis stands erect: taut, imperious, undeniable. On other occasions a vision of the immense hunger of Mavis's vagina wells before him, flush and moist, her anticipation evident on her glistening thighs. And once, to his astonishment, in the middle of his meditation he became disembodied and hovered a few inches below the ceiling and watched a fantasy of himself locked in passion with his wife as they fed one another the various nourishments of love.

Whenever these distractions emerge in his mind he acknowledges the folly of resistance. He tries to return to his mantra two, three, four times but soon he understands the struggle is hopeless. Besides, why ignore the joy of intimate marital lust? It's life, and the love of life, free of persona and resident in the here-and-now. When they both accede to the power of their erotic energy, he sits before her cross-legged and she straddles him, drawing her heels behind the small of his back as she wraps her arms around his neck and eases herself onto his lap, slowly enveloping his erection. After a few moments of shuddering, breath-taking pleasure as their flesh binds together, they establish a measure of composure and their foreheads touch just above their brows and from here they enter one another a second time: a double-bonded copulation of their second and sixth chakras. The effect is so intense that they slip into a kind of hyperbaric containment in order to discharge (slowly, slowly) the energy streaming through their bodies. Finally settled, they enter a state of harmony that can last for over an hour. Then their carefully constructed sexual engine rises and intensifies and finally the chaos of sex explodes between them. Spent, exhausted, useless — they fall into the emptiness that embraces all requited lovers.

And now, perhaps an hour later, in the midst of this void James stumbles onto an image of Teejay. At first he's surprised to see her. What is she doing here, how did she wander into this private bliss? But his surprise gradually transforms into conviction. His eyes blink open and he gazes at the ceiling, takes a moment to confirm this strange apprehension. Is it possible? Yes, but can it be true? *Yes.*

He turns his eyes and examines his wife, dozing, naked at his side. He loves the lassitude of sexual exhaustion in her face, the unspoken declaration that she's sated. For now.

"She's pregnant," he whispers.

"What?" Mavis hears him speaking but can't piece these two words together into a single meaning. "Pregnant? *Who's pregnant?*"

"Teejay." His head nods with certainty. He has no doubt. "After watching her, at the ice cream parlor, I just realized that she's pregnant."

Mavis lifts herself on one elbow and sweeps her eyes over James's face. Then she looks through him, past him into her own intuitions about Teejay. Yes, that was exactly what Fay had been telling her. About the child's *child*. The grandchild.

"My god," she says, not wanting to believe it. She pauses to consider everything she knows about Fay and Teejay and what *Inner Trialogue* really means to Fay. How could she have missed this? "But who?..." she mutters, not yet convinced. But she can't say anything more, not while a new question presses into her mind: *Who is the father?*

## Chapter Two

It sees all, but knows nothing.

Like most Geostationary Operational Environmental Satellites (GOES, as NASA calls them) GOES 12 floats — unblinking, digitally synched, tireless — at a fixed altitude of 22,240 miles above the Equator. At a coasting speed slightly over a thousand miles per hour, the weather bird is locked into a stationary holding pattern at a pace that matches Earth's counter-clockwise rotation and at a height that ensures it will neither spin off into space nor tumble into the lower atmosphere where it will be ripped into a cascading spew of twisted shrapnel. Depending on the capabilities of the other GOES birds, GOES 12 is either on active duty or assigned a standby role if more reliable satellites are available.

Alas, GOES 12 does not have a perfect operations record. In fact, it's failed to respond to orders on three occasions. However, in each episode extraordinary technical maneuvers managed to return GOES 12 to active duty. Usually it's stationed above the Amazon Basin or redeployed over the eastern Pacific Ocean. From either position it maintains an excellent perspective of the lower forty-eight states, Mexico, and southern Canada. And depending on the number of umbrella cocktails imbibed by the technicians who monitor the GOES fleet, some of the NASA staff claim that the satellites' visual acuity is so sharp that it may be possible (with a few minor system tweaks, that is) to see a sparrow fall.

We can say with confidence, however, that while GOES 12 may have *seen* the Red-Tailed Hawk that flew into a power line in the hills of Yuba County in mid-September, it did not comprehend the consequences of this seemingly innocuous collision. Nor did the dozens of meteorologists and TV forecasters who relied on GOES 12 for satellite imagery to broadcast news of the escalating drought and fire hazards building up to the moment of the Red-Tailed Hawk crash. Prior to the collision, temperatures in California's Great Central Valley ran above one hundred degrees for twenty-five days without a break. Humidity dipped below thirty percent and the carpet of baked pine needles scattered across the forest floor in the hills above the valley crumbled under foot. When the power line snapped on impact with the hawk, it emitted a spray of sparks that cascaded down the ridge below a transformer tower. The resulting inferno was instantaneous and the Yuba wildfire joined the conflagration that had scorched the eastern flank of California's Great Central Valley during the previous months.

A few weeks earlier, the State of California, balanced precariously on the edge of fiscal insolvency, had laid off hundreds of internal employees and contracted fire suppression duties to a number of private companies to respond to any emergencies. One of the contractors, A&J Enterprises, had cash-flow problems of its own. Al and John Milewski, the father-and-son proprietors of A&J Enterprises, had released all of their permanent staff when the state resorted to paying its contractors with IOUs.

Discussing their problems over a few beers at Bob's Wildcat Bar 'n' Grill, Al fixed on the idea of staffing the fire suppression teams using a state workfare program that an old army buddy, "Scooter" Schlosser, had told him about the previous afternoon. As Al understood the game, CalWorks employers gave the laborers their daily room and board, and after they completed a month of full-time work the state gave them a one-month supply of food stamps intended to cover the workers while they made the shift into paid employment — assuming they could find it.

If A&J Enterprises could establish itself as an accredited employer with the CalWorks program, Al figured they could bring hundreds of drifters onto the wildfire suppression teams, put them up in tents wherever the fires broke out and feed them state rations provided on the job. Since A&J already had service contracts with the state, they'd likely be rubber-stamped as a bona fide CalWorks employer. The cost to A&J would be zero, but at some point down the road — "God knows when," John mused, "and maybe even He's in the dark on this one" — they could trade in their hoard of IOUs for cash. Sure enough, within two weeks of making their application, A&J Enterprises became a duly certified CalWorks partner. When the paperwork arrived in the mail, John was shocked at the government's near-instant turn-around time. "When the need arises, the machinery of state becomes a rocket launcher," Al said, his tone a bit dismissive of his son's skepticism and his off-handed slight against the Good Lord.

Before the Yuba County fire could be contained it tore

through six square miles of the hills just north of the state capital, Sacramento. Rare as it was for fires to purge the valley's northeastern slopes, the devastation continued long after the initial breakout. During the final days of the mop-up, A&J was instructed to haul thirty new CalWorks laborers to the scene ASAP. As the men from the last crew to arrive slid off the box of Al's Ford F-150, each grabbed a shovel and staggered in the direction of the smoldering remains of six houses perched on the hillside.

"Keep shoveling through the rubble until the smoke clears," Al told the newcomers. "Word has it that rain's on the way, but until you're toe-deep in puddles, boss-man says to keep shoveling."

The men gazed at the spectacle of charred ruins. It was madness; there appeared to be nothing left to save on this smokey ravine. Along the pock-marked hillside stood the concrete foundations of a destroyed housing tract. One of the men pushed his boot onto the throat of the shovel and turned some shards to one side. Another, Raymond Guzman, took a deep breath and started to dig, too. What the fuck, he muttered to himself. It beats digging your own grave.

Raymond settles on top of his blankets and stares into the sky. His lower back, cramped by the ribbons of muscles knotted above his buttocks, flutters with pain as he adjusts his weight against the hardpan soil. He'd started working with a shovel as a kid spading potash into the artichoke crops south of Monterrey and he knows from experience that it takes about three days to work out the kinks.

Regardless of the lingering pain, his stomach is still full with the evening meal and none of the work crew has caused him any trouble. Most of them would stick to themselves the first few nights and Raymond figures it will take two or three weeks before a few gangs can form and several days more before any fights will break out. By then everyone would be counting off the hours until they're released and handed their workfare payout and bus fare to San Francisco. Odds are that he'll survive this detail unscathed, a calculation based on his two previous gigs in the bush that he completed uneventfully, at least as far as his own person was concerned.

Others found trouble if they were looking for it. He was particularly impressed with the damage Jack Dulbert had inflicted on some half-wit with a Rawlings baseball bat during the fires outside Modesto. While he never looked for this kind of trouble, Raymond keeps a folding barber's razor tucked in his boot just above his ankle. He's never had to use it, and worries he won't know what to do with it if a situation calls for a flash of steel. Mostly it's for show, for whenever show-time arrives. Hopefully, that would be never.

As the clouds roll in from the Pacific, the night air finally cools and he pulls his blanket over his shoulders and drifts off. After a time he slips into a dream state and once again he finds himself back home with his daughter.

Despite all his troubles with Fay he loves that little girl. And while the child has none of their features — her looks, her voice, her thoughts all seem to come from someone else entirely — Raymond remains convinced that there's more of him in her body and soul than the ounce of juice that Fay somehow managed to squeeze out of her blood and put into the girl. Teejay is all and everything that a good girl could be.

When Fay had the police kick him out of his own home,

Raymond was forced to play out his hand with stealth and deliberation and he began to monitor Fay's comings-and-goings to know the best times to visit his child without interruption.

That's how he found himself in her dark room that night. She lay fast asleep, but shivering for lack of a warm blanket. It was only natural to cover the girl. There was no decision made, no thought nor contrivance to harm her. He simply did what any good father ought to do and warmed his child's body to the point where her shivering ceased. He himself lay quietly asleep when Fay opened the door to the room.

And that precise moment is where the dream always begins, and seconds later, ends. The door opens and with it a narrow shaft of light sweeps over the bed. The light stops on Raymond's face, clicks into his eyes and in that instant he is awake, panicking, horrified that Fay's discovered him like this, in the same place as Teejay. He gasps. Always the nightmare ends with him gasping, sucking in a long draft of air before he suffocates. *It's just a dream — just a dream — just a dream!* As he screams he bats his hands against the blankets as though he's tamping out a fire that's ignited the world around him. When he comes to his senses, realizes that yeah, *it is* just a dream, he settles down again, thankful to know that Teejay slept through it all, oblivious to the nightmare. Still innocent, still pure. His beautiful Teejay, as good as a girl can be.

When the rain begins in earnest Raymond tries to wait it out where he lies. But soon the blanket is saturated and he has to pull his clothes and kit together and make a dash along the dry creek bed to the mess hall. A&J had erected a canvas tent on the bank just above the Feather River and most of the men gather there grumbling, calling for an early breakfast. During the twenty-minute wait, everyone keeps their eyes on the downpour washing against the ridges where they'd worked on the fire. The rain completely douses the smoking ruins on the slope and for the first time in days the air smells clean and refreshed. Above them the toasty wheat flavor of warm baked bread fills the canopy. They can hear bacon and eggs popping, the flop of pancakes turning on the griddle. The mix of fresh air, the anticipation of a feast, and the drumbeat of rain on the canvas roof generates an atmosphere of festivity. The men begin to smile. They can sense the change coming toward them. Something unknowable, but hard and forceful.

While they eat, some of the men joke about all the work they've done over the last week, how useless it was and if they'd just waited for Mother Nature to take her course, not one shovelful of dirt was needed to damp the fire. Instead, CalWorks should just feed them and let them watch the flame-out for free. Like watching the sunset at a beach served up with wieners and toast. Who ever heard of trying to douse a sunset? Only the government would come up with such a scheme. Probably attach a taxation program to it, too.

The rain falls without mercy and by noon the dry bed creek begins to flood below the bank where the tent stands. As the runoff flushes the detritus from the Yuba County fire into the river, everyone can see the water will soon be riding the high edge of its banks. Raymond watches the rising danger and imagines that at some point the flood will wash out the floorboards of the mess hall. The canvas ceiling begins to bulge under the weight of rainwater that fills a dip above the grill. John Milewski presses a shovel blade against the depression and just as he's making some progress in elevating the canvas to the point where all of the water might roll off the roof, a massive tear shears the canvas in half. The waterfall cascades over John and the entire tent splits into two pieces and flaps across the sides of the deck. The men burst into laughter, a sound that briefly overcomes the rush of the storm above them. In seconds they're soaking and most of them scramble back up the ridge and squat amongst the rocks and root stumps, feet planted downhill, their arms wrapped across their knees to brace themselves and tuck their bellies out of the rain.

Raymond finds a perch above a clump of burnt shrubs and he sets both feet against this prop. He yanks his blanket around his torso and holds the edges to the sides of his face while he watches the scene below. The Feather River, the main conduit of all the streams pouring off this section of the Sierra Nevada, is now swollen two or three feet above its banks. He imagines that a steel towing line is dragging along the river bottom and from that line a web of invisible cables catches the deck of the mess hall. First it pulls one joist away from the flooring, then another, and all at once, the entire structure breaks away and disappears into the torrent of the flood. The two sheets of torn roofing canvas follow as a kind of after-thought: the first, a flag waving a truce, then after it disappears under the cascade, a second flag of unconditional surrender.

A gasp rises from the men on the slope as the deepening river attaches another cable to the rear axle of John Milewski's F-150. The truck swings around and then the wheels slide a foot or two into the water. In a panic, John climbs into the cab and starts fussing with the steering column.

"What the fuck," Raymond says aloud. *What is he doing?*

Seconds later the engine burps to life and John sets the

truck in reverse to drive it backwards up the bank to safety. It tugs a little, starts to win the fight and when things look promising, Al Milewski braces himself on the outside of the cab and starts pushing. "Come on," he yells to no one in particular.

In that moment Raymond realizes that Hell itself has opened wide and instantly the Feather River rises another foot and drags the F-150 and the Milewskis into its fury. Al, still pressing his weight against the truck, is swept under the front wheel and disappears. John, now distracted by the disappearance of his father, tries to open the door to the cab. Is he hoping to swim after him, or just looking where Al might have gone?

Raymond presses his hands to his face and as he watches yet another surge rises through the river. As soon as the truck door opens a crack, the river floods into the cab. The engine coughs and dies. Every particle of this situation unfolds so slowly, Raymond thinks, as if someone has cut each second into a cartoon and pasted them onto a long sheet of paper separated by tiny gaps. Then in one long, lazy sweep of the burgeoning waters, with John pinned inside the truck, the river tugs ever so gently at the hub caps, the bumpers, the tailgate, and finally the rear box — once it floods — absorbs the F-150's inertia into the river's momentum. The truck slides into the rushing waters half-afloat, then submarines and disappears with John still gripping the steering wheel.

The men sit frozen on the slope. No one can believe what they've just witnessed. Few of them can move. When the foundations of the homes that had burnt in the fire begin to shudder, Raymond realizes the entire slope of the ridge is about to collapse. He stands up and glances around him.

"Slide." His voice is a mere whisper. He can barely hear himself speak. "Mudslide!" he cries, this time in a scream that brings dozens of men to their feet. "Climb above the foundations!" he adds and crawls uphill until he's well above two concrete pads that he knows are about to be washed into the river.

When he finds his footing on the broken ground he looks down into the flood plain. He nods his head as the soil begins to wash from beneath the foundations of the homes destroyed by the fire. It's the only time he is sure of what will happen that day. The only thing he sees coming before it hits. In one long rip that tears through the slope, both foundations break away from the hillside and slide into the flood below pushing two more men into the water ahead of them.

Raymond scrambles above the crevice opened by the slide and collapses in exhaustion on his stomach and braces his elbows in the mud. He turns his head from side to side, desperate to find solid ground. Everything is in ruins. His life, his body, his mind, his soul. He presses his face into the palms of his hands and for the first time since Teejay was born he begins to weep uncontrollably.

A handful of survivors, about twenty by Raymond's count, made their way down the valley into Sacramento. When the rain abated, they realized they'd been cheated out of their meal vouchers and bus fare, and with the Milewskis swept away, they had no one to verify their claims. Who could save them? "The governor," someone offered. "Let's go straight to the top." The idea seemed perfect, no question about it. CalWorks was Governor White's doing. And so was the food-stamp program, and all those state IOUs. It was time for the governor to pay up and if he didn't make good on his debts then someone would have to force him to it. The men drifted into the city hitch-hiking alone or in pairs, each finding his way to the State Capitol on L Street. From there Raymond crossed into Capitol Park where he found a dry patch of lawn under a park bench that would serve as a roof for the night. To his relief he passed into an easy, dreamless sleep.

The next morning as Governor Edmund White is driven along 16$^{th}$ Street, he casts his eyes up to the edges of the park through the gray, shatter-proof glass windows of the limousine. He sees the homeless wrapped in discarded newspapers and cardboard sheets, their shopping carts angled defensively against the terrors of the night. Some of them sleep with dogs snuggled at their bellies. A few of the newly dispossessed have backpacks and proper sleeping bags. But taken altogether most of them are broken and lost, he admits. Alcoholic, crack-heads, psychotics — whatever their personal tragedy, all are utterly destitute.

This is the price, he whispers to himself in dismay, the price we pay for decades of greed. He shakes his head. He knows many of the greedy, too. Indeed, some of them made generous campaign contributions to his bid to return to the governor's mansion after his years in the political wilderness. So many of them believe that they can barter wealth for safety. That's the deal they strike, the grand bargain that allows them to barricade their homes, their children, their infirm fathers and mothers, even their future generations as yet unconceived and barely imagined.

As the limo waits at the lights to turn onto L Street, the first bird hits the steel roof with a soft thud. Phil, the governor's personal driver, and McMurphy, the lone security staffer assigned to the morning detail, turn their heads toward the retractable dome window.

"What was that?"

"Don't know, sir." Phil sets the transmission in park as a second bird crashes into the trunk of the car. Everyone shifts and turns to gaze out the rear window. A third bird strikes the hood of the limo and lays lifelessly against the windshield.

"They're sparrows," Governor White announces. "They're all sparrows. See what's going on, Phil."

McMurphy shifts in his seat. "Sir, I strongly advise not to open the car doors. We have no idea what this is. It could be some kind of ... gas attack ... or something." McMurphy hesitates just enough to make his theory sound ridiculous.

"Completely ludicrous," White says as two more birds smack into the hood and roll onto the asphalt. "I want to know what in the world is going on!" With that he opens his door and Phil and McMurphy join him as they walk around the parked limo. Dozens of other drivers also climb out of their cars to survey the damage to their vehicles. As they stand there numb, disoriented, glancing into the sky, hundreds of sparrows begin to fall onto the street, the sidewalk and the boulevard.

Across the intersection, two hundred feet ahead of the cars, some of the men from the Feather River flood recognize the limousine stalled in the middle of the road.

"That's the governor!" one of them calls.

"Bring the bastard over here!" A dozen men jog toward the car, bearing the weight of their shovels and backpacks. But one by one they stumble to a halt as the birds crash down on them.

"Back in the car, sir!" McMurphy takes Governor White

by the arm and squeezes him into the rear of the limo and slams the door. "Back to the residence," he barks. "Full court press," he shouts at Phil, who immediately turns on the limo flashers and siren. "Go, go, go!"

As the car peels onto the sidewalk and around the chaos of parked cars, dead sparrows continue to slam onto the car and roll to the ground.

On the far side of the park, well out of sight of the escaping governor, Raymond is roused not by the falling sparrows, but by the screaming siren as the limousine speeds past the park and back up 16th Street toward the governor's mansion.

As soon as he's awake, Raymond rolls out from under his bench and is struck by a dead bird on his forearm. He looks at its lifeless form, at the bib of chocolate-brown feathers flushed under the bird's throat. When it doesn't twitch or flap either wing, he prods the beak with a fingernail. Nothing. He sees two more sparrows fall and quickly rolls back under the bench to protect himself from the torrent of death. He runs a hand over his eyes. Can you believe it? He tugs the blanket over his shoulders and pulls his knees up to his belly. He watches as hundreds of birds plunge onto the park lawn. He feels hungry, but he can't think of that now. All he can think about is the chaos around him. Where am I, he wonders. What has become of me? Then he realizes the rain of madness is the price he must pay for his sin against Teejay. He bunches his fingers into tight fists and begins to beat his chest and shoulders. Beg for forgiveness, he whispers to himself in rhythm with each blow. You must beg Fay and Teejay to release you.

A miracle. In the weeks after she realized that her daughter's period was late, Fay Flood prayed for a miracle of the flesh. She petitioned Saint Jacinta and her childhood companions to intervene on Teejay's behalf with Jesus and Mary. But she knew her prayers would go unanswered because the sin was too great. Teejay had her first two periods and then, nothing. She knew that sometimes irregularity was normal, especially for a girl just beginning her cycle. But a growing fear started to gnaw at Fay when Teejay missed a second month. It was then that she began to pray several times a day. She prayed that Raymond had done nothing to their child. The night when she'd found him in the apartment with the girl, Fay prayed that he'd been too drunk to violate her. For a short time she thought that was most probable. After all, Teejay said nothing about her father to raise any suspicions, nothing about touching her in that way. In fact, Teejay didn't even seem to remember her father wandering into her room that night, something that she surely would've mentioned since Raymond hadn't come near the apartment for at least two weeks before Fay caught him there red-handed. She threw him out and threatened to call 9-1-1 if he came around the apartment again. That seemed to give him a good scare. He'd been in and out of jail twice before and he knew that the three-strikes law meant he'd do hard time for a good long while if he went before a judge. Especially for harming his own daughter. And if word got out about that, someone in prison would cut him.

When Teejay started to show the tiniest swelling in her belly, Fay began to pray for a second miracle. She prayed that Teejay would never know what her father had done. That any memory Teejay had of the conception would dissolve and somehow she could escape what was coming.

For a while Fay prayed that the pregnancy might be transformed into another immaculate conception. Truly a miracle, with word sent from Gabriel that Teejay had been chosen for her purity and innocence to bear His own being into the world as a message of peace. Of joy. Of His renewed commitment to the salvation of the world and all the creatures in it.

She painted a hundred versions of this miracle, worked on them feverishly to get one right, thinking that if she could create the perfect painting of this vision, there was a chance that its reality might follow. Nonsense. She twisted her head in anger and silently screamed to herself: *Non-sense.*

After a few days she realized that only more craziness could follow this logic and it was then that she decided to see a psychiatrist for help. Within five minutes of her meeting with Dr. Benson at the walk-in clinic she was handed a sample pack of Clozaril and told to return in two weeks for a follow-up visit or sooner, if her symptoms failed to settle down. *Her* symptoms? It was her daughter who was pregnant, but she couldn't reveal this to anyone. If she told the truth to Benson or her social worker, Janice Slitz, she knew they would demand to know who the father was. And when they uncovered that mystery, Teejay would be taken from her the same day, and that — *that* — would be a death without end. Amen, she whispered to herself. That would be her final amen.

She determined that she had to be very careful, and her next step was to confine Teejay to the apartment. Twenty-four-seven, three-sixty-five, no exceptions. She had to keep Teejay out of sight until she solved this somehow. It was doubly important to keep her away from Raymond. If he discovered Teejay's pregnancy, what would he do? The volatile bastard was completely unpredictable.

Then Fay began to pray for a third intervention: that he would die. And for this blessing to be granted, she knew she would have to pray to the devil Himself. It was then that she began to paint "Trialogue," the picture she presented to Doctor Box and Mavis Helm. It was the vision that held the most power over her, the one most likely to bear its poisoned fruit.

As she lies in bed each night, Teejay sweeps her hands over her belly, pressing, testing her flesh to uncover the new mystery growing within her body. Once, well after Fay had drifted off to sleep, she could feel herself detach slightly, and except for her feet (which seemed to remain tethered to her actual, physical toes) she began to float about ten inches above her body. She immediately understood that this experience provided proof of the soul, and the body lying so heavily on the bed below her was merely a form that held her, for now anyhow, in place on Earth while her soul, the real Teejay, sorted out what she was supposed to be doing here.

She suspected that if she could figure out her purpose in life, she would have no need for her body anymore and wouldn't have to worry about what was happening to it. She could simply release it and the real Teejay would float away. Then she felt another cramp in her tummy and her soul immediately fused with her body and she felt stuck again. Stuck, stuck, *stuck*. It was the one word that applied to everything right now. Because she couldn't free herself, each night as she lay on her mattress she spent hours trying to perfect her levitation, to find the combination of words and prayers, of breathing and silence that would lift her into the air once again. And the instant she achieved this first moment of flight, she would cut the tether that joined her soul to her body and disappear forever.

Over the past week she's developed a fantasy of leaving a note for her mother telling her not to worry and asking her to say goodbye to Mavis, who'd been so kind to them. The worry of her disappearance would be less than the worry of her enlarging presence, and she thinks this idea could provide the opening sentences to her parting note: *Dear Mom: Never think that I have left you. I am a vapor hovering above you, an angel watching over your soul and preparing the way for you.*

Teejay never manages to think of a third or fourth sentence. At the beginning of her third month a pervasive nausea seizes her body. If she's not vomiting, she can only think about vomiting. Finally, when her body quakes and her stomach cramps as never before, she concedes that she has to talk to her mother.

"Something's wrong," she whispers as she studies Fay on the far side of the living room. Over the past few weeks she's never seen her mother in such a frenzy of painting. "I think I'm sick," she sighs. "In my stomach."

With her easel propped next to the window, Fay adjusts the sliding legs up, down, up again. Nothing ever seems to be just right. She looks at her daughter and shifts her jaw to one side. She turns the setscrew on the rear leg of the easel and dabs a brush in a pool of crimson paint and draws a broad stroke on the paper before her.

When Fay ignores her, Teejay continues in a more insistent voice. "Something's making me vomit."

Fay works quickly; two strokes multiplied into twenty. "What have I told you when I'm painting?" Miracles require this kind of industry; if you want a miracle you have to work with a divine frenzy. "What have I told you?" she bites into each word in rhythm to the mad dashing of her paintbrush. "What are the rules?"

Not to interrupt, Teejay murmurs to herself. But she knows this cannot wait another day. Not another moment. "*Mom.*" She lets this word stand. There's just the two of them, the small apartment, and this solitary word. When Fay stops her brushwork and turns her head to her daughter, Teejay continues. "Something's wrong with me. I feel like I'm going to vomit all the time. Yesterday I vomited twice. And the day before that and on Wednesday, too. I'm sick and I don't know what's wrong."

Fay lobs her brush into the paint pot. She looks at her daughter and at the moment when she can hear herself about to order another banishment to the bedroom, she observes something new standing before her: this child, her own innocence, is pleading for her help. She can now see what Mavis observed in an instant. How could she forget this? She draws a long breath and walks the three steps to where Teejay is standing, shoulders slumped, both hands embracing her stomach.

"Okay," she says and her head nods as if acknowledging the unspoken secret that apparently only she, Fay, has discovered. That would be the first step, to find out what Teejay actually knows. She takes her daughter's hand in her own, leads her to the sofa and sits beside her. "Tell me something, first. When was the last time you saw Raymond?"

"Raymond?" Teejay has to think. Neither Fay nor Teejay refer to him as *your father*, or Dad, or Padre. The both call him by his given name, usually with a dismissive tone, as though he were a dishonored uncle or older brother who drifted away and returned two or three times a year, repentant but more hopeless than ever before. "Not since your birthday. When he gave you the flowers. Don't you remember?"

"Yeah, yeah. I remember." Fay curls her lip. Even the memory of his gifts imparts a bitter taste. Then she smiles, thinking that Teejay is still unaware of his midnight sojourn three months ago. This is the second miracle she prayed for and, thank God, it has come to pass. Maybe all her worry is for nothing. Maybe, in fact, Teejay isn't pregnant at all. Last week, when she guessed that the truth (and that this conversation) couldn't be avoided much longer, she'd picked up an ELISA pregnancy test kit at the local clinic.

"I knew you were having trouble," she begins. She isn't used to this kind of talk, but she thinks of how Mavis would proceed: just go out to the edge and stand there without worrying about falling into the abyss below. She takes another deep breath and continues, "So I went to the clinic and the doctor gave me a little test that might tell us what's going on."

Teejay leans backward. It's unusual for her mother to prepare for something. To be looking ahead.

She finds her bag, sorts through it a moment and hands Teejay the small plastic cup from the ELISA kit. "So, I know it sounds funny, but I want you to pee in this a cup and then bring it back to me."

Teejay examines the cup. "That's *gross*." For a moment she hesitates and then realizes how important it is to follow orders. Her mother is trying to help her and gross or not, Teejay needs her more than ever. She forces back another gag of nausea and walks to the bathroom.

When she returns to the kitchen, Fay rereads the test instructions and dips one end of the test strip into her daughter's urine. Moments later the strip turns red. As expected, her prayers for the first miracle have been dismissed. "Well," she says flatly and looks into Teejay's eyes. "I'm not sure, like one-hundred percent sure, what this means. But I think we should talk to someone about it." She pauses to re-establish her balance and slowly backs away from the precipice. "Would you like to have another visit with Mavis?"

Teejay has seen it many times before, this distant look in her mother's eyes and she understands that for the moment her mother has lost her way. But that's okay; they'd always found another way to move forward in the past and a new direction had always appeared from somewhere, someone, somehow. She nods. "Okay." Her voice returns to a whisper. "I bet Mavis will know what to do."


That night Fay finds herself tangled in her bed sheets, in a mess so twisted and snarled that she has to turn on a light and sort the blankets and covers and pillows before she can get back to sleep. After she settles in a second time, she begins to weep. At first she's surprised, shocked that her face is flooding with tears. As a child, the neighbor kids in Oakland used to taunt her with her last name to see if they could get her to cry: "Fay Flood is a flood-face. Flood-face. Flood-face." Why she has to relive this childishness now is beyond her. She wipes her palms over her cheeks and props herself up in the bed. When the tearing stops she realizes that sleep has moved beyond her grasp and she reconciles herself to another night of waking dreams. Oh, what she would give just to sleep. *To sleep*.

She pulls herself from the bed again and begins to pace through the living room. She glances at her most recent attempts at painting, drops her chin into one hand and frowns. The work seems hopeless but she can't say this aloud, can't even murmur it to anyone other than the ghosts of lost sleep. They would gossip amongst themselves, of course, and everyone knows their rumors can never be trusted. No one should pay them any mind. Better just to continue with the work each day and take what pleasure it offers as each vision reveals itself before her eyes. That's what Monet did, he bore witness to the birth of the imagination. He found all the wisdom he needed in the paintings as they revealed their mysteries to him one at a time. Those were the true miracles, and he'd seen so many of them.

After another hour Fay feels her mind settling and she moves to the window to look onto the alley. Things are usually quiet at three in the morning and she doesn't expect to see much more than a veil of fog floating overhead as she pulls the curtain to one side. She leans her head against the glass and scans the row of buildings on the far side of the lane. At first she shakes her head in disbelief. Then she sets the curtain back in place, careful not to ruffle the edge and draw attention. After a moment she peels the curtain away from the window frame just enough to peer into the bleak air a second time. She gasps lightly. Below her, in the shadows cast by a garage lamp opposite the apartment, stands Raymond Guzman.

Now that he's settled into a routine, Doyle Mere is making steady progress on his memoir. He's about ten per cent into the project, he figures — not very far, but the words are coming easily to him and each morning after he scans the *Chronicle* and finishes his breakfast at the Caffe Mediterraneum, he returns to his apartment to write five or six hundred words a day on his Dell laptop. Once he's comfortable with this pace, he sets five hundred and fifty words as his minimum daily goal and uses the word-count tool in his word processor to calculate his output and then registers the tally in a spreadsheet that computes his total productivity. In the early afternoon he makes himself a sandwich and some tea and after his lunch he sets out to explore the city. In the evenings he reads or watches videos on his laptop, or talks to James and Mavis or some of the White Light acolytes who stream through their apartment every day.

At least once a week he Skypes one of his sons. They are the only link he maintains with his old life and he clings to them fiercely. Tonight he connects with Wyatt late in the evening, at a time when he assumes Wyatt has finished his shift at the marina. He's been lucky enough to keep his job as the maintenance manager after the last round of layoffs threatened to close the marina entirely. The economic slump had been especially dramatic in the pleasure-boat industry where yachts now sold for a fraction of their original price and the demand for high-end moorage facilities collapsed. At least Wyatt doesn't have a wife and child to support. Unlike Jesse, who, thank God, seems to be hanging onto his job as a physics and math teacher at Gulf Islands Secondary School.

"Yeah, it's pretty slow," Wyatt confesses when Doyle asks him about his workload. "But I just don't see how they can close this place. What would they do? Untie three hundred boats and let them drift into the strait?"

The image of his son flickers momentarily and Doyle presses the power cord securely into place at the back of the laptop. The computer battery failed long ago and he has to ensure the machine is plugged into a wall outlet whenever he wants to use it. When he's sure everything is properly connected he settles in his chair and gazes at the screen again. "So, they're still paying you?" He studies Wyatt through the liquid crystal display: examines his curly hair, the boyish smirk that undercuts every smile.

"Oh yeah. How about you? They depositing your pension check down there?" Wyatt can't imagine his father not having a bulletproof cash-flow system, but he needs to ask, just in case. Both boys worried about their father after his departure to the States following their mother's death. He'd waited nine months, decided to take early retirement and then rented the family house to a couple from Texas who claimed "they just wanted out of the USA" after they'd lost their jobs and home in the sub-prime financial debacle.

"You bet," Doyle says brightly. "I'm fine," he adds. He'd decided not to tell either of the boys that he'd been robbed twice in one day and that his wallet, passport, and credit cards were stolen. He realized that his failure to report the missing passport revealed his psychological inertia. As if reclaiming his passport meant he had to reclaim his previous identity. To go back in time, to the loss, the pain, the old life. He'd read the government web pages about how to report a stolen passport. He'd even strolled past the consulate office on California Street but promptly walked beyond it, happy to dismiss the bureaucratic tangle that would ensue if he reported the theft. He knew that technically, if he were challenged, he could be arrested as an illegal alien. But the odds of that are very long.

"And how are my Texan tenants treating the house?" he asks to divert further questions about his well-being.

"They seem happy enough." Wyatt doesn't like thinking about the Texans, Frank and Frances Bernard and their two kids, living in his old house. He and Jesse often discussed their common fear that Doyle might get used to living on the road and for some reason, or for no *apparent* reason, since almost everything their father had done in the past six months was unpredictable, he might choose to sell the house and then disappear. "They seem to think the air's fresher here," Wyatt says and then decides to shift the focus back to his father. "And how's the memoir going?"

Doyle nods. He can feel the narrative opening before him. It helps to control the chaos of his grief, put some order to it and assign the entire episode a beginning, a middle and an end. "You know, Wyatt, I think it's the best thing I've done. Since Mom passed away, I mean. I'm writing every day. I think it's helping me sort things out."

"Yeah?" Wyatt listens for any hint of false positives. He talked with Jesse about having to drive down to San Francisco to fetch their father if his situation became too strange. If he started drinking, or found a woman who might derail him. Neither possibility seemed likely, but with their father out of their orbit, they could only guess what might happen.

"And I'm seeing a new side to things," he adds, tuning his voice for positive effect. "I'm living in a house with some save-the-world, new-age mystics. Mom would've liked them. Sometimes that's why I think I'm drawn to them, too. Because of her. Seems like everyone's got religion down here. That, and hand-to-your-heart 'God Bless America.' They just don't see it for what it is."

"Which is what?"

Doyle flips a hand in the air searching for an answer. "That they've substituted belief for knowledge. That they prefer religious dogma and nationalist propaganda to hard facts. I worry about it."

Wyatt nods in agreement. More than anything else he's pleased to see his father worried about something else, someone other than Mom or him and Jesse. "Really? What's to worry about?"

"I don't know." Doyle considers this a moment. "It's as if they think there's a conspiracy underway to steal everything that's rightfully theirs. Their heritage, their constitution, their freedom, their money. *Their manifest destiny.*" Yes, that was the root of the problem. "Generous as they are individually — and I mean it, they will *give* — they refuse to trust one another. It's like there's no social contract. It's all so contradictory."

Wyatt shrugs. "I guess that's what happens when you live in a place with more guns than people and more ammo stores that gas stations."

"Really?" Doyle's surprised to hear this. "Who told you that?"

Another shrug. "I don't know. I just heard it."

"Well, there you are." He pauses, doesn't see the point of challenging these incredible factoids.

"So when do you think you'll be back?"

Doyle mulls this over. After his first week he was ready to pack up and go home. But now that he's settled in Berkeley, grown attached to the Bay Area's variety and funkiness, found something of a friendship with James and Mavis, and grown used to the homeless people on the streets, he isn't so sure. "Maybe a few more months."

"Really? Jesse and Bess and Gale all miss you, you know."

"Well, maybe sooner." Happy to hear the tender urgency in Wyatt's voice, he adds, "So how *are* your brother and his clan?"

"They're beautiful."

"You know, I love the three of them."

"Everyone loves them. You should read the tributes they get on Facebook."

Facebook. It was a party he refused to join. "Well, I

don't know about that," he says and then continues, "but I know I love you, Wyatt."

"Yeah. Me too, Dad."

" — "

Without warning the power cuts out and before he can add another word his connection with Wyatt drops out of the ether. He jiggles the cord on the back of his computer and then realizes another power failure has hit the entire building. He glances out the window and sees the street lights are out across the boulevard and in the buildings beyond the park. Doyle was going to ask if Wyatt needed any money, but later he realizes the conversation concluded on a high note. In fact, he couldn't have orchestrated it more perfectly. *I love you,* he whispers to himself and unplugs the laptop and slips it into the vinyl case and draws the zipper around the shell. *I love you so much.*

When the power is restored Doyle washes his dishes and listens to a feature broadcast on National Public Radio about new trouble in the Pacific Ocean. Biologists have detected mass extinctions of marine life in de-oxygenated sections of salt water. *De-oxygenated oceans* — could they ever be restored? When he can't bear to hear to any more, he clicks off the radio and eases into the living room chair to read the copy of Seneca's *Consolations* that James had pressed into his hands with the hope that Doyle would find some solace from the text. Indeed, Seneca offered a sort of "lived wisdom," the kind of prudence that comes from both joy and misery, the mortar that held the bricks of life in place.

After an hour he settles into his bed and sleeps until he hears an intermittent tap of pebbles striking his living room window. He rouses himself, walks to the half-pulled curtain and glances outside. Below him Fay Flood stands on the sidewalk holding her daughter's hand.

"Doyle," she calls in a hushed voice. "It's me. Fay and Teejay.'

Doyle checks the time: almost four-thirty. He pushes the window slide open and presses his head to the opening. "What's wrong?"

"Emergency," she calls back. "I need to find Mavis and James."

Minutes later Doyle leads Fay and Teejay to his living room and settles them on the sofa. Each of them carries a backpack and when Doyle raises his shoulders and waves a hand in a welcoming gesture, they slip their bags onto the floor. Fay is trembling through her arms and legs. Teejay, nuzzled against her mother's shoulder, dozes in a faraway fog. He can tell she needs to sleep.

"Why don't we put Teejay to bed?" he asks. "I've got fresh sheets on there and she can slide under the covers and forget about whatever it is that brought you here."

When Teejay rouses enough to murmur, "Uh-huh," Doyle guides them to his bedroom and lets Fay tuck her daughter into the bed. Within seconds she dissolves into unconsciousness. "God, I wish I could sleep like that," Doyle says as he watches the sleeping child. "I remember my kids going off like that. Snap of the fingers and they'd be gone. Used to give me a kind of faith to watch them slip off. Faith in what, I don't know. Maybe in the power of complete exhaustion." He laughs at this little joke but when Fay fails to respond he tiptoes out of the bedroom. A moment passes before she follows him back to the living room.

As she sits on the couch Fay feels a measure of reassurance that she's made the right decision to come here, even if Mavis is out of reach. "You've got kids?"

"Twins. Two boys." He holds two fingers aloft, V-shaped.

Fay glances around the room. "Do you mind if I turn off the lights?"

Doyle's eyebrows rise reflexively. His surprise is overcome by a feeling of resistance. "What for?"

Fay pulls her lips into a determined frown and walks to the wall switch and turns off the overhead light and then she clicks off the pole lamp next to the sofa. When she feels secure she props herself against the couch armrest once more and tries to focus on Doyle. "Look, I'm sorry to bother you, Doyle. Really. I was hoping to find Mavis. I knocked on her front and back doors. Do you know if she's in?"

In the gray light Doyle studies her a moment. Pushy. Needy. Insistent. He realizes he doesn't have to account to Fay for anything, but he knows Mavis reserves a special fondness for her and Teejay. So does James. "She drove down to LA with James for the weekend," he offers. "Some special meeting came up for James's foundation."

"Oh." Fay gazes into the middle space of the room. Her immediate plan has come to an end and she doesn't know where to go next. In the past there's always been some contingencies that simply appeared before her. Now there is none.

"Fay, what's going on?" Doyle leans forward a little. "Why do you need the lights turned off?"

Fay startles from her brief reverie. "I'll tell you later," she whispers. "I just have to listen for something."

They sit together in complete darkness. Doyle considers

their situation more carefully and decides to wait before he asks any more questions. Whatever drove Fay and Teejay to his apartment is certainly an emergency in Fay's eyes. Would it push her into reliving some nightmare if he starts to interrogate her now? Certainly he'd feel uncomfortable if anyone began to prod into his recent past. *Why did you move to San Francisco? What did you leave behind? And what, really, are you running from?*

They absorb the silence for another minute or two, listen to the hush of the world outside, the footsteps of strangers on the sidewalk, the stillness of the air adrift in the curtains of fog. Finally Doyle accepts the undisturbed presence of his guests. He doesn't require any answers. After a long while he whispers, "Fay, you can stay over if you want. It's no trouble for me at all."

In response all he can hear is Fay's light sawing, the sighing of the night air traveling in and out of her lungs. Doyle pulls himself from the chair, wraps a blanket over her shoulders and gradually tilts her torso to one side until she's horizontal on the couch and he can lift her legs onto the seat cushion and slip a pillow under her head. Like her daughter, the next instant she falls into a dead sleep.

Late the next morning, Doyle notices a man propped against a bus-stop pole on Dwight Way. A stranger, clearly dispossessed, living rough and penniless and now gazing in an unbroken trance at his apartment building. A bus chugs to a stop, discharges a few passengers and moves on. A second bus repeats the process, then another. Through each interval the drifter barely moves, rarely takes his eyes from the window where Doyle stands, invisible, he assures himself, behind the curtain.

"Fay," he says, his tone purposely low, "do you know this guy?"

A pallor crosses Fay's face as she peers through the drawn curtain. "It's Raymond," she whispers. "We have to go."

Within twenty minutes Doyle, Fay and Teejay slip out of the building through the rear door on the main floor, make their way down the alley and onto a bus connecting to the BART trains. As they settle themselves in a subway car and travel under the bay to San Francisco Doyle tries to patch together the snippets of Fay's broken narrative. But it's impossible to make complete sense of all of it, he realizes. Her panic, the unfocused loathing and revulsion. However, it's clear that the need to protect Teejay from Raymond is her single, guiding imperative.

When he was back in his apartment, the only solution that came to his mind was to call Louis Laporte, the manager of his old room in Haight-Ashbury. He might know of a vacancy, someplace available for immediate occupancy on short notice. When he called him, Louis informed Doyle that a two-room unit had just come available on the third floor directly above his old bachelor suite.

"Doyhul, it's good to see you again," Louis shakes his hand with surprising vigor, greeting him with the robust welcome of an old friend. "And these must be the two *demoiselles* in distress, am I right?"

Doyle introduces Fay and Teejay and watches Louis embrace them with his broad smile. If anything, Louis has added five pounds since Doyle last saw him, but he seems more content. Perhaps he's making money again.

"I do have a furnished apartment with two rooms upstairs at the center of the building," he explains and begins to walk them down the hallway toward the flight of stairs. "Here, I'll give you the key, Doyhul, and you can show them. It's not the Hotel De Bourgtheroulde in Rouen, but I can rent it to you by the week. And four days are already *prepaid*," he adds with a wink. "The other tenant just disappeared. Left me the key and then, poof!" The fingers of his left hand explode outwards in a display of prestidigitation, as if a gold coin clutched in his fist has vanished.

Fay brightens when she hears this. "Do you know Rouen?"

*Roo-awn*. Louis smiles at Fay's passable pronunciation. "C'est ma ville natale. Parlez-vous Français?"

Fay shakes her head. "No, no. It's just I know that Monet painted there."

A hopeful note fills her voice and for the first time since she arrived at his apartment in the middle of the night, Doyle feels some warmth for her. "And Flaubert's hometown, too," Doyle adds and smiles at Louis knowing this will induce a flash of sentiment from him.

"I'm going back," Louis confesses. "Next week. That's why I'm so happy, now that I've decided."

"Really?" Doyle can see now that the expectation of a homecoming, not money, has inspired his friend's good mood.

"I can't stay any longer. You can't make a good life here," he sneers and shakes his head to confirm that it isn't his own failure that caused his change of heart. "It's the collapse; it's going to take everyone down from the governor to the millions of people already on food stamps. Forty-nine million across America. Did you know that?" He sweeps his hand toward the door as if to indicate an impending disaster is at the gate. Then he shrugs, and a hint of embarrassment crosses his face when he realizes that the situation obviously includes Fay and her daughter, the two demoiselles in distress who stand at his side.

"Anyway, you look at the rooms with Doyhul," he concludes, "and if you want them they are yours." He turns and walks toward his room and then circles back to Fay. "And later, if you wish to talk about Monet and Flaubert, I am at your *ser-veese*!"

The rooms are a larger version of the bare-bones flat that Doyle remembers from the two days he spent in the neighborhood. Twin beds are positioned on opposite sides of the bedroom, and in the main room are a few chairs, a sofa, lamps, a TV, a stove and sink, some cutlery and cooking essentials. He checks the windows and is pleased to see that no fire-escape ladders are attached to the outside cladding, which means no one, including Raymond Guzman, can scale the three stories and break into the apartment.

His only remaining concern is for Teejay. Through the entire twelve hours he spent with them, from the moment Fay had pleaded for his help, up to now as he settles them into Louis's building and closes the door, Teejay has barely spoken. The bright girl he remembers from the afternoon he'd spent with James seems to have vanished and been replaced by this sullen child who clings to her own belly. No matter, he's done what he can for them and when they seem content he bids them farewell, climbs down the open staircase to the main floor and makes his way to Louis's apartment to say good-bye.

"Ah, good. You've got them settled in. You are very nurturing, Doyhul *Mére*." Louis looks up from the sofa where he sits watching clips of the riots in Greece on an old Sony TV. He holds a bag of Cheetos in his lap and chews on one of the cheese curls as he speaks. "Do you know what your last name means in French?"

"Mother."

"Oui."

"But in Irish it means meagre."

"Really?" Louis seems genuinely surprised. "Well, perhaps they are the same thing!"

It's a distasteful joke, one that makes him think badly of Iris, but Doyle forces a laugh to give Louis a sense of camaraderie. After they shake hands, Doyle leaves the building and walks to the bus stop and begins the journey back to the east side of the bay. When he arrives in Berkeley he takes ten minutes to circle the block around Peoples Park to see if he can find any traces of Raymond Guzman.

Satisfied that Guzman has moved on, Doyle climbs the stairs to his loft, re-heats some beef stew and eats it with a sense of contentment as he sits next to the living room window and watches the world passing on the street below. At least you helped someone today, he tells himself. Fay and Teejay needed someone, anyone, to guide them to a safe haven. Iris would approve.

Louis cannot tell which came first: the panic fluttering in his heart or the sound of the fire alarm wailing in the hallway next to his apartment. Both arrive with an explosion in his sleep and before he can think he pulls on his pants and shoes and swings open the door and stands in the front foyer of the building. He clicks on the hall lights and sniffs the air. A whiff of smoke enters his lungs and the racing in his heart revs up a notch. *Fire!* This is no false alarm.

"Fire," he calls into the empty hallway when he realizes none of the tenants is taking the alarm seriously. "Fire!" he screams and walks down the hallway and bangs the palm of his hand on the apartment doors lining the main floor.

Then in a moment of clarity, he returns to his apartment and dials 9-1-1. As he waits for the call responder to answer he keeps his eyes on the open door, scanning for tenants as they exit the building.

The punk boy, an aspiring poet from Doyle's old apartment two doors down, is the first to poke his shaved head through the doorway. "Fire?" he asks and brushes a few fingers over his sullen face.

"Yes, yes. What do you think?" Louis asks and waves his free hand as though he's whisking the kid out the front door. He makes a mental note when the boy darts toward the exit. It will be his job to report to the fire chief precisely who has vacated the building and who might be left behind.

Finally the responder comes online and talks him through the details: his name, address, number of occupants, scale of the fire. During the conversation, three more tenants slip down the hallway past his front door. It's probable that some of them would exit through the rear entrance. How could he know who they were?

After he hangs up the phone, Louis pulls on a shirt, grabs a jacket and considers the essentials he might need: his glasses, his wallet, his passport ... Mon dieu, *his ticket to France*. He bundles all of these together and pats his pockets, fleeces himself to ensure he has the bare necessities in hand and returns to the hallway. "Fire! Fire!" he calls again and again, each time feeling his heart flutter, bulging against his ribs. The widow, Mrs. Arjoon, stumbles down from the top floor and as she passes him he asks, "Did everyone on the third floor make it out?"

"I don't know," she mutters and coughs through her fist. "The smoke up there is building up."

Louis accepts this as a satisfactory reply and follows Mrs. Arjoon onto the street. A small crowd is gathering, their eyes cast up to the third floor where a cloud of smoke escapes from an open window.

"That must be where it started," she says and Louis tries to calculate which tenant occupies the room at the center of the fire. He counts over from the edge of the building and works backwards: 309, 307, 305.

"Did you see if a woman with her daughter got out?" Someone nudges Louis's arm as he's in mid-calculation. "She has big, curly hair," he adds and sweeps both hands around his head to illustrate a storm of hair.

"I don't know," Louis has to start counting again: 309, 307.

"A woman and her daughter."

Louis blinks. Yes, of course. He terminates his calculations. The fire must have started in the next room; he watches the smoke pour from the window beside Fay and Teejay's apartment. "No. I didn't see them," Louis stammers and in an instant his panic reignites and he strides back into the building.

As he enters, Jurgen and Jenny Weiss pass him and stumble onto the street. He looks up the staircase leading to the third floor. A haze, a sort of black smudge, hangs suspended from the ceiling above the top of the stairwell. He tries to assess its dimensions. It doesn't look too bad. Certainly not as serious as the view from the street would suggest. In the distance he hears the SFFD approaching, two trucks, maybe three, their sirens breaking through the clamor of the night. Richard Hoogendorn appears at the top of the stairs holding a white handkerchief over his mouth. He seems to be in no panic. When he descends to the second landing, Louis calls up to him, "Did you see if the new tenants made it out? Fay and the girl, Teejay," he adds when Hoogendorn shrugs.

Whatever inspires Louis's confidence now — the apparently benign haze of the smoke, the absence of flames, the calm descent of Hoogendorn, his brief friendship with Doyle — it's enough to spur him up the first few steps on a mission to retrieve the girl and her mother, or at least to ensure they've safely vacated the building.

How strange, he tells himself, here you are going up three flights in a fire, when normally you don't trudge up here more than once a month, and then only to determine the cause for someone's unpaid rent. *Tu es fou.* When he reaches the second floor his heart pounds wildly. The pounding reminds him of the river bass he and his brother, Paul, had yanked from the Seine onto the pier, how it flopped about with a desperate, convulsive need to escape, yet they did nothing to ease its misery. All they could do was watch as it expired at their feet. They were mere boys and Louis had the feeling that a mystery of the universe was being revealed expressly for his edification. A lesson absorbed into his body as the fishtail began to flutter in rhythm with his own heartbeat.

When he reaches the third floor he has to cover his mouth with an open hand. He can hear the SFFD trucks on the street below. He approaches Fay's door and pounds against the wood veneer with the back of his fist. The smoke bites at his eyes and he shuts them tightly and bends his knees and places his ear to the door panel. To his amazement, he can hear voices inside.

"It's Louis!" he coughs. "There's a fire!" Hadn't they heard the commotion outside?

"Louis?"

How can they still be in the apartment? "Yes! Open the door!"

Their door cracks open slightly. At the same moment a broad tongue of orange flame blasts through the doorway of the adjoining apartment into the hall and a loud bang echoes along the corridor as a wave of water flushes under the flames.

Louis is pleased to see the water gush along the floor. Perhaps the SFFD are going to contain this. Still, he can feel the fish pounding in his chest now, desperate to survive.

"Come on!" Louis grabs Teejay by one hand and Fay follows them into the corridor. Their initial hesitancy evaporates and they begin to run behind him, bent over and coughing hoarsely, and then they sprint alongside him and when they reach the staircase they overtake him and tumble down the stairwell ahead of him. He watches them hit the second floor landing in full stride, hand-in-hand. Then he feels the fish make a final frantic leap into the air and in one last, startling moment there — *there* — beside his brother, it crashes through the wall of his chest and expires, dead and gone forever.


Following James's self-realization, or satori, as he called it, Zachery Philbin, a renowned Hollywood talent manager who practiced yoga with James, said that he wanted to learn more about the new experience that James called White Light Meditation. James was happy to teach him the simple technique and after he practiced the method for three or four months, Zach started to proselytize the musicians, actors and artists in his management stable. Within a few weeks some of them found their way to James's yoga studio. As each discovered his or her own white light, one-by-one they began to abandon their pretense and bravado. Meditation helped them in ways they hadn't imagined and soon many of them wanted daily sessions with James to perfect their technique. Some gave up drugs and alcohol. Others approached their parents and children with more honesty and genuine feeling. They opened themselves to their friends and lovers. They embraced personal vulnerability.

"We're living without a safety net," Zach said, and within six months he and his circle of the LA glitterati decided to finance James's new charitable foundation, The White Light Community Foundation.

But now, eight months later, Zach feels as if he's inhabiting a different planet. His face is drawn, his hair pulled in four or five different directions, a snarl of chaos that could pass for a new style if it wasn't matted and sticky with dried booze.

"I'm sorry, James, but it's over." Zach plunks himself in the overstuffed sofa opposite James and Mavis and wipes both hands over his face. "I'm just glad I can explain this to you in person rather than in some fucking email."

As his hands drop into his lap, his face falls into a weary frown. Over the next ten minutes Zach reveals why he called James to LA for an emergency meeting. Barry Maddleman, the financial mastermind whom Zach entrusted to manage all of his clients' money after the tech crash in 2000, had engineered a Ponzi scheme that ensnared many of Hollywood's most famous names. Over the past two years he'd used Zach's celebrity network to funnel hundreds of millions of dollars into the top of the money pyramid to finance new dividends to the early investors. Once the scam was exhausted, it all collapsed within a week, taking the assets of the White Light Community Foundation with it, including every cent promised to James.

"It's a complete disaster," Zach concludes with a sigh that rises from the bottom of his lungs.

"My god, you must be completely drained." James leans forward to comfort him but as he does, Zach averts his eyes and turns his head away. His face is riven with deep, vertical lines running from his eyes down his cheeks to his jaw line.

"You have no idea. Hundreds of people have been wiped out. My friends ... my *family*...." His voice trails into a bleak silence and he lifts his hands briefly and then they collapse on his thighs.

"Zach, listen to me. It's all right, man." James's voice softens to a lower tone with each word. "We'll be fine. We've got everything we need to carry on."

"What about you? Were you personally involved in this thing?" Mavis studies the gray pall in Zach's face, the cords of tension lining his neck.

"Yeah," he murmurs and gazes into the glass coffee table separating them. "Oh yeah. I'm fucking ruined. All of us are." He waves a hand at his cherished wall of fame, a series of thirty-odd celebrity photographs that line the south wall of his office. His clients at the peak of their individual careers.

"Take a breath," James offers after a brief silence. "You're being blinded by anger. And fear. Step back a minute and you'll see that you still have *everything* that's important."

At one time he'd been James's most ardent acolyte but now Zach raises his head and gazes at him with a look of disbelief bordering on contempt. "James ... they're going to *jail* me." Again his arm sweeps toward the pictures of his friends. "Everything. Is. *Ruined!*" His teeth cut into each word separately. "Barry Maddleman committed suicide last night. He shot himself."

"What?!" Mavis slumps against the back of the chair and covers her open mouth.

Zach turns his gaze to her briefly, nods once and then with a shrug of distraction he shifts his eyes to the Persian carpet at his feet and studies the tangle of knotted fringe at the end of the mat. Someone should sort that out, he thinks. *Merna.* That's her job, where the fuck *is she?*

"You're not going to do that," James says evenly. "I want you to promise that you won't do that."

"You don't understand," he confesses. "I've been there before."

James licks his lips as he considers this. "Where?" There's a missing piece that he doesn't understand. "*Where* have you been before?"

Zach lifts his head and whispers: "In prison."

James glances at Mavis. Her face is pale, her eyes unfocussed. He turns back to Zach. "Look, that doesn't matter. *The past is gone forever.* It doesn't have to determine what happens next."

" — " A pant of exasperation wheezes through Zach's mouth and he rolls his shoulders in a gesture of submission.

James presses on. "Look. I want you to promise that you won't do anything *extreme.*"

Zach lifts his head and sets his eyes on James as if he's witnessing the arrival of a phantom.

"Promise me." James realizes that he needs to be very specific. "Promise me that you won't harm yourself."

Zach appears to complete an inner calculation, the reconciliation of the past to future considerations, and then he relaxes his mouth and draws another deep breath. "Of course," he says flatly. "You got it." He presses the palms of his hands together, lifts them to his face and covers his eyes.

Six hours later Mavis and James pull into Berkeley exhausted and still fretting about Zach. When they open the front door to their building, Doyle stands before them, his hands burrowed into his pants pockets, his French beret pushed to one side, barely covering the bald spot on his head. "Thank god you're here," he says. His voice is flat. He's been rehearsing how to break the news for hours but now that his friends are here he can utter only two words: "Something's happened."

He draws a long breath and continues, "It started last night. Fay's been calling me every three or four hours. It's crazy. She can barely breathe, let alone speak coherently."

Doyle follows Mavis and James into their apartment and blurts out the essential details about moving Teejay and Fay to his old building in Haight-Ashbury, and then what he'd heard from Fay over the phone about the fire and their narrow escape from the apartment. As he watches Mavis and James slump into the opposite ends of their living room sofa he realizes how exhausted they are, that maybe he should let all this wait until the morning.

"Tell me that again?" Mavis pauses to piece the fragments of Doyle's report into a coherent story. "Fay and Teejay were chased out of their apartment in the middle of the night? And came here?"

"And *who* chased them?" James rubs his thumb and index over his closed eyelids as though he's trying to break himself from falling into a deep sleep.

"Her ex," Doyle says. He doesn't know if he should add more, then decides to let it all out: "They're in San Francisco General Hospital right now. Recovering from smoke inhalation. I called the duty nurse to try to sort it out. Then I called the fire department. The building they were in, where I used to live, the top floor was badly scorched. The dispatcher said it looks like arson. Except when you think about it, the fire started on the third floor and most arsonists know enough to set a fire in the basement or at least on the ground floor. And ... *god, I still can't believe it* ... Louis collapsed and died from what looks like a heart attack. He's the one who got Fay and Teejay out of the building. I saw him just yesterday." Doyle's voice drops to a whisper. "It was the last thing he did."

Mavis shakes her head. "Who's Louis?" she asks after a moment.

"Louis Laporte, the property manager," James answers, his voice distended, almost strained. "He handles the rentals for all the residential buildings owned by the Capelli family. Including this one." He drops his head into both hands and rubs his face three, four times.

Doyle continues to stand next to the apartment door. No one's invited him to sit down. He can see the inertia dragging through James and Mavis, see it sinking into their flesh and bones. He tries to assess the situation and determine if it would make any difference if they drove to the hospital right now. With Teejay and Fay in a hospital, surely they must be in competent hands.

When the silence extends too long and becomes yet another barrier to surmount, James lifts his head and tries to organize a plan. "Look, we can't do anything tonight. We're too tired to be helpful. In fact, we'd probably make a worse mess given the kind of day we've already had. Mavis, maybe you should call the hospital and tell someone to assure Fay that we'll all be there in the morning. Eight

A.M." He pauses and shakes his head doubtfully. "Make that *ten* AM. What do you think?"

Mavis nods, yes. Ten at the earliest, she tells herself. She can't say anything more and she's thankful to have a suggestion about how to proceed. She digs through her purse for her cellphone, determined not to say another word until she can speak to a nurse on the ward.

"See you in the morning," James says to Doyle and waves a hand goodbye. "Give us the details then."


A little after midnight Fay realizes that she can draw a deep breath of air into her body. Finally. She has to be cautious, to sip the vapors through her pursed lips and then carefully pull the thinnest part of it into the base of her lungs. Thank-you, dear God, she says to herself. She'd never come close to suffocation before and until now she didn't understand that it could happen gradually, over a day or two by incremental closure of the lungs as the tissues fail to absorb the oxygen wheezing down her throat. She'd always imagined suffocation would be like drowning: terminated within minutes, physically painless, with a brief flash of overwhelming panic flooding every cell in the body. But the experience of smoke inhalation is the exact opposite: it's a python coiled around her chest in which every exhalation becomes an opportunity to cinch the knot tighter. Then tighter. And tighter again.

Until she and Teejay broke through the line of firemen chasing up the staircase towards Louis, she didn't realize the danger they were in. But in the race down the stairs she and her daughter had inhaled so much toxic smoke that within minutes of their escape, Teejay fell to the sidewalk and Fay collapsed beside her. The medical team pressed air masks to their faces and loaded them both onto stretchers, and then the ambulance drove them to the hospital.

She couldn't believe what happened next, it was such a rarity, a blessing so pure and unexpected that it exceeded the miracle of their escape from the fire. As they raced through the midnight traffic, Teejay reached across the gurney and took Fay's hand in her own. Fay turned her head to gaze into her daughter's eyes and suspended herself in the warm glow of the child's face. Because of the masks they couldn't talk but that was better, she realized, since every thought and feeling had to be expressed through the touch of Teejay's fingers and the wonderful, wonderful glow in her eyes. As they drove on Fay began to pray that the ambulance would become lost, would take a wrong turn, run out of gas, anything to prolong this gift of love that her child had offered so spontaneously.

Now that she can breathe freely, once again she turns her head to Teejay, lying in the bed across the room, and she whispers, "Are you okay?"

Teejay stares at the ceiling. She knows that her mother is referring to her breathing. That's all the doctors focus on. "Yeah," she sighs, "I've been okay for most of the night." She doesn't say anything about the knot unraveling in her stomach. Not yet. She's used all of her powers of concentration for the past few hours to make it disappear. To cut the knot or unstitch it, it doesn't matter which, but soon she will have it out. This is the place, here in the hospital, where she can excise this terrible pain gnawing inside her.

Fay studies her daughter's face, worries about her distraction, the way the child has become so disaffected in the past month. "I love you," she whispers again and then as if it's an almost-forgotten question she calls her name aloud when the girl fails to respond. "Teejay?"

"I love you, too." Teejay's voice is a shallow echo, bounced from the ceiling where she concentrates her attention on a small crack of imperfection in the plaster a few feet from the window frame. This is where you can flush out the pain, she thinks. Into that little hole that nobody in the whole world knows about but you. There, there, *there*.

When Mavis enters the ward a doctor is holding a stethoscope to Fay's chest. Opposite them, a woman holding a clipboard and pen in one hand appears to be observing Teejay, who lays propped on two pillows with her head turned to the ceiling.

"I know it feels a little scary," the physician says, "but I want you to cough."

Fay coughs lightly and the doctor presses her. "Harder. Cough just a little harder." Fay does her best to comply but the feeling of suffocation deepens and she waves a hand in defeat. "Can't," she wheezes and, like her daughter, turns her face toward the ceiling.

But her mood changes the instant that she sees Mavis, James, and Doyle standing at the entrance. She waves her hand again, this time begging them to come in, to join the celebration.

"This a bad time?" Mavis offers, looking at the doctor to suggest they could return if necessary.

"Not at all. You must be Mavis." He smiles broadly. "I'm Doctor Kumaritashvili and this is Janice Slitz from family services." He shakes Mavis's hand and then moves on to James and Doyle.

"You're family members?" Janice Slitz directs this to Mavis with a stern look.

Mavis shrugs, unsure how to reply. She'd met Janice

briefly, at the door to Fay's apartment on the Saturday they'd taken their girls' day out. With luck, Janice has forgotten their encounter.

Before Mavis can respond Doyle presses forward and braces Fay's shoulder with one hand and says to Slitz, "Yes, absolutely. You can't believe how glad we are to see everyone's all right!" He turns to address the doctor. "Thank you so much. How are they?"

Kumaritashvili lowers his voice to address Doyle and Mavis as if Fay and Teejay were in another room. "Their pace of recovery from smoke inhalation is typical. I expect we'll probably release them tomorrow. The girl seems to have a situational depression. Maybe from the trauma of seeing the janitor die, especially just after he saved them both. If necessary we can treat her with some Elavil for a few weeks. But she should be fine," he adds with a slight twist of his head.

"Can we talk to you later?" Doyle leans forward, as though there are personal issues that require consideration.

"Of course. I think ten minutes with the family would give everyone a boost. Janice, let's give them a few minutes, then you can finish up." Kumaritashvili waves his partner through the door ahead of him.

James presses his head to Doyle's ear. "We're family?" His voice is amused, surprised by Doyle's quick thinking.

Doyle smiles. "We all share a few common strands of DNA, don't we?"

Fay grasps Mavis's hand and pulls her close. Her face flushes and for a moment she's overwhelmed and tears slip from the corners of each eye. There's so much to say, but she can do little more than gasp. When she gasps, she coughs and then she has to settle herself and once again come to grips with the overwhelming, but inexpressible, emotions churning through her.

"It's all right," Mavis says, her voice a soothing balm to ease Fay back onto the bed. "Doyle told us everything."

When she says this Fay pulls herself up on the mattress and motions Doyle toward her. "Thank you," she whispers. He nods, his eyes narrowing to acknowledge her tribute. Then she turns to Mavis and adds, "He got us away from Raymond." She squeezes Mavis's hand to convey the importance of their escape. "He was going to take her — " she begins, but cuts herself off and tips her head toward Teejay who maintains her unbroken vigil, her eyes locked on the tiny flaw in the ceiling plaster.

When he sees her pronounced distraction, James steps over to Teejay's bed and tries to draw her attention. "I hear you're going to be okay," he begins.

The girl says nothing as she continues to breathe deeply into the crack above her and compresses the enlarging pain in her belly into a tight wedge that she is certain will soon explode through her.

"I guess it helps to be younger than your mom," he continues. "All the pink tissues in your lungs will get you through this way sooner than I could." He lifts his eyes, tries to locate the center of her unbroken concentration.

She clenches her jaw. To speak now, to break the iron rivets on the hinge of her attention, will destroy everything she's been so carefully containing within the chaos of pain. Soon, soon, *soon*.

How it happens, he cannot tell, but gradually James enters the stream of her concentration. He follows the path that her eyes have settled on and finally sees the broken plaster above them, a tiny speck of imperfection, and he realizes that she's constructed a tether between it and some inner part of her body and that the power of this invisible line is a conduit of some kind. She's traveling, or trying to travel, not to any particular place, but anywhere outside her own being.

Doyle steps beside him. "Everything okay?"

James lifts a hand, a cautionary signal: do not enter.

Doyle takes a step beside Teejay's pillow, just out of her line of sight. He looks toward Mavis and then to James and Teejay.

"Let it go," James whispers, his words barely audible, then he repeats this again and again, each time his voice rising slightly but with calm certainty. "Let it go, Teejay. That's all you have to do. Just let it go."

Teejay inhales deeply. Her chest burbles as she releases the air, then she draws another breath and pumps it from her lungs. She begins a cycle of compressed, tight breathing that builds as she clenches her jaw. Her hands grip the bed sheets and her chest arches. The sound of her chugging fills the room and Fay climbs out of her bed and stumbles forward. Then in one primal outburst Teejay screams an inhuman sound that is torn from the lowest part of her belly up through her stomach and lungs through her throat and out the wide jar of her lips into the sanitized air of the room, down the corridor past the nursing station, through the locked windows into the pointillist San Franciscan fog where it is finally absorbed and discarded into the bleak nothingness. Exhausted, Teejay flops back onto the pillows, her body soaked with perspiration. A moment later a dot of blood appears on the sheets below her pelvis, and soon the dot becomes a brilliant crimson puddle — and then a pool of rank disaster.

"Doyle, get the doctor," James says as he swabs Teejay's face with the edge of the bed sheet.

Doyle takes a step to the doorway where he sees Dr. Kumaritashvili, Janice Slitz and a nurse running along the corridor toward him.

"What's going on?" Slitz demands when she enters the room.

James ignores their panic as he mops Teejay's forehead. "I think she's had a miscarriage," he says.

"What?" Kumaritashvili lifts the sheet, blinks once and drops the cover over Teejay's belly. The moment of disbelief is broken when Kumaritashvili kicks the brakes on the bed wheels and begins to roll Teejay toward the door. "Help me get her down to 4-C," he barks to the nurse. "And call Dr. Wagner in obstetrics. Tell him we've got a spontaneous abortion coming down."


"Frankly, I'm not sure where to begin with this." Dr. Kumaritashvili tips his tented fingers away from his lips and looks at James. Mavis and Doyle are seated on either side of him in the windowless office off the 6-D corridor that serves as a consulting room. Beside Kumaritashvili, Janice Slitz sits mutely, inscribing some notes on her clipboard pad. "It's a good thing Teejay was here when she miscarried. She says she didn't know she was pregnant." He pauses to see how this registers with the others. When no one responds he continues. "I hate to think what might have happened if she let the bleeding go without seeing a physician. Apparently she just started her period a few months ago."

"We just realized that she was pregnant, too," James begins.

"Yes," Mavis affirms. "And I'm pretty sure that she didn't know it, either."

"Do you know who the father is?" Slitz looks up from her notes to look at Mavis.

Mavis shrugs, no.

"Well, obviously, we'd like to find out. The girl could have died." Slitz narrows her eyes and holds Mavis in her gaze.

"You'll have to ask Fay," Mavis responds flatly, certain that Fay will reveal nothing.

Kumaritashvili senses the tension between the two women and decides to redirect the conversation. "So tell me how you're related to Fay and Teejay." This question is pitched, underhand, to Doyle who sits up a notch, rolls the pads of his fingers over the bald patch on his head and smiles at James and Mavis before he speaks.

"I'm not," he confesses, his smile brightening now that the truth is out.

"You're not.... Earlier this morning didn't you say you were a family member?"

"Yes ... and honestly, I was wrong to mislead you. I just knew how important it was to Fay and Teejay to have someone who cares for them to be on hand. Fay was calling me every three hours yesterday. I didn't want the typical bureaucratic rules to get in the way. And to be honest, since I've known her, that girl has become like a niece to me." He smiles at James and Mavis once again.

"And where are you living, Mr. Mere?" Slitz's eyebrows arch into her forehead.

"In Berkeley. In the apartment above James and Mavis."

"And Ms. Helm, aren't you in some kind of therapeutic relationship with Fay?" Slitz's formality is honing in on a point. Obviously she's recovered her memory of their first meeting and the previous lapse has heightened her wariness.

"Not exactly. I'm an intern with Dr. Philip Box. I first

met Fay through a routine screening session." Mavis frowns slightly as she conveys this correction.

"But you saw her independently as a therapist, did you not?"

Mavis senses a trap about to snap shut. "Once. At our house, but socially. As a friend."

"You should know that I've been in touch with Dr. Box. He's quite surprised to hear that you've seen Fay Flood in any capacity."

Mavis decides not to respond to this. She takes a deep breath and settles into the chair. What would Box say and do? Perhaps he'd been in touch with her graduate advisor, Dansky.

"Well," Kumaritashvili says and settles his hands on the desk. "I don't mean to be dismissive, but while your friendship will be very important to both Fay and Teejay in the coming months, you have no legal standing as far as their case is concerned." He's much less formal than Slitz, but suddenly every bit as bureaucratic.

"Their *case*?" James leans forward, a puzzled look on his face.

"Yes." Kumaritashvili shrugs as though the situation is self-evident. "A statutory rape has been committed."

"And there's another case to be made," Slitz adds. "Of gross child neglect."

It takes a moment for Doyle, Mavis and James to digest this last point. The charge of neglect can only be leveled at Fay.

"That could be very damaging," Mavis replies with a firm tone.

"It already is, Ms. Helm." Slitz cocks her head at Mavis and taps the butt-end of her pen against the clipboard. "Wouldn't you agree?"

He'd never appreciated the full dimensions of the condition, in fact he used to consider it a ruse, an artistic phantom, but once he analyzes his situation, Doyle realizes that he is in the grip of a classic case of writers block. It takes several days of idleness before he understands that his inability to continue with his memoir has nothing to do with laziness or loss of motivation, nothing to do with the drama that played out in the hospital. Actually the confrontation with Janice Slitz and Dr. K. (as everyone now calls him) became a new source of motivation to complete the story of his life as soon as possible.

He knew that a brush with death, like Teejay's miscarriage, could inspire him. That's exactly what had happened when Iris died; he moved to San Francisco to begin something new in his life. But now when he sits in his apartment at the window overlooking at the passing cars and busses, after reading the morning *Chronicle* and eating his blueberry bran muffin and sipping his coffee and talking absently with the baristas and a few regular customers that he's met over the past month, Doyle is unable to write a single sentence on his laptop. Instead, he gazes through the window onto the street and drifts aimlessly in time, tries to weave the episodes of his life into a meaningful yarn, if not in words, then in some visual narrative that remains honest to his memory of events.

Each afternoon following his lunch, after toying with the impossibility of continuing his work, he leaves the apartment and begins his daily walk. After several days wandering through Berkeley, in a flash of revelation, Doyle discovers the reason that he cannot continue his memoir: Louis's death and the role that Doyle played in delivering his dispatch.

He knows it's bizarre nonsense, this idea of positional

redeployment. Even less sensible is his crazy metaphor of human transit illustrated by satellites redeploying from one orbit to another to escape the escalating frequency of crack-ups predicted by Kessler's Syndrome. But when he thinks deeply about it he has to admit that Louis would almost certainly be alive today if Doyle had not *redeployed* Teejay and Fay into Louis's sphere. Not only would he still be alive, but as of today Louis would be home in Rouen, reunited with his brother and who-knows-how-many relatives waiting to greet the man who left France as a young artist to pursue his dream of illustrating rock 'n' roll album covers.

Admit it, Doyle shakes his head confirming the weight of this judgment, it was *you* who witnessed the collision of Raymond Guzman into Fay and Teejay, you who then suggested they escape across the Bay to that decrepit apartment in Haight-Ashbury. And there you left them, unattended except for the hapless Louis Laporte, who had no inkling of the impending crash headed his way. You could at least have given Louis a warning. Instead you made a few jokes and moved on when the anxiety of knowing what might happen began to gnaw at your stomach. That was a warning sign. One you ignored.

Doyle settles on an empty bench overlooking Strawberry Creek in the middle of the university campus. A pleasant enough place he admits, so foreign to the likes of Fay and Teejay. And Guzman. In the murky well of his mind he replays the episode in his apartment when Fay peered past the curtain through the window and identified Raymond staring up at them. Did he actually see Fay? Impossible to tell. Guzman might have noticed him and Teejay and Fay depart through the back entrance to the building, or if not that, he could have observed them ghosting through the alley as they made their way to the BART station and over to San Francisco.

Doyle remembers their transit — refugees in full flight, carrying a few personal possessions in their bags, the look of dread in their faces, the questions in their eyes about where they were headed and where they might spend the night. Now a greater question presents itself. Was it Guzman who set the fire in the apartment adjacent to Teejay and Fay's sparsely furnished rooms? He hasn't mentioned this possibility to Mavis or James. He decides to wait until he sees Fay again, whenever that might be, and to put this question to her with the tact required to ensure she doesn't enter a new mania or panic. He smiles dismissively. A *manic panic*, Fay's specialty.

As to his own direction, Doyle now determines that he must move on. He couldn't allow his recent course corrections to terminate with Louis's heart attack. You need to add a new chapter to your life, he tells himself. Once you have something new in place, something *positive* to report, you might be able to carry on with the memoir. Maybe it's time to return to the boys, to go back home. In any case he's sure that he must leave Berkeley, find an exit strategy that will take him out of harm's way. And not just an exit from Berkeley or California, but an exit from America. To get back up to Vancouver Island, or better yet, over to Salt Spring Island, somewhere near Jesse and his wife and his granddaughter. It's so obvious. The boys have said as much for months. What better option is there?

James leans against the doorframe and gazes at his wife. He is so thankful to have her here, in this house, in this very room. No matter that she's preoccupied with something on her laptop, the on-going labor of her thesis, trading email with Box and Dansky and now this new interloper from family services, Janice Slitz. But he doesn't care about all that as long as Mavis is simply present.

"Something wrong?" She maintains her focus on her computer screen and after a moment of silence looks up to see James standing, absent-minded with the phone clutched in his hand.

"Yeah," he sighs. "More bad news, I'm afraid." He holds the phone aloft and shakes his head.

Mavis flips the screen onto the keyboard and pats the chair beside her, an invitation to sit. "What?"

"Zach's office manager, Merna Swensen, just called." He settles into the chair and rubs his face with his free hand. "Apparently Zach's dead. His girlfriend, Vera, found him in his garage, sitting in his car with the windows sealed and the engine running."

Mavis presses her fingers to her mouth and chokes down a spasm that grips her throat.

"I know." James looks at her. What more is there to say, he wonders, but to reveal the spotty news he's gathered from Merna. "It was just last night. I guess the carbon monoxide was so dense ... just from opening the garage door ... that they had to hospitalize Vera after she found him. Sounds like she's going to be okay."

"Oh god," Mavis murmurs bleakly, her voice barely audible.

"I didn't think he meant it," he continues and his mouth draws down at the corners. With his right hand he pulls his hair through the web of his fingers and ponders what exactly Zach meant to do. "I mean, he wouldn't have wanted anything to happen to Vera. Anyone who knows him, who *knew* him, would know he didn't want that to happen to her."

"I doubt he knew what he was doing," Mavis whispers when she finds her voice. They'd seen Zach when? Three days ago? Four? She tries to push time backwards and place him in the last moment they spent together, as if it might revive him long enough so that she could make a better goodbye of it, instead of their awkward, uneasy embrace at the doorway of his LA office.

James nods absently and looks into her eyes. He can feel the loss in his belly rising up through his chest.

"Shit." This is a bad place to be, in the middle of this conversation, she decides. All the allocations of blame and responsibility that have to be considered after news of a suicide. Nothing good can come of it. "Do you want to go back down there? Would that help?"

"I asked that. His family members are holding a private service. There'll be no memorial. No flowers." He pauses to wave a hand as if he were brushing off a noisy housefly. "Nothing." He glances away, gazes through the window at the pitter-patter of a light rain hitting the glass. A sun-shower.

"Well. We have to see Vera when she recovers." Mavis's voice is firm, certain of a pending duty that requires respect.

"Yeah." James still clings to the telephone and he runs his thumb over the buttons on the handset. They glow under his touch, a brief dance of light in the midst of gloom. He smiles at the compatible intelligence bred into consumer electronics. An early form of cyber DNA, he muses. After a moment he can no longer contain the emptiness rising though his body and he begins to weep a tearless form of crying. He drops the telephone on the sofa pillow and presses both hands to his eyes. "Oh god, what have I been doing?" he sobs. "I told him there was a new way. And he *believed* it."

Mavis curls her arm around his waist and draws him toward her. "At least he *had* that," she whispers. "And for a time, that was enough. *That was plenty.*" She brushes the back of her fingers across his cheek, across the chub of his cheekbone down to his chin. She's never seen him like this, an apostate to his own creed, and she can feel the uncertainty well through him as he withdraws from her and she wonders how deep this might go, how far and wide the floodplain of his doubt might extend.

James decides to spend Wednesday morning in retreat, as he calls it, in a two-hour meditation to restore his equilibrium.

Mavis, on the other hand, knows she's headed for a confrontation. She received an email from Alice Bonasteel, the dean of Berkeley's graduate school, asking to meet with Mavis at ten AM. She also wrote that Lorraine Dansky and Philip Box would be sitting in to "advise them." Mavis's initial concern — advise them *about what?* — is immediately replaced by the more urgent question: *what the hell* did Janice Slitz disclose to Box about her situation with Fay and Teejay? At the very least they would give Mavis a formal warning not to engage in any therapeutic relationships until she's duly licensed, and furthermore not to see any clients while she's still a student under the direction of Box and Dansky. Mavis prepares herself to accept these conditions as she enters Bonasteel's office. They're logically acceptable and simply a reiteration of the professional standards set out in the internship contract she signed when she began the program.

But her resolve dissolves the instant that she sees Janice Slitz sitting beside Box at a small boardroom table at the far end of the room. Opposite them, smiling an empty grin, is Alice Bonasteel, who rises to shake Mavis's hand. "I think you know everyone?" Bonasteel's bright Dublin accent rises on the last few syllables.

Before Mavis can respond, Lorraine Dansky slips through the open door with a bicycle helmet braced under her arm and settles in the chair beside Bonasteel. Dansky has a new look: jet-black hair pulled into a shoulder-length ponytail that exposes a row of seven studs pierced into her ear lobe.

"Did you get my second email this morning?" Bonasteel narrows her eyes as she addresses Mavis. "The one advising that Janice Slitz would join us today?"

Mavis takes the one remaining chair at the narrow end of the table between both pairs of her inquisitors. "No. Not yet." She tucks her chin a notch lower and examines Slitz's outfit: a silk blouse with ruffled sleeves fluttering outside a buttoned tweed vest. "Though I'm not surprised."

When he hears this, Dr. Box turns in his chair to acknowledge Mavis's presence and smiles slightly, a microscopic turn of his lips that barely hints at his discontent.

"Sorry; I just found out myself. It's a request from Dr. Box. I sent it twenty minutes ago." Bonasteel adjusts a bluetooth telephone headset planted in her left ear, a tiny device that Mavis hasn't noticed until now. "Perhaps we should begin?" She glances at the others and then sets her attention on Janice. "Ms. Slitz, since you alerted us to the situation facing your clients, maybe you can start by giving us some background and describing your concerns as you see them."

"Certainly." She lifts a legal file folder from her bag onto the table and opens it to expose a sheaf of documents about three inches thick. "Fay Flood and her daughter, Teresa-Jacinta Flood, have been clients of family services on-and-off for a little over three years." She scans a cover sheet that summarizes the key data and facts as she continues. "I believe that after working briefly with Dr. Ernest Benson, Fay came to consult you, Dr. Box, about six weeks ago to get a new prescription to manage a bipolar disorder."

Still suffering from his neck injury, Philip Box closes and re-opens his eyes, a pause that conveys a measure of his pain. "Yes, that's correct."

"Then during a routine client visit that I had with her following your meeting, Fay Flood advised me that she was no longer working with Dr. Box, but had submitted herself to the care of Mavis Helm." For the first time Janice settles her gaze on Mavis, then returns her attention to her files.

"Her ex-partner, and the child's father, Raymond Guzman, has been living outside the family setting during this entire period. He's been convicted twice, once for theft under two hundred dollars and a second time for assault. The police don't have any knowledge of his current whereabouts. However, Fay told Dr. Kumaritashvili at the San Francisco General Hospital that he began stalking them in the last few weeks."

When Box hears this news he interrupts, lifting his right index finger from the table to press for clarification. "Stalking them? In what sense?" His tone suggests that this may well be an exaggeration by Fay.

"In the sense that they had to flee their home to an apartment in Haight-Ashbury." Slitz continues the narrative: the arson, the death of the building caretaker who in the course of saving them suffered a massive coronary, their hospitalization, Teejay's miscarriage, the implied statutory rape, and Teejay's apparent ignorance of her own pregnancy. She delivers these last details at a rising pace and with an increasing sense of incredulity.

"Actually it's quite possible the child has no conscious awareness of the trauma." Dansky strokes her earlobe between her thumb and index finger and glances at Mavis. "Just as some victims blot out an attack, some women completely block the reality of pregnancy. Think of it as a self-protective mechanism; the subconscious mind eliminating events that otherwise are totally immobilizing. Even rape can be blocked."

"Situation-specific psychogenic amnesia," Box adds as a point of clarification. He's seen this all before and far too many times. "It's more common than most people think. A bit like the post-traumatic stress disorder that's now endemic in the military."

"Do we know the man involved?" Dansky asks.

"No, since she won't acknowledge it.... Maybe with hypnosis...." Slitz stumbles and then to re-establish a tone of certainty she adds, "But we have the DNA from the fetus."

"Have you checked her father?" As soon as she asks this single question, Mavis joins the same team as everyone else in the room. Despite the realignment there's a brief lapse while they individually consider the implications.

"The father?" Janice Slitz appears stunned. She turns a few pages in the folder searching for something.

"Yes, Raymond Guzman," Mavis adds quickly and leans forward to draw Janice Slitz into her gaze.

Janice closes the folder now and returns Mavis's glare. "I think we all know who Raymond Guzman is."

Box can sense the tension between the women and

decides to interrupt. "The Department of Corrections may have a record of his DNA. You'll need a court order to get it, but I'll add my signature to the application. It may expedite matters."

"That should help. Meanwhile," Janice continues, "I've already submitted an order to have the daughter apprehended and the mother declared unfit. It should be certified this afternoon. I can append a request for the father's DNA as soon as we finish here."

Alice Bonasteel places both hands on the table. The smile on her face gradually dissolves and as she looks at each person individually her lips transmit a feeling of despair. "An unfortunate situation, I'm afraid. It'll be interesting to see what you can do with it Ms. Slitz. And now I think we have to turn to another matter in confidence." She tips her head to Janice, an invitation to excuse herself. When Janice fails to respond, Bonasteel applies the formality of her Irish brogue to conclude: "And thank you for your time. Do let us know if we can be helpful in clarifying your case."

Janice Slitz bundles her file back into her bag and after a nod to Dansky and Box she rises from the table and walks to the door without another look at Mavis. When the door closes, Mavis sighs deeply. She knows the real meeting is now about to begin.

"I'm assuming this case is not typical of what our interns are expected to address." In a quick sweep of the room Bonasteel's eyes gather Box, Dansky and Mavis together. Her face now bears a hopeful, but nonetheless glum look of depression.

"Of course not." Dansky leans back her chair. "Not at this level."

"Well, much as you'd like to tailor the clinical experience for your students, I have to disagree." Box maintains his rigid pose, his neck staff-straight. "Most clinicians are seeing these situations every day. Family breakdown is chronic and gathering momentum. The state resources assigned to cope with them have evaporated. For the past year all of the clinicians I know are being paid with IOUs, all our work with this sector of the population is essentially pro bono. In fact I'm amazed there's someone like Janice Slitz who's able to handle her case load on-site and still make family visits."

"She won't be making any future visits once the state budget is passed. And as you know in the next few days we face a state-wide strike. In fact, I'll be picketing — me, *actually* picketing — in Sacramento." Alice Bonasteel shakes her head as if she cannot believe the situation facing her. Everyone is taking cuts, and more are predicted by anyone who manages a faculty budget. She can't say it aloud, but she knows that Mavis's entire graduate program will be terminated next year. Unless she can convince Box to continue her internship to the end of this term, Mavis won't be able to complete her program requirements and consequently she will never graduate. "At any rate budgets are not for us to decide. Instead we" — she waves a hand toward Mavis — "have a procedural issue we need to discuss."

Here it comes, Mavis thinks. Thankfully, this safe, technical adjective, *procedural*, hints that things might not be so bad, that disaster may still be averted. "Yes, I understand," she offers.

"And what is it, precisely, that you understand?" Bonasteel asks.

"Uhm ... that I might not have followed all the proper procedures with Fay." She knows she must own up to this. To state her transgressions simply and with humility. She pauses here but the others remain silent, a void she suspects she must fill with the details of her procedural crimes. "Dr. Box, I have to apologize to you, and to both of you," she adds and inclines her head to Bonasteel and then to Dansky, "for carrying on a relationship with Fay Flood after you referred her to another clinician."

Philip Box swivels the base of his chair toward Mavis. "Well, thank you for saying that. I have to tell you that since we've been working together every Monday morning since mid-September, I had no idea you were seeing Fay outside the office. To hear this now, frankly, I'm shocked."

Mavis draws in a long breath. Her stomach churns, an ocean seems to swell beneath her and she can only manage to utter a few words in response. "I can understand that."

Dansky tries to brighten the mood. "Mavis, it would help us to know what the situation was from your perspective. The context. Can you tell us how often you've seen Fay, and in what capacity?"

Mavis takes a moment to reflect on her history with Fay. She begins with the visit to her apartment on the first day she met her, then describes her encounter with Teejay hiding in the bedroom in such obvious distress, then she reveals the remarkable Gestalt session with Fay in her apartment, Teejay's outing with James, their neighbor's rescue of Fay and the child the night Guzman had terrorized them, and the subsequent fire and their meeting in the hospital and finally, Teejay's miscarriage. She presents all this as though her relationship with them has delivered both Fay and Teejay from enormous harm. "I hate to think what might have happened," she concludes. "Without our support, Fay's safety, and Teejay's, was at risk."

The reaction to all this is suspended briefly, then in a tone of disbelief Bonasteel whispers, "Good lord."

Dansky is more forgiving. "You shouldn't have had to

endure this on your own, Mavis. I wish you'd told me what was happening."

Philip Box, however, responds as though he's a prosecuting attorney. "Mavis, you badly misjudged the situation," he says in a sympathetic but firm voice. "Do you think for a minute that any responsible psychologist would have tried to handle this on his own? Without a social worker? The police?"

Mavis casts her eyes to the wall. She has no idea how to respond. "I don't know," she says flatly. "Who else was there to help Fay? She refused to go back to Benson and you won't treat bipolar disorders. You said yourself, *there are no other resources.*"

Box presses his lips together firmly. "Do you remember signing our internship contract in September?" He holds aloft three stapled pages, flips to the last page and points to Mavis's signature.

"Yes."

"Do you recall the article asserting that you would maintain a confidential relationship with all our clients and respect the decisions of the mentor clinician?"

" ... Yes."

When Box senses that he's punishing her, he turns the contract face down on the table. "Mavis, I've been hosting interns for at least, what, ten years?" — he glances at Dansky, who nods and then expels a long draft of air from her lips — "and you are certainly in the top five per cent of students I've known who demonstrate an aptitude for psychotherapy. But do you realize that you've now thrown it all away?"

Mavis wobbles slightly as the sea beneath her swells and tosses her off balance. "Thrown it away?"

Box leans forward an inch, almost imperceptibly. "Yes.

With this breech I can no longer trust you to maintain client confidentiality. Fay's case has been thrown open to your husband, your neighbor, his landlord, and I don't know who else! *My patient* is about to be declared legally incompetent and her daughter is going to be apprehended and assigned to foster care in *god-knows-where*. Can you imagine what will become of her? Because I can't, or least I won't let myself think of what — or *who* — lies in wait for her!" He stops and looks at Dansky and Bonasteel, then in an even, defused voice he says, "Unfortunately, I can't continue to sponsor Mavis in my clinic."

Another silence fills the room and Mavis looks at Dansky and Bonasteel.

"I'm sorry." Box slips the intern contract into his shoulder bag and in a series of wincing movements, he stands. "Really, I'm very sorry your internship has to end like this."

As he reaches the door, a burst of adrenaline pulses through Mavis's body. She has to say something, anything that can prevent him from dismissing her. "By the way," she says firmly, "She's not bipolar."

Box turns away from the door, rotates his body in one brittle motion toward the women at the table. "What?"

"The manic-depressive behavior was just masking her condition," Mavis continues with the hope that if she can provide him with this one insight, he will decide to bring her back into his clinic. "In fact, Fay Flood is teetering on the edge of psychotic depression. If I hadn't helped her, she could be catatonic right now."

"You see?" Box directs this question to Dansky and Bonasteel. "You can imagine how sorry I am," he concludes and steps though the door.

After he leaves the office, Mavis clasps her hands

together. The ocean rolling beneath her crests and she has no idea how to get to shore, wherever that might be. She opens her hands, lifts her palms to the ceiling. "Does this mean my internship is finished?" Despite her determination to remain stalwart, a tear slips from her eye and she quickly brushes it away.

Bonasteel and Dansky look to one another. Finally Bonasteel, the patented smile once again securely fixed to her lips, replies, "We'll need to consult on this, Mavis. This is quite *unprecedented*." She glances at Dansky, and when she nods, Bonasteel adds, "Please, give us a few days?"

After she leaves the dean's office, as she steps down the staircase to the main floor, Mavis feels numb. She's found her sea legs now, and is able to walk along the sidewalk at a steady pace. She's taken a new mantra from the meeting, one word that rolls through her mind over and over. *Unprecedented. Unprecedented.*

Then in a sharp rebuke to herself she realizes that she should have told Bonasteel one last thing. She stops where she stands and turns back toward the dean's office and screams into the open air, "All of life is fucking *unprecedented!* But that doesn't mean I did anything wrong!" She grinds her teeth together and then adds, "*Assholes!*"

Mavis finds James sitting in Papa Helm's wingback chair in the makeshift office next to their bedroom. She glances at him, waves a hand, a regal half-twist of the wrist, and then she wanders into the kitchen to make some tea. She's pleased that he doesn't follow her, gives her time to adjust, to consider how to break the news.

"Want some tea?" she calls when the kettle boils. When he fails to respond, she decides to make enough for him anyway, in fact decides to brew a pot of his favorite blend, Vanilla Plantation, a specialty import from China. She places two cups on a black, lacquered tray along with the teapot and two granola cookies and returns to the office. "Finish meditating?" she asks and sets the tray on the desk.

"About an hour ago." His voice is flat, disaffected. "How about the inquisition? Did Dansky and the dean take your side?"

"I don't think so." Mavis pours two cups of tea. "In fact, it was about as awful as it could possibly be. Without me actually, physically dying, I mean." She pauses to consider Zach's suicide and shrugs to acknowledge the terrible choice of words. "Sorry," she adds and sits in the desk chair.

"At least your sense of humor survived." He reaches for a cookie. "What happened?"

Mavis tests the spring action of the swivel chair as she calculates how to deconstruct the meeting. She describes the heaviest impacts in short, impressionistic bursts as if they were delivered in a boxing ring. As she talks she realizes that her memory of the session, the *sequence* of points and counterpoints is already jumbled except for Bonasteel's concluding insight that her situation was "quite unprecedented" and that Box had dismissed her from the clinic, and thus she could not complete the requirements of her MA, and that the door for appeal seemed all but closed. All these details tumble out of her in random order. As she relives the scene she realizes the benefit of distance, slight as it is, provides an anesthesia of sorts, a way to insulate herself from Box's dismissal and especially the accusations from Janice Slitz. She stops her monologue for a moment and draws a deep breath as she thinks about Fay and Teejay. Tears begin to roll from her eyes and she dabs at them with a tissue.

James leans forward and takes her hand. "Is it that bad?"

Mavis nods, yes.

"I've never seen you like this."

She nods again, draws her hand from his, wipes both eyes and then adjusts her composure. "I'm just like you last night. Because of Zack," she manages. "Except this time it's about Fay and Teejay."

"What about them?"

"Janice Slitz has secured a court order. Fay is going to be declared incompetent. And Teejay will be taken into foster care."

"What?" James stands and walks two steps toward the door and then turns back to Mavis. "Where will they take her?"

Mavis shrugs and sips at her tea. The feeling of numbness returns. There's a gap between the world and her senses, a gray void of nothingness that could easily envelope her in its mist. Part of her hopes she will disappear and never be found.

When she offers nothing more — no thoughts, no ideas, no feelings — James sits in the chair again and leans toward his wife until he is just a few inches from her face. "Don't worry. We can help them." He takes her hands in his fingers and gently rubs his thumbs over her skin. This time she makes no effort to slip away from him. "You'll see. Like everything else, this will fade and they'll be free of it soon. We'll all be free of it," he adds and leans a little closer and kisses her forehead.

At first Fay doesn't grasp what Dr. K. is saying, or at least the implications of what he's telling her. He isn't exactly panicking, she decides, but his sense of urgency is taut, edgy. She should immediately leave the hospital with Teejay, he explains, no later than the start of the evening nursing shift.

"That's about an hour from now," he says. "But you want to be gone before then. Everyone's going on strike and we have to clear all the ambulatory patients from the wards so the management team can handle those who are left."

"Everyone's on strike?" Her voice is still suppressed, squeezed into the narrow ridge at the top of her throat. At least she feels able to carry on a conversation again.

"State-wide. Nurses, teachers, police, firefighters. Do you have all your clothes and Teejay's?" He swings open the narrow closet next to the hallway door. "Is this yours?"

"Yeah, yeah." Fay starts to feel energized by Kumaritashvili's momentum now and she swings her feet to the floor and walks over to Teejay's bed.

"Now listen carefully, Fay." Kumaritashvili ensures he has her attention before he continues. "Even without the labor strike I'd discharge you both tomorrow. Teejay's well on the way to complete recovery. I'm giving you a week's supply of pills to handle any pain she might have. The discharge nurse will give her some pads; after a week the spotting on her pads should turn brown and then finish up just like her period. But if it lasts more than a week, you'll have to come to my office for help." He hands her the discharge papers, his business card and a plastic vial of white pills. "Do you understand?"

"Yeah, yeah. How often does she take these?"

"One every six hours until they're all gone or she has no pain. Now get her dressed and out the door as quick as you can." He turns to Teejay and smiles at her. "Time to go, kiddo," he chirps. "You're all better. Time to go have some fun."

Teejay props herself onto her elbows. She feels as though she is waking from a long, complicated dream that has exhausted her — but now that it's over a sense of renewal is imminent. "We're going? Like, now?"

"Yup. And I've got something for you. A going-away present." He slips a hand into his blazer pocket and lifts the other hand, palm facing toward Teejay. "First, close your eyes."

As her eyes close a faint smile crosses her lips. When he says "open" Teejay sees a fleece teddy bear, barely the size of his palm, staring at her.

She looks at her mother then at Dr. Kumaritashvili. "For me?"

"Yes, for you. For a beautiful, young woman," he says and passes the teddy to her and then turns to Fay. "One last thing." His voice drops a semi-tone. "Once this strike is settled Janice Slitz will want to … go over things with you."

Fay thinks about this. *Go over things.* "All right. I guess I should expect that. Is she on strike, too?"

"Everyone who's paid by the state is going on strike in stages over the next week. So you never know when. But some people will go to work no matter what." Kumaritashvili shrugs obliquely. He can barely believe it. All of California is about to come to a grinding halt. The health care system could easily crash within a day or two. "Okay then. I've got another dozen patients to discharge. Good luck!" He smiles a last time at Teejay and whisks out the door and down the hallway.

When they're on the street outside the hospital Fay sorts through her bag for money. She can find little more than three dollars. "Teejay, do you have any money with you?"

"Just bus tokens. And sixty-five cents," she adds after sifting through an inner pouch in her backpack.

Fay pulls a strand of hair into her hand and releases it. Apart from the belongings in their apartment everything they possess in this world is in their daypacks, along with their clothes, the same clothing they wore as they escaped from the fire. She draws a shallow breath into the top of her lungs and steadies her voice. "Can I borrow the tokens, Honey? We'll need them to get over to Berkeley."

Teejay thinks about this word, her mother has never called her *Honey* before. And rarely asked to borrow anything. "We're going back across the bay?"

"Yeah. We're going to visit Mavis. Would you like to see Mavis again?"


When their bus pulls to a stop and parks next to a curb along Telegraph Avenue everyone is surprised to hear the driver cut the engine. "Last stop," he calls over the PA and flicks the overhead lights.

"What? Don't be shittin' me!" This cry of anger booms the length of the bus from a man sitting two seats behind Fay and Teejay. "It's another three miles to my stop!"

"Yeah, mine too!" A chorus of complaints begins to ring up and down the aisle.

"Welcome to the Bay Area Rapid Transit strike," the driver says calmly and he opens the front and side doors at once. "It's four PM. We've got orders to shut 'er down at four. If you want this bus to move, call Governor White. See if he'll drive it for you. Last one out, close the doors!" He laughs with a hollow, staccato trill and then systematically shuts off the PA, turns out all the head lamps and deck lights, locks the brakes and steering column, tucks the keys into his pocket, steps out the door and waves a hand at a car parked just ahead of the bus stop, a beige Chevy sitting next to the curb, its engine idling. Without a backwards glance he ducks into the car and it immediately pulls away from the curb and drives into the dusk.

The stranded passengers sit pondering their situation for a moment and after yelling out a few complaints and slanders against the state and the unions and the way everything in America is going to hell in a handcart, they begin to exit through the bifold doors.

"Looks like we're walking the rest of the way," Fay says and leads Teejay out the rear door behind the line of desolate commuters who wander onto the street. "Your tummy feeling okay?"

"How far is it?"

"Not far, Honey." She likes the feeling that this new word imparts. And now that her girl has reached the vague adolescent limbo between child and woman she knows she'll be using it a lot more often. Honey is sweet and soft but something you still have to bottle up, the very place the girl has come to.


"When did you get out of the hospital?" Mavis steadies herself against the doorframe. Although no one had made any specific plans, at some point Mavis expected Fay and Teejay to knock at her door. Now that she sees them, their eyes hopeful but heavy with fatigue, she embraces them both and leads them into the living room.

"Dr. K. discharged us four hours ago." Fay flops her bag on the sofa and motions Teejay to do the same. She glances at James when he enters the room. "They pushed everyone out the door because of the strike."

"We could have been here sooner," Teejay says, "but the busses are on strike too, so we had to walk the last two hours." Despite her vibrancy, and her remarkable recovery following the miscarriage, Teejay's voice still wheezes from the effects of smoke inhalation.

"Do you want some milk?" James offers as he crosses from the kitchen to the front door. "Or coffee? And we've got chocolate chip-oatmeal cookies too."

As the four of them sit at the table eating cookies and drinking milk and coffee, Fay and Teejay relay the details of their last day in the hospital and the journey across the bay. It reminds James of the sagas of World War Two refugees: in constant fear of betrayal, the destitute searching for the next safe house. He suspects their situation is worse than Fay lets on; she offers no hint that she's been declared an unfit mother and that she's about to lose her daughter. She's still overwhelmed by the exhilaration of her escape from the fire, the miscarriage, and the exceptional Doctor K, "a name *nobody*, not even the nurses can pronounce," she adds. As the evening grinds on beneath Fay's growing mania, James nods to Mavis and suggests something new.

"You know, I think we should make a plan for the next day or two, at least until these strikes are over and things get back to normal."

"Good idea," Mavis says and she carries the plates and mugs into the kitchen. As she sets them on the counter next to the sink she pauses to assess the situation. Fay *doesn't* know, she murmurs to herself. Complete catastrophe is just ahead of her and she doesn't see it coming. After their abandoned apartment, this will be the first place Janice Slitz and the police will look for them. And what about your own interest in all this? If there's any hope of re-establishing some credibility with Dansky and Bonasteel, you can't have any contact with Fay or Teejay ever again. Even this little milk-and-cookie visit will have to be denied. She shakes her head. More lies and cover-ups. Which will lead to more excuses, more meetings, more dread.

When she returns to the living room, James and Teejay are standing next to the front door. "We're going to visit Doyle," James says and winks to confirm their shared, private knowledge. "Just to see if Teejay and Fay can spend the night with him again. In the meantime, why don't you bring Fay up-to-date. About your meeting today," he adds, and leads Teejay out the door.

Mavis nods, a bit flummoxed by this ambush, but she realizes it must be done. She has to tell Fay what she knows. The trap could spring at any moment and she must be warned.

"What meeting?" Fay eases into the sofa. A visible change comes over her face. Her energy level drops as if a switch has been flipped and an overload of energy is discharged into the air. When Mavis doesn't respond immediately, she presses her. "Something's happened, hasn't it?"

"Let me sit a minute." Mavis sits at the far end of the sofa and rests her hands on her thighs.

"What is it? *What?*"

"I've got bad news, Fay," she begins. "It's about as bad as news can get. I had to meet today with some people at Berkeley. At the meeting were Dr. Box and Janice Slitz."

Fay drags her fingers through her hair and locks them in place below her ears.

"They told me something about you and Teejay."

Fay arcs her head slightly and narrows her eyes to try to glimpse what is coming toward her. It is at once huge and invisible, bellowing and silent. A monster of contradictions. "No," she whispers.

Mavis blinks and brushes a hand over her left eye.

"Janice has a court order from the state." She glances away. "An order about you and Teejay."

Fay tightens her jaw and she draws a breath.

"Do you know what the order is?" Mavis immediately regrets saying this. It's so gutless. So cruel. Nobody should have to guess the means of her own execution.

Fay braces herself once again. "You tell me," she whispers without taking a breath. "You're the only one who can tell me without it killing me." She swallows and loosens the tendons in her neck.

Mavis draws a breath and begins. "Janice is going to take Teejay and put her in foster care. The only way they can do that is if the court declares you an unfit mother. That order went to the court for approval this afternoon."

There are no tears. No crying, no wailing. Instead, Fay sinks deeper into the sofa, melts into a pool of despair. Mavis pulls one of Fay's hands between her own and presses them together. She knows that she has to revive her before Fay slips into a catatonic state and is completely immobilized.

"Fay," she says firmly and turns Fay's hand to the left. "You can*not* go there. I know what you're feeling and if you want to save Teejay and yourself, you have to fight back. We're going to help you. Me and James. And Doyle. And we're going to help Teejay. But we cannot do it without you. Do you understand what I'm saying?"

Fay stares into a gray space about two feet above Mavis's head.

"Fay, I want you to say that you hear me. I want you to say 'yes.'"

She lowers her gaze slightly. To Mavis's mouth. To study the shape of the words she is speaking.

"Say 'yes' Fay."

This is a game you played before. Mavis tells you what to say and then you say it. What are the actual words she's saying right now? *Yes*, she's saying yes. Now you say it. "Yes."

"What was that?"

"Yes."

"Good. Now let's go upstairs and see what Teejay's doing with James and Doyle. Then we'll get some sleep and fix everything up tomorrow. Okay?"

"Okay. I know," she says and her voice breaks through the plug of suffocation at the top of her throat. "Don't worry. I'm going to be all right." As they pull themselves up from the sofa and step towards the door she adds, "Thanks. I can't believe I'm saying it ... but thank you."

---

Once Doyle is certain of his departure plans he decides to Skype Wyatt and tell him the news. There are a few problems, like his stolen passport, that he has to sort out before he can return and he knows that Wyatt should be aware of them.

"You lost your passport?"

"I didn't lose it. It was stolen."

"When did this happen?"

"The day after I arrived in San Francisco." Doyle shrugs. The confession reveals that he'd hidden the episode with ¡Ouch! and Kandy from his son. By now he'd dismissed it as a minor misadventure but when he sees Wyatt wince, he detects a look of disapproval: *How could you be so naïve?*

"Anyhow, I need a new passport to get back into Canada. So I'm wondering — "

*"Wondering?"* Wyatt interrupts, "They've got to have a Q-

and-A page about stolen passports on their website." Wyatt's voice rises with each word. He restrains himself from asking the obvious: *Why didn't you deal with this when it happened?*

"Of course they do. I've checked it all out, I just haven't gotten to it yet." Doyle exhales a long sigh. Neither of the boys has ever spoken to him like this. As though he's the wayward child. He recalls his bout of inertia. His difficulty (*his refusal*) to report the lost passport, thereby renewing his old — abandoned — identity. It made no sense, of course, but that's just the way things were. Until Louis died he didn't feel any immediate pressure to move on. But now each passing day presses more heavily upon him. Without your intervention, he reminds himself, today Louis might be home in Rouen surrounded by his family.

"I need to re-deploy," he adds in the well-known code he and the twins developed after years of studying satellite orbits on the back deck of the house.

"Well, you'd better be quick. Did you hear what the Americans and Chinese have been up to?"

"What?"

"It came out in a new Wikileaks report." Wyatt loves Wikileaks. The conspiracies brought to light, the lies exposed, the righteous revolutions unleashed. "Apparently the Chinese were concerned that Bush 43 had revived Reagan's Star Wars system by developing laser technology to take out their satellites. So to demonstrate their cred they struck first and used a missile to destroy one of *their own* birds. Then the Yanks did the same thing a month later and blasted a non-functioning US satellite."

"When was this?"

"Back in 2007 or 2008. As usual there's a little confusion in the report."

"What? That pre-dates the Kosmos-Iridium collision in 2009!" By now the debris from all three strikes would be scattered throughout the geostationary band surrounding Earth. Due to the Chinese-American skirmish the exponential collapse of orbiting systems predicted by the Kessler Syndrome was probably multiplied by a factor of five or six. Maybe more. At some point this madness would take down the entire global communications network. Had they no idea what the implications were? "They both took out their own satellites? They're crazy!"

"I know. Gives new meaning to that old saying of Mom's. Don't cut off your nose to spite your face."

"True enough." Doyle frowns. For once he doesn't want to talk about Iris with his son. Maybe because of Louis Laporte's heart attack. But neither does he want to mention any of that to Wyatt. It's one thing to reveal that he'd lost his passport, however, the story of Fay and Teejay and Louis is too much to impart right now. Besides, he hears someone knocking at his door.

"There's someone at my door. Can you give me a minute?"

"Sure. I've got to go anyhow. A client wants me to sail his ketch around to Sooke Basin tomorrow."

"That's a good day's sail." He pauses to consider the voyage around Vancouver Island with the boys when they were sixteen. Afloat on a boat. "Remember the *Snail's Pace*?"

"That old tub? Of course! Think you could make a trip like that again, Dad?"

"I'd do it tomorrow." The knocking at his door is a little louder now. "Look, I've got to go."

"All right. Email me if there's anything I can do to fix the passport thing. I'll do what I can."

"Okay." Doyle inches closer to the screen to ensure he

can see his son's eyes clearly. "I love you, Wyatt." He always reminds the boys of his love every time he speaks to them. It's a lesson you can learn too late in this life.

"Love you, too."

Seconds later the laptop screen freezes, locks up as it does from time to time. He jiggles the power cable. The connection's good. Doyle taps the ESC button two, three times. Nothing. The image on his screen holds the blurred pointillism of electronic scramble. You see, *there is no escape,* he muses to himself as he walks to the door rubbing the arthritic knuckles in his left hand. How easy life would be if you could just hit a button and — poof! — escape.


"Mavis is talking to Fay downstairs, so we thought we'd pay you a visit. You know, if you've got some time." James peers at Doyle through the pale light of the upper hallway. The look on his face this late in the evening reveals a neediness Doyle has never seen in his neighbor. Usually James appears so confident, assured that he's found *the way* through White Light Meditation, the public lectures, the private gatherings of ten, fifteen, twenty people that meet in his living room most afternoons, all of it driven by a momentum of certainty confirmed in James's strong face and bearing. But since he returned from LA and confronted Fay and Teejay's disaster in the hospital, James's self-assurance seems to have vanished.

"Hi Teejay." Doyle smiles at the girl and waves them both into the room, over to the table next to the front window. Everything about her physical movements and gestures suggest a deep exhaustion, but Doyle is taken with her bright demeanor, the latent energy in her steel-gray eyes. It's hard to believe that a few days ago this child had a miscarriage. "I just finished talking to my son, so yes, I've got time. Lots of it. How did it go in the hospital?"

She presses her lips in a wry pout and shrugs. "I can't remember much of it. Except for Dr. K." She sets her pack on the floor and deftly changes the topic. "You have a son?"

"Yes. And you know what he is?"

*"What he is?"* An odd question, she thinks. From an odd man. She considers asking if he's a Martian. Or kept in a circus because he has two heads. But that wouldn't be very nice.

"He's a twin. I have two boys who are identical twins."

"You can't tell them apart?" She settles into a chair at the kitchen table and wraps her hands in separate strands of her long, strawberry-blond hair.

"Well, *I* can. But most people take months before they can tell them apart. Some of their teachers could never sort one from the other."

While Teejay considers this James sits beside her and scans Doyle's face. "We have a favor to ask." He props his elbows on the table, weaves his fingers together and balances his chin atop this construction. "Would it be okay if Teejay and Fay spent the night with you again?"

Doyle adjusts his head a little. There is so much unspoken in this request. He knows James would never ask this if something were not at risk. Nor would Mavis.

"I can explain the details later," James adds when he sees Doyle hesitate. "It'll just be better for everyone. Just for tonight, I mean."

"Of course." Doyle waves a hand to dismiss any doubts. "Teejay, do you want to sleep in the big bed again?"

"Yeah, I'm getting sleepy," she says. "But I have a pill I have to take first. Could I have a glass of water?"

Doyle gets her a glass of water. "Do you remember where everything is?"

"Yes." She opens her bag and finds her toothbrush and the vial of pills from Dr. Kumaritashvili. Barefoot, she makes her way to the bathroom, brushes her teeth and wanders past James and Doyle who are speaking in whispers in the living room.

"Can I just get into the bed?" she asks, her eyes now dim with lethargy. "Will you tell Mom that I'm here?"

"Yes and yes." Doyle nods at her and smiles. How can she be so self-reliant? Taking her own pills, getting herself ready for bed. The twins were never like this. But this twelve-year-old child seems closer to twenty. And just when he dismisses everything about Teejay's childhood, certain that she must have managed the necessities of life on her own for the past ten years, Teejay calls him from the bed.

"Can you tuck me in?"

Doyle looks at James and shrugs with amazement. Neither of them can fathom this mix of independence and need. For a moment they are confused; which of them is Teejay asking for? James tips his head to Doyle: you go.

Doyle leans over the bed and pulls the sheet and blanket up to the girl's chin. As his sight adjusts to the dim light cast from the living room, he can see that she's holding a small teddy against her cheek.

"So how do you tell them apart?" she whispers.

"Who?" He can barely see her lips move in the darkness.

"The twins."

"Oh. Well, I could tell from the day they were born," he says in a whisper. Now he remembers how to tuck children into bed. The art of it. The delicate nuances, the tenderness, everything done in a hush. "Wyatt came out first and

Jesse waited inside their mummy's tummy a good twenty minutes or so before he decided to put in an appearance. Since then, Wyatt's always been a leader and Jesse a follower. But I never tell them that."

"Why not?"

"I guess I never want them to feel different from one another. I just want them to always be friends."

"I wish I had a twin." The stuffed bear is snuggled in the palm of her hand. She kisses the tiny pink lips and then holds it against her cheek again.

Doyle ponders this notion, something he'd considered many times, of course. But in all his years, he never wanted to take the boys' place. Never wanted to be a twin. In Teejay's case, however, he could appreciate her point of view. As a twin she would escape the loneliness, the isolation, all the imponderables of dealing with Fay on her own.

"Yeah, me too," he says after deciding this harmless lie would soothe her, and thinking of his sons when they were twelve years old, he leans over and kisses her forehead just the way he put the boys to sleep every night, year after year.

"Amazing," James says when Doyle returns to the living room. "I can't believe how she does it." He crooks a thumb to the bedroom. Already Teejay's breathing has softened into a light wheezing. They smile at one another, at the good fortune of witnessing a child's heavy sleep, and they both savor the rare pleasure provided so late in the evening.

After a moment Doyle leans toward James. "So, where's Fay?"

"Long story, my friend." James shrugs, rolls his eyes and begins to relay what he'd heard from Mavis. With each new blow — the declaration of parental incompetence, the pending seizure of the child, the threat of foster care, the collapse of Mavis's internship — Doyle sinks deeper into his chair. James explains that the court order probably will be delivered the day the strike ends and that family services staff and the police will certainly look for the girl and her mother in his apartment.

"Well, they won't stop there," Doyle frowns. "I told that woman that I lived upstairs from you. They'll knock on my door two minutes after you tell them to fuck off." Doyle surprises himself with this word. He rarely swears, but in this case he knows it's warranted. "No, we're going to have to get them to re-deploy."

"What?"

"To move on." He jabs an index finger toward the window, to a destination well beyond Berkeley. "They need to get a fresh start. Somewhere a thousand miles from here."

James considers this. When nothing comes to mind, he realizes that new ideas have abandoned him. Always he's had the ability to try something new, take a fresh approach, run a new strategy through his head. All that has vanished now. Maybe, he tells himself, you need to re-deploy, too.

"Why can't they just move to Oregon and forget everything? Are these court orders just local, or are they national?"

James shakes his head and frowns. "If you're wanted in one state, you'll be wanted in the other forty-nine," he says. "With all the child abuse scandals in the past ten years, I think they take it pretty seriously."

"Amazing." Doyle covers his mouth with his fingers. "You can't walk down the street without stumbling over the homeless. *The San Francisco Chronicle* says forty-nine million people are living on food stamps. But despite all that" — he turns a hand in the air and then flattens it on his knee — "tomorrow the full weight of the law is going to come down on *Teejay.*"

There's little more to say. As the evening completes its covert shift to nightfall they stare through the window in a mutual recognition of the stalemate confronting them. Below them on the sidewalk, strangers pass looking for a new place to sleep in the shadows. Meanwhile, not more than ten feet away from the homeless, a steady stream of BMWs and SUVs whiz by on the cracked asphalt, the drivers locked securely in their cars, their hidden steel gas tanks filled with a blend of home-grown biofuels and refined light sweet crude shipped through the Straits of Hormuz from one of the new revolutionary Arab states. Our allies? Doyle wonders. Sure, add that to the unfolding illusion of sustainability.

When Mavis taps at the half-open door and then enters the room with Fay, James is instantly relieved when he sees his wife smile and the calm resignation in Fay's face. "Teejay's asleep," he announces as if a bit of magic has been rendered while they were all looking the other way. "It's Doyle's doing. The master-dad," he says and ceremoniously bows his head toward his friend.

Later, after James and Mavis have returned to their apartment and Fay has checked on her daughter and settled onto the living room sofa, a blanket drawn snugly around her body, she whispers to Doyle. "Doyle, I know you didn't ask for this."

Curled on a foam pad laid on top of the living room carpet, Doyle tries to adjust his back in preparation for what he is certain will be another night of near sleeplessness. "Don't worry about it, Fay. I know *you* didn't ask for all that's happened to you and Teejay."

Fay thinks about all that can come your way. All of it uninvited. "Well. Thank you, anyway. If I had my way," she continues in a whisper, "you wouldn't even have met me, let alone had me sleeping on your sofa and Teejay in your bed. Though I'm glad you did," she adds, in an effort to turn this confession into a compliment.

Doyle draws a long, uneasy breath and turns onto one side. People meet one another and sometimes it feels as if the meeting is ordained by blind luck, if that makes any kind of sense. Consider your own particular case. What possible combination of events could conspire to deliver you to these exact coordinates: aged sixty, widower, itinerant, self-employed as an memoirist (currently blocked), attempting to sleep on the hardwood floor in a rented attic in that celebrated center of the liberal-intellectual world, Berkeley, California, lying next to an incompetent mother and her brilliant child who has just had the bud of life ripped from her body. How is it possible to calculate the permutations of these variables in order to predict what might come tomorrow? Better not to think of all this, especially not to talk with Fay about it now that she's fading. No, best just to kiss the long day one last farewell and try to drift off. "Good night," he whispers into the darkness.

" 'night," she replies and a moment later her snoring begins to wheeze through the room.

Since he learned the news about Zach's suicide, James is increasingly preoccupied with the likelihood that he's deluded himself. It's not a matter of ignoring small details, of passing over inconsistencies. No, this is about a broad misunderstanding of reality. Of wishing and hoping that the simple act of meditation can change individual behavior and then one-by-one change all of society. After all, if his chief benefactor from the White Light Foundation has fallen by the wayside, what hope is there for the mass of citizens thrashing about in the day-to-day struggle to survive? Maybe the economic environment is just too toxic to support the solution he has to offer.

The situation reminds him of an environmental analogy he heard on National Public Radio a few years ago: the modern fable of two frogs and the stew pot. A stew pot is filled with room-temperature water and set on top of a stove. A healthy, mature frog is dropped into the pot where it swims about, exploring its new environment. The stove element is turned to a medium heat. Since the water warms very slowly, the frog never experiences a shock-point that generates a fight-or-flight response. Instead of jumping from the pot to save his life, the frog makes tiny incremental adjustments to his situation, swimming about until it's too late, until the water rises to a boil and he's cooked in mid-stride. At this point a second frog is dropped into the same pot. But the second frog's reaction is immediate. The instant his feet touch the boiling water he jumps out of the pot and leaps to safety.

The question posed by the fable is unavoidable: how can we tell if our environment is approaching a boiling point? Almost every day reports of calving glaciers or species extinction fill the airwaves. Seemingly impossible events like the thousands of birds plummeting to their deaths from the sky in towns and cities around the world. But who could prove all this hasn't been going on for millennia? Maybe we inhabit a new world — a hyper-manic digiworld — where the continuous reports of catastrophe are *normal* and the media have concentrated our perceptions so acutely on disaster that we believe that Armageddon is nigh. Maybe mass media is the problem, after all. The *only* problem.

Despite the media mania, James is confident there is one sign post we can count on: the ocean water table. This is the mercury bubble rising in the glass thermometer, an indisputable scientific marker that reveals the true condition of global warming. Since the oceans are rising millimeter by millimeter, year by year wherever measures are taken, there can be only two reasons for the unrelenting increase. First, warming the ocean water causes it to expand. Second, the rivers of glacial melt pouring into the oceans cause it to rise. Since the ocean mass is undeniably growing at an unremitting rate, then likely both causes are in play.

Therefore, given the near certainty of global warming, the pot you are swimming in, he concludes, is about to cook you in your own juices. Whether humanity is to blame is a totally separate issue. What matters is survival, which means jumping out of the pot and finding a new place to live out your days. But what a crazy proposition! When has anybody ever had to face this same challenge? Perhaps during the last ice age. Or seventy-five thousand years ago following the eruption of the Toba super-volcano when the human population was probably reduced to a thousand breeding pairs. But nobody *foresaw* these events and the survivors had to scramble from day to day in a hand-to-mouth existence that would shock the Starbucks habitués with its grim brutality. Luck had to be a huge part of their success. And perseverance.

But in your case, James assures himself, you can apply forethought and planning to the situation. Each moment reveals a number of possible future outcomes. If you can envision the future you desire, you can chart a course to get there.

Twice before, James has immersed himself in a meditation that lasted a full day. The process is simple and now he prepares for the journey by setting aside a pint of unfiltered apple juice to quench his thirst and a few firm pillows to keep his posture upright. He clicks off the phone and opens the window half an inch to provide a stream of fresh air.

Once everything is in place he begins a series of yoga stretches. Over the next hour he mobilizes and releases the muscles, tendons and organs in his body, but more importantly, he contacts the physical reality of his being. As he stretches, he focuses his attention on his breath and breathes into the light pain of his muscles as they distend and then he relaxes in each posture until the tension dissolves and the normal limitations of his body seem to dissipate with it.

When the yoga exercises are complete, he takes a sip of juice and squats on Mavis's wing-back chair, crosses his shins on the cushion, and closes his eyes. After a moment he props one of the pillows against the small of his back and folds the edge of two others under his thighs. He closes his eyes again and rests his hands, palms up, on his knees. He curls his index fingers into Guyan mudra, a closed circuit formed when his fingertips touch the ends of his thumbs, tip to tip. He draws a deep breath and exhales. He waits a moment and breathes again and then again, letting the parachute of his diaphragm rise and fall with the air that streams in and out of his lungs. Soon his awareness of breathing fades as if the room itself takes on the unconscious requirement of breathing. After five or ten minutes the double mantra comes into his mind. Sa-ta-na-ma, om-ma-ra-ma.

He lets the monosyllables hum their quiet song and the only control he applies is to slow it down so that each consonant and vowel becomes a paragraph in the long narrative of the here-and-now. Sometimes there are breaks in the sequence. Sometimes there is nothing at all, just the uncluttered well of his being. When these moments of emptiness arise, he can see a white dot appear just above his closed eyes, and in this small bright space he watches the tiny flutters and aberrations of light, the expansions and dissipations, the gray clouds that shade the center of light and then are burnt through, first at the edges, then as the white space crystallizes and the cloud is completely illuminated, the brilliant expanse occupies all of his awareness until he achieves the streaming entry into the white light of his being.

The effect can be very powerful and this time he gasps slightly and has to return to basics: breathe in and exhale, let the mantra present itself, let it sing as slowly as time itself and then ... let go ... let go ... let go. Once again the flood of light sweeps through him and this time he's able to swim into the waves rushing through the room, up through the ceiling and into the air above the Victorian house on Regent Street where he pauses a moment and realizes that he is anchored by a gravity field generated from the triangulation of each hand locked in Guyan mudra and joined to the third eye in the center of his forehead, the chakra which bears the pulse of his white light. From this anchor a long tether begins to unravel as he drifts higher, a secure line that he ascends up the long flight that takes him high above San Francisco Bay.

Out of his body, discorporate, he examines the expanse of the Pacific Ocean, turns to the flat contours of the seacoast, over to the Sierras and north to the long chain of mountains rolling into the distance. He hears nothing. There is no wind, no fragrance, and he has no tongue to taste the air. *But what he can see and feel!* The distances sprawl before his eyes and his body-less being absorbs the comfort of oneness that envelops him. *This is ...* but he blocks the thought, lets the mantra slip through his mind and rides higher again, this time to some supernatural perspective of the world, a place where he can see in the distance five or six other beings floating in a state of white light. Yes, there are several of them, each an orb of light attached to a long thread fluttering to Earth below. Is it possible? Are there others inhabiting this realm with him? He lets the question dissolve in this place where no questions exist, where nothing matters.

He rolls through another slow rotation and finds himself transfixed by one point, a point far to the north along the coastal mountains where there are no other orbs aloft, and then instantly he is transported there. Looking down he can see hundreds of islands: green, bright, sparsely inhabited. The archipelago shimmers beneath him, cool in the surrounding waters, the peaks of their beige hills stretching up to him, offering an invitation to live and thrive. Yes, *there*, he thinks and he draws a long breath that travels along the length of his tether and returns him to Papa's wingback chair in the little office. *There*, he whispers to himself over and over again until the sound of his voice is a wind that awakens him and he opens his eyes. The clock on Mavis's desk shows 9:37 PM. He's been gone for almost ten hours. "Yes," he says aloud and takes a sip of juice. "*That* is the place."


He finds Mavis in the living room hunched over her laptop. "Hi," she offers tentatively, wondering how she would handle a day of solitary meditation. The physical and mental stillness required almost frightens her, but the one time she witnessed James after he emerged from a "journey," he seemed completely refreshed. He spent the next day without sleep, totally absorbed in a new project which turned out to be the formation of the White Light Foundation. "Did it go okay?" she adds when she sees him sorting through the bookcase looking somewhat disoriented.

"I think so. Do you know where the atlas is?"

"The atlas? It's on the top shelf, extreme left," she says and then asks, "Why not use Google Maps?"

He pulls Papa's *Reader's Digest World Atlas* from the shelf and taps the cover with a finger as he approaches her. "No, I think I want to study this awhile."

"Thinking of a trip?"

"Maybe." He sits beside her and finds the section containing the charts of the Pacific Northwest. He closes the book and takes a moment to consider his situation. Here he is, living happily in Berkeley with his wife, and until recently everything between them has been calm, untroubled, steady. Is the water really about to come to a boil? And perhaps more important, does that question make any sense at all?

"What is it?" Mavis sets the computer aside and touches his arm.

"You know there are times when I think I'm deluding myself." He draws a long breath and shoves the atlas against the arm rest. "I've told you that before."

"Mmm, I know." She nestles beside him, happy to release her own troubles for now. "Everyone has doubts; no big revelation in that. But in your case, everyone wants to believe in your certainty. That probably makes it harder for you to say that you're not sure of things."

He hasn't thought of that before, that his wall of certainty is higher than others' and that it could be important to those around him. "Sometimes when I meditate, I wonder if all I'm doing, what we're all doing, is just *wishing*. What if it's all simply an elaborate wish-fulfillment fantasy? I mean on a colossal scale. The millions of Buddhists and yogis, the Dalai Lama, the TMers — all of us lost in an utter fantasy so grandiose in its deception that it would startle Sigmund Freud and Carl Jung."

"Wow. You had quite a trip in there." She crooks her thumb in the direction of the office and the chair where he'd been meditating.

"Yeah. It was fantastic until I just sat down here." He draws a hand over his chin and then adds, "But they've got nothing to do with you. The delusions, I mean."

"But what about the research? There're volumes of neuro-psyche papers that have replicated all kinds of double-blind studies that show the effects of meditation. They're all brilliant. It's like Darwin's evolution or Einstein's relativity, they're not *theories* anymore. It's proven, already."

"Maybe." James presses his lips together and shrugs. "But has anybody used the same tests on people who sit for an hour once a day and simply *wish* for a better world?"

Mavis pulls away from him and studies his face. "So what are you thinking? I mean, this is different. From the normal you, I mean."

James shakes his head. Should he go on? "Okay. So first of all, everything I'm going to say will sound crazy. It already sounds crazy *to me*, so don't worry, I'm not going to be upset by your reaction." He pauses to look at her and opens the atlas again, flips to the maps of the Pacific Northwest, tries to identify the island he'd been floating above half-an-hour ago and then taps it with a finger. "I think we should move here," he says and watches her face to gauge her first reaction. When she stares at the island under his fingertip, he moves it a little and adds, "Or to an island around there. I'm not one hundred percent sure which island yet, but I think it's this one."

"That's in *Canada*. Here's the San Juan Islands in Washington State, but you've picked out Salt Spring Island. Which is in Canada."

"That's right." He shrugs, tries to interpret any underlying judgments in her tone. "I've never been to Canada. Have you?"

"Once. To Montreal. Papa was born there and moved to Boston when he was nine. He had pretty clear memories of it."

"And?"

"Good." She rubs a hand over her forearm and settles it on her knee. "Canada's good. Everybody knows that. It's just kind of … *remote*."

"Which is why we want to move there."

She tries to hold his eyes, blinks, and shifts her attention to the atlas. "Which is *why*, exactly?"

"Because of what's going to happen, Mavis. Happen here, I mean." He waves a hand across the breadth of the room, a broad gesture to indicate an area within a thousand-mile radius. "Everybody can see it, a huge part of Southern California blows up in wildfires every fall. Even the Yuba Valley had that firestorm last month. And it was followed by floods that washed dozens of homes away."

"But that's because there's too many people and — "

"Exactly. And there's too little food, too little water. The aquifers are drying up, the Colorado River no longer flows to the sea. My god, flocks of birds are dropping from the sky, dead on arrival!" He realizes he should stop here. A mania is rising through him, as though he's about to feel the temperature hit the boiling point. Then he remembers the most important fact of all. "But what's absolutely irrefutable is that the sea levels are rising around the world. It's all going to mean disaster." He pauses again, shakes his head obliquely. "Sorry, I cut you off."

" ... I was just going to say ... " she continues with a slow emphasis that surprises him, "it's not just the environment. It's the social breakdown, too. It's been going on so long, the pace is so gradual that it's hard to see the actual change. Then you get an economic crash like we had and it's in your face every day."

"Like Fay and Teejay."

"Yeah. Times ten million."

The next morning James is awake at six-thirty and slips out of bed and into the kitchen. He mixes a double batch of granola, toasts it in the oven, happy to know that the aroma of oats and honey, sunflower seeds, raisins and kamut flakes will fill the air when Mavis joins him. He brews their coffee and sits at the table savoring his breakfast, poring over the atlas, absolutely certain now that Salt Spring Island is the fertile, isolated paradise he'd come across yesterday evening. The contour lines on the map reveal multiple elevations in the landscape and the highest point of land, Mount Maxwell, is close to thirteen hundred feet. Plenty of room to escape the rising tides.

"Still thinking about it?" Mavis asks when she sees him peering into the map. Her hair is damp from the shower and her bathrobe is tied at her waist. "Mmm, smells good." She sniffs the pan of granola on the stove and kisses him behind his left ear. "I just don't know what to eat first. Or should I say, *who* to eat first?"

"I think you mean *whom*.

"No, I mean *you-mmm*." She spoons some granola into her mouth.

James smiles and rolls his hand over her waist to her thigh.

"Hey, this is good." She fills a bowl and adds some skim yoghurt, sits at the table and begins to eat.

"Thanks, kiddo." He pours her a cup of coffee, adds a drizzle of cream, just enough to bring a dollop of almond color to the surface. He wants to talk to her in a serious way about moving to Salt Spring Island but he knows the time has to be right. He moves the atlas beside her and he points out the island again. "Interesting just to look at, don't you think? It's got a zig-zag shape."

Mavis nods and eats another spoonful of cereal. "You should ask Doyle about it. I think he's from around there. He told me one of his sons lives on an island."

"He does?"

"One of the twin boys." She nods. "Makes sense that he has twins, don't you think? He is *such* a daddy-man." Somewhere her cell phone rings and she glances around to echolocate her phone.

"Night table." James nods in the direction of their bedroom.

Mavis returns to the kitchen and with the phone in her hand and shows James the caller-ID. "Dansky," she moans. "It's not even eight o'clock. Damn it, this can't be good." She takes the call and wanders into the living room, responding in monotones to Dansky's brief expositions.

"She wants me to meet her off-campus," she says when she returns to the kitchen. "Apparently the students have blockaded the entrances to the campus and she doesn't want to cross the picket lines."

"Good luck." James shrugs with a look of resignation.

"The strike's not restricted to the university. People will be picketing all across the city."

"Will someone give me a break? *Please,*" she begs and walks briskly into the bathroom. "I've got to dry my hair."

A moment later the whine of the hair dryer fills the apartment and James takes his mug of coffee and the atlas into the living room. He'll have to cancel the last of his seminars and wind down the advertising for White Light Meditation, he decides. Figure out what to pack, what to sell, what to give away. Then rent a U-Haul, sort out all the details for the move. He draws a long breath and considers how far down the road he is already, whereas Mavis has yet to agree to anything. He decides she can have the last word. If she doesn't want to go, it's understandable. With her masters degree up in the air, this might be the worst time to move on. Or, perhaps the best.

"See, that's where Jesse lives. Ganges. He teaches physics and math in the high school. It's a beautiful little spot, right on the waterfront, just a few thousand people in the town itself, then another ten thousand scattered in farms and cottages around the island and in the other two villages, Fulford Harbour and Vesuvius. Both of them have ferry landings." Doyle leans over the *Readers' Digest World Atlas* and shifts the tip of his little finger from place to place marking points of interest for James to consider. "I love maps," he adds with a sigh of contentment.

"Me too," Teejay says as she looks over his shoulder at the table.

Doyle smiles at her. "I used to be a geography teacher. I had hundreds of maps. Big ones you could spread across the floor."

"You did?" Teejay inches closer to him.

"And before that I was a gold prospector in the Yukon."

"You were?" Fay, sitting in the corner of the room, is sketching in her pad. Last night, when she was sure neither Guzman nor Slitz would be looking for her, she'd returned to her apartment in Emeryville to dig out the sketch pad along with her case of Derwent graphic pencils, some clothing and a few other prized possessions. She puts her pencil aside and looks directly at Doyle as if she's seeing something new in him that had been invisible until now. "Up near Dawson City, you mean?"

"Thereabouts. For about six months," he adds. "After I finished university. I had a stake roughly fifty miles up-river. Have you been up there?"

Fay shakes her head and continues to study Doyle. The only person she's known with an interest in Dawson City is her father. That was the destination he'd set out for when he left her. She was a six-year-old girl and he abandoned her and her mother and never returned. "No," she says. "But I wouldn't mind seeing it."

"I thought I could make some money. Instead I just about went crazy from loneliness. Besides that, it's damned cold." Doyle turns to James and in a more assuring tone he continues, "But Salt Spring Island has the warmest climate in Canada."

James smiles. "Which isn't saying much."

"Hey, it's not as cold as Russia."

"I heard it is." Fay continues to study the two men and Teejay from her chair. "I heard it's colder."

"One day that might be an advantage." James looks at the map of the island from a distance now. He's looked at it from several perspectives and continues to reach the same conclusion. "Yeah, I think it's good."

"It's pretty," Teejay says and when something catches her eye she walks toward the window overlooking the street. "Hey, look at that," she says and waves a hand to bring the others to her side. "They've started a fire."

James and Doyle join her at the window. "Jeez. That's going to create a lot of smoke," Doyle says as he watches five or six people roll two car tires toward the center of the park and dump them into the flames.

"I'm not surprised." James holds a hand to his face and considers the chill that's come over the bay in the last week.

Fay closes her sketchpad, pulls herself from the chair and peers over her daughter's shoulder into the park. "They're going to have to do something to stay warm. There's a lot of tires on all these cars. Probably enough to see them through the winter."

Lorraine Dansky carries her grandé gingerbread latté to a table next to the washrooms. As usual, Starbucks is crowded with people sipping their five-dollar drinks as they surf the internet on their laptops and smart phones. They tap at the glass tablets, each one feeling untouchable in their invisible silos, a digital drape drawn snugly around them. What magical distractions we've made for ourselves, she thinks, knowing full well there are disasters a-plenty beneath the surface life of half the people in the room. Many of them are mere moments away from outrage or madness, but these toys keep the demons at bay. For now.

When Mavis joins her, Lorraine is quick to explain her situation. "Sorry, but I refuse to cross the picket lines on the campus," she says. "Let me buy you a coffee."

At first Mavis declines, then assents to having a cappuccino and waits alone for five minutes while Lorraine buys the drink and returns to the table.

"Sorry," she says again as if she's at fault for requesting the last-minute meeting. "Starbucks is the most pedestrian of all places in the U-district," she adds, "but it's the one place everyone can find."

When they're finally settled Lorraine continues to talk about the general strike. She knows the conversation is a delaying tactic, a way to put off the bad news she has to deliver from the dean. But it provides a context based on the narrative universally known as *good things gone bad*. "The government is expecting all kinds of sabotage," she begins, "if this business isn't settled in the next few days.

"Sabotage?"

"Because of the double-bind the governor's created. Later today he's going to sign an order forcing everyone back to work. Those who don't report to their employers tomorrow will be fired. But because of the budget cuts, which take effect on Monday, something like fifteen percent of the union workers are going to be laid off next week." She leans forward to share a confidence. "And I know they're expecting trouble with the utilities. I mean, can you imagine the chaos if the power grid goes down?"

Mavis shakes her head in dismay. She hasn't been following any of this. She shuns the press and clicks off the TV every time some new disaster flares up. "How do you know all this?"

Dansky inches closer. "My partner works in the governor's office. She's been monitoring the email traffic. It's *seriously* bad." She shakes her head and explains the trouble is everywhere, with the union, the government, the students. There's even some talk about conspirators planning mass disruption.

Mavis leans back in her chair and blinks. What's going on, she wonders. Why are we talking about this? After a moment she tries to shift direction in the conversation. " ... So ... "

Lorraine sips at her latté and glances away. "So, yeah." She lowers her head slightly and forces herself to look Mavis in the eyes. "So I have bad news. From the dean. I decided I owe it to you to tell you in person before it arrives as a form letter from our illustrious school of graduate studies."

Mavis presses her lips together. She can already feel it coming. This is how Fay felt when I had to break the news about Teejay's pending apprehension. "All right, what is it?"

"The day after our meeting with Dr. Box, the dean and our department chair decided to terminate your internship. They also determined that it's too late in the term to assign you to another clinician. Believe me, they're not acting out of malice. In fact, when you look at the big picture, they may be doing you a favor"

Mavis feels her chest stiffen. She takes a shallow breath. "But the internship is a requirement of my degree."

Lorraine nods once. "You can appeal the decision, of course. And if you do, I'm willing to write a letter of support for you. But even if you won an appeal, you wouldn't be able to start a new internship until next year." Lorraine's voice is flat.

Mavis draws a long breath, unsure what to say. "Well ... if I can appeal, at least that's good news." But Mavis detects something in Lorraine's face that suggests there's more bad news ahead. "That *is* good news, isn't it?"

"It would be," she says drawing a hand along her jaw, "except Dean Bonasteel just told me that the entire program will be wound up next spring."

"What?"

"Yeah. And get this. The program funding is being *redeployed*. Wonderful word, isn't it? To something even more wonderful called nanotechnology-enabled geo-engineering."

When she hears this, Mavis is surprised to feel a perverse sense of relief. Sure, she's being dumped from the program, but the program itself is being dumped from the university. Suddenly she's been freed. The implications begin to ripple through her mind. "What about you? Will this affect your job?"

Dansky raises her eyebrows and frowns. "Since I haven't made tenure yet, yes, probably. They'll make a decision sometime in January."

"What'll you do?"

"I don't know." She casts her eyes over the crowd of people hunched over their laptops and smart screens. "Face it. We're both part of the ninety-nine percent. I'm ready to surrender to the underworld any day. Maybe one of these tech-geeks can turn me into some kind of avatar. A persona in a virtual reality with a lot of money and an organic garden living on a lake where no one can touch me."

A lake and a garden. Mavis considers the contentment she used to share with Papa as they harvested their veggie patch on the south slope of the cottage on Lake Tahoe. Beets the size of Papa's fists. Tomatoes ripe on the vine, their bright skins hot in the sun. "I used to do that," she says and smiles, assured that she owns something Lorraine Dansky will never possess. "We had a garden on a hill beside a lake." She glances at the crowd swelling around the cash register and thinks, yes, and I can do it again. Maybe on Salt Spring Island.

Mavis is pleased she left her car at home. With the bus drivers on strike, the roads are clogged with traffic snarled in grid lock. While the air is cool, the sky is clear and a festive mood seems to invigorate the pedestrians wandering along the sidewalks. Couples walk hand-in-hand, girls are shopping in groups of threes and fours, men are reading newspapers in the coffee shops or uttering curses about the unions or the government or the collapsing pension funds, dogs lie at their masters' feet content and undisturbed. It's a carnival atmosphere, she decides, the rare public euphoria that emerges when everyone enjoys a shared adventure. There are no buses, the schools are closed, a burst fire hydrant floods the avenue. What will come of it all?

Despite the sense of release, she knows that unless there's a return to the social routine things can unravel in a serious way. Looting, murder, fires, rape — the chaos can quickly consume everyone. She shakes her head in consternation and crosses Haste Street toward the park. The fact that her masters degree is ruined, the dream she had of working in a clinic, the fantasies she'd secretly created of working at a real job, owning a little house with a yard, having children with James, all of that was gone. Effective immediately she needs to construct a new view of things.

Or maybe not. Maybe it would be better to have no view of things at all. For a little while at least, she could simply *live*. Become a living, breathing member of the human flotsam, lost in Dansky's underworld, drifting wherever the currents lead, eyes wide open, senses attuned, absorbing the mysteries of life without having to make sense of it all or designing a career plan intended to take her somewhere else. Somewhere beyond all this. But why try to make yourself into someone else? James had once asked this question at one of his introductory lectures. *You can only be you.* It seems so simple; how did he manage to make what is completely obvious into such a huge enterprise?

When she reaches Peoples Park, Mavis notices a teenage boy and girl pulling a tire off a silver-gray Mercedes. She crosses toward them and when she realizes they are working without a tire jack she stands at the curb, surprised a little by her own curiosity. "Got a flat?" she asks when the boy wrenches the tire free.

"We're good," he says and glances at Mavis. Once he frees the tire he turns his attention to the girl. "Okay, Kandy, slide that block off slow so we can throw it on the fire."

The girl presses her foot against a block of wood that they'd braced under the frame of the Mercedes and after a few tentative shoves, she kicks it hard and the car slumps forward so that it teeters on the remaining three wheels. With another assured kick, she knocks the block to the curb and lifts it into her arms.

Mavis watches the boy roll the tire into the park toward a few people gathered around a small fire jetting a black stream of smoke into the air. He's wearing a shirt with something hand-stenciled across the chest: *¡Ouch!* He has wonderful hair, she thinks. Lovely blonde dreadlocks that bounce with every step, a wave of lyrical freedom surfing through the breeze. She could be like them, she thinks. Gypsies living day-to-day, taking what they need from the bounty of the world surrounding them.

## Chapter Three

Over twenty-three hundred miles southwest of Berkeley and San Francisco, in his Uncle Murray's condo on Kona Bay on the west coast of the Big Island in Hawaii, Justin Fry leans against the balcony railing as he savors his first scotch-and-soda of the day. He holds the cocktail tumbler to the light reflecting from the surf in Kona Bay and admires the liquids swirling together as they sparkle around the fractured ice cubes. Pressing the chilled glass against his throat, he sighs. *Ahhh, life.* He takes another moment to assess the expanse of ocean that rolls beyond the horizon.

"So small. So tiny," he says aloud, and ponders what these words might imply. "You. Us." His free hand sweeps above the guard rail, a brief gesture. "We, *them,*" he concludes and then he steps back into the living room, bends over the coffee table and peers into the window of his laptop computer. "Mmm ... back to reality," he whispers and narrows his eyes. He taps a few keystrokes and soon finds the CNN.com newsfeed for Governor Edmund White's scheduled press conference in California.

Over the past two weeks Justin's plan has proceeded with military exactitude. Although he's never been in the army, he considers himself an expert when it comes to precision planning. As an Information Technology Systems Manager for PG&P he has to ensure the best computer technology is in place to support California's electrical power grid. His success requires a detailed knowledge of the state's entire power infrastructure so that when disasters strike, his team can quickly devise an array of solutions, select the most effective option and implement corrective action. If that means shunting power from region to region based on unpredictable load demands, then Justin handles it. If it means deploying emergency solutions when extreme weather hazards take down parts of the grid, Justin handles it.

When the position of Information Technology Systems *Director* came open after Jay Gramen retired from the post last year, everyone in his team looked to Justin. His broad perspective on the grid, his front-line experience, his hacker-honed computer expertise and coding savvy made him the perfect candidate for the job. But on the day that the posting was awarded to Ben Ferrazzano, Governor White's *son-in-law*, Justin Fry's loyalty to PG&P faltered, and over the next month his career path careened through several wrenching detours.

Two weeks after he re-decorated his office suite, Ferrazzano accused Justin of mishandling the series of power failures that plagued the capital city during the floods and firestorms that raked the Sacramento Valley through the last weeks of summer. Then came Ferrazzano's charge that Justin couldn't guide his ITS team as the demand for climate-change management strategies emerged. "We need a big-picture thinker. Someone with strategic vision,"

Ferrazzano told him, "and, let me be clear on this, there's absolutely no personal offense intended, but you ain't the guy."

"You ain't the guy. *You ain't the guy*," Justin mutters as he adjusts the laptop screen on the coffee table to compensate for the mid-day sunlight streaming over his shoulder onto Uncle Murray's lanai. *What the fuck does Ferrazzano know about the California power grid?* "Nothing!" he shouts and twists his jaw until it cracks with the familiar sound — "*clktz*" — that almost always relieves the tension pulsing through his head.

When Governor White approaches the dais at the rear entrance to the state mansion in Sacramento, Justin taps the "expand" button on his web browser. Edmund White's face fills the screen. "You've turned my job into a political spin machine!" Justin yells at the governor and then, worried that someone in the adjoining condos might overhear him, his voice drops to a whisper: "You *fuck*. You *asshole-fucking fuck!*"

Governor White adjusts the microphone. He smiles. He winks at his press secretary and fumbles some off-the-cuff remarks congratulating the volunteers who saved a yachtsman from the waters off Santa Cruz during the tsunami generated by a western Pacific earthquake. He then turns his head to the camera and begins to recite his prepared text. "Ladies and gentlemen, as you know, we are facing difficult economic times...."

Justin can barely listen to the monotone. "You are *so* white." He glares at the laptop as if he's just recognized exactly how pale the governor is: white hair, white face, white teeth, white shirt, white lies. He's a political albino. The Moby Dick of politicians. "You're already half-dead!" He downs the dregs of his cocktail, turns up the volume on the laptop and retreats to the kitchen to prepare another scotch-and-soda, and then strolls back to the computer, drink in hand, to witness the governor's finale.

" ... as a result, today I have signed the return-to-work order. Any employee of the State of California, or its supported organizations and institutions, who fails to report for duty tomorrow, whether he or she is a union member or not, *will be fired*." Governor White pauses to stare into the camera and nods once to emphasize his conviction that shirkers will suffer the consequences.

"Your mistake, Governor." Justin shakes his head and closes the news feed from CNN. It's a shame the old man would employ these tactics. Not that Justin has any sympathy for the unions but the governor has to appear to pay a price for *something*.

Years ago, in this very room, Uncle Murray spelled out his belief that most union members can't fend for themselves. "They represent a certain kind of un-American weakness that takes shelter in like-minded crowds," he'd said. "Perhaps they're decent individuals, some of them, but none possesses an innovative mind. Can't create anything of their own, and consequently they band together to squeeze their livelihoods out of the men and women who do bring something new and vital into the world."

Justin stands and walks in a tight circle around the room, then returns to the coffee table and waves an open hand at the laptop. "You're *all* garbage," he barks, condemning the governor, Uncle Murray and their tribe of millionaires, a disparate group he imagines barricaded in their mountaintop compounds in the days after the pending collapse.

Shaking his head in exasperation he sits at the table and

unravels a foil-wrapped nugget of cocaine the size of his little toe. With a razor blade fixed between his thumb and index finger, he begins to shave the crystal into fragments on top of a hand mirror. As he dices and slices, he considers all the elements of the plot that he'd concocted over the last month. First, writing the computer code. It's a triumph of ingenuity, a mixture of the CIA's Stuxnet virus, Chinese cyber-espionage, and geek programming with no return address. A hacker bomb that he will launch following a few toots of this precious coke. With three mouse clicks he will precipitate a rotating, massive overload of the California electrical power grid that will result in a cascading failure designed to fry, perhaps even *melt*, every power sub-station throughout the state. Even he, himself, can't know the precise extent of the collapse. Would it take down the neighboring grids in Oregon or Nevada? Trip the wires in Baja and Sonora? "There's no precedent, buddy," he murmurs as the razor lacerates the growing dune of cocaine. "No precedent at all."

Above and beyond the genius of his coding, delivering this blow from the remotest edge of the Union constitutes his real masterstroke — here, from the lanai of his Uncle Murray's condo on Kona Bay on the west coast of the Big Island in Hawaii. When it was clear that the State of California was heading for a do-or-die confrontation with its employees, Justin booked his vacation for a time when he guessed, correctly, (…uh…*HELLO!*) that the political crisis would peak. When the grid collapsed he would be off-stage and minutes later, as the panicked calls came for his assistance, then everyone would realize that Justin was on vacation. Nowhere to be found. Had simply disappeared. Ferrazzano and Governor Father-In-Law would come *crawling* to find him.

A quantum of boredom ticks through him. He pauses from the delicate art of fluffing the cocaine to search his iTunes collection for his favorite mind-whacker from the 1960s, Jimi Hendrix's "Voodoo Child." As the song rolls into its opening verse, he pumps his head to the rhythm.

Once the coke is prepared in two parallel lines of finely granulated powder, he rolls a twenty-dollar bill into a tight flute and presses one end to his nose. He sets the other end at the top of the line and drags it toward him, deftly snorting the fine particles into his right nostril. A pause. A deep breath. A tweak to his sinus. Then he funnels the second line into his left nostril and eases back in the chair. A nodule of hyper-perceptive lucidity attempts to penetrate his mind, bubbles through the fog of his scotch-and-soda combos and then settles atop his cerebral cortex, where it's strategically positioned to direct the ebb and flow of his thoughts. Suddenly, and quite unexpectedly, a blitz of temporal tendonitis ripples through his face and anchors in his jaw. He cranks his mandible sharply to the left. *Clktz.*

When everything settles down and he's centered in the axis of the turning point of the moment, just as "Voodoo Child" rises through Jimi's extended guitar solo, he opens a file on his laptop computer and he clicks on an icon resembling a bass drum that he'd named "Drumbo." A text box appears below the drum that asks, "Do you want to launch Drumbo now?" After he clicks the box marked YES, he enters a password and a follow-up text box appears: "Are you sure you want to launch Drumbo? This action is irreversible." He draws a shallow breath and clicks a button that reads "Launch now." The bass drum disappears in an animated cloud-burst sequence that concludes with a puff of smoke fading into the ether.

As he rides the escalating finale of "Voodoo Child,"

Justin overwrites all the files related to Drumbo, checks to ensure they've been completely eliminated from his computer and then shuts down the laptop. After a moment of contemplation he wanders into Uncle Murray's bedroom to fish his new Abercrombie & Fitch surfer shorts from his suitcase.

Ten minutes later, as he dips his feet into the surf rolling below the high-tide line on Kona Bay he realizes that a stealth surgical team working within the division of cocaine analgesics has pinned rivets into each of his jaw hinges. The rivets are fixed to fibre-thin stainless steel threads that are in turn attached to microscopically small grappling hooks that have been hurled upwards, one through each nostril, where they are now embedded in his sinuses. Probably better to keep your nose and mouth above water, he cautions himself and a spasm shakes through the core of his body when he realizes this advisory is emanating from the recently-appointed Strategic Clarity Director located in his head office. *Remember*, the robo-voice continues, *it's been over twenty years since you last tried to swim.*

He considers the rolling surf coming toward him in rows of five, each one crashing above Jimi's guitar solo, which is now locked in a repeating loop that pulsates in rhythm with the ocean. Despite their height, six or seven feet, he figures, the spray from the imploding waves radiates the warmth from the early afternoon sun. And from that warmth emerges a feeling of security. Of comfort and safety. He pauses a moment to squiggle his toes into the sand beneath the surf. A baby crab is dislodged by his left foot and it scuttles somewhere behind his heel. *Ahhh, life.* Then he steps two, three, four paces forward, feels the sheet of water rising over his thighs. He detects the wet tickle as his testicles wash under a wave that rises to his chest, and then with a sense of certainty, of his *victory*, he dives under the surface.

And as his arms spear before him, in the last instant in which he could push to the surface and breathe, he forces himself down into the long throat of the undertow. From there, close to the very bottom of the world, the sound of the surf submerges in his ears beneath the pounding guitar riffs of Jimi's suicidal genius. His last breath bursts from his lungs in a cascade of bubbles that is instantly swallowed and dissolved in the ebb tide. He feels his face loosen and the muscles that have so long held his being in their grip, relax.

*Clktz.*


Unlike the blackouts over the last few months, Teejay immediately realizes that this episode is different. In the past the lights seemed to fade, fight back, fall off, revive, sputter and then finally expire. Within an hour or two, they'd click back to life as if someone had simply flipped a wall switch in the middle of the night. But this time, as she sits on the toilet in Doyle's apartment, the twin lights above the bathroom mirror glow brighter and brighter, testing the upper limit of their possible radiance. Then with a final gush of brilliance the lamps make a tiny popping sound and the windowless bathroom falls into darkness.

"Jeez. Can you believe it?" she whispers as she completes her inspection of one of the cotton pads from the San Francisco General Hospital. When she and Fay passed the nursing station on their way out of the hospital, one of the nurses slipped a small bundle of pads under Teejay's forearm. "Some spotting will be normal for the first while," the nurse said. "Then it should turn a rusty brown. But if it gets worse, worse than your period, say, then you need to see Dr. K., even if the strike is still on." She stared at Teejay without blinking. "Do you understand?" Teejay nodded. Apart from her mother, she'd never talked to anyone about her period before. She'd had it twice and then it stopped completely until the miscarriage.

She liked that word, a word that Dr. K. used after she came out of the obstetrics ward. *Miscarriage*. It sounded like she'd dropped something, as if it were just an accident. And like all accidents you were told to clean it up and then forget about it. "There's no point crying over spilt milk." That's what her seventh grade teacher, Ms. Stokes, used to say before Teejay left Anna Yates Elementary School to start home-schooling. She missed Ms. Stokes and wondered if *she'd* ever miscarried and had to check for spotting.

And at this exact moment, while she thinks about Ms. Stokes and as she examines the pad, the electric power surges in the twin light bulbs above the bathroom mirror and then it fails completely. In the black silence it takes her another few minutes to finish the routine she'd developed in the past two days. To adjust, she pretends to be blind, to imagine how an unsighted girl would clean herself and dispose of the pad, apply a new one, flush the toilet, wash up, make sure everything is perfect so that no one, especially Doyle and James, will know her secret.

"Teejay, you okay, Honey?" Her mother calls softly through the bathroom door, for the second time in two minutes.

"I told you, I'm okay. It's just dark in here." She slips one of the pills from Dr. K. onto her tongue and washes it down with a handful of tap water.

"Yeah-yeah, the power went out everywhere." Fay stands at the door listening for her daughter, her ear hovering an inch from the wood paneling. "We're going to have something to eat. Okay?"

Teejay opens the door. "All right," she says, her eyebrows notched expectantly with the obvious question: *Why are you so worried?* She scans Doyle's living room and sees that Mavis has returned from her meeting. "Okay, let's eat."

James lights three candles in the kitchen alcove while Doyle sets a platter of chicken salad sandwiches on the table. He's decorated the rim of the plate with strawberries and finger-length spears of pineapple. He places a second dish beside it, a serving of homemade French fries. "Why not celebrate?" he chirps and scans the guests in his home. A rarity: four friends ready to enjoy a meal at his table.

"What're we celebrating?" Mavis lifts a wedge of sandwich from the plate and begins to eat. She's hungry and needs to restore her spirits after the meeting with Dansky.

"Well," James begins, "while you were gone, we were all looking at the maps." He points to the *Readers' Digest World Atlas* lying open on the floor.

"Did you know that Doyle has twin boys and one of them lives on Salt Spring Island?" Teejay sits next to Mavis, takes a sandwich and then adds, "His name is Jesse and he has a baby girl named Gale. You spell it *Gale*, as in storm," she continues, "because she was born during a blizzard. And since Blizzard is hopeless as a name, she became Gale."

"A baby?" Mavis nods at Doyle, smiles as though she's just starting to sniff their conspiracy. She takes another bite of her sandwich and surveys the group. The mood of expectation is visceral. She can tell they're excited by the possibility of ... what? A holiday in the northwest? "So?"

"So we want to visit Salt Spring Island," James says. "Just to see what it's like."

"You're all welcome to stay," Doyle says. "I talked to Jesse just before the power went out. They've got a five-acre hobby farm and there's room for everyone. At least for a few weeks." He places a canary-yellow teapot in the middle of the table and sets a mug in front of each of his guests. "And you should get used to this. Canadians brew tea in tea*pots*, not cups."

Everyone studies him as Doyle tugs a wool-knit cover over the pot.

"Why did you put a hat on the teapot?" Teejay begins to giggle at this bit of madness, shakes her head as she looks from Doyle to the teapot and back to the others.

"It's called a tea cozy. With the power off we have to keep the tea warm."

"A tea cozy?" Teejay's laughter rises as her face breaks into a broad, unrestrained grin. "*A tea cozy?*" She can barely speak.

Doyle watches the elation flood through Teejay's face. Her eyes begin tearing as she laughs. For the first time Doyle feels as though he's completely arrived in San Francisco. Here he is, all ten trillion cells of him harmoniously united in one place and time, in the company of friends and all of them full of good cheer. "Yes," he says and he knows if he repeats this once more, Teejay will go over the top. "It's a *friggin' tea cozy!*"

The room erupts. Teejay's laughter is now uncontainable and she flops onto the floor and rolls toward the atlas, hugs the open pages to her chest as she gasps for air. Doyle, convinced that he's the source of this craziness, howls and barks and yelps. James slaps the palms of his hands on the table in a broken drumbeat. Only Fay experiences any hesitation. Her giggling falters and she begins to cry, but after a moment her laughing resumes. Wrapping an arm around her shoulder, Mavis brushes a tear from her cheek. Everyone is transfixed by Teejay sprawling on the floor. She is breathless, ecstatic — once more infused with joy.

"Can we talk?" A few hours later, as dusk approaches, Fay takes Mavis aside and slants her head at an angle to the door.

"Sure," Mavis says and then turns toward the kitchen where James and Teejay are washing the dishes. "We're going for a walk around the block," she tells them.

She opens the door and leads the way down the staircase and onto the street. As they turn the corner onto Dwight Way they can see the fire in People's Park, now tended by a group of thirty or forty people. Occasionally someone will toss another chunk of wood into the flames. Something about the atmosphere worries Mavis, but she decides not to say anything about it to Fay. Instead, they turn away from the park and saunter past the homeless wanderers beginning to stake out a place for the night along the sidewalks. They pass a few other pedestrians, people out on a stroll together, laughing nervously as if they are entering an uncertain world.

"So look," Fay says when it's apparent that Mavis is waiting for her to speak. "For the first time in months, maybe even a year, I can feel things getting better."

"Really?" Mavis flattens her voice, an attempt to conceal her surprise. "Tell me about it."

"The crazy part is that it started getting better after the

fire. I know how horrible this sounds, but when Louis got us out of that apartment — and it's so terrible that he had to die, that I can't even *think* about that part of it — but from that point on Teejay and I turned a corner. Even in the hospital, with the miscarriage and everything, no matter what Janice Slitz is planning, things are so much better."

"Like what?" Mavis steers them toward an empty bench next to the sidewalk. It would be nice to sit and talk for as long as Fay needs to get everything out that she's been holding back. The list of disasters that have befallen them seems to grow with each passing day. It's remarkable that Fay can consider any of this as a turning point.

"Teejay, of course." She angles her thumb back toward the apartment and smiles as she remembers the uncontainable joy in her daughter. "I mean, I haven't seen her *laughing* like that in months."

"It was wonderful. It really was." Mavis brushes the bench with the sleeve of her jacket and sits. "Hey, let's sit here."

"She just seemed so" — she waves a hand — *"free."* Having found the word she needs and surprised by the simplicity of it, she settles beside Mavis and smiles.

"Mmm." Mavis nods. She knows this of course, she just needs to let Fay articulate it in her own way. "Free of what, do you think?"

Fay fixes her eyes on a house a few doors along the street, a white stucco home with a wrought-iron Juliet balcony on the second story. "Free of the pregnancy," she says after a moment. She's never talked about this before. Never used the word pregnancy in reference to her own daughter. "Do you think that makes me a bad mother? Because of what happened to Teejay, I mean."

Mavis turns her head to Fay and catches her eyes. "No."

"No?" Fay presses the palms of her hands together. "So what do you think it makes me, then?"

"At this point in the game," she says, "I think it makes you free, too." Then she remembers Janice Slitz and the meeting with Philip Box and adds, "At least for a while."

"Yeah-yeah. For a while." Fay makes a comb of her fingers and drags it through the length of her hair. "Which is what I really need you to tell me. You've already explained it in general, but I need the details. About what will happen next. And *how*."

"Well." Mavis exhales a long stream of air and glances at the homes along the street. Without the street lamps and house lights, the neighborhood seems unfamiliar, unknowable. "The governor announced a back-to work order and…." she stops herself and looks at Fay. "You know, Fay, what they're going to do … it's not very good."

Fay nods. She still holds a band of hair in her fingers. She gives a light tug and then her hand falls to her lap. "But you have to tell me." She looks away and then back to Mavis. "And you have to be honest."

Mavis narrows her eyes. It's true. Ready or not, Fay needs to hear what's coming so that she can prepare. "All right." She considers how to proceed. "So the court has already received an order to apprehend Teejay. Once the family services unit is up and running after the strike, she'll be taken into custody and given up to foster care. That means she'll be assigned to foster parents. Likely at a group home." Mavis lets this information settle in and then she adds, "You might not see her again until she's twenty-one. Even then, it's not certain."

Fay's head wobbles backward. She can feel the old chaos welling in her stomach, ready to burst through her again, into her hands, into the paint brushes, into the mad paintings that will rush into the world. She tightens her chest and forces it down, caps the well and locks it shut. "When?"

For a moment Mavis is unsure what Fay is asking. Then she realizes that for Fay, there is only a single, isolated, turning point in time: the moment when her daughter will be taken from her. "It could take a while," she says, but she knows it all depends on the individuals involved in the case, and she frowns when she considers who they are. "On the other hand, it's up to people like Janice Slitz. And Dr. Box. With them involved, it could be tomorrow."

Fay pinches her lips together. "I hate that bitch."

Mavis looks away and nods in sympathy. "I guess we both do."

"So be it." Fay draws a deep breath, relieved to know that Mavis shares her opinion of Janice Slitz.

They sit for a few moments. A few cars pass along the road, their headlamps the only illumination sweeping through the failing evening light. Above them an array of stars begin to blink. Mavis admires them in silence, calmly, happy to assign the next few hours to Fay, knowing that all she has to do is wait for Fay's fears and doubts. Whatever misery might emerge from Fay, Mavis will embrace it despite the question that has been prying at her conscience over the past week: why does she, Mavis, *care*? What is it about this broken woman and her remarkable child that has anchored itself in the middle of her life? And it's not just her. It's the same care and attention that flows from James and now from Doyle, too. Maybe in some abstract, ideal world there's a corresponding balance between poverty and plenty, between need and generosity. Was she trying to turn this fantasy into reality? Is that what they're all trying to accomplish? Yes, that must be it: to bring Teejay and Fay into balance with their own lives.

When she's had time to gather her thoughts, Fay leans forward to make sure she has Mavis's attention. "When you said that Teejay was finally free, and that *I'm free*, that means we have a choice." Fay bunches her fingers into fists in front of her. She weighs one fist in the air, and then the other. "When do you think *I ever* had a choice about *anything* in my life?"

Mavis feels the gravity in Fay's voice and shakes her head. "I don't know."

"I can either take what they're trying to do to me" — she releases the fingers of one fist to reveal its emptiness and clenches the other with renewed force — "or I can take my child and go. We can *disappear*," she whispers with certainty, and her second hand flutters open and glides into the air, a newborn sparrow taking flight.

Mavis smiles. "You know," she says, "I think you probably can."

"We're going up to Canada and we're not coming back."

Fay's certainty is something so rare that Mavis doesn't want to dilute it with any more talk. She stretches her spine up and through her shoulders, and with her hand she gestures that they should be getting back home now. In the distance she can hear the brief wail of a police car or an ambulance and she feels a vague reassurance that some part of the city's emergency network is still intact. The sound of African drumming rises from the far end of People's Park where a dense crowd of people surrounds the well-tended fire. Nightfall is descending and the neighborhood is full with the hoots and cries of young men and women usurping new powers in the darkness.

As they near the apartment, Mavis decides to ask the question she's been harboring for days. "You don't have to tell me this, Fay. But I was wondering something about Teejay.... About the baby's — "

"The baby's father." Fay finishes the thought, the one statement that she could never bring herself to express openly until now. She feels the blood pulsing through her body. Everything good about her life seems to be opening up with all this talk.

"Yes."

"I'm not saying it's certain, but it could be Teejay's father. Raymond Guzman. " She pauses to let this horror sink in and then pass from her thoughts. One day perhaps it would pass away completely. "But I never married him," she adds and realizes this was the last time she ever made a choice that counted for anything, even though it was not a choice but a kind of default. An evasion of things, not a way forward like the path she is set to embark on now.


By the time Mavis and Fay return to Doyle's apartment everyone else has reached an unspoken consensus: that they're all going to Salt Spring Island, that they would leave first thing the next morning, and that they want to drive there with Mavis in the Prius. When Mavis thought about it later, she realized that no specific decision was ever made, no council held, no votes taken. Maybe that was why things later seemed to wander on a course so random and unpredictable: no one sat down to make a plan, to figure out how much money they'd need, the food, the clothing, the gas for the car. No one realized they'd need passports, except Doyle, and that idea only occurred to him when they'd driven halfway through Oregon.

Fortunately, Doyle's travel preparations are dead easy. All he needs to do is load his belongings into his bag and walk out the door, lock it, and leave the key under the mat. Since Fay and Teejay have been living out of daypacks for the past week, their arrangements are even more basic. But this spare simplicity is complicated by the blackout and the fact that everyone has to navigate the small space of Doyle's apartment with the three candles he borrowed from Mavis. And soon they all have to confront the psychological blackout that accompanies the collapse of the power grid. There's no TV, no radio, no internet or cell phone connectivity, no word on how long the city will have to endure without light and heat, no confirmation from the mayor or the governor that food and water will be available tomorrow or in the following days.

Once they make their way downstairs to their own apartment, James and Mavis enter a void of possibilities. James, whom Mavis has always seen as nearly clairvoyant when it comes to making the right decisions, begins to navigate by such microscopic measures that she worries he's completely lost sight of the big picture. Instead of determining what highways they need to take to the border, and where to board the ferry to Salt Spring Island, and how many days the journey will take, he turns fitful about minutiae: whether he should take sandals or hiking boots. Did it make sense to bring his books, and how many? Should it be his old favorites, or just those he hasn't read?

"This is crazy," she says to him as she sorts through her drawers and loads a few items into her suitcase. "I mean, how long do you think we'll be gone?"

After bumbling through his own internal blackout James manages to divine an organizing principle. "I've just figured it out." In mid-stride between the bathroom and the kitchen he stops himself and looks at his wife. "Pack as if we're not coming back."

"We're not coming back?"

"No, we might come back, we very probably will come back, but pack now, tonight, *as if* we're not coming back." He smiles at her, at the zen-ness of the organizing principle he's discovered.

Mavis pauses to study James's face to determine just how serious he is. But in the candlelight, everything appears shadowed and elongated including his intentions. "Well *I'm* definitely coming back. Don't get me wrong. I'm committed to getting Fay and Teejay to Salt Spring Island, but after that — I mean, we still have a life here. I'm still thinking of this as a holiday. Like a vacation," she adds when James doesn't respond.

James looks at her and shrugs, a gesture suggesting that the life they possess in Berkeley has changed so fundamentally in the past week that the traces of their past existence is quickly fading.

"What about all our stuff?" Her hand sweeps across the apartment, to their bed, their dresser, their clothes and books, and Papa Helm's chair.

"I thought about that," James says. "I'll get Rosa to look after everything. She always says she loves this place. And I know she'd like to move up here from her suite in the basement. We'll let her take over the rent. Just while we're gone."

Mavis sits on the edge of the bed to think this over. She likes Rosa and knows she wouldn't damage anything, or worse, sell it off for a few hundred dollars. "But what about the *us* that's still here?" She considers the wonderful dinners they cooked together. The times they meditated together, their long sessions of glorious, unforgettable sex. They had *tantric* sex on this very spot where she now sits.

"That," — James sits beside her and kisses her ear and

then continues in a murmur — "we can take *that* with us no matter where we go. In fact, we can have it again anytime. Right now, if you want it."

As Raymond Guzman walks along the sidewalk toward Berkeley he settles his Lil' Slugger baseball bat against his shoulder so the fat part of the wood stock rests on the nylon strap of his backpack instead of slapping against his collar bone. Despite its three-quarter size there'd been a few times in the night when all he had to do was shift the bat in his hands or over his shoulder and soon the shadows that were following him faded into the distance. No surprise to that. But what did surprise him was the smoky haze building above San Francisco. This was no mid-autumn fog rolling in from the ocean. From the east side of the bay he could see a steady glow intensify through the night and in the still air the smoke seemed to hang above the concrete towers as if it was waiting to flush through the entire city.

God's own redemption, that's what it was. He'd heard a few sirens wailing, cop cars and fire trucks, he figured, but after a few hours they began to fade. No surprise to that, either. Without power, they couldn't fill their gas tanks and apart from the generators running the hospitals and a few other emergency centers, everyone was still trapped in the blackout. He knew the chaos in the city could get out of hand when the fires started spreading from one park to another. With the fall chill pushing down to the freezing mark in the middle of the night and no electric power to warm the street shelters it was understandable that people would build fires just to keep warm.

By the time he reaches People's Park Guzman figures it's about three or four in the morning. About a dozen people linger around the fire at the far end of the block and he makes his way there and squats on the ground just close enough so the heat can warm his face, but far enough to one side so that he doesn't have to talk to any vagrants.

He sets the fat tip of the baseball bat on the grass and rests the knob end against his knee. He slips the pack from his shoulders and opens a can of tuna with a pocketknife and begins to eat. All these things he'd found: the food, the backpack, the bat, the knife. All of it abandoned, waiting for him, it seems, to pick up and make his own. Matthew, chapter 7, verse 7: "Ask and it will be given to you; seek and you will find." Besides the Lord's Prayer and the Twenty-Third Psalm, it's the only Biblical passage he ever managed to memorize by heart.

And what's most important to him now will emerge from Matthew 7:7. What he is seeking and what he must find is a few minutes of time, in person, with Fay and Teejay, a moment when he can confess to them the terrible crime he brought into the world. It's all the more crazy because the sin is already known both to Fay and to his girl, Teejay. But what's not known by anyone except to him, Raymond Luis Guzman and to Jesus Himself, is his own naked contrition. He knows the only people who can relieve this pain are Fay and Teejay. And he knows they don't have to forgive him. He's sure they would never do that even if it were within their power, which it is not, of course, because only God possesses such powers. But if they will just hear him, just listen to the pain in his voice as he lays the poison fruit of his trespasses at their feet and then smashes it before their eyes, then his confession may deliver him from evil. That is his hope and his prayer. The miracle he seeks.

When he sorts all this out in his mind and once more rehearses exactly how he will approach the confrontation, he wanders across the park and settles opposite the white apartment building where he believes Fay and Teejay are sleeping through the night. They slept there the day before he followed them to the third-floor apartment in Haight-Ashbury and now, in this brief time before the end of days, they are sleeping here again. In the morning, when they emerge, he will speak to them. And he prays that God Himself will make them listen.

By six AM there's just enough power left in Janice Slitz's cell-phone battery to trip the alarm clock app and rouse her from bed. By seven AM she's showered in the tepid water, eaten a breakfast of sliced banana and room-temperature yoghurt, and in the absence of fresh ground coffee, forced herself to down a glass of tap water.

As she walks up the last hill to her office she wonders how long the city water supply can be sustained without electrical power. There'd be some interesting physics involved in calculating that answer, she figures. A combination of gravitational pressure generated by the water flowing along the two-hundred-mile transit from the Hetch Hetchy Reservoir, the volume of water still available in the city pipe system, and the rate of usage. How different her life would be now if she'd stuck out her science degree instead of switching to sociology. Still, her new job in family services has one huge advantage, the driving force that inspires her day after day: providing help — genuine physical, moral and emotional support — to the people who need it most. Children like Teejay Flood.

Much to her dismay, when Janice finally climbs the stone staircase and enters the lobby of her office, she immediately encounters a new roadblock to achieving her mission. No doubt one of the many she'll encounter in the years ahead, she assures herself. In fact her brief career has dished up a series of impediments and blockades intended (she might even say *fated* if she believed in such things) to stem her from her task. And Gerrard Jackson is the new barrier-du-jour.

"Simpson told me this morning that only class-A apprehensions can be filled. At least until someone figures out how to switch the power back on." Gerrard Jackson stares down the length of his nose and holds his eyes on Janice as he tells her this. He's twenty years her senior and very skilled at relaying direct orders, especially orders that keep him in the office and away from the usual terrors involved with prying trembling children from their hysterical parents' arms. *Nobody* likes that, he tells himself, except for Janice Slitz. She's the only staffer who possesses an actual zest for the job. Whatever her motivations, Gerrard can't bring himself to ask her to reveal the beliefs that drive her particular zeal; he simply doesn't want to hear much of anything she has to say. She's what Wayne Simpson calls a *career jetliner*. Upwardly mobile and cleared for lift off. She's everything Gerrard isn't: young, educated, a talker, a looker, a woman, ethnic. Ethnic, that is, if you consider her second-generation German roots to be ethnic, which somehow manages to trump Gerrard's standing as a thousand-plus-generation black man.

"This *is* a class-A apprehension," Janice counters. She waves a file containing the certified apprehension order in front of Gerrard and scans the office. Besides Wayne Simpson, whom she spies cowering in his corner office, there're only four staff on hand. None of the other hundred and sixteen employees reside within walking distance of the office so they're staying at home, she figures. Or using the blackout as an excuse to extend the illegal strike and defy Governor White.

"Don't you think it's odd?" she asks, pondering the possibility that the union is behind the blackout.

"What's that?" Gerrard tilts his head, surprised to hear her asking his opinion.

"That minutes after the governor issued yesterday's back-to-work order the power cut out."

Gerrard purses his lips and wipes a hand across the stubble on his face. "Likely a coincidence," he offers.

"Or a conspiracy. You can find coincidence anywhere you look for it," she replies and tilts her head toward the garage at the rear of the building. "Come on, let's grab a car. And make sure you pick one that's gassed up, okay? None of the gas stations will be open."

Gerrard narrows his eyes. Somehow, she's brushed off his idea about the blackout being coincidence without giving him a chance to show her that pure coincidence is much more likely than some cock-eyed, one-in-a-million conspiracy. It's simply statistical. Damn it, without any of her diplomas and degrees, he understood probability theory and knew the underlying mathematical facts. He'll have to explain it all to her once they get into the car.

He grabs his jacket and hat and walks down to the dispatch cage where Mickelson stashes the keys in the second drawer of the filing cabinet. Maybe you should've stayed home today, too, he tells himself. Instead you'll be playing chauffeur to the career jetliner. Prepare for lift-off.

By the time Doyle and James load their bags and packs into the Prius it's almost nine o'clock. Apart from the smoke from the fire that's been burning in People's Park through the night, the air looks clear and dry in the distance. A good day for a long drive, James decides as he presses his fists into the backside of his waist and stretches the kinks out of his spine. "Do you think it's too early to knock on Rosa Zane's door?" he asks.

"Why, does she want to join us?" Doyle shrugs, unable to imagine how anyone else could fit into the Prius. It'll be crowded enough, even with Teejay, slight as she is, straddling the middle of the rear bench.

"No, not that" — he waves a hand — "I just want her to handle the rent and mind our furniture and belongings once we leave. And to tell her to let the landlord know where we've gone."

"You sure about that?" Doyle frowns and a look of doubt clouds his face. "I don't think anyone should know we're even leaving town, let alone where we're headed. I mean, given Teejay's situation," he adds when James seems unable to recall the court order to apprehend Teejay.

James blinks as the realization sinks through him. "Right. Of course. I'm not awake yet," he explains and briefly drifts in the memory of the long night he spent in Mavis's arms. He waves his hand again and makes his way around the side of the building to Rosa's apartment door. "I'll just tell her to keep an eye on things."

Doyle frowns again and shuts the hatch-back on the Prius. He knows he's not the only one to understand the gravity of Teejay's situation, but once he and James and Mavis enable Fay and Teejay's escape they'll all be legally liable for some damn thing, he's sure of it. He can imagine drawn pistols, handcuffs, screaming, gun-shots. Just make sure you get home in one piece, he advises himself. When he sees James return from Rosa's apartment Doyle walks back to the house to tell Fay and Teejay that everything's ready and they can climb into the car and begin the long drive through Oregon up to the north end of Washington State. And then, back home.

As the landlord leads Janice Slitz and Gerrard Jackson through Fay's Emeryville apartment they soon suspect that Fay and her daughter haven't been living there for the past week. They descend the long narrow staircase and stand on the sidewalk below the old "Buxton's Meats" sign and Janice considers their options.

"We had to check there, first," she explains to Gerrard and leads the way back to the car, a mid-90s Ford Crown Victoria, one of the re-purposed (and re-painted) SFPD cars with a secured cage in the back seat that Mickelson always has gassed-up and ready for emergencies. "I know they don't have any money, so that means they're probably taking shelter in Berkeley."

"Is that where the father lives?" Gerrard strolls behind her, takes his time to reach the curb before he clicks the door locks open, just so she realizes that she has to wait on him before things happen. Before doors will open.

"Guzman?" Janice shakes her head in disgust. "Nobody's seen him for months."

Gerrard climbs into the driver's seat and contemplates the neighborhood. Very few cars are moving along the road. On the other hand, the sidewalks are busy. Everyone's pushing forward looking wary, distressed. He watches them with an abstract interest, and as Janice buckles her seat belt, he fits the key into the ignition and waits.

"What are you stalling for?"

Gerrard ignores this. "So where is it exactly, that we're going to? In Berkeley, I mean."

When she detects a note of insubordination, Janice narrows her eyes. "To her therapist. Actually she's not even certified." When this fails to prompt Gerrard to start the car, she continues. "I have good reason to suspect that Fay and her daughter have taken shelter with Mavis Helm. I've got her address. Let's go!" she says with exasperation as Gerrard simply nods his head and the fingers of his right hand idly stroke the key chain.

"Let me see the court order," he says in a flat tone moderated by years of procedural routine. "You don't see many orders covering more than one victim address. You told me we'd find the girl and her mother here. Now you're telling me they're in Berkeley."

"Fuck." Janice's voice is narrow, icy. She digs through her bag and produces the file. "Here. And the address is *not* restricted."

"Don't you be saying *fuck* to me." Gerrard doesn't bother to glance at her as he flips through the file. He's dealt with too many of her kind too many times to know the rules of their game: give an inch; she'll take a mile.

"All right, I'm sorry." She draws a shallow breath, realizing that she could be on the edge of a harassment charge if she doesn't cater to Gerrard. Just a little.

"*You're* sorry?" Gerrard savors the moment before he closes the file. "I don't see any address in Berkeley. And no reference to Mavis Helm."

"*That's* in my phone." Janice clutches her phone in her fist and gives it a shake. She decides not to tell Gerrard that the charge on the phone battery is so low she might not be able to retrieve any contact numbers or addresses. Then she remembers the charger in her purse and plugs it into the slot for the cigarette lighter below the dashboard. When the phone fails to begin its charging sequence she stares into

Gerrard's eyes. "Could you at least turn on the ignition so I can charge my phone?"

Gerrard tightens his lips and after a moment he turns the key. The engine starts and a flashing amber light dances across the cell phone display.

"Thank-you," she says, a little more brightly, trying to inject some warmth into her voice. She gazes at the screen on her phone and clicks on her contacts. "They live in Berkeley. On the corner of Regent Street and Dwight Way, next to People's Park. Do you know where that is?"

"Yes, I do." Gerrard checks the traffic and when he figures he's made his point, he pulls the Crown Vic into the street. "But for the record, I'm telling you this is outside normal protocols. *Jetliner,*" he adds under his breath.

*Jetliner?* What the hell is Jetliner supposed to mean? Janice decides to let this go and settles in for the drive. She knows that soon enough she'll have to rely on Gerrard and there's no point wasting the delicate truce she's established by trying to de-code some personal jargon. Not now. And most definitely not today.


When everyone is settled in the Prius a giddiness seizes Mavis, the sort of light-hearted expectation she shared with her sister whenever they were about to start a long trip with Papa Helm. "Everybody buckled up?" she asks, her voice in mock baritone to resemble her grandfather's resonate confidence. "Teejay? You buckled up?" She looks in the rearview mirror, adjusts it slightly. Teejay is positioned between Fay and Doyle in the back seat. They appear to be crowded but not completely uncomfortable.

"Yup."

"Fay? Doyle?" She smiles, convinced by the authority of her voice.

"Yeah-yeah."

"Ready for lift-off!"

She looks at James and he smiles, pulls his seat belt with a thumb and lets it slap against his chest. "All set, Captain America. Did you fill the tank?"

"Two days ago, thank god. Plus a wash and wax job," Mavis says with a measure of pride. "It could be a long time before we can get gas, but we should be able to drive at least four hundred miles on what we've got." She presses the start button, pulls on the wheel and begins to turn into the traffic lane. But before she can drive two feet someone jumps in front of the car and waves a hand as if he's flagging down a taxi.

"What the *hell!*" She pumps the brake and the car lurches to a halt. *"Who is this?"*

Mavis soon realizes that the interloper is no passing pedestrian desperate for a ride. Directly in front of the car Raymond Guzman drops to his knees on the asphalt and turns his face toward the sky, his lips murmuring a private incantation. As he kneels he peels off his shirt, kisses the crucifix that hangs from his neck and then lifts the Lil' Slugger baseball bat in both hands above his head so that his extended arms and the length of the bat make an equilateral triangle with his head anchored in the lowest angle. He stares into the car and when he sees Fay, he locks his eyes on her and drops the thin end of the bat from his left hand and begins to tap the knob against the back of his shoulders.

"Forgive me!" he cries and he soon establishes a rhythm by alternating the strikes to his shoulder blades with tight, bruising whacks to the front of his broad chest.

"Fay, you must forgive me!" he moans in a weeping lament.

A jolt of panic grips Fay and she stabs at the door lock to ensure it's closed. "It's Raymond."

"Who?" James swivels around and immediately sees the fear in Fay's eyes.

"Raymond." This time her voice is a whisper and a hand curls over her open mouth.

"Teejay's father," Mavis says evenly. When she sees the desperation in Raymond's face, she turns off the engine, worried that somehow Raymond will fall under the wheels and she'll drive over him.

Guzman, his eyes still locked on Fay, continues to flail himself. After three, five, ten strokes he realizes that he can endure this penance, that he can rise above the pain and accept the punishment that will yield his redemption. He begins to turn the bat against his biceps, slapping one side and then hitting the other. With each strike he calls out, "You must forgive me."

"My god, stop him," Doyle says and he opens his door and steps out of the car. But before he can move forward, James swings his door open, blocking Doyle's advance.

"Raymond." James walks around the car door to Raymond's left side, just out of reach of a wild swing that might come his way. "Raymond, you're going to hurt yourself."

A layer of sweat glistens on Raymond's face and he tightens his jaw. He can hear James talking to him, but he knows that he cannot break the execution of his penance until Fay grants him forgiveness. He begins to strike his neck and jaws and he clenches his teeth as the beating reduces him to a point of submission.

"Raymond. Take a deep breath." James eases a step

closer. "If you don't take a deep breath you're going to pass out. Then you'll *have* to stop," he adds hoping this bit of logic will force Raymond to pause long enough for James to seize the baseball bat.

As Doyle stands beside the open door he can hear Fay whimpering in a low, wheezing pant. He looks back into the car. Teejay clutches her mother's hand, rocks it back and forth in time to the sound of the bat striking Raymond's flesh. A crowd is beginning to build on the sidewalk, everyone in horror at what they are witnessing.

"The guy's crazy!" someone exclaims.

"Yeah, but don't be tryin' to stop him."

"Dumb fuck'll slug you, too."

As the commotion stirs, more people drift over from the fire pit at the far end of the park. Doyle works his way toward James, but ensures the car door is still ajar in case he has to dash back to safety.

"Raymond, just try to feel the air going in and out of your lungs," James continues, his voice low and steady as if he's describing the mechanics of breathing to someone who has lost the capacity to live.

Raymond's face now drips with beads of perspiration that run down his neck to his shoulders. His chest and arms are swelling with prune-colored welts. The pain has reached a point of numbness and a fog has filled his mind. The air is thick with noisy anarchy: the soft thunking of the bat on his flesh, the crowd moaning, some of them egging him on, the muffled exhaust of the odd car passing in the street. But through the chaos he can make out the voice of this stranger standing before him, talking as steady as a tidal flow pulling the loose pebbles from the shoreline: "Take a deep breath. You can feel that, can't you? That's the outside world going inside you, man. It's a gift. *A gift.* Take it in and feel it." For a moment, Raymond pauses, takes a sip of the air, *tastes it* as it enters his mouth and funnels into his chest.

And in that brief pause James steps forward and clamps the bat in both his hands and lifts it straight into the air and out of Raymond's clenched fist. "You can stop that now," he says and he stares at a strand of damp hair fallen across Raymond's forehead. "No one wants you to do that. Least of all Fay and Teejay."


"There they are!" Janice Slitz points her hand to the Prius still angled half-in, half-out of the parking slot at the curb beside People's Park. "We've got to get them before they make a break!"

As he lifts his foot from the accelerator, Gerrard Jackson stares across the road. A crowd of about thirty people stands in a crescent-shaped arc across the lawn facing a blue Prius with its two right-hand doors swung open toward the sidewalk. Three or four of them are recording the spectacle on cell phones. A badly beaten man kneels in front of the vehicle and above him stands a bearded six-footer holding a bat in his fist, and behind him stands another man, perhaps five years older than Gerrard, waving everyone back toward the sidewalk with an calm, open gesture of his left hand. Gerrard eases the Crown Vic forward as the engine idles and he looks around for a place to park. "I don't see the girl. Or her mother," he says to Janice.

"They're in the back of that car. And Mavis is driving it. Come on, we don't have time to park!" As the car coasts along the road she opens her door and unclips her seat belt.

"Don't you — " But Gerrard is too late. Before he can say another word, Janice steps out of the moving vehicle. Instead of planting her foot on the asphalt, her right ankle twists under the gliding motion and she crashes headfirst toward the road. As her hands break her fall, the flesh of her right palm tears open. Gerrard pumps the brake and the rear tire stops inches from Janice's foot. He cuts the ignition, clicks on the emergency flashers and races around the car to pick her up. As he lifts her shoulders and props her against the side of the Crown Victoria all he can think of is the series of mistakes that she's making.

Janice bites her lower lip to divert the pain in her ankle and her hand. "I'm okay," she insists. "Just help me get up and get the girl."

Gerrard braces her under the shoulders again and when she can stand she takes another moment to brush herself off. Her right hand is gouged. A two-inch patch of skin is shredded and blood seeps into her palm. She clasps it in her left hand and leads the way around the car toward the park. "Come on," she calls over her shoulder, the pain evident in her voice.

This's going sideways, he tells himself, but despite his intuition Gerrard straightens his jacket and follows as Janice hobbles across the road to the Prius.

"Fay Flood, I've got a certified order from the State of California to apprehend your daughter, Teresa Jacinta Flood." Janice sets her jaw and braces herself about a foot from the car door. When Fay fails to open her door Janice peers through the smoked-glass window and pries her fingers into the door handle and heaves upwards. When she realizes it's locked, her hand slips away leaving a trace of blood on the blue paint of the Prius and she limps around the back of the car to the open door on the right side.

Gerrard follows five steps behind her and as he begins to assess the situation, he calls to Janice in a voice just loud enough to be heard above the noise of the crowd. "If it comes down to it, you let me lift the girl out of the car."

Janice leans into the open doorway and when she makes eye contact with Fay she does her best to apply a smile to her lips. "Fay, we're going to make this as easy as possible on everyone. Please unbuckle Teejay's seatbelt and help her out of the car."

"Mom?" Teejay looks at Janice and then to her mother and over to Mavis. "Mavis? What's happening?"

Mavis turns her head toward Janice and narrows her eyes. "You have no legal right to enter this car without a warrant."

"I have something better than that." Janice turns her chin just enough to suggest that she has everything she needs to do whatever she pleases. "I have a court order to apprehend this child." She reaches into the car, across Teejay's waist, and tries to unclasp the seatbelt.

A loud wail of despair bursts from Fay's lungs and she begins to flail her hands against Janice as she struggles with the seatbelt. "No!" she cries, "NO-NO-NO-NO-NO!"

"What the hell is going on?!" Three women in the crowd standing closest to the car have diverted their attention from Raymond to Janice and Gerrard.

"Hey, let that kid alone!" one of the men yells and steps toward Gerrard.

Two others begin to record the unfolding scene on their cell phones.

"Please, let me handle this," Gerrard's voice drops to a near whisper as he speaks to Janice. "Just back out of there and let me do it."

The pain ripping through Janice's ankle and her hand begins to surge through the rest of her body. With a final stab at the seat belt buckle, she realizes she cannot fend off

Fay *and* free the child. A moment of clarity strikes her. She realizes she has to back out of the car and she decides, all right — *okay*, let Gerrard handle this now, especially now that she sees the blood from her hand smeared across Teejay's jeans and t-shirt. She pushes herself backwards with both hands, stumbles a little as she transfers her weight to her feet, and then rolls against the side of the Prius where she braces herself and lifts the heel of her injured foot a few inches off the road so that just her toes are touching the asphalt.

Then Gerrard slides into the car, sits beside Teejay and nods to her, his head bobbing up and down as a warm, homely smile draws across his face. "Honey, your mom and your friends can all come with us. We're not about to take you *from* anyone." He continues to smile and in one motion, he gently reaches over Teejay's waist and unclips the seatbelt.

"No," Fay says, the terror now depleted from her body. Her cry has been reduced to mere bleating, the struggle dissolved to acceptance.

"Get out of my car." Mavis's voice is steely, unforgiving.

"Yes, ma'am, I will," Gerrard replies and draws Teejay by the elbow as he steps onto the street and slides her out of the car.

The crowd has now completely surrounded the Prius. "Let that kid go," someone yells with contempt. "Don't you think you've done enough damage already?" Six people are now recording the episode on their phones.

Gerrard's left hand maintains a grip on Teejay's elbow as he scans the crowd. He eyes Janice Slitz doubtfully. Her face is drawn with thin rivulets of pain, a smudge of blood is streaked under her right cheek and she's balanced on one foot as she leans against the car. "I want you to go slow," he whispers to her. "I want you to lead the way through the crowd to our car. Find a way through the women and don't say a *fuckin'* thing." He looks at her directly, just so she knows who can use that word and when.

Janice gnashes her teeth together and with one hand frog-hopping on the trunk she presses her way behind the Prius and when she finds an opening she hobbles toward the middle of the road and, finally, out through the crowd. Gerrard is inches behind her, his head still bobbing ever so slightly, the hint of a smile still on his lips. As Teejay is towed along, she turns her head back to her mother and Mavis and begins to cry aloud. Her voice beings to rise with every step she makes toward the Crown Victoria: "Mom? *Mom! MOM!*"

When Teejay reaches the middle of the road, Raymond, still kneeling in front of the Prius, can see his daughter as she's led away. The fog now partially lifted from his mind, he realizes what is happening: Teejay is being escorted toward an unmarked cop car by a man in a gray uniform. Her shirt and jeans are smeared with blood. She's crying out for her mother, and no one is coming to help her. *No one is coming to help her*, he says to himself in astonishment. He blinks and in an instant pulls himself up, tugs the Lil' Slugger bat from James's hand and stumbles over to confront Gerrard and Janice.

"Let the girl go," he says, gulping at the air. "That's my little girl you're taking away. You let her go. Now."

Janice's body floods with adrenaline. The shock of this terribly beaten man poised in front of her with a bat clasped in both hands forces a gasp from her throat.

Gerrard's bobbing head wobbles to a halt and he freezes where he stands. He sees Raymond's eyes are fully dilated, a void seems to tunnel through to the back of his head. "Let's be calm," he says and licks his lips so he can talk his way through this. "We aren't here to harm nobody."

"I warned you." Raymond's voice is steady now and he plumps the bat in the palm of his hand and locks his eyes on Gerrard. The muscles in his forearms coil and uncoil with every stroke of the bat. "I won't tell you again. You let her go. *Right now.*"

When she realizes the depth of Raymond's despair Janice conjures the idea that if she can unravel Raymond's wired tension, she might be able to divert his attention for a moment. Get him to think of something else, anything, and then they can secure Teejay in the car and deal with the father. "You'll be able to come down to see her," she says, remembering what Gerrard said as he coaxed Teejay away from Fay and Mavis. When this seems to have no effect, she adds, "If you want, you can come with us right now." She extends her uninjured hand toward the Crown Victoria, a gesture of reprieve and openness.

But this tiny movement, Janice's delicate fingers extended casually from her open hand, ignites the tendons in Raymond's arms. There is no consideration, no thought, no preparation, no plan for what might follow. With one swing he bats Janice's hand to the side with such force that she falls to her knees and begins to wail from the pain of her broken fingers. Gerrard is so shaken that his grip on Teejay's arm tightens and the girl calls out in pain.

*"Daddy!"*

When he hears this cry Raymond lowers the fat end of the bat to his waist and in a swift upper-cut he drives the wood shaft under Gerrard's chin with a force that snaps his head to one side. As he collapses onto the road Gerrard releases Teejay's arm and she slumps backward and then regains her balance.

Raymond drops the bat and gazes blankly at the clot of people behind him, the cars, the fire still smoking at the far end of Peoples Park. As Teejay backs away, he smiles slightly, knowing that he's saved his little girl, that of all the things he's done in his life, he's done this one good thing: he's saved Teejay from who-knows-what horror. He sees Mavis and Fay jog across the street to embrace Teejay, and as they lead her back to the car and settle her into the seat and buckle her into place, James and Doyle step into the Prius and shut the doors.

A moment later the car glides silently away from the curb, and he sees it carry Fay and Teejay to the place where they have to go. And it doesn't matter where they go, Raymond realizes, so long as it's new and very far away. With this new clarity he looks down at Gerrard, watches the blood drizzle from his mouth as he spits one, and then another tooth onto the road. Raymond steps forward and kneels at the man's side. It's good to see that Gerrard can still breathe. He'll lose a few teeth, sure, but he'll be okay, he tells himself and when Janice's cries begin to subside, he looks at her and says, "You'd better call an ambulance."

She grimaces at him and shakes her head and begins to wail again, but Raymond holds his hand aloft to calm her.

"Don't worry," he says. "I'll stay here until help comes. Then I'll leave with you." Yes, he murmurs to himself. I'll go with you, just like you wanted and that'll give me a place to go, too. A new resting place. Somewhere I can stay and wait for the days of final atonement.

As the Prius rolls down the length of the road beside People's Park, Doyle feels as though he's being transported from a war zone toward a dystopian fantasyland. All the pent-up *frisson* from the tens of thousands of homeless men, women and children that have swarmed through the city streets since his arrival in the Bay Area is exploding before his eyes. Despite the trauma, the cries and screams from Fay and Teejay abate sooner than he could have guessed. The breathless panic quickly transforms into a rush to ensure Teejay is whisked away unharmed. When Mavis reaches the end of the block, James commands her to slow down and then come to a stop.

"Pull over," he says softly. "Once you turn the corner just pull over." Despite the adrenaline pulsing through all of them, James manages to constrain his voice to a steady calm.

After she turns the corner onto Bowditch Street and is certain the Prius is out of sight from Janice Slitz, Mavis eases the car against the curb. "What?" she says, incredulous that anyone wants to stop now. "Why are we stopping?"

"Okay, Teejay, let's have a look at you," James says as he opens his door and then nods to Doyle to slip out of the back seat. "Just to make sure you're good to go," he adds lightly.

Doyle stands at the curb as James helps Teejay out of the car. The smudges of blood on her t-shirt and jeans are still damp. "Think you've got any cuts or bruises?"

Teejay glances at her waist and pulls the shirt away from her skin with a look of dismay. "No. That blood's not mine. It must be from that woman."

"Good." James's sense of relief is evident in his face. He turns to Mavis. "Let me have your phone. I've got to call Rosa." James gestures with his hand and after Mavis slips the phone into his palm he finds Rosa's name in the index and then clicks on her number.

"Right. Okay." Mavis glances at Doyle and Teejay, and

then, through the rearview mirror at Fay. "Rosa's a nurse," she says to Fay and forces a smile to her lips. "She lives in the basement suite below us."

As James holds the phone to his ear, Doyle whispers doubtfully, "I don't know, James. I've heard that all the cell relay stations are power hogs. They'll be the last thing brought back on-line."

After a moment James realizes the cell phone is useless and returns it to his wife. "All right, this is what we *can* do. Mavis, why don't you and Fay get Teejay into some clean clothes and tidy her up. Meanwhile Doyle and I are going back to the house to get Rosa."

"All right. But don't be long, okay?" Mavis brightens now that James is taking control again. As soon as she started the car and tried to pull onto the road, everything began to slip out of synch. Finally someone was re-establishing a sense of order.

James breaks into a jog and Doyle follows as they cut through People's Park, through the make-shift lean-to's and huts, past the circle of boys tending the open fire, along the well-worn lawns to the far end of the block. As they cross the road they can see Gerrard still crumpled on the asphalt, tended by two or three by-standers. Janice Slitz crawls to the curb and squats on the concrete lip, cradling her injured hands against her breasts.

"Look at that," Doyle says when he sees Raymond propping Gerrard against his bruised chest and patting Gerrard's damp forehead with an open hand. Raymond's face radiates compassion and sensitivity. His fingers stroke Gerrard's broken jaw in soft, even caresses. The bat is nowhere to be seen.

"Yeah. Unbelievable," James whispers through a heavy pant and then jogs along the side of his house toward Rosa's door. He knocks once and Rosa appears before him, covered by a knee-length bathrobe.

"Rosa, there's been an accident right in front of the house. Do you have a first-aid kit?" James glances from Rosa to the street and back.

"What?"

"Look, I don't know when the phones will start working again, but no one can get through to 9-1-1." He focuses on Rosa's eyes, imploring her. "We need your help."

Rosa cinches the waist of her bathrobe in one hand and dips her head toward the street. "Right out front?" she asks as though the impact of the emergency is just hitting her.

"Three people are in pretty rough shape. You'll need some compresses and some finger splints. Maybe something for a jaw fracture. And some pain killer."

"All right. Give me a half-sec."

When Rosa closes the door, James jogs back toward the street and calls over his shoulder to Doyle. "Let's go." Moments later they're back at the car. Teejay and Fay are settled in their seats, Mavis is at the wheel.

"All cleaned up and ready to go?" James asks as he climbs into the Prius.

"Much better," Mavis says as her mouth dips in a down-drawn smile. Her unspoken message is that the worst is over, hopefully. "Teejay's got a fresh shirt and jeans. And I told her I'd buy her new clothes tonight or tomorrow.

"Excellent!" James turns his head to Teejay and then to Mavis. "Rosa's helping to patch them up."

"And guess what," Doyle says to Fay. He buckles his seat belt and locks his door. "Raymond's helping the guy who fell." He steers away from saying *the guy he slugged*. "He's holding him against his shoulder while he's waiting for Rosa."

"Raymond?" Fay can't believe it. Can't believe he didn't kill someone.

But later, when she has time to consider everything that happened that morning, Fay would admit that it was Raymond who sprung them loose. It was Raymond who set her and Teejay free. She knew that she would be grateful to him forever, and for that she prayed that God might forgive him for his sins despite the grief and shame he'd brought to so many people.

## Chapter Four

A war zone. Doyle has seen thousands of pictures and videoclips of cities devastated by napalm, atomic bombs, mortars, howitzers, IEDs. But their drive through the streets of Berkeley reminds him of the neutron bomb, that cold-war-era weapon engineered to destroy all lifeforms, but to preserve the surrounding buildings, cars and highways. Within an hour they manage to navigate their way past the empty cars abandoned around every intersection and drive onto the freeway. He feels as if they are driving through a dream without ghosts. Without phantoms. Without a soul.

Without anyone suggesting it, they collectively decide to disregard the whole, horrible episode with Raymond, Janice Slitz and Gerrard Jackson. At one point Fay utters a low, unintelligible wail but Doyle turns to her and presses a finger across his lips to coax her into a new silence. Meanwhile Mavis takes every opportunity to direct their attention to various road-side highlights and diversions: splash-down water parks, historic sites, the mileage marker to Seattle. "Just under eight hundred miles to go!"

But such distractions fail to keep anyone from noticing the increasingly snarled traffic along the highway. A few vehicles appear neatly parked next to the highway shoulders in groups of three or four, straddling the crushed gravel that borders the asphalt. It's as though the drivers and passengers decided to meet in one place and walk down the bank to a river or park, or whatever local attraction might inspire an outing next to the freeway, and from there, the revelers disappeared. But the further north they drive, and the further from any functioning gas stations, Doyle figures, the more abandoned vehicles they pass: cars, trucks, SUVs, semis, each one ditched in increasingly random disarray. Mavis has to slow the Prius to thirty, then twenty, and then to ten miles an hour to weave around the growing chaos.

Soon three trucks appear locked together in the middle of the traffic lanes where they seem to have collided and jammed together in the middle of the road. "That's number two hundred and fifty-four, fifty-five, and fifty-six," Teejay announces in amazement as they swerve around the trucks.

Apparently tallying the score of derelict vehicles offers her an effective distraction from the crazy drama she witnessed with her father, Doyle tells himself. He has to admire her, the thing in her that refuses to be squashed into despair. Once again she proves to be resilient, indefatigable, a master of psychological jujitsu. It's something he could learn from her, he realizes, something he never witnessed in the thousands of high school students he taught over thirty-two years. Maybe that's because none of them had been pushed to the extremes that Teejay's encountered. As he sits in the back of the Prius, dozing in and out of his thoughts, Doyle realizes the child will be all right. No matter what might lie ahead of her she'll always be able to assert herself over anything this life can throw her way. Miscarriages, street fights, battles with the law. It's a kind of miracle, he decides, and he's grateful — honored, in fact — that he can travel with her and witness the unfolding of her eternally optimistic spirit.

Later they encounter scores of hitch-hikers. Men, women, teenagers, groups of families with their thumbs dragging through the air, a dispirited look drawn on their faces as they trudge along the side of the road carrying their packs, brief cases, and shoulder bags. The Prius is one of the few vehicles still moving forward, and as they continue it's apparent the freeway will be difficult to navigate much further.

"We'd better take one of these exits," Doyle says when the way ahead looks impossibly snarled. "Maybe the back roads are less clogged."

Mavis and James agree and at the junction near Williams, Mavis turns west onto Route 20, works her way above Clear Lake until they merge with Highway 101. Although the road is narrower than the freeway and meanders back and forth to follow the contours of the hills, the number of abandoned cars diminishes as they drive on, especially when they enter the rural areas, the forest, the small farms and acres of vineyards, the pastures of grazing cattle who seem oblivious to their passage and all the trouble they carry with them.

"I'd like to be a cow," Teejay muses as she gazes at the pasture on the left.

"Careful," her mother warns and then adds, "Make sure you become a *dairy* cow. Otherwise you might end up as someone's dinner."

Teejay thinks about this a moment. "Right, of course. A

*dairy* cow." She considers their situation and then asks, "Mavis, what would you like to be? If you could come back in another life, I mean."

Mavis purses her lips, tilts her head back and forth, indulging the fantasy of a selected reincarnation. "Well, if I came back as another animal, I think it would be a yellow Labrador Retriever."

"Really? Why?"

"Because when I was your age, we had one. Her name was Carmen, named after my grandfather's favorite opera character. And you know something?"

"What?"

"She was the best friend I ever had." She dwells on this and then adds, "Next to you guys, I mean."

Everyone chuckles at this and an air of relief fills the car. The increasing number of miles between them and Berkeley has diminished the power of the morning trauma and allowed them to enter a soft, feminine space contained by the shell of the speeding vehicle and the transit of their collective anima. Their giggles soon turn to outright laughter and everyone wants to encourage more of it.

"What about you, Doyle? What would you come back as?"

Doyle smiles, happy to be included in the fun. "Oh, I don't know." He recalls the moments yesterday afternoon when Teejay rolled on his apartment floor in sheer abandon. "I think I'd like to come back as a tea cozy."

More laughter. But Teejay insists on re-directing him: "No, I mean what kind of *animal* would you come back as?"

"You mean I can't be a tea cozy?"

"Of course not. Nobody comes back as a *thing*. Be *serious.*"

"All right." This time he doesn't hesitate. "I'd be a sea

otter." When the boys were young and played this game he used to fantasize about being a sea otter. Here's another chance, the closest he'll ever get, he figures, to do it all again.

Teejay is temporarily silenced as she ponders how to properly structure the diversion she's devised. "Okay, people. You have to say *what animal* you want to be, *and why*. So Doyle, *why* a sea otter?"

"Because all they do is play all day long." He tells Teejay about the summers when the boys were young and they'd watch the sea otters steal onto the shore on Vancouver Island, rob some food from a local picnic, swim back into the shallow water, and then flip onto their backs and lounge about on the waves, their sopping bellies glistening in the sun, happily munching away on a sandwich or chicken thigh. "They're the pirates of the animal kingdom. Equally at home on land or water, living the gypsy life. The real question in my mind is, who *wouldn't* want to come back as a sea otter?"

When Teejay is satisfied with Doyle's response she turns to the front of the car. "What about you, James? What would you come back as?"

The Prius is driving through a long stretch of open road now. There're no cars visible and Mavis has set the cruise control to sixty miles an hour. James turns in his seat so he can see Teejay and the others without concern that he'll have to help Mavis navigate their way past any surprises. "Can I tell you first what *thing* I'd come back as if I didn't have to be an animal?"

"Only if you tell the animal part, too."

"Okay." He glances through the roof window. "I'd like to be a magic carpet. So that I could fly using my mind to take me wherever I want."

"I can see that." Mavis nods as though James has just revealed a not-so-well-hidden persona. "I can *so see that*."

This answer makes perfect sense to Teejay, too. She can imagine him as a Persian carpet flying above the car guiding their direction even though flying carpets don't actually exist, a fact she's compelled to impart. "Okay, but since they *don't* exist, what animal would you be."

"A goat."

"A goat?!" She begins laughing again. "Nobody wants to be a goat!"

"I would!" James takes mock insult from her laughter. "Goats are very independent. They can travel just about anywhere they please. All they need for food is a patch of grass. They have a lot of friends, friends like sheep and chickens and farm dogs. And, most important, they give us milk. And *cheese,*" he says with gusto to underline the value of the lowly goat. "Frankly, I can't imagine life without goats! It would mean the end of civilization as we know it."

"James, sweetie, admit it, *you* could only return as a *boy*-goat." Mavis wags a finger. "And everybody knows that Billy-goats can't make cheese."

"Then I'd come back as a Jilly-goat."

"No. Not *you*. Sorry, I know you too well. Besides, girl goats are called nanny-goats. Jilly-goats are yet another product of your over-fertile imagination."

When the laughter subsides, Teejay turns to her mother. For a moment she thinks of letting her off the hook, knowing she might take the game in the wrong direction, but then she decides to press a little, just once. "What about you, Mom? Have you thought of one?"

"I don't know." Fay turns her head to the window and watches the countryside stream past, the tall trees, the green canopy reaching higher and higher overhead as they approach the redwood forests. She's never seen this part of the world before. Much of her silence is simply due to the quietude of awe — that, and the release she now feels from Raymond and all the threats that have haunted her for the past few months. "I really don't know," she says again.

Fay's silence stalls in the air. The party atmosphere deflates a little and when Doyle can feel it about to collapse completely, he looks across Teejay directly at Fay, tilts his head toward her and smiles. "With all the painting you've done over the years? From all that, you haven't ever imagined *one* animal you'd like to be?"

"I don't know. Well…." Her voice hints at a concession. "Do you consider *people* to be animals?"

Everyone speaks at once, their voices overlapping: "Yeah." "Of course." "Sure." "Absolutely."

"Well," she says, and lifts Teejay's hand in her own. "I'd like to come back as your mom again. And just try to do a little better job of it next time. Yeah-yeah," she concludes, "that's what I'd do if I could come back again." Pleased with this answer she presses her lips together, and then adds, "I mean it, too."

After another twenty miles the surrounding forests have grown thick and tall and the late afternoon light diminishes in the shadows. "Look! The power's back on!" Teejay points to the porch lights on a small, cedar-shake house as they round a bend in the road. As the car slows everyone cranes their necks to observe a string of lights draped in a series of garlands from the outdoor rafters of the porch. "They're Christmas lights. And all white, too."

"Could be they're on a generator," Doyle offers, but

when the Prius rolls into the town of Myers Flat, it's evident that the entire community is back on the power grid.

James tries the radio again and manages to tune in a country-and-western station broadcasting Johnny Cash's "Folsom Prison Blues."

"All right, we're pulling in here." Mavis parks the car in front of the Poke-in-a-Hole Thrift Shop and sets the emergency brake. She cuts the ignition and the radio goes silent. "Time to get Teejay into some new duds," she says and steps into the crisp, fall air. "Wow. It's chilling down."

"Let's find a place to stay for the night," James says to Doyle and leads the way across the road to a gas station, past the twin gas pumps and the line of parked cars waiting for fuel, and pushes open the door to the shop. Inside he sees a tall, lean attendant ("BEN," according to his name tag) flipping through a magazine. No one else is present, but he can hear someone washing dishes in a back room.

"Afternoon."

"Hi." James glances about. The few shelves surrounding the cash register have been stripped of snack foods and candies. The noise from the dishwasher stops. The absence of any sound makes him hesitate briefly. "We're looking for a place to stay the night. And some gas for the car."

"Can help you with the first, but not the second." Ben rolls his thick purple lips together to re-moisten them. He sets aside his copy of *Fish 'n' Fly* and flattens his hands on the countertop next to the cash register. "What kind of place you needing?"

"Something like a KOA would be good," Doyle says. He turns to James and adds, "I used to stay at Kampgrounds of America with the boys during summer holidays."

"There's a KOA up in Eureka, thirty-seven miles north of here. And another in Crescent City. I expect they've got more than a few cabins open this time of year." Ben says. "But with the blackout, everything's gone haywire. I sold out all the gas I had yesterday. Hoarders," he says with a shrug. "I'm not expecting another delivery of gas for a week."

"Really?" James takes a few steps closer to Ben, leans against the glass counter and glances at the empty shelves. "That would account for it, the line of cars trying to get gas."

"Yeah. I told everybody just to lock up and leave 'er in line. Park at the end of the line if you like. But I can't guarantee when we'll be back in business. From what they're saying on the news, there's a helluva mess to sort out." He rolls his ulcerated lips under his teeth as though the gentle motion provides a measure of relief.

Now Doyle steps a little closer. "You know, this is going to sound crazy, but we haven't had any news at all. What happened to the power grid?"

"Can't tell for sure." Ben shakes his head skeptically. "Seems to have shut down everything from Redding to Tijuana. And a little bit into Nevada. Apparently some places are coming back on line, bit by bit. Anyway, we were never touched by it up here." Ben hesitates a moment, calculates if he should say any more to these two strangers. When he arrives at a decision, he nods his head and continues. "Governor White and the president have called a state of emergency. The National Guard had to put down some riots and looting in Los Angeles. There was trouble in San Francisco, too. Apparently the Occupy Wall Street gang. Some are saying it's because the unions can't abide the governor's back-to-work order. Or it could be al-Qaeda again. Others, like the greens, say the grid's so over-cooked, it was just a matter of time before it fried anyway. You hear ever' possibility." He narrows his eyes. "These days the news is just what people say. Not what actually is."

The kitchen door swings open on a pair of loud, sprung hinges. "Careful what you're saying, Ben-bo." Another bean-pole of a man ducks his head under the doorway and enters the room as he wipes his hands on a dishtowel. Doyle imagines the two men could be twins, but they're now so old that they've been re-shaped into a stark dissymmetry by time and separate histories. "They could be unionists," he murmurs and with a nod indicates Doyle and James.

Ben doesn't offer a blink of acknowledgement to his brother. "Anyway. As I said, there's some KOAs up the road. And you might find gas further up the 101. Or most likely in Oregon, if the hoarders haven't taken the whole stock. Good luck to you," he concludes with a tone that suggests they'll need it.

"Mavis. Wake up." Fay kneels beside the canvas cot and tugs at Mavis's shoulder with her fingers, a delicate motion intended to ensure James will sleep through the distraction in front of their cabin.

"What?" Mavis's eyes blink open. Instinctively she realizes that she must whisper, that whatever has brought Fay to her side in the middle of the night can be easily broken. Words alone might shatter the fragility of the cool night air.

Fay presses a finger to her lips and steps away from the bed, motioning with her other hand to follow. Mavis slips out of the blankets, pulls on a sweater, her jeans and shoes, and with five or six steps she is in the living room and peering through the cabin window to the fire pit outside. There, squatting on a block anchored in the concrete pad, she can pick out the profile of someone hunched over the flames rising and falling as if they are alternately aroused by a bellows and then choked for air.

"It's Teejay," Fay murmurs. "I just realized that she wasn't in bed. Then I saw her at the fire pit."

"What's she doing?" Mavis rubs her eyes, still unsure of what she is witnessing.

"She's burning her clothes." Fay releases a sigh. "I asked her why, but she can't tell me. I don't think she can talk to anyone right now. She has no words left." She waves an empty hand and shrugs.

Mavis pulls on her fleece and zips it up to her throat. Then she opens the cabin door and steps onto the deck. "Come on," she says to Fay and heads toward the girl. As Fay follows her, Mavis hears the gravel crunching underfoot, the ocean breakers banging into the beach below. The clouds are thick above them and except for the glow of the fire, the only illumination in the darkness comes from the naked light bulb on the porch of Jerry McCallum's cabin, the KOA manager's office at the far side of the campground. Mavis treads cautiously, aware that the ground is uneven and clotted with roots from the surrounding forest.

The fire pit is well constructed, "manufactured" as Doyle described it earlier in the evening as they roasted marshmallows donated by Jerry when he met Teejay and wondered if she'd like a campfire treat. They sat around a discarded steel brake drum — the actual fire pit — which had been salvaged from a wrecked semi-trailer and then embedded in the concrete pad surrounding the pit. The steel-and-concrete fabrication minimized any fire hazard, and so everyone felt comfortable retiring to the cabin to sleep while a few embers remained to warm the night. It was from these cinders that Teejay constructed her fire.

"Hi Teejay," Mavis whispers as she approaches the girl.

Teejay draws a deep breath. She appears to be mesmerized, lost in the rising and falling flames as she lifts and dips her blouse on the end of the wire marshmallow stick.

For a moment Mavis considers the girl's deep distraction before she sits on a concrete slab beside her and watches the flames claw at the blouse. This is the same blouse Teejay wore when Janice Slitz tried to pry her out of the car. The blood stains are still evident, even as the flames begin to consume the cotton sleeves. They watch the fire char the sleeves and bodice while Teejay damps and engorges the flames with her steady up-and-down manipulation of the rod. Finally the plastic buttons ignite and melt in a series of waste-chemical blobs that drip into the flames.

"That part's not very pretty," Mavis offers when she hears Teejay sigh. The blouse is gone now and they both pause to consider what comes next.

"No, not very." Teejay's jaw pushes forward and Mavis can see a tear give way from her eye. Without another word, Teejay pulls her soiled pants from her pack and drapes them over the wire rod and hoists them above the flames. As they watch the first lick of fire brush against the denim, Fay walks behind Mavis and sits on a third concrete cube. She folds her hands in her lap and says nothing.

In the flickering light Mavis can see these jeans are blood-stained, too. As the flames catch one pant leg — and seconds later, the other — she realizes what this is about. "So ... " she says, tuning her voice tentatively, to a delicate speculation about the pain welling in Teejay's eyes, "So, did you already burn your socks?"

Teejay presses her jaw forward. "Yes."

"And your shoes?"

Teejay looks at her, at the openness in her face, the invitation that Mavis is offering. "Yes." She wipes her eyes with the back of her left hand. "And my underpants. I burnt them *first.*"

"Oh, Honey." Fay leans forward and wraps her arms across her own chest. How she would love to wrap the child in her arms, but she knows she cannot. All she can do is observe this ritual, this long, quiet passage that her daughter must navigate alone.

When her jeans are engulfed by the fire, Teejay dips the metal stick and lets the pants fall into the flames untended, as though she's lost interest in governing the pace in which they are consumed. Instead her tears begin to stream down her face and she drops the steel stick and presses both hands to her cheeks.

"Honey," Fay moans and moves to embrace her.

"Let her finish," Mavis says and waves a hand and forces a smile that convinces Fay to wait.

The women sit and watch as Teejay rubs the last of the tears from her eyes. She's managed to render her crying in silence, controlled by the same silent strength she's always found in the midst of chaos.

When a measure of composure returns, Mavis leans forward, turns her head to the left so that she can take Teejay in completely. "And is there something else?"

Teejay considers this and shrugs when she realizes that there may be more to this pain, a torment that finally seems to be subsiding. "Something else?"

"Yeah." Mavis tips her chin toward Teejay's pack. "Anything else you want to get rid of. I mean, it might be a good time ... while the fire's still burning." Her head slips backward an inch and she smiles, opening her lips just enough to suggest this notion could be taken as a joke if Teejay wants to ignore it.

She looks down at the fire and then reaches into her

pack. "Maybe," Teejay says with new seriousness. "There's this."

In her hand she holds the palm-size teddy bear that Dr. K. gave to her after the miscarriage. "I can't decide if this came at the end of everything that went bad," she says and looks into its face, "or when things finally started to get better."

Mavis watches Teejay pondering the decision before her, as if she's trying to determine if this mock-child, a felt teddy, belongs with her anymore.

"No," she concludes and in one motion she pitches the doll into the fire. "I think I'll just remember it." Turning to Mavis and her mother she adds, "Instead of hanging on to it forever."


The next morning new worries escalate in Mavis's imagination as she sorts through the gear in the back of the car. At least there was plentiful water at the Crescent City KOA and everyone loaded up on tea or coffee over breakfast. She had the foresight to bring enough blankets for everyone, but apart from the supply of sandwiches she'd packed they aren't carrying enough food to see them through another two days. Unless they can find an open grocery store their situation will grow desperate in short order.

As far as Mavis is concerned the food shortage is symptomatic of other problems. So many of her expectations are proving to be wrong. She assumed they could draw money from ATMs on the way north, but because of the blackout there's been a run on cash and every bank machine they come across has been emptied or is out of service. Among the five of them, they have a total of two hundred and sixty-three dollars. She figures that will last for four more days, assuming they pay cash for gasoline, if they can find some. They'd spent twenty-five dollars on the cabin in the KOA, and a little more than fifteen on some used clothes for Teejay. Thank god for that, especially after her midnight meltdown at the fire pit. At least Teejay is happy with the clothes that they found for her, thanks to the staff who directed them to the "barely used" clothing section at the back of the store. The women at the thrift shop blamed the shortages on hoarders. All the gas stations were sold out of fuel and most shops were locked and shuttered as if the proprietors were waiting out a hurricane.

While Mavis figures it will take two days to reach the Canadian border if they return to the I-5, it could take three or maybe four days if they continue along the meandering 101 which hugs the Pacific shoreline through most of Oregon and Washington. Yesterday they'd only managed to travel three hundred-odd miles. While the scenery along the road was gorgeous and nobody seemed to object to the long drive, the total distance they had to travel is greater than she'd calculated. The Prius would certainly need to be refueled within the next hundred miles or so. Maybe by then they'd be far enough away from the blackout zone that the panic hoarding wouldn't affect them.

Fortunately their collective fantasy of Canada provides a diversion. They need that, an image of what lies ahead. A new beginning, a new life, she thinks as she waits for the others to wander up to the gravel parking lot from the KOA campground. Doyle seemed to know the entire area all the way through the redwoods and up the coast of Oregon and Washington, and the fact that there are a dozen KOAs along the route gives everyone a sense of security knowing they could find a decent place to sleep each night.

Doyle and James are the first to emerge from the woods and join her at the car. James has his face turned to the sun, welcoming it into his day. But Doyle seems to bear some new worry as he tips his bag into the trunk.

"I've got some bad news," he begins. "I realized last night that I'm going to have to part company with you just before we reach the border." He nods his head in a short, tight motion to suggest that there's no disputing this conclusion. "I forgot to mention that I lost my passport. It was stolen the day I arrived in San Francisco and I'll need it to get back into Canada."

"What does this mean?" James glances at him and then at his wife. "Can we hook up later?"

Mavis tries to think this through. What are the implications of losing their guide on the trip to Salt Spring Island? Another worry. One more unplanned turn in the road.

"Eventually they'll let me in," he continues. "They have to. I'm a Canadian citizen after all. But there'll be a lot of questions, paperwork, the entire Kafkaesque inquiry. I'm worried that if you're with me, they'll start checking on Fay and Teejay. There might be a warrant out for them. Do you think that's possible?"

Mavis shakes her head. "It's not just *possible. It's a fucking certainty.*" Her voice is heavy, as though she's now picked up Doyle's burden and realizes she can't carry it. "And *we* don't have passports, *either.*" She curls her hands into fists and pumps them once. "I mean ... *shit!*" She spits out this word with bitterness and turns away, walks around the car and then returns to confront James and Doyle. "Look, I know we're only doing this because of me. Me and Fay and Teejay. But this is *crazy*. Do you know what happened to her last night? The meltdown she had?"

Doyle and James glance away, speechless.

"How can we *be* so naïve?" Her voice exposes the well of doubt and fear within her. "How much longer can we go on with this, this *fantasy*, before admitting *it's just not on?*"

Doyle stares down the stretch of road ahead. There's a long way to go yet, he tells himself, and we all need one another if we're going to move forward. "It's not just because of you, Mavis. We all agreed to this trip, separately and together," he says. "Look, let's drive on into Oregon. There's got to be a coffee shop in Port Orford or Coos Bay with a wireless internet connection. I'm going to Skype my son. Maybe Wyatt can help us."

At first James and Doyle can't distinguish anything in the long shadows of the warehouse. The shallow, enclosed space is tucked behind Hartley's barn, completely invisible from the long gravel driveway leading up to the farm. A good place to stash your hidden wares, Doyle tells himself. Gold, marijuana, rocket launchers, stolen cars — or sealed barrels of gasoline. When his eyes adapt to the darkness, Doyle can make out ten tidy rows of fifty-five-gallon barrels, each one propped on parallel train-track rails to lift them three or four inches off the compacted dirt floor.

"It's not what it looks like," Hartley tells them in a low voice. "I don't have more than twenty barrels of gasoline. The rest is corn, oats, beans and such."

James quickly calculates the quantities involved, over a thousand gallons of fuel alone, and nods his head with a look that he hopes will be recognized as one of gratitude for Hartley's generosity. "Well, that's a hundred times more than we could ever use," James says and sweeps a hand over the top of one barrel and then another. He can tell the drums were recently wiped down; despite the whiff of petroleum in the air, not a trace of gasoline smears his fingers. "In fact, that Prius only holds eleven gallons."

"Eleven?" Hartley frowns and walks past three or four barrels and then swings back to James. "These days, even eleven gallons is precious."

"Well, we wouldn't necessarily need to top 'er up." James looks to Doyle for some kind of confirmation.

"Yeah, I think a little under ten gallons would give us enough to make it as far as Port Angeles," Doyle says and then he turns to Hartley. "I've heard the gas stations are running at full capacity in Washington State." When Hartley doesn't reply, Doyle adds, "Is that what you heard?"

Hartley nods doubtfully.

"Well, if we could purchase ten gallons from you," James says to push the deal forward, "that would certainly get us out of this jam, Mr. Hartley."

Hartley sets his jaw and looks into James's face. He seems to have no trouble adapting to the dim light in the shadows. "All right. I'm doing it for that little girl of yours. But it'll cost you twenty dollars a gallon."

James blows a broad stream of air through his lips. Two hundred dollars would immediately impoverish them. He glances at Doyle who turns his head away and shrugs. "Well," James says when he realizes he must say something, "then would you consider filling the tank for two hundred?"

"You mean all eleven gallons?"

James nods, yes. "Probably a little under," he says in a near whisper.

"Cash only."

James nods again.

"All right, pull the car up to the door here. And don't let no one see you coming or going."

As the only other licensed driver in the group, Doyle takes the wheel to provide a driving break for Mavis, who squeezes next to Teejay on the narrow back seat of the car. While he's happy to pitch in (and, thankfully, to extricate himself from the rear of the Prius) Doyle conceals the fact that he's not actually *in possession* of a drivers license since he was robbed and the replacement he was promised failed to materialize. Best not to dwell on these legal niceties, he counsels himself, and decides to steer the conversation elsewhere.

"I don't know how you did it, or what you said, but the only reason we're still on the road is because of you, Teejay." Doyle glances at Teejay in the rearview mirror as he turns the car north onto Highway 101.

"I just told him the truth." She shrugs her shoulders and raises her hands to reveal that nothing could be more simple. "At least to start off." She reveals that during the long wait at the gas pumps outside Coos Bay she'd wandered into the restaurant attached to Hartley's Gas 'n' Grill to make her way to the washroom. When she was inside, Hartley's boy, Jeb, asked her where she was from and where she was going. When he gave her a square from his Cadbury Burnt Almond Chocolate bar she told him that *if* they could get some gas, she was going to Canada to see the twins, Wyatt and Jesse, who she'd never met although they were both twenty-five, to which Jeb said it was totally obvious that they'd be the same age if they were genuine twins, and so rather than honestly explaining any more about who they actually were — especially if Jeb intended to be so smart about everything *she* said — she told him Wyatt and Jesse were her *cousins*. "I guess I shouldn't have lied," she adds, "because it led to a few others."

"A few other *what*?" Mavis asks.

Teejay hesitates. "Well, you know ... a few more" — she spreads her index finger and thumb an inch apart — "*little* lies."

"Now just hold it there," Doyle interjects. As the Prius enters a long, empty stretch of road along the shoreline he sees an opportunity to clarify the situation. "First: that particular prevarication falls into the category of a *white* lie, since nobody's hurt by it, and, second: really, practically speaking, how else were we ever going to get the gas? and, third: as far as I'm concerned, Teejay, they *are* your cousins, insofar as I consider myself your uncle. Which I would consider an honor if you'd allow it," he adds and glances at Fay through the mirror to ensure she's not dismayed by this proposal. When she smiles at him, he relaxes and with another glance at Teejay, he encourages her to continue.

"Except I told him you're my *grandfather*. And that *James* is my uncle."

"What?" James begins laughing and slaps Doyle on the shoulder. "Too bad, old man! But don't be offended. It's just a *white* lie."

When the laughter subsides, Teejay returns to her story to describe how Jeb reported the conversation to his mother, who then enlisted Mr. Hartley himself to come to her aid. Hartley approached the Prius, which was parked at the end of a line of fifty-odd cars waiting their turn at the gas pump. "The rest is history." She shrugs again, leaving unspoken Hartley's brief dialogue with James and Doyle and his suggestion that they leave the women and Teejay at the Grill, so that his wife could serve them some soup and sandwiches, and follow Hartley along the ten miles of gravel road to the family farm, where he "might have something that would be helpful."

Helpful indeed. They now have enough gas, maybe, to

drive to the north coast of Washington's Olympic Peninsula. And while they'd been waiting at the gas station, Doyle found a coffee shop with an internet connection. He'd been able to Skype Wyatt and ask him to sail the *Sustenance* down to Pillar Point where they could meet just outside the abandoned village of Pysht, about thirty miles west of Port Angeles.

Wyatt Mere slips the *Sustenance* from its moorings and with his right foot he pushes the sloop away from the wharf into the slate-gray waters washing through the Sidney Marina. Normally he'd use the outboard motor to propel him into the center of the bay, then cut the engine, lift the mainsail and set his course. But tonight he'll let the tide draw him away from the shore and run everything "according to Doyle."

That's the expression Wyatt and Jesse use whenever they employ an unassisted, natural system. Their father always liked to demonstrate the "mechanics of nature" to the boys and then get them to observe how much more satisfying the results are compared to engine-powered systems. Like the gravity-fed shower bag Doyle rigged from a sturdy tree limb whenever they went camping. Or the hot-rock saunas he helped them build below the high-tide line in mid-winter. He maintained that sailboats were the ultimate naturally-powered systems and they represented a way of life outside the closed-loop tyranny of fuel-based machinery, and therefore, outside the global economy and all it entailed: money, jobs, debt, despair, pollution, and all too often, war. On a sailboat you could fish, collect rainwater and edible kelps, and let the winds propel you to almost any coastal destination in the world. It's an entirely self-contained framework that conforms to the principles of the natural world.

To ensure they absorbed this message in their bones Doyle enrolled the boys in the local Sea Scouts troop and volunteered to assist the group leaders on their trips. On a weekend sail up to Coffin Point, Doyle and the boys had so much fun that he promised to help them purchase their own boat, and when they did, they'd make a voyage around Vancouver Island. Two years later, when they were fifteen, and after Doyle earned some extra money tutoring Geography in the evenings and then taken on a line of credit to make the downpayment, he purchased the *Snail's Pace*, a fractional rig sloop that was just big enough to sleep four if the boys shared a berth. During the following summer the entire family spent seven weeks in a leisurely circumnavigation of Vancouver Island in balmy weather that barely stirred the rolling swells off Cape Scott. The experience enthralled Wyatt and since that summer he'd spent his life with boats in one way or another. Selling them, repairing them, crewing them, painting them — and now, living on one.

Once the *Sustenance* clears Trial Island Wyatt settles into the cockpit and tips his head to the stars and scans the familiar constellations: the Dippers, Canis Major, the Belt of Orion. The full moon and open skies make for clear sailing. Just as well, since he's shut down all the running lights.

That's illegal, of course, but so is the voyage he's undertaking. Picking up his father *sans passport* along with four illegal aliens and transporting them across the international boundary. It's so odd, so unlike his dad. Never in his life has Doyle asked for any help from either of the boys, let alone a rescue mission. And now he wants to stow away some friends who, for all Wyatt knows, are about to claim refugee status! After the last conversation with his father, a Skype call from an internet café in Coos Bay, Oregon, he discussed the mission with his brother and talked about the power failure in California. The crisis normally would have made headlines around the world, but the collapse was eclipsed by news of massive uprisings in the Arab world and the deflating debt bubble in Europe that pressed the international banking cartels into ever more desperate bailout schemes.

After weighing their concerns, his brother said, "Look, just do it. And if *you're* arrested by the Coast Guard, I'll take the ferry to Port Angeles and drive you *and* Dad back here. And for god's sake, don't lose *your* passport!"


After the Prius crosses the The Astoria–Megler Bridge, a four-mile-long transit over the mouth of the Columbia River to Washington State, the ebb and flow of traffic seems almost normal. Or whatever passes for normal in an area like this, Mavis figures. Logging and construction trucks climb in and out of the feeder roads along the 101. In the villages the traffic lights are in running order and the shops are open. Most of the gas stations have lines of three or four cars and an orderly procession of service appears routine. When they reach Aberdeen, a mill town down on its luck for the last forty years, Mavis spots a bank machine and withdraws five hundred dollars from her account. She tucks most of the cash in her pocket, but waves two twenties in the air as she climbs back into the car. "Anyone for lunch?" she calls with a taunt that she knows cannot be refused. Ten minutes later they're settled in a plastic booth at Abbey's 50s Grill eating pan-fried oysters, fish-and-chips, iceberg lettuce salads and a chocolate sundae for Teejay.

On the way out of Aberdeen, they top up the tank with gas and then Doyle outlines the next phase of their journey. He's arranged for Wyatt to meet them in two days on the beach near Pillar Point, a remote spot he says he visited ten years ago, a place where no one will see them climbing aboard his son's sloop, especially in the dark of night, which is when Doyle has set their rendezvous. They'll have nothing to fear from anyone, he assures them. The Coast Guard maintains an under-staffed patrol along the shore during the day, but at night it's satellite surveillance you have to be wary of, and lately, drone observation planes are rumored to be cruising overhead. Once they clear the shoals surrounding the point, within an hour or two they'll cross the boundary into Canada. After that, depending on the wind and tide and currents, it will take them perhaps a day or two, three at the most, to reach Salt Spring Island where they'll meet Wyatt's twin, Jesse, and his wife and baby. And until they find a place of their own, Mavis, James, Fay and Teejay can live in one of two out-buildings on Jesse's property, a five-acre hobby farm a half-hour walk from the village of Ganges.

Funny, Mavis thinks, but she hasn't put the twins' names together before. As they drive east along 101 and turn down the service road toward Pysht, she asks, "Doyle, the boys are named Wyatt and Jesse, right?"

He nods.

"Is there some sort of *cowboy connection* there?" She hopes the emphasis will provide a comic diversion, but her question emerges with a hint of urbane sarcasm and she immediately regrets it.

"Iris is from Wyoming but she grew up in San Francisco," Doyle says after a moment and leaves it at that.

Hmm. Maybe she's from Wyoming, Mavis muses,

knowing full well that Iris passed away earlier in the year. But obviously she still maintains a home in your heart.


When the sign for the Koivu Bed and Breakfast Inn catches her eye Mavis turns onto a gravel side road that passes along a stand of spruce trees. She's delighted when she pulls up in front of the B'n'B, a two-story cedar house decorated in the Finnish style and surrounded by a screened porch trimmed with white paint. A set of six matching Adirondack chairs positioned in a semi-circle on the lawn offer a commanding view of Butler Cove and the abandoned cabins dotting the shoreline.

Once inside the Koivu home, Mavis is presented with a basket of hot dinner rolls before she can sign the guest register. Now that's hospitality, she decides, especially coming from the sole surviving homestead in a ghost town with not a vowel to its name. Unless you count the "y" as an "i" Mavis concedes, which you have to do in order to pronounce it properly: *Pisht.* She's informed by Betsy Koivu that "Pysht" is a native word meaning the wind blows from many places. Even with a vowel, Mavis is tempted to blurt out "Pissed," which she dreads, in case it might upset Betsy Koivu.

"You'll find everything in Port," Betsy explains when Mavis asks where the ferry terminal is for the crossing up to Canada. "About thirty-two miles east on 101."

Mavis assumes that *Port* is the handy abbreviation used by the locals to designate Port Angeles, the central hub in Clallam County. Although the only locals she's met so far are Betsy and her husband, Aarne, and their three sons who are planning (everyone but Betsy, that is) to ship out at four in the morning so they can run with the early tide and set off for a week of fishing in their trawler. The men make a decent living from "the catch," Betsy says, and she operates the bed and breakfast to provide for extras, which appear to be plentiful enough to Mavis.

The next evening, after a day spent wandering the sparse downtown core of Port Angeles, Mavis has finalized her decision, a nagging problem she's had to resolve before she sets foot on Wyatt's boat: what to do with her car? She toyed with the idea of ferrying it across the strait to Canada and meeting the others after they arrive. But without a passport that option is impossible.

Satisfied now that she's making the right choice, she locks the Prius and walks around it once to ensure that everything's secure. The windows are up, the lights off, the emergency brake set, everything cleared from the trunk. She shuts the hatch-back and passes the key fob to Betsy Koivu. "I guess that's it," she says as Betsy tugs on the garage door with a rope pull that eases the door along a track and then swings it gently to the ground.

"Don't worry, nobody'll be joy-riding in your car while I'm here," Betsy says with a crisp nod. She smiles with a calm assurance and tucks Mavis's fifty dollar bill, the garage rental fee, into the front pocket of her jeans. "And like you said, if you're of a mind to sell it, I can handle that for you, too. Just call me and I'll fax the papers to you from the department of motor vehicles in Port."


In the clear November darkness the sound of a hundred paddles slips through the cold air. You would never hear the water splash as the canoes pressed across the strait to the far shore, but if you were attentive you might detect the wood blades stroking the breeze as they lifted from the water and then silently plowed into the next wave. The sound of birds' wings, of geese pressing south without issuing a cry. The sound of clouds forming in the west, pushing up from Hawaii. You could hear all that if you knew how to listen, hear the traffic of a million voyagers tracing their way up and down this coast over the course of twelve thousand years. A long, long time, Wyatt thinks as he sets his eyes on the North Star, the distant mirror that has reflected the hopes and worries of the sailors who shared this same journey so many times before. Where had they come from? Where had they gone? He shares this space with their ghosts and with all the ghosts still to follow. *He* is the living spirit now, now the spirit living this dream, this passage through the clean air on the water that washes through every living thing and then devours them all in one continuous draught. Ah, the godliness of human existence: he can feel all eternity in this pin-prick point of time. As the dots of salt water dash against his hand on the wheel, his eyes absorb the endless rotation of the stars. He revels in this — in life, multiplied by the awareness of life, divided by the certainty of his pending non-life, and subtracted by the loss of these thoughts, which added a flash of lucidity in the midst of the darkness. O great myriad of mysteries! He takes sustenance from the assurance that other ghosts will follow him, would know this passage through the world, this same tidal pulse and star scape. It doesn't matter that their memories will be forgotten, too. It doesn't even matter that a day might come when there will be no humans left to conduct this voyage, or if Earth were scorched by the sun's explosion and the oceans evaporated into space. Other stars would still churn, and from their grindstone the dust of existence will scatter into the cosmos and then another path would unfold and await discovery.

Wyatt sails alone through this dream, content with it. Soon enough he'll have to put away these thoughts and turn his attention to his father and navigate the shoals surrounding Pillar Point. Ten years ago with Doyle and Iris and Jesse, he'd darted in and out of every cove along this shore. It was a "rum-runners paradise" his father claimed. During the American Prohibition dozens of high-powered cutters darted back and forth across the Juan de Fuca Strait loaded with government-inspected, certified Canadian whiskey. Canadian Club, Seagram's VO, Black Velvet. Fortunes were made by those who escaped the Coast Guard, fortunes that still trickled their dividends into the pockets of old-money, west-coast families. Wyatt knew a few of them, too. The Saint-Lamberts. The Broomfields. Families with streets named after them. Families with political and business connections. Maybe that was what his father was bringing home with him this time. Connections and possibilities. Or perhaps the exact opposite: termination and a blockade of impossibilities. But in this frame of mind none of it matters. He's happy to navigate the tide and currents, to dodge the shoals and sandbars and let the future find its own way forward.

It takes over an hour to walk from Betsy Koivu's house down the hill, past the cluster of collapsed loggers' cabins near the estuary and through the cedar forest out to the gravel beach along Pillar Point. In the dark, without streetlights or the moon looming above to guide them, and with their bags and blankets weighing on them, the march is made in fits and stops. While no one is complaining, Doyle can sense a new tension in the others, an edge that he assigns to the breach that is opening between him and his companions. While he's inching closer to his family and his native country, the others are about to depart the familiar and enter a land of strangers. But he doesn't mention this insight to anyone and simply bides his time in silence, occasionally calling out directions ("left near that cedar tree," "right at the boulder ahead") to Teejay and Mavis, who are holding hands as they saunter along the trail followed by Doyle, Fay and James.

At the end of the dirt track Doyle turns on his flashlight and without saying a word he points out a path through the forest that he knows must eventually open onto the shore. This time Fay leads the way, walking just ahead of Doyle, two or three feet into the beam cast by the flashlight. How odd for her to be leading them now, he thinks, but why not? The most surprising change of character has come from Fay, who carries on silently, almost stoically it seems, as if she's discarded her anxieties and mania and inner rage and adopted a new personality. It's an osmosis of some kind, a way she's found of absorbing the tempo and spirit of the physical environment and making it part of her inner life. Perhaps the same principle of osmosis guided her life in San Francisco, too. He recalls the frantic traffic, the steep urban hills and valleys, the homelessness in the midst of exorbitant wealth and the ever-present threat of violence percolating just below the surface tension in the streets. That was San Francisco Fay, he tells himself. And now as they slip through the forest and emerge on the seashore, he's witnessing the appearance of fern-and-fennel Fay: sensitive, quiet, in tune with the nuance of her surroundings.

Twenty or thirty yards along the shore a row of logs is hung up on a bank near the high-tide line. Doyle switches off the light and leads them to the largest log and slips his pack onto the ground. He finds a large flat boulder below the log and squats on it, splaying his feet before him.

"Try to keep low and stay out of sight," he whispers, but the rush of surf scraping the rocky shore drowns his voice. "We'll wait here," he says a little louder. "Wyatt'll be along soon." He adjusts the collar of his jacket over his neck and passes two blankets to Teejay and Mavis. "Try to keep warm."

"Thanks." Mavis tugs a blanket around her shoulders and over Teejay's back so that the two of them are bundled together and then she wraps the second blanket over their legs. Fay sits on the other side of Doyle and folds a blanket on her lap, and James settles beside her at the far end of the log, a log so massive that it conceals all of them completely.

"Mavis, if you give me your phone, I'll check in with Wyatt," Doyle says when everyone is settled. Mavis digs her phone from her shoulder bag and a moment later Doyle sorts out the details of their rendezvous with his son. " ... All right. I'll flash the light once.... Okay, I'll have the phone on vibrate, so call me when you launch the dinghy.... See you soon."

"I guess we're a little early." Doyle checks his watch and hands the phone back to Mavis and asks her to set the ring mode to vibrate. "In about half an hour Wyatt will row in and take us out to his boat in two trips. Mavis you and James can go first, then I'll follow with Fay and Teejay."

Everyone assents to the plan. A light wind flutters above the log. A chill dampens the breeze and Mavis pulls her blanket tight around Teejay.

"I don't see him at all," Teejay says staring into the darkness above the waves. Twenty feet out she can't tell where the horizon line falls, the precise point where the water surface ends and meets the night air. She's never seen blackness this deep.

"You're not supposed to see him," James says. "You won't see him until he slips his dingy onto the beach."

Doyle draws a long breath and sets his gaze on the invisible distance past the crawling surf. Now that he's spoken to Wyatt he feels a longing to embrace him and hold him to his chest. That longing — and he can't quite determine how this impulse has crept up on him without any warning — pushes through his torso up into his head, into his face and up to his eyes. He has the sense that he's about to break into tears. He brushes his eyes and takes another breath. How could this be happening? The last time he cried was when Iris passed away. When she left him to sort things out for himself and determine what came next in his life. And now here he is months later, after *failing* to complete the memoir that was supposed to answer that damn mystery (the precise root question which he is still unable to articulate) here he is, squatting on the shore with four companions *who mean exactly what* to him? Answer *that* question, he tells himself. If you can't answer that question, be very careful because the last time you introduced Fay and Teejay to someone you knew, he died. Yes, embrace it. Louis is dead and departed because of your previous redeployment operations and now you're about to bring these same people into the sphere occupied by the boys and Bess and baby Gale. Do you dare to imagine you're some kind of master navigator who can pop freely from orbit to orbit without consequence?

"You're awfully quiet, Doyle." This observation is whispered by Fay who still sits with a blanket folded on her lap, her hands at rest — for once, Doyle notices — *not* spinning the rings around her fingers.

"Mmm." He glances at her briefly and returns to his

inquisition. First, he asks, who is the lord-high-priest asking the questions here? And second, what kind of proof can you present to demonstrate the connection between Louis's death and me? Doyle startles a moment when no reply ensues. When he realizes there's no one to answer him, he continues: just try to prove that I'm at fault. Why am *I* supposed to be responsible for all this? And who the hell put *me* in charge of human death and survival? Then, as if the next question is carried to him from an off-shore breeze, he asks, *and why am I guilty just because I outlived her?*

"Doyle?" Fay's voice is breathless; over the constant roll of surf only he can hear her. "You all right?"

He brushes a hand over his eyes. He's got to do something to hold this back. With Wyatt rowing toward him and everyone waiting to take this last step of the journey, he'd better shape up. His front teeth bite into his lower lip with just enough pressure to block the tears. After a moment his mind clears and he concentrates on the unending *shush* of the surf grinding below his feet. *Shush.* Let's get back to the first question, he says as though he's continuing a lecture to his senior geography students: What exactly do these people mean to you that you would sacrifice your future for them? Answer: *everything.* After Wyatt and Jesse and Bess and the baby, and the memory of Iris, they are the *new* now. And the memory of Iris is the root cause. Her embrace of humanity. Her willingness to offer help to anyone in need. Yes, her love of others had infected him. He sees the long chain of individual moments extend from the past up to the present instant, sitting here with Fay and Teejay and Mavis and James. They mean everything to him now. When he understands this he wraps his arm around Fay's shoulder. He's never touched her before, he realizes, never shaken her hand in greeting or embraced her narrow shoulders to say goodbye.

"Your wife?" her eyes stitch onto to his.

He nods and tips his head away. His arm falls from her shoulder to his lap.

"Everything all right?" she asks. She takes his hand into her own, slips it under the blanket and presses it to her leg. "You know, I owe you a lot." She guides his palm along her thigh. "I was wondering ... if there's anything I can do." She lets these words hang and studies his face, the soft weariness in his eyes. When he draws a deep breath and dips his shoulders, she continues, "And I mean *any*thing, Doyle."

He withdraws his arm, sets his eyes on the sky and teases himself with this offer. "Mmm," he murmurs, pleased to know that he could still play the game. "Not now, Fay. But who knows?" he adds, unsure if he should lead her on.

"Doyle." Mavis passes the phone to him. It vibrates in his hand, insistent and strange. He's never completely adjusted to the near-sentient quality of cell phones. He touches the answer button and holds the phone to his ear.

"I'm anchored just off the point," Wyatt whispers through the darkness. "Flash the light and I'll come in for you."


At first he appears as a shadow, then as a silhouette emerging from the darkness. "There he is!" Teejay cries in a suppressed cheer. Seconds later she can make out the motion of his back and arms pulling on the weight of the oars as he presses through the rolling surf toward them. "Over there," she adds when Doyle and Mavis claim they can't see him. She lifts her hand from the blanket and points to the white dingy bobbing in the waves as it hits the shore.

Once he steps ashore Teejay is surprised that Wyatt doesn't match the image of the lone twin she held in her mind over the past few days. He doesn't look at all like Doyle. He's a little taller and broader and his hair is blond and it curls over his ears in loose bundles that shake this way and that as he heaves the dingy onto the rocky beach.

Doyle hugs him for a long time and then he turns to introduce Wyatt to everyone one at a time as if he can't get enough of saying over and over, "This is my son, Wyatt."

When Wyatt shakes Teejay's hand and smiles, she finally finds a sure connection between the father and son. His eyes are identical to Doyle's: ice blue, thoughtful-looking, and above all, very kind. She nods her head to affirm this new insight to herself. Doyle is the kindest man she has ever met, even a notch kinder than Dr. K. And now she recognizes this same kindness in Wyatt.

The next half hour is spent loading the dingy and rowing everyone out to the *Sustenance* in two trips just as Doyle planned. Once they're all on board Wyatt summons everyone below deck and after a "gray-light tour of the boat," as he calls it, everyone settles into their berths to sleep while Doyle and Wyatt climb onto the deck and let the sailboat slip with the tide into the Salish Sea.

As she lies beside her mother in the rear berth, Teejay adjusts the pillow and presses it against her cheek. "I've never been in a boat before," she whispers above the sound of the waves slapping against the hull.

"I know. I haven't either," Fay replies. "It's kind of fun, don't you think?"

"Yeah." Teejay feels a wave of exhaustion slide away in

one long sigh as she submerges under the heavy currents of sleep.

"Everything's kind of fun these days," Fay adds as her eyes adjust to the darkness and she scans the compact design of the berth. "Don't you think so?"

"Shhhhh." Teejay expels another sigh and settles her tummy against the curve of her mother's hip.

Feeling the warmth of her daughter as she sleeps at her side, Fay closes her eyes and begins to pray. How often in the past has she prayed and then been disappointed? But this time, finally, some of her prayers are answered. *Thank You, dear God, for Your blessings.* She folds her hands together and murmurs silently to herself, pressing her fingers into a steeple the way her mother taught her. *Thank You for the comfort and guidance of my friends. Thank You for the new life You have given us. I promise I will dedicate the rest of my days to You through the love of my child, named for Your saints, Teresa and Jacinta.* A moment later Fay falls into sleep, a long rest that will last ten hours.

As soon as Wyatt stows the anchor he can feel the *Sustenance* turn northwest into the tidal flow. He zips his jacket up to the collar, walks across the deck and joins his father in the cockpit of the sloop. Then he pours two cups of tea from his thermos and checks his watch: one-thirty. Not bad; pretty much on schedule.

"Earl Grey?" Doyle asks as he draws a sip of tea over his tongue.

"Yeah. Miss it?"

"Not as much as I missed you," he says and ropes an arm around his son's shoulders and presses him to his chest once more.

Wyatt sets the wheel to align the sloop with the tide. They'll be drawn out into the Pacific by morning, but at the same time the currents will drag them across the international line, and even without a favorable wind, they should be clear of the US by daylight. Despite the simplicity of the plan, there are dangers on both sides of the border. On the Canadian side, they risk interception by patrols from the Canadian Coast Guard and from random checks by Fisheries and Oceans Canada. But a greater threat lies with the US Coast Guard, who could be alerted to their movement by images downloaded from the constant sweep of satellites, or worse, direct detection by unmanned drone surveillance.

"It's ridiculous if they're using drones out here. It's too expensive," Doyle says after listening to Wyatt report the recent rumors about robotic surveillance. "Especially when they can get the same information with satellites." He jabs a finger toward the heavens and glances into the night sky. It's bejeweled with stars, a sight he can never forget, but one that always startles him the instant he gazes into the void. He's convinced there's a direct exchange between the stars and human awareness of them. We are illuminated by their presence, he thinks, and the that fact most people no longer witness the stars' nightly brilliance — and thus, our own human radiance — renders us mere smog-dwellers sifting through the detritus of the urban world.

"But the drones provide more detail," his son continues and locks the wheel in place and settles on the cockpit bench next to his father. He pulls a blanket over their thighs and smiles. Good to have the old man back on board.

"Maybe," Doyle concedes and leans his head back so his eyes can take in the expanse glittering above them. "Keep an eye out for Big Birds," he says with a short laugh. *Big*

*Birds* is the game he used to play with the boys at night when they sat on the back deck of the house during the new moons every summer. They kept a log of their sightings and after consulting with various authorities, they were able to identify the names, origins, and orbits of over twenty satellites and eventually learn to predict their scheduled passage overhead. Years later, aboard the *Snail's Pace*, each of them used the same game to keep awake during the solitary night watches.

"There's one," Wyatt says and points directly overhead.

"Right. Got it." The arc of the bird unfolds slowly, traced by the satellite's on-board lights blinking mechanically against the void. Doyle recognizes a deep ambivalence welling through him. They represent the ingenuity of humanity, yet at the same time they litter the atmosphere with the shrapnel of their increasing collisions. "It's a Timex watch draped over the wrist of Infinity," Doyle says, a little surprised by this metaphoric flourish. Normally he prefers precision in speech, not some literary allusion.

Wyatt chuckles. "That's a good one. I'll tell that to Jesse. He won't believe you said — "

At that moment the satellite explodes above them. The single, blinking light bursts into a hundred sparks that dash across the sky.

*"Holy shit! Did you see that?"* Wyatt grabs the binoculars and presses them to his eyes.

"Yeah!"

A few of the bigger embers burst a second time, a detonation within an explosion, firing off one at a time as they spin in brief, crazy dances of exhilaration and then expire in the surrounding silence.

"Did you see that?!" Wyatt asks again and looks at his father and then back to the sky.

"Yes. *Yes — I saw it!*" Doyle can't believe the intensity of the dwindling electrical discharge glittering above them.

It takes a moment before either of them can say another word. They keep scanning the sky for any trace of the satellite, but none emerges. When it's clear the event is complete, Doyle holds his mug of tea aloft. "Cheers," he says to his son. As they clink the mugs together they smile in mutual recognition of what they have seen. They are eyewitnesses to the Kessler Syndrome made manifest, possibly the first people ever to behold a satellite collision in real time. A feeling both divine and melancholic seeps through them. For years they've been certain that everything Kessler predicted would come to pass. In ones and twos the satellites would continue the long sequence of smash-ups. It was just a matter of time before they're all rendered into a hail of ripped debris speeding around the earth and then transformed, piece by piece, into ashes and dust.

Wyatt feels a breeze come over his shoulder and he decides to adjust the mainsail. "There's one thing we can count on," he says as he sets his mug on the deck. "With that satellite out of commission, the Coast Guard won't see us moving across the line. At least not from that bird."

"True enough." Doyle nods and watches his son draw the sail tight against the wind. In the spare shelter of the cockpit he relaxes on the bench and wraps a blanket around his back and over his chest. The journey has taken a toll on him and he can feel the long grind of exhaustion in his bones. In a moment he'll step into the cabin and climb onto the empty berth. "I guess it means we're home-free," he says, realizing that Wyatt is too preoccupied with the sail to respond. Nonetheless, he shrugs and says it again to himself just so he can hear the reassurance the words provide. *"Home-free."*

"Are you hungry, Teejay?" Wyatt sees the tip of the girl's head poke through the cabin doorway. Since first light, well over an hour ago, he's been expecting her.

"Yes, a little," she offers and sits beside him next to the wheel. She glances at the deck of the sloop, studies the shoreline in the distance and the forests rising through the mist on the hills. "Are we going to be there soon?"

"Hard to say. It all depends on the wind and the currents and tides. You see those colored streamers on the edge of the sail?" He points to the tell-tales fluttering in the breeze. "Those are called tell-tales because they tell you which way the wind is blowing no matter which way the boat is going."

"Tell-tales?" She smiles at this and examines Wyatt's face to identify any resemblance to Doyle.

"Right. And the tide schedule is published in printed tables. But the currents are indicated on maps." He points to the laminated chart stowed under the wheel. "So if everything aligns we should be there tomorrow or the day after. We have to sail around the southern tip of Vancouver Island and then up the Baines Channel to Salt Spring Island."

"I've never been on a boat before," she says, and grasping a rail in one hand she stands up to take in the view over the low, curving deck of the *Sustenance*.

"I guess that means you've never gone fishing, then."

She shakes her head, no.

"Do you like fish? For breakfast I mean."

"Well, I like *fish burgers*, if that's what you mean."

Wyatt laughs and glances away. "You're funny," he says and then adds, "If you like fish burgers, there's a chance you'll like fish. In which case, I want you to pull on this rope and see what we've got for breakfast." He tugs on a cord that descends from the stern into the ocean and hands it to her.

Teejay steps beside him and grips the rope and begins to reel it in, hand-over-hand until the heads of three salmon emerge from the water. A flash of panic courses through her and she releases the rope and the fish dive back into the water. "Yuck! What are they?"

"Salmon." Wyatt laughs again and decides he shouldn't try to surprise her. "Pinks, we call them, because of their color when you cook them."

Teejay edges to the stern of the boat again and stares into the wake slipping behind the *Sustenance*. She draws a long breath and begins to haul the fish toward her once more, pausing briefly when she sees their open mouths break the surface. As she lifts them from the water, she's pleased to see that each fish head is still attached to a fish body and that the fins and tails are located where she assumes they should be. Taking another breath she tugs on the line and pulls the catch of fish along the side of the hull. "Where do I put them?" she asks when they are up to the gunwale.

Wyatt points to an empty styrofoam ice chest and when he sees her hesitate, he decides to take the line and lays the fish into the chest himself.

"Are they alive?"

He shakes his head.

"Where did you get them?"

"I caught them. While you were sleeping."

Teejay glances away, scans the water surface and in the distance spies three trawlers heading toward the Pacific. "So now what do we do?" she asks.

"Can you cook?"

"Yes. A *little*," she adds, to suggest that she's never come close to cooking fish before.

"Have you ever used a frying pan?"

"Sure. To make grilled cheese sandwiches."

Wyatt smiles and nods his head, a gesture to assure her that if she can cook grilled cheese sandwiches, she can pan-fry six salmon fillets. "Here, take the wheel," he says and he slips a half-step toward the bench allowing her to scoot behind him.

Teejay looks at the wheel and then into Wyatt's face. "You mean you want me to steer the boat?"

"Of course. I've got to clean these fish if you're going to cook 'em."

Teejay eases forward and places the fingers of one hand on the wheel. "Like this?"

"Yup. Except you have to get a solid grip on it."

She places her second hand on the wheel and studies the horizon beyond the bow. "Where do I steer it to?"

"Just keep her going straight. Pick a spot on Vancouver Island and keep the bow pointed toward it. You don't need to turn the wheel too much." Wyatt turns his back to the girl and begins to cut the fish with a filleting knife.

"What's the bow?"

"The front of the boat."

Teejay locks her eyes on a log cabin perched on a point of land jutting into the water. She steadies herself and turns the wheel a few degrees each way to determine how much force she has to apply to ease the boat to the left and right. She glances at the tell-tales and after a few moments she asks, "Is that Vancouver Island?"

"Yup. Everything on the left is Vancouver Island. Everything on the right is the US of A." Wyatt cleans the fish quickly: fins, tails, heads, guts, scales.

"How am I doing?"

He laughs again. "I can see why Dad likes you," he says.

She glances around and sees Wyatt smiling at her. A smudge of fish scales has splashed onto his wrist. A few others are speckled on his cheek.

"Why?"

There're so many reasons; he can't choose just one. "Because you're so funny," he says.

"No, *you're* funny. You look like a fish! You've got fish scales all over your face," she replies and starts to laugh, too.

"All right, all right. It's a tie. We're *both* funny." He finishes cleaning the fish and tosses the remnants overboard. He rinses his hands in the ocean and wipes his face with the cold water.

Teejay turns her attention back to the horizon off the bow and realizes they've drifted to the right of the island. The tell-tales won't do this for you, she tells herself and fixes her gaze on the little cabin standing on the distant point. She braces her feet on the deck and leans against the wheel and when everything feels just right, she locks her body in place and holds the *Sustenance* on course. How long will it take to reach that cabin, she wonders. Maybe an hour she decides, maybe more, depending on the wind and the currents and tides.


The next day the afternoon air is cool and breezy. Everyone has come onto the deck except Wyatt, who is taking a turn to sleep in the berth next to the head. The *Sustenance* presses toward the city of Victoria and in the distance everyone can see the lighthouse on Trial Island. Once they pass Trial Island, Doyle tells them, they'll turn north and make the run up Baines Channel, past the

Sidney Marina, where Wyatt lives, and on to Salt Spring Island.

Teejay wedges herself into the cage formed by the aluminum tubing of the bowsprit, a cramped spot that allows her to obscure the view of the rest of the boat when she leans forward and extends her head above the water. She's pretending to be an explorer like the Asians that Wyatt told her about, the first people to paddle this way twelve thousand years ago. She tries to see the world as it was then: the unbroken surface of the sea, the steep hills on the island, the virgin forests. Whenever another boat comes into view, she holds a hand up to block it from her fantasy. But when she spots a few of the nineteenth-century mansions behind the shoreline of Victoria, and in the distance the classic white lighthouse with its red roof perched on Trial Island, she sits up and imagines she's entering another era, a time with horse-drawn carriages and clipper ships and women dressed in long skirts who sip tea and discuss the coming debutante ball.

"Can I draw you?" Fay steps behind her daughter, comfortable enough with her sea legs now to venture from the cockpit onto the deck. She holds a letter-size drawing tablet in one hand and she cocks her head to take in this new image of Teejay: alone at the front of the gliding ship, happy with her solitude.

"Sure." Teejay wipes a strand of hair from her face and rearranges herself so that she faces the stern. Doyle is holding the wheel. James and Mavis are holding hands. She settles herself on the deck and scans the freighters and pleasure craft coming and going in every direction. "It's pretty here," she says and plumps a smile on her face.

"I like it, too." Fay listens to the waves slap at the bow and then squats on the deck and leans against the mast a few feet from Teejay. She places the tablet on her bent knee and with a stick of charcoal she draws a curving line on the right side of the page. This is her daughter's cheek. Another line: her chin. "Seems like I haven't drawn anything in weeks," she says.

"I know." Teejay nods. "Since before the fire."

"I guess that's about when it was." She sketches an ear and the threads of hair curling under the earlobe. She wants to say that the fire took everything she had, but she knows it's not true. In fact the fire *gave* her everything she now possesses: a new beginning and a new life with her daughter. Most important, her sanity. "Are you still taking those pills from Dr. K?" she asks as she lays some texture into the hair.

Teejay shrugs and watches James and Mavis. Whenever Doyle looks away, they steal another kiss. "I haven't in two days. There's no more pain. None at all. Do you think I should take any more?"

Fay relaxes her shoulders, pleased to be asked for advice. "I don't think so. Not if the pain's all gone." She pauses, just long enough to ensure her voice is neutral and then continues, "And what about the spotting, Honey? Has that cleared up?"

"Yes."

Fay smiles without looking up and she rubs a finger on the charcoal behind her daughter's neckline. A little smudge suggests the gray waters pooling in the background. "I'm not taking my pills anymore, either." She looks into Teejay's eyes to gauge her reaction.

The girl considers this, how it fits together with where they are. "That's good, Mom. Really good."

"I know. It really is."

Teejay sits quietly while her mother continues to sketch,

waits for the right moment to ask a new question. "Have you been thinking about Raymond?"

Fay draws a breath and slides the drawing tablet into her lap. How sad, she thinks. Teejay can never bring herself to call him her father, or simply Dad. "A little," she says and casts her eyes to the lighthouse. "What about you? Do you think of him?"

"Not much." She presses her lips together as if she's pressing the memory of him to the back of her mind. "I know what happened," she says. "I know what he did."

Fay gazes into the sketch and then forces herself to look at her daughter. "You know what he did?"

"Yes." She nods and holds her mother's eyes. "And I know that what he did made everything go ... bad."

Fay glances away. She can barely contemplate the special hell he made for her and Teejay. "That's true," she says, "It was his doing."

"But I don't think of that part," she continues. "Not very often. And when I do think of it, I just want to believe he didn't mean to. It was like ... *a mistake.*"

Fay places the tablet in the well of her lap and nods her head with a sense of relief. How smart, she thinks. How wise to dismiss his crime with this kind of forgiveness. So much better to deem it a mistake than a crime. That way you can think of yourself as a survivor instead of a victim and then you can take control of your life again.

"Do you think it could have been a mistake?"

"I think *he* believes it was a mistake. That's why he came to see us. To ask our forgiveness. But here's what I think now. For the first time since you were my baby, we're free. What's in the past is gone, Teejay. And what we have now, right now, is good. As for what lies ahead...." She shrugs and considers how to explain her view of things. "It's like this boat. All the water behind us, *that ocean behind us,* who knows where the individual drops of water that make it all up have gone? And as for what's ahead, we just have to pick a place and steer toward it. That part's up to us. Yeah-yeah, that's all up to us," she says again and braces the tablet on her knee and continues her sketch. "Does that make sense?"

Before she can respond, Teejay's attention turns to Doyle, who caps his eyes with one hand and then points past the lighthouse.

"Whales!" he cries. "Two of them breaching at one o'clock!" When he sees them — one small, one large — breaking the surface in unison, he adds, "Looks like a cow and her new-born calf."

Everyone turns in all directions, unsure what Doyle means by one o'clock. Then they align their eyes with his arm pointing to the stark black-and-white humps of the Killer Whales. Again and again the two whales breach the water beside one another, each time jetting an enormous spray into the air and then diving in graceful arcs that reveal their broad, wing-tip flukes before they disappear into the sea.

Mavis has been trying to sort it out all morning, trying to calculate the precise instant when everything about the journey from Berkeley changed for her. After hours of doubt and speculation, she's finally able to pinpoint the transition to the moment when she handed the key to her Prius to Betsy Koivu. Not that there has to be a turning point, but she knows there are specific times in life that are temporal *hinges,* and this was one of them. Another example: the second you first saw James, she tells herself. When you enter one of these precisely contained instants, your life turns and for better or for worse you begin a transit along a new path.

In her current situation, Mavis now realizes that her latest transition depends upon the simplicity of *release*. The release of her cozy apartment in Berkeley. Letting go her dream of becoming a Gestalt Therapist. Parting company with Dansky and Box. Abandoning her MA degree. Leaving Papa Helm's wingback chair to Rosa. The oddest thing about releasing so much of her past is that the effect didn't truly impact her when she *began* to abandon these diverse components of her life, but at the *end* of the process. It was only when she dropped the car key into Betsy's fingers that she completed her divestment. As she walked from Betsy's house down the hill toward the ocean she took Teejay's hand in her own. This was a new thing, holding the surprisingly strong hand of the girl she so admired. Then came the next new thing, clambering into the wobbly dingy with Wyatt and James and paddling into the night. At one point she couldn't see the shore behind them nor the *Sustenance* bobbing about in the darkness ahead of them. She'd entered a moving center of darkness, a place occupied only by her awareness of it. The single force propelling her forward was a sense of blind trust. That was when she realized she was on a new transit, and from there, she worked backward to piece together the actual turning point: the instant of final release. From this point of discovery she wonders if maybe all the things we try to acquire through life — money, houses, furniture, credentials, cars, vacations, clothing, safety, protection — if maybe, the more of them we possess, the more they possess us. It's a deceptive form of slavery. One you think you want until you have too much of it. And once you have too much of it, the only salvation is *release*.

She smiles again. She's been smiling a lot in the last few hours as they glide across the surface of the water in the open air of the cockpit. There's so little to hang onto. James's hand, the thin metal railing along the edge of the deck, the wheel that Doyle allowed her to steer for ten minutes when the wind fell to a calm. She sits in the embrace of James's arm, shares a kiss from time to time and when the Killer Whales break the surface, she can feel the forces of nature whirling around her, a kaleidoscope of energy, all of it humming the coda to a grand symphony: release, release, release. From time to time she turns her head to study Fay squatting against the mast, lost in the sketch she's creating of her daughter, who sits at the tip of the bow, an angel about to take flight — the flesh-and-blood embodiment of a figurehead flying above the waves. All this swirls within her and when Wyatt emerges from the galley stretching his arms and yawning, she whispers to James, "Why don't you come with me." It's not a question, but a command. An appetite for desire. "Just come inside for a little while."

She takes his hand and leads him below deck to the master quarters that Wyatt surrendered to her and James when they started the voyage. She steps over the sill and closes the door behind James and sets the sliding latch in place.

"What's this?" he murmurs, but she places her hand over his lips and leads him to the bed that extends from the rear wall. Tucked beneath the bow, the tiny room employs a mariner's efficiency to shape the walls and floor and ceiling into a bright cell illuminated by an arc of six circular windows positioned a foot above the waterline. There are hidden bookshelves, a built-in stereo system, a rack of CDs, places for candles and incense, flashlights, a set of drawers where Wyatt keeps his clothes and snorkeling gear, a collapsible desk. She could take a day exploring this intricate cubby-hole, but she will not take another moment away from her consideration of James.

She slips his jacket to the floor and begins to unbutton his shirt. When her fingers unclasp his belt, he cocks his head and asks, "What's going on?" She holds a hand to his mouth again as her left hand reaches into his pants. "No talking," she whispers. "You'll disturb the whales. Besides, you *know* what's going on." She lifts his testicles into her hand for a moment and sighs, then pulls the bed sheets aside, and settles him onto the mattress. She begins to strip her clothes away and when she's naked she pulls his pants from his legs and rolls onto him. "And you know what *these* are!" She laughs into his ear and presses her breasts to his mouth, first one, and then the other and then back and forth again and again as she releases a stream of lust through her nipples into his mouth, passing it from her body to his, nourishing him with her need simply by opening her body to his — to become the well that will quench them both, the deep, deep well of her inner world and all the mystery hidden there, flooding (so moist and slick) with her new liberation. When he turns her onto her back and mounts her, she feels herself pressed down into the pool of her desire and as she falls through the abyss into the simultaneous blessing and disaster of sex, she can feel one last burst of freedom, a release that has been opening ahead of her for the past two weeks, that has lured her relentlessly and finally pinned her to the bed in this unexpected junction of time and place, in a tidy berth skimming above the Salish Sea in a place between two invented countries. Then she can feel it: the explosion of millions of sperm and their mad dash toward the lone egg that waits patiently to receive the chosen one, and then at the moment of their union — *then* — she feels the instant conception of her child. To think this solitary egg once rested in her own mother's womb, already fully developed in one of Mavis's tiny ovaries while Mavis herself lay *in utero*. They made a set of three Russian dolls: grandmother, mother, child. And now, following the release of her penetration, she *knows* the child is truly conceived and she rolls her belly up and away, away from James's spent body, as if she's secreting the embryo into the wall of her uterus, to its sacred hiding place. *Yes*, she whispers to herself as she tucks her head into the curve of James's shoulder and drifts in his sweet sexual aroma. In a final rush of passion she drags her tongue over his nipple and bites his flesh until he moans. He should know what has been divined from their bodies and if he cannot guess it, she will soon tell him. How odd, she thinks, that in the moment of her liberation the child will now take possession of her body. It's just one more hinge in time. But fortunately, she now knows how to turn.


When the *Sustenance* passes the Sidney Marina, Wyatt and James are the only people still working on the deck. The others are in the galley preparing fish chowder and warming the poppyseed bagels that Wyatt purchased before setting out on the voyage. Dusk is approaching and a damp chill is heavy in the evening light. "There's the spot I call home," Wyatt says and he points to the wharf where he moors his boat. "It's the third finger down," he tells James and extends an arm past the port bow. "There's a village a few kilometers up the peninsula where I share a car with a few buddies, so I never have any trouble getting into the city."

James nods with a sleepy satisfaction as he studies the passing islands. *Kilometers.* Another small signifier that they are entering a new world. Like Doyle's fondness for tea cozies. Since he returned to the ship's cockpit after his spontaneous romp with Mavis (and her insistence that they'd conceived a baby) he's been considering the variety of cottages and cabins that line the shores, wondering who might live in this one or that, speculating how durable they might be in the winter storms that surely must rip through this channel, and if the land would support a garden and a pen of chickens and goats. "Do people live here year-round?" He points to a group of small islands in the distance.

"On some of them." Wyatt pulls his jacket collar over his neck. "There's over two hundred islands in the Gulf. Some are parks, some privately owned. Salt Spring Island has over ten thousand residents. There's schools, hospitals, cafés. Lots of ten-acre farms. It's got everything. My brother's a teacher on Salt Spring."

"Like your dad."

Wyatt adjusts the wheel. "Yeah. Jesse's the one who followed in Dad's footsteps. As for me?..." He smiles and lets this sentence hang, as if his career direction is a matter of family speculation.

"You could wonder the same about me." James claps a hand onto Wyatt's shoulder and lets it fall onto the railing. They're both standing now, observing the boats passing in and out of the marina as they sail past it and bear north toward the Gulf Islands. "I would say my career path is somewhat checkered."

"A good word for it. Since it's all a game."

When the *Sustenance* rounds the eastern point of Coal

Island, Wyatt angles his arm to the left of the bow. "There's Salt Spring," he says.

"Really?" James narrows his eyes. "What's that behind it? With the mountains."

"It's all part of Salt Spring. That's Mount Maxwell and Mount Tuam. They're both surrounded by dozens of hills, lakes, back roads. Here, take the wheel, I'm going to phone Jesse."

James holds the wheel in his hands and Wyatt indicates a distant point of land on the far right of the island and advises him to steer behind any ferries coming or going through Swartz Bay. "Just keep her heading toward Beaver Point and we'll be fine."

As Wyatt calls his brother and begins to plan when and where they'll meet, James tries to match the shape of Salt Spring Island to the image he carries in his memory. In the looming darkness the hills appear more blue than green. He can't make out specific details of the roads or houses but the mountains are unmistakable. The only difference between his vision of them and their stark reality is the scale. Everything is so much bigger than he imagined. As the wind carries them forward he tries to purge his mind of any more preconceptions. They are all illusions.

Perhaps everything he's ever perceived is a form of reality in disguise. *Exhibit A: your transcendent apparition of the Salish Sea.* James tries to calculate how many days have passed since his out-of-body journey to Salt Spring Island. Was it a week ago? That was his last opportunity to meditate and now, like every other occasion when he's dropped his daily practice, he begins to doubt the substance and reality of his clairvoyance. What's worse is that whenever he falls out of the daily groove of White Light Meditation, he struggles to overcome the inertia of what he calls *mere mortality.* He's never discussed the idea with Mavis (or anyone else) because he knows how elitist it must sound. How spiritually fascist. Mere mortality suggests the world is inhabited by the *merely mortal,* a kind of sub-human species that is unable to recognize its inherent radiance, a herd of sleep-walking drones who decline the gift of illumination when the opportunity welcomes them with each passing day.

*That* is the tragedy of humanity, he decides. He tried to point the way with the White Light Meditation Foundation but the folly of his mission was revealed with Zack's suicide. Going forward, if you want to overcome the inertia dragging you down, he tells himself, then embrace this single lesson as a guiding principle. Remember the one truth imparted by your own illumination: The purpose of life is *to be, not to believe.*

Paranoia. The word sticks in Doyle's mind as he stirs a saucepan filled with salmon chowder on the stove in the galley. In the 1960s he experienced the cultural paranoia prevalent at the time. Sometimes the drama was inescapable: the National Guard shooting innocent bystanders next to a Vietnam anti-war protest (Kent State). Other times the feeling was nuanced and phantasmagorical: visions of faceless bureaucrats concocting phony charges to arrest artists and agitators (Joan Baez, Timothy Leary). Then came the episodes of invisible dementia: the steady drip of environmental collapse under the stress of acid rain and lead poisoning (Lake Baikal being the worst, so far). Looking back, he can see these myriad fears had a basis in reality. But the dread in him now is so specific, so tied to his present circumstance that he can't shake the premonition that his arrest is imminent. He can feel his arms twisting behind his back, hear the handcuffs clicking into place around his wrists.

To ensure he's not being paranoid *about being paranoid* (the ultimate psychotic double-bind, he figures) he pulls the pocket dictionary from Wyatt's library shelf and thumbs through the pages to find the definition of his possible affliction: *par·a·noi·a, n: 1. An unreasonable mistrust of others and their intentions. 2. A psychiatric disorder involving systematic illusions of persecution.*

He eliminates definition number two on the spot: no *systematic* illusions; if anything, they are more erratic than systematized. Definition number one is arguable, perhaps, except that his mistrust isn't unreasonable. Specifically, he's worried that the Royal Canadian Mounted Police will board the *Sustenance* moments after it docks and arrest everyone on board for the entirely reasonable cause that four of them are illegal aliens and that Fay and Teejay are evading a warrant for their arrest. More worrisome, Wyatt is involved in transporting the aforementioned illegals, a crime which carries serious jail time. Not to mention the almost laughable offense that Doyle has returned to the country without his passport. So, he murmurs as he stirs the soup, while his might not be a textbook case of paranoia, this grinding dread is completely justifiable.

He decides to put on a game face and asks Teejay to bring him the soup bowls. "And a basket for the bagels," he adds. While the fear is real, he continues, the possibility of capture is remote. After all, the *Sustenance* sailed across the international boundary without incident. And when they slipped past the Canadian Coast Guard station in Victoria, Teejay had the temerity to wave to the crew on one of their ships and persisted until three or four of the uniformed men waved back. And now in the gray dusk, as Wyatt guides the boat to meet Jesse at the dock below the Hamber's cottage, the chance of being busted as they land is so remote that it's negligible — within the same range of possibilities, for example, of Kosmos 2251 slamming into Iridium 33. He tries to smile at this crumb of irony but the best he can do is drag the corners of his lips into a frown.

"You're being very quiet again," Fay says. "Something wrong?" She takes a soup bowl from Teejay and sets it in front of Mavis on the galley table.

"No, no. Not at all," he says a little too brightly in an effort to deflect her recent fixation on his moods. "I'm just a worrier. It's in my nature. As a *grandfather,*" he adds and winks at Teejay as he hands her the basket of bagels. "We should be arriving in the next hour, so you folks enjoy the soup and bagels. I'm going to take some up to the boys. Teejay, open the door for me, will you?"

When he climbs into the cockpit, Doyle is surprised to see the *Sustenance* has already rounded the eastern point of Ruckle Park. He passes one bowl of soup to his son, the other to James. He tugs a warm bagel from each of the front pockets of his jacket and passes them on and then takes the wheel in his hands so that Wyatt can eat. "How much further?"

"Twenty minutes, maybe." Wyatt pours the bowl of soup into his empty coffee mug and sips it between his lips. "Nice and warm," he says.

"Twenty minutes?" James squints through the failing light. He can see the rocky beaches to the left and the stand of trees rising above the stacks of loose driftwood scattered along the waterfront but in the lengthening shadows it's difficult to distinguish anything in the distant shoreline. "How will you know where the dock is?"

"Jesse will signal us." Wyatt sets the mug aside and bites

into his bagel. After a moment he takes the wheel from his father and says, "I'll take us in, Dad."

Doyle passes the wheel to his son and rubs his face with both hands as though he's shaking off a long night of troubled sleep. When he's revived he takes a moment to gaze at the foreshore of Ruckle Park. The arbutus trees climbing above the grass fields are so familiar, even in the dusk. "How did you decide to dock at the Hamber's place?"

"Jesse says they've gone to Calgary for the week. And since their property is midway between the park and the marina, I wouldn't expect anyone to be keeping a watch over it at this time of day."

"And as I remember it, the road down to the cottage is pretty well screened." Doyle contributes this detail as a compounding piece of logic. It's almost certain now that the RCMP cannot have devised any traps. As they approach the pier the likelihood of arrest diminishes with each passing band of kelp floating on the water's surface and his fear recedes to a narrow blade of anxiety.

They skim over the water in silence for another few minutes listening to the screech of two Great Blue Herons fighting for turf on the rocks off the beach. When their battle is over, Wyatt passes his flashlight to Doyle. "Do you want to do the honors?"

Doyle nods and points the flashlight to where he imagines Jesse might be stationed. He clicks the lamp once and turns it off. As everyone peers into semidarkness he can feel the air fill his lungs and then flatten in a slow exhalation. A light flashes from the shore off the port bow. One burst, exactly the way he'd taught the boys so many years ago. "That's him!" he whispers.

"Yeah." Wyatt pulls hard on the wheel and releases the tension on the sail. It flutters briefly and with the slacking momentum the *Sustenance* drifts toward the dock. "You can call the girls up to the deck," he tells James. "Tell them we're here."

James sets his soup bowl on the deck and slips his head through the transom. A wedge of light from the cabin illuminates his face and he waves to Mavis and Fay. "We're here. Tell Teejay."

Moments later the women emerge with a gust of light laughter. Doyle tries to hush them. "Shhh, shhh, shhh," he whispers with a forced severity. The chance of disaster is now close to impossibility, he figures, but still, they must steer away from it, reduce it to nothingness.

"Throw me a line."

Doyle can hear Jesse's voice at the edge of the dock. Now he sees him. "I'll get it," he tells Wyatt and he tosses the nylon rope to Jesse.

"Hi, Dad." Jesse's voice is low but full of cheer. He snugs the line around a metal cleat on the wharf and quickly cinches it in place.

"Hi son." He wants to hug him, but he knows he should get Mavis, Fay and Teejay onto the dock before he disembarks. "God, it's good to see you. Did you bring Bess and the baby?"

"Yeah, they're at the end of the dock."

Doyle waves. He can see Bess's hand fluttering as she sits on a wood bench near the shore. Yes, they're all here. Even his granddaughter.

He helps Mavis and Fay step over the rail onto the dock. Then he takes Teejay's hand. "You see," he says to her as her foot steps onto the planking, "there's Wyatt's twin, Jesse. I *told* you I had twins."

"Of course!" As Teejay looks from Jesse to Wyatt and

back to Jesse again her face widens into a broad smile. "Did you think I didn't believe you?"

"No, it's not that." He briefly considers her question. "I just like to say it out loud once in a while. To remind myself."

She turns her head and waits for James to step onto the pier behind her. Even in the dusk Doyle can see her radiance. He follows James and then Wyatt joins him on the wharf, everyone taking a moment to adjust their sea legs to the stability underfoot, to accept their moment of arrival. When he has Jesse in his arms and tucks Bess and the baby against his waist, and when Wyatt throws his arms around them all — then he realizes that he's beat the odds. Finally, he's sure of it. He's made a safe landing after all.

# More by D.F. Bailey

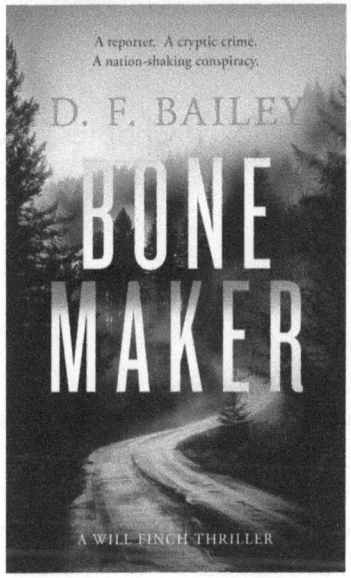

vinci-books.com/bonemaker

**A relentless reporter. A cryptic crime scene. A conspiracy that could shake the nation.**

Will Finch, a tenacious San Francisco crime reporter haunted by tragedy, stumbles upon a chilling mystery in the Oregon wilderness. A deserted car, a wounded bear, and a town gripped by a ruthless cop – all connected to the murder of a senator's daughter's fiancé. As Finch investigates the multimillion-dollar bitcoin scam behind it all, he uncovers a sinister conspiracy that threatens to consume him.

Turn the page for a free preview…

## Bone Maker: Chapter One

A whiff of blood in the air.

The bear rose on his back feet, turned his head upwind, and flared his moist nostrils. He needed food — anything to slake the deep hunger that clawed through his empty belly. The forest, thick with fir and cedar trees, surrounded him. In the distance, he could see a blur of rocks on the hillside. His ears filled with the sounds of the spring melt rushing down the creek beds and the heavy tree limbs pulling in the wind. He listened for the sound of more gunshots and car engines but they had passed now. Still, he felt a lingering danger. He set his forepaws on the ground and made his way up the slope to the gravel road. He paused and looked along the muddy track and then walked with purpose toward his prey. As he approached, he could make out the scent of several men and their machines. He hesitated and moved forward again — a force of nature.

Hungry, willful, unrelenting.

When Ethan Argyle first caught sight of the bear he assumed it was a boulder that had fallen from somewhere above the ridge onto the gravel road. The bear stood motionless, hunched forward, about fifty yards up the track from the Mercedes GLK. But since something was obviously amiss with the car — the driver's window wide open, despite the late morning drizzle — neither Ethan nor his son Ben focused on the animal. Until it began to move.

"Look at that, Dad." Ben pointed toward the bear with his gloved hand. He dug through his pocket for his binoculars. "It's big enough, but it *can't* be a grizzly. Not here." He pressed the glasses to his eyes, then gasped at the size of the animal gnawing away at something on the roadside. "Have a look," he whispered and passed the binoculars to his father.

"It's not a grizzly." Ethan focused the lens with the nose screw. "It's a black bear. He's feeding on something," he added but he couldn't make out what it might be. "No wonder we haven't come across any deer all day."

The father and son worked their way down the hill onto the switchback. There were dozens of dirt roads like this that cut through the forest above the coast, gravel tracks barely wide enough for two cars to squeeze past one another. But today no cars were visible and no trucks could be heard struggling up the long ravine. Nothing except the Mercedes, Ethan whispered to himself. The car looked abandoned; its engine was silent. A spray of mud caked the exterior, a dusty-gray paste that had hardened in the sun and then smudged under the light rain. He figured it had been parked here at least a day, since Saturday, when it had been sunny through the entire afternoon.

"There's just something wrong about that open window," Ben said as they approached the vehicle from the rear and then stopped about five feet away. He eased his rifle into the crook of his elbow and studied the car.

"Yeah." Ethan kept an eye on the bear, who seemed oblivious to them as it nuzzled a carcass on the roadside. They stood downwind from the animal and as Ethan sniffed the air he caught a whiff of fresh kill. "He can't smell us," he whispered to his son, "but he might hear us. Keep 'er quiet." He made a downward motion with his left hand and then brought his rifle from his shoulder into his arm. "Let's look at that window."

They walked silently beside the big SUV and peered into the black interior. It took a moment for his eyes to adjust to the lack of light, and only a few seconds longer for Ethan to make out the pool of blood that soaked the driver's seat. "Good lord!" he moaned, much louder than he wanted. He looked toward the bear to see if he'd startled.

"Dad ... I think that bear took him." Ben's voice was breathless. He wiped a hand over his mouth and angled the barrel of his gun towards the bear. A defensive move, nothing more. He kept his eyes on the bear, sure that it was more important than whatever might remain in the Mercedes.

"Doesn't make any sense," Ethan said and drew a long breath before he forced his head back through the top of the window. He could see the key fob lying in the CD tray. An opened pack of cigarettes, Marlboros, lay above the dash. A half-empty bottle of water stood uncapped in the drink caddy and beyond it a discarded Starbucks cup had spilled across the passenger seat. A rain jacket had been tossed onto the back seat and a duffle bag tucked in the rear footwell. He tried to imagine what could have transpired: a lone driver crossing the switchbacks is confronted by a rogue bear who refuses to yield an inch of the road ahead.

"He's starting to move, Dad. He might be onto us."

Ethan turned his attention to the scene up the road. The bear now stood upright over his kill with his eyes fixed on Ethan and Ben. Must be six hundred pounds, Ethan murmured to himself. The bear stole a step toward them and paused as if to consider his next move.

"I might have to take him out, Ben." His voice sounded apologetic but firm.

"Yes sir." Ben stood behind his father and readied his gun. They'd done this a dozen times before when they were after deer. They hunted the old-fashioned way, with bolt-action Winchester Model 70 rifles. If one missed his shot, the second fired the insurance round. But Ben never had to make a shot like this. Not with his fingers this damp, his heart pounding.

The bear lurched another step forward, then charged. Ethan had to shoot before he was fully prepared. Still, when he fired, he thought he'd hit squarely in the bear's torso. The bear bobbed and weaved, paused to sneer with a look of puzzlement, and then staggered forward again. A second later Ben fired his rifle. The bear roared and wheeled away as its front paw dissolved into a red pulp. It clambered into the scrub brush at the edge of the road, moaning loud wails that filled the depth of the ravine below.

"Damn. Now we have to go after it," Ethan murmured and fixed his jaw with a weary determination. "It's my fault, son," he said to dispel any misgivings the boy might have. He set their pace toward the bloody, abandoned carcass sprawled next to the weed-infested shrubs beside the road.

As they neared the corpse they staggered backward in an uneven motion that forced Ben to miss a step and move behind his father. The cadaver lay on its back, the chest cavity ripped open. Nothing of the man's throat — or his face — remained. Already the corpse was abuzz with flies.

"Oh no," Ben whimpered. He sunk to his knees and began to vomit onto the gravel.

"Give me your phone," Ethan said as he turned away from the mess that lay at their feet. "We've got to call the sheriff." As he punched 911 into the keypad, he prayed for a miracle. But he knew they were off the cellphone grid and they had little hope of connecting with anyone. They'd have to hike over to the switchback above the Lewis and Clark River where he'd parked the four-by-four, then drive down toward Astoria before they could make a cellphone connection.

He pulled his son by the forearm and braced him against his side. "Come on, it won't take us more than an hour," he said with forced certainty as he directed them back toward the ridge under Saddle Mountain.

Above them he saw two hawks surfing the aerial drafts in wide, easy circles. Somewhere below he could hear the bear crash through the bush, dashing loose rocks down the ravine into the rushing creek. Jesus, he moaned to himself and set his jaw once more. What kind of mess have we stumbled into this time?

## Bone Maker: Chapter Two

"Well, well, well. Will Finch — welcome back!" Wally Gimbel's wide face emerged from his office doorway when he saw Finch walk toward his cubicle at the far end of the writers' pool. Gimbel held his landline phone in one hand, the mouthpiece covered with a thumb.

"Good to see you," Will replied with a nod. Gimbel's face looked puffy and more inflamed than Finch remembered, but the voice retained the same edge of authority.

"Take a minute to dust off your keyboard," Wally whispered with a hint of fondness, an affection that he hoped the other reporters would not hear. "Then get back here in ten minutes." He winked and for a moment Finch imagined Wally was glad to see him again. "And bring Fiona Page with you," he added and turned his attention back to his phone call.

Finch continued down the aisle through the narrow labyrinth of walled pods known as "the bog" by the staff writers who complained that despite their urbane surroundings, they worked in a swamp seething with leeches and snakes. Most of them ticked away solemnly at their keyboards, a few others spoke in low tones to the digital images on their screens. The reporters had quickly learned the optimal volume to employ during Skype calls: a narrow spectrum between barely audible, and a murmur which could not be heard in the adjacent pods.

No one made eye contact with Finch until he reached Fiona Page's station. "Will!" Surprised, she pulled the earbuds from under her hair and leaned back in her chair. "Welcome back," she said and wheeled her chair to one side and waved Finch toward the guest chair.

"Thanks." He forced a smile and dropped onto the padded seat. Settled below the five-foot wall baffle, he was now invisible to everyone else in the bog. Hiding in the trenches, he thought. A good place to spend his first few minutes back on the front line.

"I didn't realize you were coming back this week." She pulled a length of hair over her shoulder and tipped her head to one side. "Sorry to hear the news." She frowned and looked away. Then she smiled a genuine good-to-see-you grin that flecked the dimples in her cheeks.

"Back at it," he said halting a little, unsure how much she knew about his situation. About Bethany and Buddy. And everything that happened after that. He forced himself to focus on the job. "So did you pick up the threads on the Whitelaw trial?"

"You bet." She opened a file on her screen and tilted it in case he wanted to have a look at her notes. "Not much to report over the last month, but I can send this to you if you want." Her tone was back-to-business.

He was silently thankful to her for immediately forcing him back into the game. Into the chase where they hunted and pecked out their daily nourishment from the world of politics, fame, sex, money, and crime — and the attempt to make sense of it all.

"Sure. Forward it, but only if Wally wants me back on the story." Finch nodded toward the managing editor's office. "By the way, he wants to see us both in five minutes in the boardroom."

The boardroom doubled as the staff meeting room at the *SF eXpress*, the internet division of the *San Francisco Post*. Willie Parson, the *Post's* CEO (and with his brother, co-owner of Parson Media) explained that the "e" denoted "electronic" and the "X" meant there would be no press machines cranking out actual papers. And no more press union, machine operators, typesetters, bundlers, truckers or paper carriers.

Like everyone else at the *eXpress*, Finch had quickly accepted Wally Gimbel's invitation to help him establish the digital version of the *Post*. If Finch had rejected Wally's offer he would have enjoyed a direct exit onto the street with a week's pay for every year of service in the old newsroom. Six years in his case. Three for Fiona. Dozens of reporters, many with more seniority, weren't offered any opportunities within the paper — print or internet. And when the cuts hit they came fast and hard. No good-bye parties, no chance to see the old news hounds off to another, better life. As far as management was concerned, the shame of teetering bankruptcy outweighed any loyalty to dismissed veterans.

"He'll want you back on the story," she said with certainty. "Did you hear what happened this weekend?"

He nodded no.

Before she could fill him in, her phone buzzed. She picked up her handset, listened a moment and said, "Okay, Wally."

"That was less than ten minutes," Finch grumbled as he

followed her toward the boardroom. He hadn't even seen his old pod, let alone dusted off the keyboard.

---

From the look in Gimbel's eyes, Finch figured a new crisis had hit. Something lower on the Richter scale than presidential assassination or global financial collapse, more likely another horrible mass shooting, or perhaps the long-anticipated closure of the newspaper.

"What's up?" he asked and leaned against the doorframe as Gimbel eased into a swivel chair at the head of the massive oak table. If needed, the boardroom could accommodate the entire digital-edition staff, stringers and freelancers. Roughly twenty people, ten sitting around the table (snatched by Gimbel from his old editorial office downstairs), with latecomers allotted to standing room only. Fiona stood beside Finch and then sat next to her boss.

"Close the door." Gimbel rolled his lower lip under his teeth and tapped a finger on his tablet screen. "You read the news feed this morning?"

Fiona shrugged with a sense of resignation. "Yeah ... it's hard to believe."

Finch raised his hands. "No time, Wally. Haven't even set eyes on my desk yet." He shrugged, a plea for a time out, and then realized he wasn't part of the game. *I need to suit up and join the team,* he told himself and walked behind Gimbel and sat on his left. They hunched together in the windowless room and stared at the list of links on the tablet screen.

Gimbel looked into Finch's eyes. He wanted to test the reaction, witness the surprise voltage on his face. "Ray Toeplitz is dead."

"Ray Toeplitz?" Finch glanced away. "Dead?"

Gimbel tapped his finger on the computer screen. A window popped open revealing the headline: *Key Witness Dies Tragically*. Below the text stood a picture of Toeplitz's worried face as he exited the front doors of the Hall of Justice two months earlier.

"It gets weirder than you think," Fiona said and let this idea sink in before continuing. "Did you hear that crazy story on Sunday? About a black bear dragging some guy from his Mercedes in the backwoods in Oregon — and eating him alive?" She paused to see if this registered, examined Finch with a hint of absolution, knowing that if he'd skipped the news over the past month it was understandable. Everyone understood.

In fact, Finch had purposely ignored all the news — TV, radio, papers, the web. He ignored her questions and set his eyes on Gimbel. "So what's the connection?"

Wally clicked on another link and the article about the rogue bear flashed onto the screen. "Toeplitz."

*"What?"* Finch brushed a hand over his mouth and quickly scanned the story. When he finished, he tipped back in his chair and gazed at the ceiling. Toeplitz: the genius with a PhD in Finance Mathematics. In his early twenties he'd made his mark on Wall Street, engineering complex hedge fund strategies that funneled millions into traders' bank accounts. Ten years ago he'd been hired by Whitelaw, Whitelaw & Joss and then promoted to the position of Chief Financial Officer.

But was Toeplitz a player in the Mt. Gox Bitcoin scam in Japan? Maybe. And was he part of the financial manipulations that defrauded investors of over four hundred and fifty million dollars? Possibly. Although he vehemently protested his innocence, as a member of his company's Board of Directors, Toeplitz was arrested and accused of fraud in a trial which everyone assumed would last at least six months. The tabloids called it "The Battle for Bitcoin."

But recently Toeplitz experienced a moral epiphany, or more likely, Finch assumed, he'd negotiated a compelling plea bargain with the District Attorney. Whatever his motivation, Toeplitz said he possessed records pointing to a massive fraud perpetrated by the senator's half-brother, Dean Whitelaw. And so Toeplitz decided to take the stand as a prosecution witness against Senator Franklin Whitelaw's investment house.

The senator himself claimed prosecutorial immunity because all his business affairs were held in a blind-trust, which he referred to as a "Chinese Wall." Another racist gaffe from the politician who'd built a populist reputation on similar foot-in-mouth blunders. Republicans loved him. Democrats laughed. Five times he'd been elected and sent to Washington.

And now came this latest episode in the most bizarre corporate saga that Finch had ever covered. Somewhere in a remote coastal forest, Raymond Toeplitz had been devoured by a bear.

Finch turned his attention back to Wally. "So there is a natural justice, after all."

"Mmm." Wally pressed his lips together and shrugged doubtfully. "I hope not, especially if we can squeeze new juice from this story. With the executive team in Parson Media threatening to roll the print edition of the *Post* back to three days a week, it would be helpful if your tale of Toeplitz and the bear could draw in a few more readers. Just to keep their office doors open another week or two." He pointed toward the floor, to the offices one story below.

They all smiled at this, at the fantasy that the digital division might save the print edition from insolvency. In any case, Finch felt relieved to have the story pitched in his direction. Something substantial to chew on instead of the bitter fruit of Bethany's guilt and depression. And the tragedy with Buddy.

"All right." Finch sat up in his chair. A jolt of energy radiated through his chest. In his gut he could feel the story coming back to life. He never expected the fraud trial to reach a satisfying conclusion. Now a new chapter opened before them. Everything had changed. "So. Fly to where? Portland? Interview the local sheriff, the coroner, and whoever bagged the bear. Right?"

"No." Gimbel smiled with a miser's grimace. "*Drive* to Astoria, the county seat of Clatsop County. Check the map. It's on the rear end of the back of beyond. Take the company car," he added after he remembered the photo of Finch's destroyed Toyota. A total write-off. "And so far, no one has found the bear, dead or alive. But don't let that stop you. Everyone loves to talk about the one that got away. I'm sure if anyone can pick up the story from there, you can." He turned to Fiona. "Meanwhile, I want you to develop the human angle. For the first time, Toeplitz appears as a victim in this sorry tale. Did he have a wife? Kids?"

"No." Finch shook his head. "No family at all. He was a childless orphan." An interesting combination, he thought and then realized it was a circumstance he and Toeplitz now shared: no parents, no siblings, no spouse, no children.

Gimbel paused. "Then get Dean and Franklin Whitelaw's reaction to Toeplitz's demise. If he stonewalls you try Senator Whitelaw's sons. They're twins. The two boys were brought into the firm in the last few years. They probably knew Toeplitz, too. Or his daughters, there's two or three of them. Remember, both of you, we don't work at a news*paper* anymore. We're looking for the human dimension here — opinions, rumors, innuendo — not *just* the facts." This was Gimbel's new mantra based on his theory that print delivered news while the internet delivered opinion. Overall, Finch had to agree.

"You got it." Fiona pulled her notes together and rose from her seat. "I'll email you the files I gathered over the last month," she said to Finch and pursed her lips, a sign that read: buckle up, we're both in for a long ride.

Finch stood, ready to follow her when Wally raised a hand and said, "Hold up a minute, Will. I've got a few questions for you."

---

Wally seemed nervous. A rare moment of hesitation gripped him. "I didn't have time to check in with you." His head wavered from side to side. "I mean about what kind of workload you can handle right now. Do you think you're ready for this?"

Finch shrugged. Good of you to ask, he thought, but what I need more than anything is to slide into the old groove. More than that, to get back into my life. "I'm ready. Hell, I'm here a week earlier than anyone expected," he said with a curt nod, and when he realized Gimbel needed more assurance he added, "Look, this new angle on Toeplitz might ease me back into the routine. After a day's drive through the Redwoods, maybe I can step into the Whitelaw story through the back door."

"Good." Gimbel raised his eyes from the oak table and studied Finch's face, unsure if he could carry the load so soon. "You know, normally we wouldn't send anyone up to Oregon to dig through this mess with Toeplitz. A few phone calls would reel in the details. But since you're back a week early and still technically on medical leave, it might prove a good way to bring you in." Gimbel raised his eyebrows as if to add, so don't treat it as a vacation.

When Finch sensed that his reliability was the issue he leaned forward and stared into his editor's eyes. "Wally, look ... it's over. It's been thirty-three days." To lighten the mood he faked a smile, checked his watch and said, "Make that thirty-four."

Gimbel gazed at Finch with an expression that softened his face. Not with pity, but with an air of empathy.

Finch could understand his concern. Gimbel had assembled the *eXpress* team only ten months ago. And eight months in, just as the Whitelaw trial began to gather a national following, Finch's calamity hit. Wally had to assign Fiona to cover the trial while Finch checked out of the bog and into Eden Veil Center for Recovery. The bucolic retreat provided the space Will needed to come to terms with the black pit into which he'd stumbled, and then been shattered.

"I'm okay now. The time off did me some good. Really. It's over, I've picked myself up and I know I have to move on," he said and swept his hand toward the wall. "It's all about my job now. That's what I do." The palm of his hand hit the table. "*This* is who I am now."

Gimbel tipped his head to one side. "All right," he whispered and set his fist against his mouth. He shifted his weight, a signal the meeting might soon be over, but then he settled again and angled his wide face toward his reporter. "And what about Bethany?"

Finch leaned back in his chair, a bit startled. This was getting personal. Six months ago Wally had mentioned Bethany's drinking. Said he knew where it could lead, that he'd lived through something similar himself. Will realized that his boss needed some assurance that this part of Finch's world wouldn't blow up again. "I haven't seen her in thirty-five days. She's...." He looked into his open hands, at the emptiness they held. "Look ... she's completely broken." He narrowed his eyes. "You want the honest truth?"

Gimbel nodded.

"With luck, I'll never see her again."

Gimbel pressed his lips together and drew a long breath. "I know you think this is none of my business, but I need to know if you can stick this thing."

*Stick this thing?* What did that mean? Could Finch stick with the job — or stick a knife into the part of his life destroyed by Bethany and surgically remove the diseased tissue? He fixed his eyes on the far wall. "Okay. Here's the bare essentials, for your ears only: she's been suspended from her job, with pay, pending the medical examiner's report and criminal investigation. Likely there'll be a trial for criminal negligence, maybe manslaughter. I hope so. If that sounds like revenge, then so be it. I'll take my slice served cold." His eyes narrowed. "As for me, I've moved into a one-bedroom place on South Van Ness while I'm looking for something better." He felt as though he'd just climbed a steep flight of stairs. If nothing else, at least he still held a grip on the facts of his life.

Will had a sense that his managing editor wanted more, that he wanted to hear something about Buddy. But he felt that if either of them uttered Buddy's name, some kind of emotional disaster could follow.

"South Van Ness?" Wally Gimbel shook his head doubtfully, then smiled, happy to divert their attention.

"Do you know how hard it is to find a place in San Francisco for two thousand dollars?" Will tried to fix a grin on his lips but instead looked away.

"All right," Wally said and exhaled another long breath,

a sigh of relief that they'd both survived this conversation — a topic that they had to resolve before they could move forward. "I'm going to give you a week," he concluded. "Then you tell me if you can stick it."

**Grab your copy...**
**vinci-books.com/bonemaker**

# About the Author

In 2015, D. F. (Don) Bailey published The Finch Trilogy — *Bone Maker*, *Stone Eater*, *Lone Hunter* — three novels narrated from the point of view of a crime reporter in contemporary San Francisco. Following the trilogy's success, *Second Life* (2017) launched a new saga based on the characters introduced in the first three books. The series prequel, *Five Knives*, came out in 2018. The Finch chronicle continues with *Open Chains* (2019), *Run Time* (2020), *White Sphere* (2022), and *Burnt Embers* (2023).

His first psychological thriller, *Fire Eyes*, was a W.H. Smith First Novel Award finalist. His second novel, *Healing the Dead*, was translated into German as *Tödliche Ahnungen*. The *Good Lie* (2008) is set in his adopted hometown, Victoria. His fourth novel, *Exit from America*, appeared in 2013.

After his birth in Montreal, Don's family moved around North America from rural Ontario to New York City, Mississippi, and New Jersey. "After years of seeking the ideal place to live", he says, "I finally landed on my feet on Vancouver Island — where I live next to the Salish Sea in the city of Victoria".

For twenty-two years, he worked at the University of Victoria, teaching creative writing and journalism and coordinating the Professional Writing Cooperative Education Program — which he co-founded. From time to time, he also freelanced as a business writer and journalist. In the fall of 2010, Don left the university so that "I could turn my preoccupation with writing into a full-blown obsession".

An Amazon bestselling author, he's also a ManyBooks.com Book of the Month Award winner and a Whistler Independent Book Award finalist.

www.ingramcontent.com/pod-product-compliance
Ingram Content Group UK Ltd.
Pitfield, Milton Keynes, MK11 3LW, UK
UKHW041113260226
468438UK00002B/73